"In The Aristocrat's Wife, Jodie Leigh Murray sets the bar high for blending historical romance with a deep exploration of social issues, personal loss, and emotional resilience in a story of redemption and the transformative power of love. Georgie emerges as the heroine she was meant to be, demonstrating that having the right people by your side empowers you to embrace your true self and discover the strength within. This is a testament to Murray's skill in crafting a compelling narrative with an outstanding cast of characters within a richly detailed historical context. I recommend this book to historical romance enthusiasts who enjoy stories featuring resilient female protagonists who challenge societal norms."

Maalin Ogaja for Readers' Favorite

"The author balances passion and restraint in a way that heightens anticipation at every turn with never a dull moment. As I followed Georgie's journey, I found myself deeply invested in her personal growth, cheering for her newfound strength and independence while also feeling the weight of her difficult choices, making her story resonate long after I finished the book. Overall, I highly recommend The Aristocrat's Wife to fans of historical romance who appreciate strong character development and a richly detailed setting that brings the post-Civil War era to life."

K.C. Finn for Readers' Favorite

"As a romance, love is at the core of the story; however, you can also see themes of independence and self-discovery. If you enjoy historical romances with richly developed characters, filled with slow-burn tension, and a mix of adventure, this book should be on your TBR list."

Priya Mathew for Readers' Favorite

Other Books by Jodie Leigh Murray:

Romantic Suspense
The Gangster's Daughter
The Gangster's Mistake
The Gangster's Game

Historical Romance
The Duke's Daughter
The Aristocrat's Wife
The Pirate's Daughter

The Aristocrat's Wife

The Aristocrat's Wife

Jodie Leigh Murray

Jodie Leigh Murray Books

Published in the United States by Jodie Leigh Murray Books
Printed in the United States

Paperback ISBN: 978-1-968598-06-8
eBook ISBN: 978-1-968598-07-5

First edition: November 2024
Second edition: August 2025

www.jodieleighmurray.com

For my brother, Nathan, who was taken from us too soon.
Not a day goes by that I don't miss you and your smile.
I will miss you forever.

Part One

A lie will remain a lie, even if everyone believes it.
And the truth shall set you free.

Chapter One

May 29, 1868 ~ New York City

I've never been the type of person to think life is not worth living. People could say I'm a spoiled brat, wealthy beyond measure, with a supportive husband and a beautiful home along a street reserved for the wealthiest in the city, the best clothing and jewels to match, and part of a society looking down from above. But they don't know what it's like to be the wife of an aristocrat.

They don't know my husband.

The Derringer is laid out on my dressing table in front of me, the stark white of the linen wrapping a sharp contrast against the dark color of the gun. They call it an assassin's weapon, easily concealed. Except I hadn't gone to the shady streets of New York City to get it for an assassination. I'd gotten it on a whim. In a moment of utter hopelessness, I thought this my only way out of a lonely life.

My reflection in the looking glass mirrored my fear. Big brown eyes stared back, blessed with heavy black lashes albeit wet from tears. I used to believe my eyes were too far apart, but my grandfather insisted they were beautiful, the same deep brown as my late grandmother's. Sybil had coiled my brown hair perfectly atop my head, with wisps framing my face and tendrils tickling my nape. As my lady's maid, I couldn't have asked for a better attendant.

Reaching up, my fingertips caressed the pearls that circled my neck. I dressed modestly tonight. Nothing to trigger anger from Charles. Not this evening. He'd be careful to conceal his emotions from our friends and acquaintances, being the model son and husband to all who knew him.

I'd never considered myself a stunningly beautiful woman, having been unsuccessful in securing a husband after my coming out. My mother, a pinch twisting my mouth at the thought of the cruel woman, had not allowed me to enter the marriage mart in London until I turned eighteen claiming I had not yet fully matured while most of my friends had come out at ages sixteen and some at fifteen. I'd been the last, much to my dread.

After years with no proposals had passed, Abigail Rutherford had been furious with me for not securing a husband. Not for lack of trying, for I'd entertained quite a few callers during the seasons in London before traveling to our summer home in South Lancashire. The men I'd met were utterly boring, interested only in their sports or businesses, themselves, or not interested in a woman who wanted to have an intellectual conversation. Prospects had dwindled by the time I'd turned twenty-four.

At the risk of becoming a spinster, my parents packed me up and brought me to America to visit the St. John family, associates in the textile business. My mother would have never considered bringing me across the sea after my brother had abandoned the family. I'd overheard her arguing with my father about bringing me along. He'd wanted the best for me, convinced bringing me to New York would be.

If not for the fact my husband is possibly one of the most handsome among the now ineligible bachelors, I may not have considered his proposal. Six months ago, I wouldn't have if not for the urging of my father. I couldn't have given a care about my mother's insistence that I marry Charles St. John. But as soon as my father told me of his desire to see me wed, I buckled.

The abrupt knock against my bedroom door startled me enough to set my hands trembling. I wrenched the top drawer of my dressing table open and laid the gun inside, closing it before the door opened a fraction. Dark hair appeared, followed by Charles's lanky frame entering without invitation and closing the door. Even without his top hat, he was the epitome of an aristocratic gentleman, from the tips of his thin mustache to his neatly trimmed sideburns.

"Beautiful, as always, my sweet."

The huskiness of his voice masked the intent of his statement when he stepped behind me, curling his hands around the shoulders where the pink sleeves of my gown covered most of the paleness of my skin. He leaned down, brushing his lips against my temple and meeting my gaze in the mirror.

"Seems like only yesterday when we wed," he continued, keeping his hands on my shoulders, trapping me from moving away. "Does it not?"

I had to clear my throat before I could reply. "Six months isn't such a long time. Imagine what it might feel like after a year."

The pressure of his hands increased a fraction, a warning to watch my tongue. "Perhaps you will bless me with a son or daughter by that time."

His eyes, holding mine in the mirror, were unmoving.

"We can only hope." I drew in a silent, shaky breath when his hands fell away and he moved to wander around my bedroom.

After we'd been married, I'd been startled by the separate bedrooms Charles insisted upon. My father and mother shared a bedroom, and while I knew of people who didn't, I always thought I would share a bedroom with my husband. But Charles said it was best to have separate rooms, giving me the excuse that business kept him up late at night and he rose impossibly early. As such, he didn't wish to disturb me.

The furnishings in my room spoke of his mother's elegant taste. Unlike most beds, mine was vast and lacked curtains, leaving it open on all sides except the back wall.

Being raised under the tight control of my mother, nothing would be out of place in my bedroom, which remained impeccably clean. If there was, the maid would be dismissed immediately. Any misstep from me and I'd learn, locked in my room or meals withheld. With my father away in London so often, and Anthony at school, much of my childhood had been spent at the mercy of my tyrant mother. I had thought marriage an escape. I couldn't have been more wrong.

When Charles wandered towards my desk, he found nothing on the surface and had nothing to do but to continue toward the tall windows to look down at Fifth Avenue. I stared back at my reflection, noting the flush in my cheeks at the sudden intrusion. Usually, Charles came to my bedroom for one thing, and one thing only.

"Father and Mother should be here shortly. We'll accompany them to the ball, if that's agreeable to you."

"I rather enjoy their company."

He turned with a smile. "As they enjoy yours."

When he strode back toward me, I braced myself. Surprisingly, he kept his hands to himself. For a moment. He reached up, touching a wisp of hair that had drifted down against the curve of my neck.

"You are truly an extraordinary woman, Georgiana." He leaned against the dressing table, still caressing the tendril of hair between his fingers.

I raised an eyebrow. My unruly nature urged me to ask him why he treated me so callously if I was so extraordinary. How could I be extraordinary when I couldn't do such a simple thing as conceive his child? Wisely, I kept my lips pressed together. I'd love nothing more than to find out I carried his child. Perhaps then he might agree to let me leave our house without supervision. At present, I must have his permission to leave and am not allowed to go anywhere else but immediately home.

His gaze dipped down to my bosom. "You'll wear the blue gown tonight. The one with the silver stitching." I opened my mouth to argue, but he drew his hand around to the back of my neck and brought my mouth abruptly against his in a brutal kiss. "You'll wear the blue gown."

When he released me and strode to the door, I pressed my back into the chair, staring into the mirror until my eyes burned.

After the soft click of the door closing, I remained alone once more, Charles having left me with a direct order to change my entire outfit to suit him. If I didn't, I could be sure he would lock me in my room and regale the guests at the ball of my change in health. It wouldn't be the first time he'd done such a thing.

Moments later, the door opened again and Sybil hurried in. "Miss Georgie?"

"There has been a requested change in what I'll be wearing this evening, Sybil. Please fetch the blue gown with the silver stitching and the low bodice."

Although her eyes widened a fraction, she nodded and went to retrieve the gown. James and Mary could arrive at any moment in their carriage to retrieve us. I'd need to hurry. Sybil took only minutes to return with the gown, but with the amount of buttons on each dress, it took time to shimmy out of one and into another.

Once again staring at my reflection in the mirror, this time in the light blue gown with a daring plunge in the bodice, I had to admit that it complimented my dark hair and lighter complexion. There had been no issue with the pink gown. Charles only wanted to exert his control.

It had taken me only a month after our wedding to understand I had traded one toxic home for another, one tyrant ruling over my life for another—my husband replacing the rule of my mother. The subtle direction of whom to make plans with, suggestions on what I might wear while not entertaining a discussion, the lack of choice over any matter. The trinkets and surprise gifts when I followed his orders, the silent treatment and days away from home when I did not. I coped with the house confinement, but his anger occasionally became too much for me. Charles did not know his own strength.

"There is no difference," Sybil said from the door leading to my private bathing chambers and dressing room. "This only heightens your beauty, Miss Georgie."

The corner of my lips lifted. No matter how many times I told her to call me Georgie rather than Miss Georgie, she still did so. "That is exactly what he wants." I lifted my chin. "In fact, I'd like to change jewels."

I met her gaze in the mirror's reflection before she disappeared into the room, taking the pink gown with her. Looking back at myself, I smiled. While my mother may have controlled my life until I married, there were always ways I would get around her. Charles was much the same, but I needed to tread more carefully. Much more.

Sybil, having an exquisite sense of fashion, returned. Patiently, I waited while she removed the pearl necklace and set it away before I removed the earrings. The diamond earrings sparkled in the light, but when she laid the diamond necklace around the slim column of my neck, I smiled. The diamonds dripped down toward the low bodice, giving a more alluring display. This would play with fire.

"Charles wishes for me to be on display this evening, then by God . . . I shall be."

Chapter Two

Voices in the foyer greeted me as soon as I swept out of my bedroom, closing the door softly behind me before hurrying down the short hallway toward the stairway. Our bedrooms were on one side of the stairway while the guest bedrooms were on the opposite, but my room was closest to the stairs, which made for the quicker walk. As soon as I appeared at the top, three heads turned toward me.

While the St. John family had wealth, Charles and I lived in a brownstone that divided the house in half with the library and parlor on one side and the dining room, kitchen and servants' quarters on the other. The foyer where the wide staircase led down was spacious enough to be considered a small dance floor. Being the end of May and still cool in the evenings, I'd already donned my cloak. It swirled around me while I descended to meet James, Mary, and Charles below.

"Ah, Georgiana." James, barely taller than Charles and a full head taller than me, leaned down to kiss each cheek.

Charles inherited his handsomeness from James, although James had the darker hair of the two and nearly obsidian eyes. While Charles had a thin mustache and always took great care to trim his sideburns, James had no mustache and had much larger sideburns. Sharp features with strong jawlines and high cheekbones ran in the St. John family. I had to admit that he and

Charles looked handsome in their suits and top hats, complete with walking sticks, even though they accessorized more than a need for walking.

I smiled, inclining my head. "Always the charmer." I turned to Mary. "We are still having luncheon tomorrow with Annabel?"

"Of course! We must talk about the charity auction at the Smith house next week." Mary had lighter brown hair than the men with pale blue eyes that accentuated her prettiness. She linked her arm with mine and together we walked toward the doors.

Fitz, our ever faithful butler, bowed and opened the double doors for us while the footman, Oliver, stood at attention. Although we'd hired an entire household of staff after our wedding when we'd purchased the home, Fitz had come with high recommendations and appeared well-aged while Oliver, at least twenty years his junior, had dazzled us with his straight-forward nature. During the last six months, none of the staff had given either of us reason to believe they couldn't carry on their duties as hired.

We strolled out into the coolness of the evening. I burrowed into my cloak further, stepping toward the coach where the coachman held the door open for us. The coach rocked as Charles climbed in beside me, his hand sliding to my knee, followed by James.

The drive to the home of Frederick and Annabel Shaw took less than ten minutes. Their grand house, on the corner overlooking Central Park, was one of the largest in the city. They were one of the wealthiest families and at the top of the aristocracy. To be invited to their home, whether for a ball, tea, or a dinner party, was a great honor. Mary and Annabel were the best of friends, and we were celebrating Annabel's birthday with tonight's festivities.

Upon entering the massive foyer of the Shaw residence, Charles moved me forward by pressing his hand against my back below the edge of my corset. Indecent if anyone stood behind us. Likely, they'd be snickering, I thought. The marbled floor shone from the lit chandeliers overhead, servants littering the area while moving from the kitchens on one side to the ballroom on the other near the back with trays of sparkling champagne and a delectable assortment of finger-foods.

My fingers shook when I undid my cloak, aware that Charles would get a full view of what I had done. While he had ordered a gown change, he had said nothing of changing my jewels. It might cost me, but then again . . . it might be worth it.

When my cloak lifted from my shoulders, swept away into the arms of the footman along with the other cloaks, I waited. Instead, I felt Charles press his hand against my back once again. A warning. James and Mary had taken up a conversation with another couple, Charles wishing to wait until they concluded before moving into the ballroom.

If there was one thing that I enjoyed, it was a ball. There was something about the excitement of dancing, the men in their formal attire, and women in their best gossamer dresses with jewelry sparkling under the light of chandeliers overhead. Music stirred emotions, laughter filled the room, and I felt like I was someone of importance.

I felt his lips at the curve of my ear, the warmth of his breath disturbing the tendrils of hair there. "Don't think I don't see what you've done, my sweet."

My chin lifted. "I don't know what you're talking about."

Laughter rumbled in his chest when he pressed closer to me, indecently so. "Oh," he breathed, "but you do. You'll no doubt have every eye on you tonight."

"Isn't that what you wanted?"

My tongue slid between my teeth and I bit down lightly, keeping myself from saying anything further. I only played with fire the more I spoke, and I knew better. I had known better my entire life than to speak so freely. Even Anthony had tried to get me to tame down my unruly tongue, knowing that someday it would get me in real trouble.

"Of course. I am a lucky man to have such a beautiful wife." His arm tightened around my waist, his fingers pressing painfully into my hip.

Not the perfect woman, poised and elegant, but bold. I wanted to speak with people I'd never spoken to. I wanted to educate myself in ways never allowed, learn of things I'd only dreamed of, experience things only reserved for others.

"Charles! Georgie!"

I looked up at the massive staircase to see Benjamin Shaw. As the only son of our hosts and my husband's best friend, he'd dressed immaculately for the occasion. Black tuxedo with tails, dark hair neatly combed away from his clean-shaven face. Benjamin always stood out, doing everything against popular opinion, including no sideburns and no walking stick.

Instead, he spread his arms wide and started down the staircase with a bounce in his step. The staircase separated the two sides of the house much like ours did, except they had a set of stairs on each side leading down to a landing with one wide set coming down into the foyer. The family's immense wealth was evident in the carved stone staircase, which was a stark contrast to the dark mahogany one in our brownstone.

"I wondered when you'd finally get here," he called out, heedless to those in the foyer listening in. "Was thinking I'd have to wait."

Charles loosened his grip on me, his hand sliding from my waist as Benjamin stepped down to us. His spirits were indeed high when he clapped Charles on the back rather enthusiastically. I promptly hid my smile of satisfaction at his grunt.

"You didn't have to wait," Charles grumbled.

Benjamin turned to me, the sparkle in his deep-set blue eyes more vibrant than usual. Only knowing him as long as I did anyone else in our circle of friends, I didn't think this celebration would cause him to be so cheery, but perhaps there was more to the festivities tonight than I thought. I studied him, leaning my head to the side as though it would aid me in discovering the true reason of his delightful mood. He hadn't been courting anyone that I knew of, although there were several ladies vying for his attention. Friends in my circle, including my dearest friend Maddie Bennett. Several gentlemen sought to call upon her, but her father, a banker of high importance and a widow, had made his reluctance known to suitors after his only daughter's hand. Settling for anyone would not do.

He reached for my hand, pulling it to his lips. "You look ravishing this evening, Mrs. St. John," he murmured. "Please save a dance for me."

Such a tease, I thought, swatting him with my fan before pulling my hand away. "I might save you a dance, Benjamin. That will depend on my dance card and how filled it becomes after Charles has his say."

The wicked gleam in Charles's eyes attested to my statement. He trusted Benjamin beyond his life, having been friends with him their entire lives. To hand me over to him for a dance or two would be nothing. Others, however, would need to fight for a dance. Married or not, Charles would not relinquish me so easily. The gown only enticed those to that which they could not have, although I'd disagreed wholeheartedly.

"Shall we go in?" Benjamin asked, sweeping his arm out.

My eyes lifted to James and Mary, seeing them conclude their conversation to follow us, but not before I noticed Benjamin's gaze dip to my necklace. And lower. I frowned. Benjamin had been cordial to me, friendly as his best friend's wife. Never had he looked twice at me. Quickly, I moved at the insistence of Charles and his hand on my back again.

I could walk by myself, I wanted to tell him but remained silent while we entered the liveliness of the ballroom awash with dancers in the center of the room. Every sconce along the gilded walls flickered, the chandeliers overhead sparkling with lights that made the room glow in merriment. Chairs lined both sides of the room while the orchestra played from the riser.

Nothing but gossamer silk and black tuxedos spun about the center of the room while we skirted around, finding a clear spot to one side. Benjamin snagged a few glasses of champagne as a footman passed, handing us crystal flutes.

"You must tell me your opinion of old Seymour making a run at the presidency." Benjamin inched closer to Charles while I sipped from my glass, eyes sweeping the room.

"That old bastard." I heard Charles mutter. "He'll never win."

"He might not, but I've got to give him some credit for opposing the draft in '63. Wouldn't you agree? God knows, we'd have seen the uglier side of the war."

While I listened with half an ear, my thoughts strayed to Anthony in wonder about what had happened to him while the war raged between the north and south. The war had officially ended less than two years ago, but the south surrendered over three years ago in 1865. Anthony had come to America in 1859 and, no matter where he may have settled, would have gotten caught up in the fighting.

There were no men who had escaped it, unless they were aristocrats like Charles and Benjamin. Sent to aid in the war but far from the actual fighting, Charles and Benjamin served under generals who were intent on preserving the elite.

"Maddie!" I said, delighted to see my friend across the sea of dancers.

Standing beside her father of considerable height, he of the darkest hair and eyes and she of the lightest blonde hair and eyes, made one question their relatability. Only those who knew of her mother before she passed away from tuberculosis knew that Maddie had her mother's beauty. Soft, light hair, beguiling blue eyes, and the porcelain skin of a doll won hearts abound. Most men fairly tripped over themselves for a word with her, but

Harrison Bennett wouldn't be called a fool. Though a business-man through and through, he guarded his daughter like precious cargo.

A single step. That's all I took. Strong fingers wrapped incon-spicuously around my wrist, holding me hostage from leaving his side to seek another conversation. I'd have bruises circling my wrist, hidden now by my white glove. Charles didn't inflict enough pain to make me cry out, but tears welled up instantly. He wouldn't dare do such a thing in public. He merely kept me from leaving his side, pulling me back and curling his arm pos-sessively around my waist. A prisoner amongst friends.

"Charles," I moved closer to him, removing the need for him to keep his hand around my wrist, "I merely wish to go speak with Maddie. She is on the approved list of those I may associ-ate with."

His eyes snapped to mine, and even though Benjamin had feigned interest in those around us rather than the conversation going on beside him, I saw his jaw flex. "You will. Once we've danced."

I raised my eyebrows but inclined my head. Benjamin locked eyes with me as Charles whisked me away to the dance floor. I couldn't interpret the seriousness in Benjamin's eyes, as I couldn't recall ever seeing him like that. Instead, I put it out of my mind while we swung into a quadrille.

"Why must we be at odds?" he asked when we came back to-gether.

"This is not the place to discuss it," came my tight reply.

His lips pinched together, but he spun me around and smiled with gaiety as though enjoying himself. The smile hadn't left my face since we'd entered the house, ever playing the happy wife. I truly enjoyed the company, as I would enjoy his company if he weren't being so possessive and controlling all the time. One wrong move and I would find myself forbidden to attend the next ball or party.

When the dance ended, Charles allowed me to escape from his side at long last, and I hurried over to Maddie. The question he'd asked me drifted through my mind. If he would lessen his control, perhaps we could be less at odds. Perhaps if he didn't blame me so much for the lack of pregnancy, we could move past it and be happy. Maybe if he didn't punish me for the slightest issue, I would learn to be happier.

"Georgie!" Maddie's smile grew when she saw me approach, hurrying to link her arm with mine. "I'm so glad you're here." She glanced up at her father. "Aren't we so glad Georgie is here, Papa?"

Harrison Bennett smiled down at me with an incline of his head. "Always good to see you, of course. Anyone who can keep some sense into my daughter's head is welcome."

Maddie tsked at him, pulling me away from him. "Have you ever seen such grand parties in your life?" I would have responded that I had while in London, especially when the queen attended, but she continued on. "This house is absolutely to be envious of, don't you think? And Benjamin! I daresay he looks as dashing as ever."

I laughed, tipping back my head and catching looks from Benjamin and Charles across the room, which I promptly ignored. "Will you allow me to answer your questions, or will you continue firing them at me?"

Her giggling carried us around the room while we strolled, arms entwined as though she were reluctant to let me go. I couldn't remember a closer friend in my life, even while in London, than Maddie. Warm and funny, gracious yet kind. She would do well as any man's wife. Especially Benjamin. Glancing at him, I noticed he watched us even though speaking with Charles. They would make a charming couple.

"You've seen grander parties than this in London?" she prompted.

"Yes, but it seems so long ago. Things are much stricter there than here, but the houses are just as grand and envious. The men, very much as stiff." I snagged another glass of champagne from a passing footman, sipping it while we strolled. "We only stayed in London during the season, you know. During summers, we were in our home in the north."

"And your brother?"

"He left after I turned fifteen."

"And you never heard from him again?" I shook my head and her smile turned upside down, but I patted her arm. "Was he handsome?"

I laughed softly this time to avoid attention. "I suppose he is."

"But you haven't heard from him in all this time?"

"I never have. He promised to write, but he didn't. He wrote to my parents, but I never received a letter from him. Perhaps he thought they would share his written words with me, but my father didn't come home often, and my mother would never speak to me of my brother after he left."

"And now they are gone, too," she whispered. "I feel so bad for you sometimes, Georgie. To have lost both your parents at the same time. I shan't know what I would do if I lost my dear Papa."

It hurt my heart to have lost my father. My mother, though she was my mother, did not hurt as much. Shortly after we got married, Charles informed me that their ship encountered a storm on the voyage home, resulting in all lives lost at sea. He'd received and read a few letters from my grandfather to me, but otherwise I'd lost all my family other than Anthony, and I didn't know where he settled or if he even survived the war.

It left me an heiress since Anthony seemed to have disappeared. Father had sent Anthony a considerable sum of money to get started and keep his adventures here afloat. Charles gave me a decent allowance, so I'd be able to make purchases for things I needed. It never negated the fact I needed permission to leave. He provided the excuse that his English rose needed safeguarding in the city streets, when questioned about it. No one knew it wasn't true. I'd never been loose with spending, and most of it I kept in my desk drawer. But it wasn't much.

"I have Charles, and his parents are lovely," I whispered. "That is enough. And perhaps someday I will find out what became of my brother."

"Look! There are Elly and Nettie. Let's go chat with them."

Laughing, we hurried as quickly as allowable, across the room to the other two ladies speaking in hushed tones. At least the four of us could have a conversation without the need to include politics, cigars, the state of the country, or world affairs. We spoke of the upcoming charity event next week, who would bring what and the newest fashions at Macy's, even a few risqué topics.

Eventually, my cheeks ached from smiling so much. I danced with James, who rarely danced with anyone. Everyone knew my father-in-law as a serious sort of man, but he allowed himself to dance at balls only twice. On rare occasions, three times. A man of few words, but he danced very well, and I enjoyed dancing with him as much as I enjoyed dancing with Charles, though

Charles usually got beneath my skin with his biting comments before the end of the dance.

"I daresay my wife is much sought after this evening." Charles, coming up behind me, took my hand and pressed his mouth to my knuckles while the other came to rest on my hip. "Have I reason to be jealous, my sweet?"

Keeping his hand to my hip, he pulled me against him into a stroll through the crowds with my arm tucked against his. "Of course not. You know your father always dances with me."

"It wasn't my father whom I referred to."

I looked up at him, my eyebrows drawn together while I tried to recall who might have paid such attention to me to seize his interest. There had been no one, any man, whom I'd paid any attention to other than James. He'd been the only man I'd danced with all evening.

"I'm a lucky man to have such a beautiful wife."

That you purposely ordered to wear such a daring gown, I thought. "Perhaps it is me who is the lucky one." Two could play this particular game. I looked at him with a sidelong glance. "I wish Benjamin would think of settling down soon. Maddie would be a wonderful wife to him, and she is so pretty."

I watched Charles scan the crowd, searching for Benjamin. If only he could persuade him. Being best friends since they were young boys, Charles as an only child and Benjamin the only boy, had an insurmountable life of responsibility awaiting. If anyone could convince Benjamin to settle down, it would be Charles. The same age as Charles, Benjamin should be considering it. As I'm sure Annabel had reminded him, he bore the responsibility to carry on his family name.

The thought dampened my mood a little. The responsibility of the St. John name came down to me. Since our wedding, there had been no luck in getting pregnant. Not for lack of trying. Charles visited my bedroom often enough, but to no benefit. And he blamed me. I studied the profile of his face, the curve of his firm jaw up to the curve of his ear.

"Would you speak to him?"

Charles looked down at me. "I've spoken to him many times before, Georgiana. Benjamin is not in mind to settle down yet. I promise you that Miss Bennett is likely at the top of his list of eligible ladies when he does."

Georgie, I thought silently. Not once had he ever called me Georgie, as everyone else did. I was Georgiana to him. Formal and stiff. "If he waits much longer, someone else is going to capture her heart. Archie is quite charming."

Charles arched his eyebrow. "Is he, indeed?"

I gave his arm a light tap with my fan, my attempt to lighten the mood and hopefully his temperament for later, having not forgotten the necklace dripping down towards the crevice between my breasts. "Do not tease me."

Leaning down, he pressed his lips to my temple. His mouth lingered. "I must go speak with others, lest they think my wife monopolizes my time. You will find Miss Bennett and when I find you again, we shall dance."

Another order. One to keep me away from any men that he might think sought my company. His behavior tested my temper. Not one single male in this room had captured my attention for longer than a passing greeting other than James.

I'd had enough pleasantries, exhausted from smiling. I merely wanted to fall back into the shadows and have a moment to myself, a time for quiet to collect my thoughts and be away from people briefly.

As commanded, I strolled away from Charles with a snap of my fan to chase away the warmth of the ballroom. With this many people in one room, it was bound to grow warm. Though directly disobeying the order, I ventured out of the crowded ballroom and down a long hallway until I'd nearly reached the end. I chose the last door on the left to open, revealing a dimly lit room, the back wall nothing but rows of books.

Closing the door softly behind me, I wandered into the library. This room felt much cooler, and I laid my fan down on a table while I meandered toward the books to gaze up at the tomes. It felt good to have quiet. To rest my smile as genuine as it might be.

"My dear, Georgie."

I turned to Benjamin's impossibly low voice as he strolled into the library, not having made a sound when he'd entered. How he'd spotted me leaving the ballroom and walking down the hallway, I didn't know. I thought I'd been inconspicuous. He had a commanding presence that no one else I'd ever known had. At least a head taller than Charles, I had to crane my neck to look at him.

The darkness of his hair complimented his olive-skinned

complexion. His forehead was high, and there was always a swath of hair that hung partially over it. Those who knew him, knew he had a habit of always pushing it back. He stood impossibly straight, making him seem more imposing.

"Am I disturbing you?"

"Not at all." I smiled. "But I believe Charles is in search of you. Did you see him?"

"No." He looked sheepish. "I was eager to take some air, and now that I find you in here, I'm glad to have done so. The ballroom was becoming quite stuffy. I'll seek him out in a few moments."

He stepped over to me, looking up at the books while standing beside me. It seemed strange to be alone with him, something I couldn't recall ever having done before. I didn't think I'd ever been in a room alone with any man except for Charles. No matter, I thought, looking back at the books. Benjamin might as well be Charles. They were so similar. Like brothers.

"Have you seen Miss Bennett?"

He chuckled. "I know what you're doing, Georgie."

"You do?"

"Trying to get me to court Miss Bennett."

"And?"

He paused for a moment. "I can appreciate your eagerness to see her happy, but I'm not ready to settle down."

"When will you?"

"When I think the time is right."

"Maddie is beautiful, is she not?"

"She's quite beautiful." He turned to face me.

I knew a lost cause when it was staring at me. "Your mother throws such wonderful parties. I envy her."

"She does," he murmured, reaching out to tuck a wayward curl behind my ear. "You do not know how particularly beautiful you are."

I frowned and moved away from him, but his hands grasped

my forearms and it startled me. My mind raced in confusion. Benjamin had never behaved in such a way before. This had to be inappropriate, although he had done nothing else untoward. He tightened his hold, refusing to allow me to move away.

"I need you to listen to me. This may be the only time I can say this, he keeps such tight control of you." The look in his eyes had turned serious, the tone of his voice hoarse. "You must realize what he is doing to you, Georgie. You must get away from him. And you can do it by becoming my mistress. I can protect you. Set up a life for you where he'll never find you."

I tugged against him. "Release me, Benjamin."

Chapter Three

Dear God, I thought, what is happening? My mind spun from what Benjamin was propositioning me with. Become his mistress? Had he lost his mind?

He loosened his hold on me, but didn't yet release me, keeping me prisoner. "I can't prove what happened to Violet, but I know enough to think the same could happen to you. I won't let that happen to you."

"Who is Violet?" His hands fell away, allowing me to take a step back. "What are you talking about, Benjamin? You aren't making sense."

"Violet was Charles' sister. She took her own life. I suspect Charles had a hand in it. And I can see the same thing happening with you. Only you can stop it before it happens to you. I'm begging you." He leaned closer to me, mouth set firmly. "Become my mistress, Georgie. You are wasting away as his wife."

"Never."

He stared down at me, a fire in his eyes that I'd never seen before. What did he think he was doing? I thought. If Charles caught him saying any of these things, or us in this position, he would be furious.

"I'll leave you some time to think about it, but I leave with a warning. Do not take overly long. Before it is too late, you need to get away from him. You will never want for anything in life with me."

I watched him walk away, his long strides carrying him across the expanse of the library in only a matter of moments. Left alone, my face burned hot, and I cried out, clasping my hand over my mouth while tears filled my eyes. I had known Benjamin as long as I had known Charles, meeting them at the same time I had arrived in New York City.

Benjamin had given no sign he had thought of me any more than the wife of his best friend. Benjamin was always just a friend of Charles. Regardless of what I thought of my husband, I would never become the mistress of another. Especially his best friend. To do so would be madness. Even I wouldn't be that foolish!

Fear washed over me. Why wouldn't Charles have told me he had a sister? James and Mary had never once said a word of her. It almost seemed as though she had been erased from their history. I leaned against the bookcase, afraid to face Charles now. A feeling of dread settled deep in the pit of my stomach.

I stayed in the library until I was confident enough to rejoin the party without looking as though death claimed me. This would be about the hardest charade I would need to play at, not only mingling with people while smiling with gaiety but facing Charles after what had happened.

Muted music wafted through the closed door, bringing me no joy as it normally would. I pressed my palm to my bodice, wishing the dread to go away so I could finish the evening with a smile on my face. But as I walked on shaking legs back to the door, I knew it wouldn't happen. I couldn't finish the evening with a smile on my face because of the dread running through me.

I slipped out of the library, my legs gaining strength as I trudged back down the hallway and into the crowded ballroom with a smile on my face. It would be a miracle if those who knew me believed my smile.

"Georgiana?" I turned, my smile faltering, when Charles slipped his hand around my waist. "You don't look well. Has something happened?"

I shook my head. "I'm suddenly not feeling well. Would you mind terribly if I had John bring me home early?"

"I'll go with you."

"No. Please stay and enjoy the rest of the evening. I'll be fine, Charles."

He brushed his knuckles against my cheek, causing me to pull away. The critical frown that appeared on his face almost made me release a groan. I quickly placed my hand over my mouth, eyes widened.

Charles took my arm and led me out of the ballroom and into the expansive foyer, motioning to the butler. He whispered to him, and the butler hurried away, only to return with my cloak a few moments later. Charles settled the cloak around my shoulders and tied the front. I waited for him to kiss my cheek, but it seemed my reaction before had created some doubt.

"Charles." My voice trembled.

"I'm coming with you."

When I noticed his jaw flex, I clutched his arm before he could move away from me. Coming with me had to be the worst idea. I couldn't think straight. He would only make this worse.

"No. Please don't. I might have had too much champagne."

"Mrs. St. John, your coach is being brought around. Please, allow me to escort you outside." I nodded while he turned to Charles. "I will make sure she gets into the coach safely, Mr. St. John."

"Thank you."

After another moment of hesitation, Charles relinquished me into the safekeeping of the butler. Our carriage was pulling up, with the coachman John at the helm. John jumped down to fold the steps down and helped me step up.

I looked at John with a smile, his white teeth flashing. "Thank you, John."

"Miss Georgie, I'll bring you home safely."

"I know you will."

Once I'd settled into the comfortable seat, I closed my eyes. My eyes remained closed even when the coach lurched into motion with an abrupt jerk. It wouldn't take long to reach home, our brownstone located only a handful of blocks down from the Shaw residence. I hoped when I woke in the morning, it would all have been a dream and never happened, removing a need for worry. How could Charles have had a hand in his sister's death, I couldn't know. Asking him was out of the question.

◆

A short time later, Charles found me sitting in bed, idly brushing my hair. Countless times I had tried without success to find sleep. Nothing was putting my mind at ease. It was well past midnight, but it didn't come as a surprise he came to look in on me. He needed to pass my room to get to his.

"I saw your light still on."

His eyebrows cinched together while he closed the door behind himself, his eyes not leaving mine. Carefully, I set my hairbrush on the table next to my bed while I watched him remove his jacket. Before sitting down on the bed beside me, he draped it neatly over the chair at my dressing table.

"I'm worried for you, my sweet." He reached out, brushing his knuckles against my cheekbone. I held perfectly still this time. "You look so pale. No better than you did earlier."

My hand crept up to cover his, but I didn't press my face into his palm or lean into his touch. I suppose if there were love in my heart for him, I would have. "I'm fine," I whispered.

"Dare I have hope that you might be . . . carrying . . . my child?" He pressed his lips to the curve of my jaw, the spot beneath my ear, followed by my neck.

It didn't escape my notice that his hand had slipped around my waist, his body leaning into mine with obvious intentions. Charles had been my first, and although I wasn't sure what to expect on our wedding night, he hadn't hurt me overly much.

His question fell heedlessly aside when his mouth took mine. I tasted the port on his tongue like bitterness, but I pulled away. Denying him tonight would anger him, but I didn't think I could after the events of the night.

He leaned back and pulled me with him. The frown marking his dark brows, the one that sent ripples of apprehension skittering down my spine, reappeared. He said nothing, but I knew his disappointment would be short-lived. After all, if he was worried about me, he wouldn't continue to press his suit.

Charles lightly drew his fingertips along the bare skin of my neck, above the fabric of my nightdress.

"Did something upset you tonight?"

His question surprised me. Confessing to him what Benjamin had told me crossed my mind, and I opened my mouth to tell him, but thought better of it. I couldn't be sure that what Benjamin had said was true. He might have been bluffing and saying something now would blow it out of proportion. Taking the chance on it coming out at all wouldn't favor me.

"No. It was entirely too warm in the ballroom this evening."

He dropped his hands away from me. "You don't think you might be pregnant?"

It felt like a lead ball in the pit of my stomach, not being able to tell him what he wanted to hear. Not even once during our time together had I ever suspected I carried his child. "I wish I could tell you differently, Charles. You know I would."

"Perhaps I should fetch the doctor tomorrow."

"That isn't necessary. I'm fine now. Truly."

When he stood up and looked down at me, it seemed impossible to tell what he might be thinking. I knew he'd likely had a fair amount to drink, but he didn't slur his words or sway on his feet.

"Goodnight, Georgiana."

My eyes followed him across the room, collecting his jacket on his way out. When the door closed behind him with a click, I turned out the lamp and lay down. If I needed to force myself asleep, I'd have to. It would simply not be good to have dark circles beneath my eyes tomorrow when meeting the ladies for luncheon.

Chapter Four

"You cannot possibly think of marrying a commoner, Georgie."

I gasped, looking up from my spot under the big oak tree at Anthony, his impossibly long legs dangling over the ledge of the low tree branch where he sat. Nearby, the river gurgled and jumped in a rush. I stayed away from the river. Not that I was afraid of it. I wasn't. I just didn't know how to swim. It didn't matter the number of times Anthony had tried to teach me. I either couldn't grasp it, or Mother would interrupt us.

At sixteen, Anthony looked like he was still a young boy with his legs swinging happily. On the cusp of adulthood, he should think of his future and the future of the family. Being the only boy, he'd eventually be the Viscount of Northrup after Grandfather and Father passed on. Both of us hoped that would be long in the future.

Four years older, Anthony was my best friend. My only friend. Anthony and I were against the world, or so it seemed. Our parents never had more children, at least successfully, after me. It didn't matter that he was a boy; we were inseparable when he was on break from school. I couldn't imagine growing up and living apart from him.

I pursed my lips. "I can marry Nigel, Anthony. You wait and see."

Nigel Chrisley was not of noble birth. He was the second son of a farmer in a nearby village, but he was handsome and kind.

Someday I vowed to marry him, even if my mother would never approve. And I knew she never would. Mother told me whom I could associate with and when. Nigel would never be on her short list of those people.

If she'd known I'd snuck out to meet with him sometimes at the very edge of our property, there would be dire consequences. With my father away in London or Manchester much of the time, she did whatever she wanted with me. Controlled what I wore, what I ate, how my hair was styled. She even locked me in my room once when my grandfather came to visit as a punishment for my disobedience. No one knew how mean she could be. It always surprised me how   I didn't have marks on my hands from her thrashing me with her stick on my palms. Withholding meals, I could live with because she wanted me to look perfect, but acting perfect would be something I had to work hard at.

"Mother would never allow it."

"Father will not deny me anything."

Kicking out his legs, Anthony jumped off the branch and landed on his booted feet right in front of me. Laughing, he stretched out beside me and plucked a thick blade of grass up between his fingers. I watched him put it between his hands and blow, making a whistling sound. Together, we laughed.

"Father will not allow this, Georgie," he whispered after our laughter softly flitted away. "He cannot. And Grandfather would not allow it, either. You'll marry a nobleman. That's your destiny."

"And if Mother has her way, no less than a duke." I rolled onto my back and snickered.

After a second of silence, we laughed again. He would leave for school soon, and I'd deal with my mother alone once again. I had learned the hard way what to do and what not to do, but sometimes my defiance got the best of me and I didn't care what consequences would come. Until they came. But I thought I'd learned enough to not repeat the error of my ways.

Abigail Rutherford was known as an ambitious woman. Even

after marrying a viscount, her visions were set impossibly high. When I'd been born the plans in her mind were already made. While Anthony and I had laughed merrily at her marrying me to a duke, that was the stark truth. The hideous list of etiquette in which I'd need to learn to live by would be beaten into my head until I became a meek, beautiful daughter who could attract a duke for a son-in-law. Boiled down, the list included keeping my mouth closed and looking pretty.

Rolling to my side, I rested my head on my palm and studied him. His dark brown hair ruffled in the slight breeze, and his soft brown eyes were full of kindness and joy. When he reached out and tweaked my nose, I giggled and pulled away.

"Try not to do anything rash, Georgie." He turned serious. "I mean it. You're at an age now. You know what will happen when I'm away and Father isn't here. Don't test her."

I flopped onto my back. "I can't help it."

"You can. And you will. Someday you will find a husband who will treat you like the wonderful girl you are, Georgie. You will be away from her and live your life happily ever after." He tweaked my nose again. "I promise you."

The next morning, I woke up with an ache in my heart and wetness on my pillow. If only Anthony's words had come true. I missed him terribly. Shortly after he'd turned eighteen, he told us he was leaving England for America, and it broke my heart. He promised to write to me, but he never did.

Sybil breezed in with a smile, even when I burrowed under the blankets, unwilling to get out of bed yet. I didn't want to face the day. I didn't want last night to be real. It couldn't possibly be. How could Benjamin ask me to do such a thing? I'd liked Benjamin. Why did he have to make me be so mad at him?

"Good morning, my lady," she sang, crossing the carpeted floors to the tall windows and throwing open the curtains to the bright morning sunshine. "Did you enjoy the ball last night?"

I sat up, reluctant to face the uncertainty of the day. I

fervently hoped that every day would not be like this. Perhaps I had misread the situation and Benjamin wouldn't recall his un gentlemanly behavior toward me. Had he been drinking overly much?

"Yes." It was only a partial lie. I had enjoyed the ball. Until Benjamin had cornered me. "The ball was every bit of Annabel's personality. It was elegant, lively, and perfect in every way."

Sweeping the blankets away, I slipped out of bed. After having my daily bath, a requirement on my long list of etiquette, I drifted over to my dressing table. A lady must take a complete bath upon rising, washing her hair once or twice within the week. I didn't mind it so much and I didn't need a tub full of water for a complete bath.

As I sat down at my dressing table and gazed at my reflection, I noticed her looking at the fresh bruises on my wrist. I lowered my wrist from the table and met her gaze in the mirror, yet she stayed quiet. Sybil knew. For six months, she'd seen bruises on my wrists, or on my arms, when Charles had been a little too forceful. She never said anything, and as my maid, she wouldn't.

It was not long before Sybil had my dark hair brushed, twisted, and pinned up in a stylish array of curls. Turning my head to each side, I nodded approval. She smiled, knowing very well she didn't need it.

"You must hurry or you'll be late for breakfast. Charles is already downstairs waiting, and you know how much he hates to be kept waiting."

Dressed in a dark blue pleated dress with tiny buttons down the bodice, I left my bedroom. The knots in my stomach did little to raise my mood. Each step down the staircase caused my heart to pick up an extra beat. Charles sat at the long mahogany table reading his daily newspaper when I rounded the corner to the dining room.

As though sensing my entrance, his eyes caught me immediately. The intensity in his gaze slowed my pace to a dramatic stop, uneasiness coursing through me when his eyes remained on me. The breath caught in my throat while he calmly folded his newspaper and set it aside, his gaze returning to me as a smile curved the corners of his mouth.

"I trust you slept well?" he asked, his tone betraying his disappointment at my rejection of his advances last night.

Finally, my feet moved again until I stood next to him. When it was only the two of us, I often sat next to him rather than the opposite end of the long table. I sat, waiting for Fitz to set my plate down. Today, the plate overflowed with an array of food. Fluffy eggs, muffins and fruit. There were times I barely had anything on the plate, and times like this when there would be too much.

I looked up at Charles. He only nodded, as if to tell me that I would eat all of it without argument.

"Well enough."

My empty stomach turned sour. Poor Maddie. I only hoped Benjamin was sowing whatever wild oats he had left before he settled down. He could have any mistress he wanted, yet he picked me.

"It should please you to know Maddie caught Benjamin for a dance as you were departing. I wasn't sure if you saw." I shook my head. "She looked pleased, but I cannot say the same for Benjamin. He didn't look quite himself."

News of Benjamin dancing with my dear friend should enlighten me, but his words replayed in my head. Had he been attempting to upset me with the proposition, or had he been serious?

"Georgiana?"

I looked up. He watched me curiously. "You're better? You gave me a scare last night. I know how much you love a ball, especially one at the Shaw house."

"I told you last night that I'm fine."

When his hand covered mine and squeezed firmly, I smiled

graciously despite the pain his grip caused. Even as controlling as he was, I knew he would take care of me. I just wasn't sure how long I could live this way, which is why I had purchased the gun.

"You have plans for luncheon today with my mother?" He withdrew his hand, allowing me to eat.

"Yes. Your mother and Annabel."

"We'll be taking a trip next week."

My heart leapt in anticipation. The opportunity to travel again after having been stationary for so long was enticing. I enjoyed living in the city with our friends, and the social engagements, but to leave was exciting.

"Where did you have in mind?"

"We'll be leaving for Philadelphia. There has been an acquisition of a new mill there."

Not overseas, as I'd hoped, as seeing my grandfather would have been wonderful. Grandfather remained my only known family until I could find Anthony, but I hadn't exactly been trying to find him since I'd been here. Charles kept a tight watch on me. He knew I had a brother, but I so rarely spoke of him it might raise unnecessary suspicion. Or that could be my paranoia from my mother taking over.

Charles could very well help me in finding Anthony.

"You will help charm those involved in this acquisition. We will leave a week from tomorrow. I trust you'll have everything in order for our departure?"

I gave him my brightest, most willing smile. Of course, I would be on my best behavior and charm his associates into bending to his every whim. After all, what else would the wife of an aristocrat do?

"Unless there is a reason you couldn't make the trip." He looked at me expectantly.

"There is no reason," I whispered.

"I thought you might say that."

Fitz strode over to Charles, leaning down to whisper into his ear. A second later, Charles pushed away from the table and threw his napkin down next to his plate.

"Business calls, my sweet. Give my love to my mother." He kissed my cheek quickly and left me in the dining room to eat the rest of my breakfast alone. But not before I caught him tell Fitz to make sure my plate was cleaned.

Following breakfast, I met with Juliette to review the menu for the following week's meals and made the beginning preparations for our journey to Pennsylvania for the following week.

Hours later, the carriage brought me to the bustling street outside Delmonico's beside the footman John, who would make sure I went inside before he left. Activity on William and Beaver Streets seemed to be always in abundance with carriages traveling in every direction and people walking along the walks or streets toward a midday destination. At the corner, I watched the surrounding commotion with a sense of temporary gratitude for the life afforded me. Young boys squawked nearby with an effort to sell the remaining issues of the daily newspaper while men dressed in their business attire sought a break from their busy day. A mother surrounded by four children carried a basket covered with a dirty cloth, my eyes following her in wonder until she was around the corner. The south end of the island was where the ships docked.

It didn't seem so long ago that I'd stepped from a ship in this new land, the tall buildings of New York a wondrous sight to behold. The urge to twirl around had been too strong for me to ignore, but just as I had stepped into a wide circle, my father had sensed my wayward mood and caught my arm. Other than Anthony, he had always known me better than most. He'd known that I would have twirled my way to the carriage had he not stopped me, despite my advanced age. Mother would have been beyond furious. My mood brightened at the joyous memory.

A couple, strolling along the sidewalk, caught my eye. They had to be married, I thought, for as close as they were holding each other. It would be indecent otherwise. The way she looked up at him, eyes shining with brightness, I envied. I could feel the love in her gaze. And the man looking down at her, lips curved in a smile that spoke of equal love. This was not the first time I'd seen people in love. But deep down, I wanted that. I needed it.

As much as I would give to have Charles look upon me with love and adoration, treat me as an equal rather than someone to command, I knew I could never look at him with that shine in my eyes. I'd hoped in time that I would, especially if we could have a child. But in the time we'd been married, nothing had grown between us. If anything, it had pushed us further apart. I drew in a deep breath. There would be no good in dwelling on it now.

After having a minor delay with my gown when I'd accidentally torn it, I didn't doubt Annabel and Mary were already waiting for me in the popular restaurant of the seven-story building. A woman journalist hosted a luncheon here over a month ago after they denied her entry to a well-known author's reading. All because she was a woman. The insistence of this group of women allowed us to dine here without our husband's having to accompany us.

Annabel and Mary sat by the window at a small table, each with a cup of tea at hand and a smile for me as I approached. I admired them for their taste in fashion for they were both dressed impeccably. It was because of Sybil's keen eye for trends that I didn't feel drab beside them. Mary wore a bright yellow dress and Annabel a fashionable light blue. While they both wore matching hats, I likened myself to Benjamin and abhorred having to wear a hat, even though fashion dictated it. I shuddered at the thought of him, still wondering what I would do about it.

Mary leaned over to kiss my cheek when I sat down between them. "I apologize for my tardiness. There was a slight tear in my dress that needed to be mended quickly. I hope you've not waited overly long."

"My dear, you've not kept us." Annabel patted my hand. "I heard you left the ball early last night. Were you ill?"

Never one to mince words, that would be Annabel.

"I fear the champagne went straight to my head with all the dancing. I'm feeling much better today. In fact, I was determined to keep our appointment." I pulled off my gloves, ignoring Mary's gasp at the sight of the fresh bruises around my wrist.

"My dear! Don't tell me you tripped on the staircase again!" Mary said, looking at Annabel. "Charles is forever having to save her from falling. One of these times, she is going to tumble and it will not turn out well." She gently touched my uninjured wrist. "I worry for you, Georgiana."

I accepted a cup of tea from Mary, her light eyes somber when she handed it to me. Lips tight, I kept control of my inner turmoil regarding what she thought of my bruises. I liked Mary, but it would do no good to correct her. Charles would forever be the hero in her eyes, never at fault for a thing.

"You look much better," Mary murmured.

"You'll accompany us for a drive in Washington Square Park following our lunch. The fresh air will do us good, I think. Benjamin thought for certain you were ill last night."

I tried not to wince at the mention of Benjamin, the very cause of my distress. Had it not been for his sudden absurd invitation to become his mistress, I would have remained at the ball much later and not given Charles a cause to worry. The rim of my cup hid my grimace when I took a sip of my tea. No one could know of the dastardly proposition he had cast upon me, especially Annabel. We would be shunned by the elite society. I couldn't do that to Mary.

"Nothing to worry about, I assure you."

"Could you be with child?" Annabel asked abruptly.

Mary's gasp echoed my shock. I considered myself to be a calm person. Even as a child, I never had a quick temper. I smiled sweetly and shook my head.

"Are you certain? You've always been one of the last to leave a ball."

I eyed her carefully, forcing myself to laugh softly. "I'm quite certain."

"My dear, you can tell us anything."

My hand rose quickly, my palm a sign of my desire to cease the conversation. "I appreciate your concern, Annabel, but I can assure you I'm not pregnant. And if I were, my husband would be the first to know such a thing."

Annabel's lips pressed together briefly before she smiled and retrieved her tea, taking a sip to hide whatever machinations she had up her sleeve. My inability to conceive during my marriage was mine to deal with. It was dreadfully embarrassing enough. While not above discussing it, I would not be discussing it with Annabel.

I'd be more inclined to speak with my neighbor, who lived a few doors down from us, as she had been equally unsuccessful in conceiving. Married for two years and no children. We'd shared many tea times in the privacy of our homes in such discussions.

"I didn't mean to distress you." Annabel's lips still looked pinched.

"I'm not distressed at all. Please think nothing of it. In due time, I shall be pregnant and announce it to all, I am sure. In fact, Charles and I spoke only this morning about traveling to Philadelphia. Perhaps that will help."

"Oh, my dear!" Mary cried. "I am delighted for you! When will you leave?"

"Charles said a week from tomorrow."

Annabel reached over and touched my hand, smiling. "Being

away will do you good, Georgiana. I am certain of it."

Annabel was right. Being away after having been married for six months is what I needed. Charles needed it as well. Together, we would enjoy traveling to another city and there would be no pressure, no responsibility to face. That would be what we needed.

We ate tiny sandwiches and drank black tea, gossiping about the ball last evening. Soon after, Annabel called for her carriage, and we were riding in Washington Square Park, enjoying the sunshine. While Annabel and Mary opted to stay in the carriage, I walked around the park with my parasol resting on my shoulder. Only the light fabric shielded me from the sun. As a woman, even married, walking alone in the park was frowned upon. I stayed within a safe distance of the carriage, but as soon as I spotted Benjamin, I regretted it instantly.

As soon as he saw me, he wasted no time approaching. The reason for his attendance in the park, I could not fathom, but suddenly I wasn't sure what to say to him. He bowed to me first before greeting his mother and Mary.

"What brings you to the park, my dear boy?" Annabel asked.

I felt a gnawing curiosity to know why he strolled in the park at the same time we were, and I was relieved when she asked instead of me. I wasn't ready to face him yet. I didn't know when I would be ready.

"Only taking a much needed walk." He turned to me. "How good to see you after last night, Georgie." His eyes sparkled with mischief. "I was distressed to hear you had left early. I trust you are well?"

"Quite."

If there was a bite to my voice, I couldn't help it. Even knowing him for nearly as long as Charles, he had never been more of a cad than he had been last night. Seeing him now showed him in a new light.

"Could I interest you in a stroll?"

I stared at his outstretched arm as though it were a two-headed snake. To decline his offer would offend his mother, who aptly listened to our exchange. To accept would mean I would have to be in his company, not alone, but alone enough for a conversation between only the two of us. It made me nervous that he would ply me with more ridiculous talk of becoming his mistress, a thought that left a sour taste in my mouth.

Resigned, I tucked my arm within his and allowed him to guide me away from the safekeeping of my companions. I would suffer through whatever else he could say to me, but I would never consider his suggestion. He waited until we were safely out of earshot before continuing his pursuit.

"Have you thought of my proposition?"

His voice was low, even though no one could overhear. It took determination to not visibly shudder in revulsion. "There is nothing to think about, Benjamin. I would never do such a thing to Charles. How you could even think of such a thing, I don't know. He's your friend! Your best friend."

"Friend or not, I don't care. It's for your own well-being."

"And you get nothing of it? What is this nonsense about me becoming your . . . your mistress? I don't understand why you are doing this. What have I done?"

He laughed. Did he truly think this was amusing? "This has nothing to do with what you have done, Georgie. Or haven't done, for that matter. It's what you could do. Get away from him! Be in the arms of a man who would cherish you."

I couldn't believe I was having this conversation. "You think Charles does not cherish me?"

"I know he doesn't cherish you. He owns you, Georgie. He will never let you go. You shouldn't be with Charles. He will ruin you in time. I just know it."

I scoffed. As unladylike as it was, I didn't care. "You are the lowest kind of bastard, Benjamin. To think that I would do such a thing with my husband's best friend."

His arm stiffened. "I hope for your sake, you see it before it's too late."

My face burned in shame. I would sooner die than succumb to Benjamin. He was worse than a cad. It was men like him who society should shun, yet he was at the very top of it. My stomach lurched, and for a moment, I thought I might vomit. Was this truly happening?

"Georgie?" Benjamin asked. "Are you ill?"

I laughed haughtily. "While you seem to think I would betray Charles, I never will. You would need to take me by force and I can assure you, if you try, I will scream it from the highest building."

Benjamin stopped, turning to face me with soft eyes. "Don't do that, Georgie. Please. Consider it."

My lips pressed together. I needed to compose myself or people would think Benjamin and I were disagreeing. "I never will. You are putting me in a terrible position."

The light in his eyes softened even more, turning us to continue our stroll as though no bitter words had sprung from my lips. "You are a passionate woman, Georgie. You will only suffocate in your marriage if you continue as you are. Or worse, follow the same fate as Violet."

"What do you know about my marriage? And why are you so convinced I will end up like his sister, that no one speaks of?"

"You forget I am best friends with your husband. I have known him longer than I have known many others. Violet went crazy, nearly had to be sent to the mental institution. Instead, she took her own life. His jealousy will snuff out whatever light you have in your eyes. He'll never give you what I can. Away from here."

"You are terribly wrong. Why did you not ask to court me at the same time he did? You made no suggestion of it." I shrugged.

He chuckled, his hand smoothing over mine. The heat of his palm was not comforting, but I kept my composure. "Your mother was intent on having Charles for a son-in-law, not I. For whatever reason, she would have no one else but Charles for her daughter."

If nothing else, I could believe that. Why else would a marriage proposal have come so soon after reaching here? No, she knew exactly who was best suited to tame my quick wit and wayward nature. Charles St. John. She knew I'd never manage to snag a duke. My aspirations in life had never matched hers.   I shook my head, still angry beyond words with Benjamin. Regardless of what transpired six months ago, my vows were now what they were then.

"I am no more ready to settle down now than I was then. All I can offer you is passion and some companionship."

If I stormed away from him, I risked upsetting his mother. Upsetting Annabel would upset Mary, and I would not do that to her. This wasn't her fight. It was mine. Benjamin was still pulling me slowly forward, only a few steps ahead of the carriage. It didn't matter. I wouldn't relent.

"I cannot do what you are asking me to do."

Turning to me, the plea in his eyes confused me more than his words. This didn't seem like a man intent on ruining my marriage, my good name, and making a fool of me. What on earth did he think he was doing? He could have any woman he wanted in his bed. Why choose me?

"You can, Georgie. No one needs to know."

"No one will know."

Despite my irritable growl, he continued, "You can be happy. I can be happy."

"Take me back to your mother. I won't do this. I can't."

"You may regret it," he whispered.

I wondered if he would cause a scene here in the park, in front of several groups of people walking in pairs and riding in open carriages. I would have called his bluff had he not turned us around and strolled toward Annabel and Mary.

Chapter Five

Wednesday evening, following Benjamin's surprise declaration of intentions, I sat at my writing desk answering invitations. The day had been dreary with rain, clouds covering the sky with no hope of allowing the sun to shine through. As evening closed in, the weather had not let up even the smallest bit. The steady downpour against the windowpanes unsettled me, with occasional flares of lightning followed by rumbles of thunder causing me to jump with every loud boom.

After changing into a suitable dress for dinner, I went downstairs to find Charles in the parlor, pacing. A letter, nearly crushed, in his hand and his brows drawn together as though pinched.

As though sensing my presence, his brown eyes lifted, and I nearly stepped back from the animosity brewing behind his glower. The look in his eyes was unnerving.

"Come in, my sweet." His words dripped with contempt.

Cautiously, I stepped in and closed the door behind me. Although, closing the door would likely do little to ward off any eavesdropping servants. If he raised his voice, there would be no stopping rumors from escaping like wildfire. People tended to believe the worst types of gossip, regardless of the truth.

"I've received the most troublesome news."

I stayed near the door, drawing my hands behind me and

clasping them together. My fingers dug into one another, twisting.

"Whatever it is, it can't possibly be true," came my whisper.

He turned to face me, the normal calmness in his eyes gone and replaced with a fierceness I had never seen before. The line of his jaw was hard, his lips pressed into a thin line. I'd seen Charles angry before, but I'd never see him this enraged.

He strode up to me so quickly; I winced. Never had he raised a hand to me. He'd put his hands on me numerous times, always in warning, but had never struck me. That didn't mean he would not do so now.

"Someone saw you at the ball. Someone saw you in Benjamin's arms."

I watched fury come over his face, even when his eyes closed. Blocking out images of what he must think Benjamin and I would look like together, I thought. It made my stomach turn.

"Who? I deserve to know who is spreading these lies."

"It does not say," he snapped. "Do you know what I think? I think that you've been preventing pregnancy because of your affair with Benjamin."

Heat flooded my cheeks. That he would dare to accuse me of such a heinous thing was beyond comprehension. I wouldn't know the first thing about how to prevent pregnancy. Stepping back from him, I could only stare at him in disbelief. That he could say such a thing to me. Believe such a thing about me. I put distance between us, and he didn't stop me. I knew Charles didn't have much decency in him, but this . . .

This had become far more than I'd imagined it could. The one thing that I'd wanted most had now turned into something against me. I'd wanted a child so badly, I'd never turned him away except for the night of Annabel's ball. I'd wanted it so much I put up with his callous treatment of me, even though I never knew why he treated me so.

"Do you deny it?"

"Yes! I deny it! I deny being with any other man but you. And I absolutely, unequivocally, deny preventing pregnancy. All I've wanted since we wed is to give you a child. That you do not believe me hurts me beyond words."

"You were seen in his arms! Less than a week ago!" He shook the crushed letter in his fist at me.

My eyes widened. Someone could not have seen me in his arms. I hadn't been in his arms. I reeled from the confusion. What was happening?

"It is not true," I whispered again.

What more could I say?

"Why would the sender of this letter lie?" I didn't have an answer for him. "Odd that both of you were absent at the ball for a time and you left soon afterwards, don't you think?"

I pressed my lips together, else I would say something I would likely regret. Nothing I could say was going to sway him. Instead, I stayed quiet.

He looked down his nose, condemning me. "I nearly shared your bed that night," he bit out. "Now I know why you denied me. After you were . . . with him."

"I wasn't—"

His head snapped up, eyes blazing with fury. "You're going to deny you were with him the night of the ball?"

"I wasn't with him the night of the ball, Charles!"

"I can only guess why you looked unwell that evening."

"Because Benjamin—"

Unsure of what to tell Charles that wouldn't make me look guilty of something I had nothing to do with, I stopped myself from saying anything further. He wasn't about to believe anything I said.

He towered over me. Defiant, at best, I tilted my chin up.

Leaning in closer, he stared at me for a moment, his eyes looking deep into mine. "I should have you committed."

My face burned. "Wha . . . what are you saying? You don't

believe me, therefore you'd send me to an institution to be rid of me?"

"I have every right to do it." His eyes narrowed. "And more."

Before I could utter another sound, Charles strode away from me and out of the room through the second door leading to the back of the house. I stood frozen, alone in the parlor, for several moments. The shock of what had transpired overwhelmed me with emotions all at once. Hot tears burned my eyelids, filling my eyes while I pulled my shaking hands in front of me to trace the gold band around my finger.

Something had gone terribly wrong. Not only that, but someone else had seen us in the library, and misinterpreted the situation at best. And it had all been his fault. If he hadn't had this crazed idea to pull me away from Charles, make me his mistress of all things, I wouldn't be threatened with being put into a place where women were treated like animals and left to die. Except now, I didn't quite know what to do. Benjamin might be the only one I could go to if Charles had me committed. But would I be able to?

Chapter Six

Attending the charity sale today seemed like the worst idea. If word had gotten to Charles about this ridiculous accusation, it had undoubtedly made its rounds. Society in New York was not very different from London, which meant people would whisper about this behind their hands for months to come.

Mary would be at the charity auction and if this malicious rumor had gotten out, I didn't want to leave her amongst wolves. I bolstered what little courage I had and left the house, escorted to and from the carriage by John. I only had permission to leave because Mary would be there. I doubted I'd be allowed to leave the house after today. While I took a tray for breakfast in my room, with no intention of seeing Charles so soon, I couldn't find him when I went downstairs to leave. Nor did I look hard.

In such a hurry to leave the house, I paid little attention to Fitz and Oliver on my way out to catch any type of betrayal or indifference on their faces. No one else had been about when I rushed across the foyer.

The moment I stepped into Elizabeth Smith's home and looked around her large drawing room, a hush swept from one side of the room to the other. The furniture had been replaced with tables covered with items for sale for the charity, from handkerchiefs to hats. All eyes fell on me as though no one had expected me to appear. Warmth grew on my face while I looked from one woman to the next, eyes lowering as I did.

When I reached Annabel, she met my gaze only briefly before looking away and leaning down to whisper something into the ear of Hazel Jaffries. I looked for Mary, but she wasn't present. Either she hadn't shown up yet or because she had more sense than I and stayed away. I only hoped it was the latter.

As I turned to leave, I caught sight of Maddie. She had her back partially to me, speaking with Elly and Nettie. Clearly, no one wanted a thing to do with me now that the rumor had gotten out. Drawing my back rigidly straight, I turned and left. The carriage was nowhere in sight, assuming I wouldn't be out so soon and giving me a chance to be out on the streets without supervision.

No sooner had I reached the street, stinging tears had burned trails down my face. The walk to clear my head would do me good. My mind raced with what I could do now that society had snubbed me. No friends, no support from my husband, no family. I had fallen to utter ruin in the matter of days.

It seemed to take longer than usual to reach my street; the brownstone coming into view and relief washing over me. I'd be able to get to my bedroom and retreat into darkness until I could figure out what to do before Charles did something so drastic such as commit me. I could book passage home. Grandfather would protect me. He would have to. But I'd need money, and to get it, I would need to get to my bedroom and hope that Charles hadn't taken it.

The street had more traffic than usual, causing me to have to dart in and out of carriages while crossing, but I reached the opposite sidewalk without issue. I heard my name called behind me, turning to see Benjamin coming for me. Oh, no! I thought. Not now. Not in front of my home. Charles could be home.

This day couldn't possibly get worse. Whirling around, I bolted for the front door of my house before he could catch me.

The door slammed loudly behind me. I leaned against the

door, my chest heaving.

Thankfully, only quiet greeted me in return. Charles didn't rush from the parlor or his office to see what the commotion could be. Only Fitz came from the kitchen to see if I needed someone. I could only shake my head, not trusting myself to speak and sure I'd looked a mess.

Strangely, my bedroom was my only safe place, but it was suffocating. Once in my room behind the closed door, I sat at my writing desk, unsure of what to do next. Word traveled fast in this house, and a short time later, Sybil came in.

"Miss Georgie," she whispered, "are you unwell? Should I fetch a physician?"

"That isn't necessary."

We fell silent while Sybil pretended to tidy the room before going to leave. The thoughts of what the day might bring invaded, wreaking havoc on my emotions that I held so tightly within.

"Have you heard any rumors within the servant's quarters?"

She didn't miss a beat, turning back toward me. "I hear many rumors. Was there someone in particular you wanted to know about?"

"Me. Someone has said Benjamin Shaw and I are having an affair, although I am without a clue to understand how we would have had such a chance to. I'm never allowed to come and go without an escort."

"Oh, Miss Georgie," she whispered.

A tilt of the corner of my lips, even a half-hearted one, was all I could manage. "It has already made its rounds within society. I'm already being snubbed."

"What will you do?"

I shrugged. Truly, I didn't know. "Charles doesn't believe me. And worse, he thinks I've been preventing pregnancy because of it."

"What will he do?"

"He's my husband. He can do anything he wants with me. You know how tightly he controls me."

Shouts from outside my window drew my attention away, my gaze on the panes of glass but not really seeing them. I felt trapped in my bedroom until I could find a way out of this mess. Perhaps I should have spoken with Benjamin. I shuddered. Anyone who saw us would have gossip traveling faster than the currents in the Hudson River.

"I can't face anyone now." When I stood, my legs still shook. "I only ask that you keep an ear out for gossip in the servants' quarters and let me know what you hear." I touched her arm. "Anything, Sybil."

When she nodded her head, I knew I could trust that she would report back. She had been the most faithful maid, giving me no reason to believe I couldn't trust her. When the blasted rumors of my failure to conceive made its rounds, she made sure I knew what was being said in the servant's quarters, although it was no fault of my own. I would at least know what was being said. And by whom.

Left alone, I settled back in the chair at my writing desk to pen a letter to my grandfather. I hoped to find solace in my grandfather. Perhaps he would send for me and I could return to South Lancashire in disgrace. Better to live in shame than to live here with those who thought me capable of such a dastardly act.

By the time I finished my letter, my hand ached from clutching the quill and I had nearly three pages full. Before my courage failed me, I tucked it in an envelope and sealed it. It would take weeks to reach home, but I had faith I could wait it out. I could lay low. What was the worst that could happen?

I strolled to the windows, pulling aside the sheer draperies to gaze down at the street. The streets were alive with activity, people strolling the streets while carriages rambled by, oblivious to the hell I'd found myself in. How I longed for companionship, but already I felt like an outsider. It hadn't been like this even when I'd arrived over six months ago. Welcomed openly into New York society, it was like a warm embrace, now suddenly missed.

My door opened and Sybil stepped in with an apologetic smile. "Miss Georgie, you have a visitor."

"Who is it?"

"Miss Bennett."

I swallowed my gasp. "I don't want to see anyone. Tell her I'm ill."

"Fitz told her as much, but she insists upon seeing for herself."

The draperies softly slipped out of my hand, my heart steadily thrumming in my chest. Hurting Maddie was the last thing I wanted to do, but I was afraid. I couldn't run anywhere now. My only choices were to turn her away and hurt her feelings or be brave and face her.

"Very well," I whispered, crossing the room. "I'll see her."

I took my time walking to the staircase even when Sybil lingered behind me. My hand slid along the banister until I reached the end, my fingers curling around the newel post.

She studied the books lining the shelves of the bookcase at the far wall of the parlor when I entered, her back to me. Although my arrival at Elizabeth Smith's house had been brief, her presence in my parlor came as a surprise. She should be at the charity sale with Elly and Nettie.

"I knew you were not ill." She didn't turn around to face me, pretending to study the books instead. "How could you do it?"

Slowly, I stepped fully into the room. "I didn't. Someone is lying about this. I would never be unfaithful to Charles."

Maddie whirled, folding her arms in front of herself. "Lying seems to be what you do."

The blood drained from my face and I put my hand on the back of the chair to keep myself from falling. I crept closer to the chair as though it provided a barrier between us. Surely, she would believe in me. Of the very few people I had close to me, Maddie had to believe that I wouldn't do such a thing.

"How could you?" she whispered.

Did everyone think I could do such a heinous thing? Was Benjamin not just as guilty of this, if it were true? "You can't think I did this, Maddie." She rolled her eyes. "It's not true."

"I saw it with my own eyes! I heard it, too!"

I gasped, my hand flying up to my throat as though to stop any cries from escaping. Had I been so preoccupied with Benjamin that I'd not heard anyone come into the library to see us?

She moved closer to me. "I was curious when you left the ballroom, more curious when I saw Benjamin follow you. Neither of you heard me open the door to the library, but what I saw crushed me! You know how I feel about him, Georgie, and yet you . . ."

How in the world could I explain this to her and make her understand it wasn't what she thought she saw? I moved around the chair toward her, but she threw up her hands to ward me off and shook her head.

"I thought you were my friend."

"He asked me to become his mistress. I refused. That is all."

Her eyes betrayed her emotions. Even knowing her for such a small amount of time, I knew she didn't believe me. If she had seen what she had, there would be no talking her out of what she thought she'd seen.

"You were the one who sent the note to Charles," I said. "You told him what you thought you saw. And because of that, my husband wants to commit me."

Her eyes widened.

"Commit me!" I shouted. "All over something I did not do. Would never do."

Like with Charles, I didn't know what to say to convince

her of my innocence. Everyone in this society knew each other well, had known each other for years. It was me who came from the outside. They didn't know me like they knew each other. I moved toward her, anger rising quickly. It didn't matter what I did, what I said. No one believed me.

"We are friends. If you don't believe I wouldn't do that to Charles, at least believe I would never do such a thing to you." She kept her back to me, rigidly straight. "You've been my closest friend, Maddie. You were the first to befriend me. Why would I ever hurt you this way?"

Maddie stayed where she was. "I saw what I saw, but if it isn't true, people will see the truth."

I doubted her words, as much as I wanted to believe in them. Maddie always saw the brighter side of things, ever optimistic. Benjamin had to be blinded not to see her worth, but I hoped Archie won her over before Benjamin could sink his claws into her. I didn't believe for a moment that Benjamin would stay faithful to her.

Chapter Seven

"Ah, there she is."

When I swept into the dining room that evening, it didn't sound like the rumors had reached the ears of my in-laws. An impossibility, I knew. They had to have heard it. Frederick and Annabel were their closest friends. Outwardly, my demeanor was cool while inside I shook in apprehension of what could come. I dared not look toward Charles, who sat at his usual spot at the head of the table. I didn't need to look at him to know that he didn't stand when I entered as James did.

Fitz pulled my chair out, and I sat, spreading my napkin on my lap as he pushed me in. I met Mary's eyes across the table and she smiled kindly. They acted as though nothing had happened, ignoring the rumors in favor of their son. The smile I returned was feeble at best, slipping away quickly when pea soup appeared in front of me. I withdrew into silence while Charles and James discussed the running of the textile mill.

"Georgiana, I hear you and Charles will take a trip," James said.

Midair, my spoon stopped. Amidst the events lately, I'd forgotten about the trip to Philadelphia. I looked at Charles, but he wouldn't meet my eyes. Silence hung thick in the air, suffocating.

"Our trip will need to be delayed," Charles said, bitterness deep in his voice.

I lost the grip on my spoon and it clattered against the bowl, all eyes falling on me. Murmuring an apology, I retrieved it quickly and continued to sip my soup with calculated movements. My ears filled with a buzzing sound, voices drowning out as I fixed my eyes on the vomit-green of my soup.

My stomach twisted and rolled. I set my spoon back down and waved Fitz over before what little soup I'd ingested came back up. "Please take it away."

After an approving nod from Charles, Fitz took it away. From across the table, I saw Mary frown. "Georgie, you don't look well," she whispered.

"I've not felt well lately, which is likely why Charles has delayed our trip." It seemed all I could offer as an excuse, even with a small smile, my stomach still turning. "I'm sure I'll be well soon enough."

Mary dabbed her mouth gently. "A trip, while not feeling well, would be a travesty. It's best to wait until you are better. Has the doctor come to call?"

"I'm certain I only need rest. I'll send for the doctor if I don't improve in a few days."

"Did you hear of the train robbery in Indiana last week?" She rambled, as she did in tense conversations. "I heard the gang got away with over ninety thousand dollars!"

I gasped. "Was anyone hurt?"

"Not that they reported. They said it was that Reno gang who's robbed other trains these past few years. They couldn't catch them."

"Seems that gang is getting bolder," I murmured.

"Dangerous times to be traveling on trains," James cut in, his voice commanding the quiet of the dining room. "Only a matter of time before they start hurting people."

"These are troubling times still. Many are still destitute after the war," Charles said, the sharpness of his tone not lost on me.

Fitz and Oliver cleared the remaining first course, leaving me to my thoughts for a few moments before they brought the second course. My stomach immediately revolted at the aroma of the roasted fish, but I kept my composure and picked at my potatoes until the front bell rang. We all looked up at the unexpected sound.

"Who on earth would ring at this time?" James asked, while Fitz motioned to Oliver to see who was at the door.

When Oliver reappeared with Benjamin behind him, I stifled my gasp. Charles stood so abruptly from his chair it knocked backward and crashed to the carpeted floor. Oliver hurried over to pick up the chair.

"You dare come to my home? After all that you've done? After all that you've caused?"

Eyes wide, I watched Mary stand weakly as though she'd try to stop Charles from rushing toward Benjamin. I'd never seen Charles so furious, even after he'd confronted me about the charges against me. Benjamin interrupting our dinner was not only damning me but causing his own repercussions. Red crept up Charles's neck, his fists clenched when he released his napkin onto the table.

I looked at Benjamin, who acted as though he owned the room with his cool demeanor. "My apologies for interrupting," he said, tone smooth. "I would like a word with Georgie."

Not so much as a *please* or *if I may*. He breezed in here and expected to speak with me. As if I could do such a thing. Even if I would allow it, he had to know that Charles would never.

If Charles's face could get any shades redder, it did. It looked purple, his lips pressing together so tightly I could hardly see them. When he moved to approach Benjamin, James stood and held his arm to stop him.

"You've no right to come here. You've no right to ask to speak with my wife, whom you've clearly already had more than words with."

This time I couldn't stop the gasp, but I stayed where I was. I needed to remain calm, having no interest in speaking with Benjamin now or any other time. Only my potatoes had my attention.

"Georgie," Benjamin said, his voice soft. "Please. May I have a word with you?"

My head snapped up at his plea. Had I heard him correctly? He sounded sincere in his request, his eyes pleading to me. If he would have reached out his hand to me, did he think I would take it and we would run away? I shook my head. I couldn't do this.

"Get out!"

I watched Charles shrug off James, heading straight for Benjamin. He got in one solid punch before they were grappling. James rushed to them, trying without success to pull them apart. Mary and I watched with wide, terrified eyes. This had gone on long enough. Finally, I threw my napkin down and stood.

"Stop it!" I shouted, having never shouted so loud since I was a very young girl. Ladies did not raise their voices.

Everything in the room came to a sudden halt, Benjamin with his hands pushing against Charles's face. Charles with his fists within Benjamin's coat lapels. Poor James had them both by their collars. Mary stood, wringing her napkin in her hands.

Pushing away from the table, I came around to them. "Stop fighting this instant," I snapped. "Fighting will do none of us any good. I maintain my innocence, Charles, so whatever he has to say to me can wait, for I wish to never speak with him again."

Charles released Benjamin and took a step back, but the grimace on his face remained. Even now, he did not believe me. Benjamin coming here and asking to speak with me only pushed me further into damnation.

Benjamin stepped away from Charles. "Georgie, I must speak with you."

My chin lifted. "Are you here to assist me in denying this

ridiculous lie?"

He frowned. "I wish only to speak with you."

Charles growled, "I want you out of my house. You will not be speaking with my wife now or in the future."

"Benjamin, I think it is best if you leave." For good measure, James added, "Immediately."

My shoulders slumped. Was there no end to this nightmare? I waited patiently while Oliver and Fitz led Benjamin out the front door before I brushed past James and Charles.

Charles reached out to grab my arm, his fingers painfully tight while holding me from taking another step. "Surely, you're not going after your lover."

I snapped my teeth together. "I am going to my room."

Wrenching my arm away, I left the dining room and did not dare to look back. I barely made it into the foyer when Charles caught my arm again, halting my steps. This had become exasperating, being talked to as though I were a disease and man-handled like a belonging instead of a person.

"Tell me the truth, Georgiana."

"I told you the truth," I hissed. "You choose not to believe me."

"There is little reason to believe it isn't true." He released my arm. "I only ask for the truth."

"And I gave it to you."

"What reason would Benjamin have to come here? To ask to speak with you?"

There were a string of reasons I could give him, but none would help my cause. "Those are questions for Benjamin, not I. Only he would have the answers you seek. Now, if you don't mind, I would like to return to my room."

Charles stared at me. "To think of you, in his arms . . . " A look of disgust passed over his face, burrowing his brows and pinching his lips. "In his bed."

"Then don't think of it. Because it doesn't have a merit of

truth to it."

Whirling, I continued to the staircase without looking back. It couldn't be clearer but he still didn't believe my word against what he'd been told, and I wouldn't wait for him to decide. The sanctuary of my room called, my steps increasing in pace the closer I came. It was blissfully quiet when I closed the door behind me a moment later.

There was hardly a sound as I sat at my dressing table, picking up the hairbrush and tracing my fingertips over the grooves in the silver. I knew I couldn't stay here. But of one thing I could be certain. Charles would not allow me to go so freely.

I set the hairbrush down, about to open the drawer that hid my Derringer when the door opened and Sybil swept in. Faithful to me, she likely heard I'd left the dinner table early and had hurried up after me. The high collar of her maid's uniform nearly brushed the edges of her hair where it swept up.

"Shall I ready you for bed?"

I sighed. "I'm sure you heard of our rather intrusive dinner."

She stepped behind me, pulling pins from my hair until my hair fell down past my shoulders.

"There was talk in the kitchen," she admitted, reaching around me to set the pins on the table and pick up the brush. "I must say, it doesn't paint a very pleasant picture."

"I'm aware."

As she drew the hairbrush through my hair, I closed my eyes. Curiosity at why Benjamin wanted to speak to me raced through my mind. The reaction to his interruption from Charles had been enough for me to decline speaking with him. Had I accepted, I couldn't imagine what Charles would have done.

"Rumors are running through the staff?"

"Yes, but I am doing my best to dissuade them from believing such things of you."

I laughed, softly. "How are you doing that?"

"There is no doubt in my mind that you would do such a

thing, but there is something you do not know about me." She fell silent, as though she didn't trust herself in outing what she had to divulge.

I swiveled around, causing her to stop brushing my hair. "Sybil? You can trust me."

"You know he had a sister."

"I have only recently found this out. Why no one ever spoke of her, I still don't understand."

"I served as Violet's maid." My mouth fell open. "She died some time ago. I was told never to speak of it, especially to you."

"By whom?"

I didn't need to ask the question to know who might have told her never to tell me such a thing. If Benjamin had been right, and Charles had something to do with his sister's death, it made sense he wouldn't want me to know this.

"They thought you might ask too many questions about her."

"They? Not Charles?"

"They do not speak of her. She took her own life. Violet went a little mad, I suppose you could say. I didn't think she did, but Charles did. He wanted to send her to the institution for tests. James didn't want to do such a thing. And Mary, well she does everything Charles wants her to do."

"Benjamin asked me to be his mistress," I whispered. "He said he would get me away from Charles, where he could never find me. Unfortunately, it's what started this entire disastrous mess. Had he not asked that, had it not been overheard, none of this would have happened."

As she brushed my hair, she remained silent about the information I told her. I kept silent when she helped me out of my dress until I was standing beside the bed in my chemise, wondering where it had all gone wrong. But if Charles was convinced his sister needed to be committed, he would have no issue with sending me away. Sybil bid me goodnight and I turned down the lamps except for the one closest to the bed. It wasn't late, but the evening had been exhausting.

Sleep should have claimed me quickly as little as I had gotten lately, but I lay in the dark for a long time without reprieve. Even sitting up to brush my hair more did little to help and I stood to pace the room. I thought about the gun in my dressing table. It had been incredibly difficult to sneak out to purchase it, and I nearly didn't make it back into the house without being discovered. It didn't matter that everything was now much worse than before. I would take my own life before stepping foot inside an institution for the insane.

My thoughts drifted to Anthony. One of my finer qualities, one my mother never found out about, had been listening through the cracks in open doors. Thank goodness for being light on my feet. Father and Mother never knew that I'd learned things about Anthony. Such as the money Father had sent to him. Regardless of whether he had abandoned his title, Father would never let Anthony struggle in life. He'd provided him enough to get started in his venture and then some.

There were still a number of things I'd never been fortunate enough to hear, such as where I could find him. And some I would never know. With my parents gone now, he remained the only close family I had, even if I hadn't heard from him in years.

"He met a girl." I heard my father say just before the rustling of papers, as though he were reading.

I pursed my lips. He promised to write to me, yet he'd written to Mother and Father. Where were my letters? Surely he'd want me to know what happened once he'd reached America. He'd promised me!

My mother clucked her tongue against her teeth, a habit that annoyed me beyond madness. "I suppose he is looking to settle down with this this girl. And so soon after having reached that godforsaken country."

"Abigail, please try to have an open mind. I do business with that 'god forsaken country,' which allows us to live in luxury."

The exasperation in his voice made me smile. It felt good to know I was not the only one annoyed with her outlandish views. I'd never known anyone more of a snob than my mother.

"Her name is Helene. He met her in North Carolina, in a city called Charlotte. Helene Ward. Sounds like a nice girl. He and his business partner, Chester, have stayed there for a time, on account that her family is there, before finding a place to settle. He'll write again soon."

"Does he ask after Georgiana?"

"Of course he does." His voice gruff. "He always does. You know how close they are. Why wouldn't he?"

"No good can come of it, Edward."

"That does not mean he shouldn't know how well his sister does. She'll be at an age to have her coming out soon. Meeting a man who may become her husband one day is a big to-do."

If he wanted to know about me, why wouldn't he write to me directly? I thought. He should write to me and ask so I could write to him back. Surely, there is a place where he is receiving posted letters.

"Georgiana is nowhere near ready to have her coming out, Edward. She is naïve, headstrong, and entirely too much like Anthony. I am still working with her to ensure she finds a suitable match."

"She will, love. She will. Georgie is a delightful girl, and while she may be headstrong, she will find a suitable match. Give her some room. You'll stifle her if you continue to control her too tightly."

I grinned, heart swelling with pride for my father. While he may be away most of the time, he knew what to say to my mother on my behalf when it mattered. Even when she never listened to him.

Hearing her clucking her tongue again, I stifled a groan and quickly backed away from the door when I saw her shadow pass over the light. Time to go! I fled from my father's office as quickly as my feet would allow, back to my room on the upper level before

I could get caught eavesdropping. She'd not caught me yet, and I'd make sure she never did.

She never caught me. Any information I'd learned from those private conversations, I tucked away in my memory for when I needed it. Anthony met Helene Ward in Charlotte and based on a conversation I'd heard a few months later, they'd been married. Still, it hurt that he'd never written to me and I had to glean this information by resorting to eavesdropping, but that seemed to be the best way to get the most information. Never mind that I'd been doing it my whole life. It's how I found out my mother wanted me to marry a duke and anyone of lesser nobility wouldn't be acceptable.

I needed to speak with Charles. Wondering what he intended to do would drive me mad. With Benjamin showing up here tonight, it could have dire consequences. Or perhaps my reaction gave him enough reason to believe me. Either way, I needed to know. I crept out of my room into the darkened hallway and walked to his bedroom, but when I opened the door, only shadows greeted me. His bed hadn't been touched, still perfect.

Thinking Charles may have gone to the club with James, I went back to my room. Voices coming from the parlor stopped me when I reached my door. I carefully stepped down the stairs and tiptoed toward the parlor. The door, left open enough, gave me all I needed to hear James and Charles talking.

In my state of dress, I wouldn't rush into the parlor. Especially with James there. I'd need to wait to speak with Charles after James left. That didn't mean I couldn't listen to what they might talk about. I sidled closer, pressing my back against the wall outside the door.

"Are we going to talk about this, or go on ignoring what happened tonight?" James asked. "What do you think Benjamin wanted with her?"

"I can only think the worst," Charles answered, a slur of his voice from too much port. "I know Benjamin. He gets what he wants."

Not me, I thought. He would never have me.

"Then he truly got to her."

"I believe so, yes."

My hand clamped over my mouth to silence my gasp. Charles believed Benjamin only because he always got what he wanted. Even when I denied it. How poorly he must think of me to believe I would fall into Benjamin's arms.

"What will you do?"

I heard his heavy sigh, wishing I could see what they were doing.

There was silence on the other side of the wall and I slid a fraction closer, barely breathing, to hear his answer. I was dying to know what Charles would do, or if he would admit to James what he would do. Charles was close with his father. If he would admit to anyone, it would be to James.

"Society is not looking kindly upon us right now," James continued. "Even your mother is being shunned. Annabel refuses to speak with her."

"It was her son that caused this mess!" Charles shouted, making me jump from the vehemence in his voice. "If he'd kept his hands off my wife, none of this would have happened! If Georgiana wouldn't have allowed him to . . . to . . . "

"Easy, Charles. We still do not know the truth about what may have happened. Georgiana says it's not true. Benjamin never said it was, he just never denied it."

"Someone saw them. Together."

With the clinking of glass, I heard one of them pour another drink. I hated this. I hated being in the center of this firestorm. To rush in there, beg them to believe that it never happened, weighed heavily on me. But I couldn't do that. Not without betraying the fact I'd been eavesdropping on their conversation.

"I know. Something must be done. So I ask again. What will

you do?"

"Commit her," is what I heard next. "I'll be a widower before long and be able to start anew. Women in those facilities don't last long. And with donations to the hospital, I'm sure they'll take extra special care of my wife."

"Charles, you can't be suggesting what I think you are."

"Father, she is an adulteress. She's my wife. It's my decision. We already dealt with Violet not so many years ago."

"Violet was not insane as you said she was, and you know it. And look what happened!"

"Violet taking her own life was not my doing."

"Do not make any rash decisions," James uttered.

It took both my hands to smother my outraged cry, my heartbeat pounding in my ears and drowning out anything else being said. I spun away from the door until my back hit against the banister of the staircase. Tears burned my eyes. No! I'd heard horrible tales of women in those facilities, used like animals for experiments, some of them becoming worse from those treatments while others died. The conditions in those hospitals were barely tolerable. Charles was right. He would be a widower if he had me committed, for I wouldn't last long.

I turned and ran up the staircase, tripping twice on my way up. Once I made it safely back into my bedroom and closed the door with trembling hands, I sagged against it. Disbelief invaded my thoughts. This couldn't be happening, could it? Pushing from the door, I went to my dressing table and slowly eased open the drawer. Having not opened the drawer since I'd put the Derringer back into it, I'd tried to keep it from my thoughts.

The open drawer stared back at me, my eyes burning down into it. The drawer contained nothing but a few hairpins and ribbons. No gun. My eyes lifted to the image in the mirror. Charles had taken my gun. That meant he'd been snooping in my room, had discovered it and taken it. When? My mind raced.

Why? If he wanted to be rid of me, what would be the difference if I took my own life? Either way, he'd be free of me. Free to marry another.

Although no longer in possession of my gun, I knew for certain there would be no opportunity for Charles to commit me. I needed to figure out what to do, and I needed to do it with haste.

Chapter Eight

Nerves nearly kept me from going down to breakfast the following morning, fearful of what I might find. After such a tumultuous day, it couldn't possibly get worse unless I came face-to-face with the men who would take me away. When I found the dining room empty, I breathed a sigh of relief. Fitz stood by, waiting to provide me with my plate of food. Luckily, all he had was a slice of toast, some fruit, and tea, which was all I could manage as I sat silently at the table to eat.

The daily newspaper sat folded neatly at the head of the table, untouched. With a sly glance at Fitz, I leaned over and grabbed it. Despite the trouble I was already in, I could withstand more for reading the paper before Charles could. I eased back, picking at my fruit while glancing at the front page. Ads were in abundance in the first couple pages, leading into news from Washington. It was the seventh page, where the telegraphic news from all parts of the world began, when my fork clattered against my plate, then to the floor. I picked up the paper with both hands while Fitz retrieved my fork. My breakfast ignored while I quickly scanned the bottom of the page was Texas written in bold lettering.

"Proceedings of the Reconstruction Convention," I whispered to myself.

"Ma'am?" Fitz asked.

I waved my hand flippantly, continuing to read softly to myself. "The Galveston Bulletin's Austin dispatch that the Convention is still arranging preliminary matters. On the fifth, the president announced the members of the standing committees—sixteen in all." My eyes skipped down as I continued to read the article of this meeting that had taken place. "A proposition to furnish a certain number of copies of various specified newspapers to each member created an animated discussion. Mr. Hamilton, of Bastrop county, opposed taking a single copy."

Fitz set a clean fork beside me. "Do you need something, Miss Georgie?"

I reached out, clutching his forearm. "Bastrop County."

"I'm sorry?"

I flung the newspaper away from me and pushed back from the table. Getting to my room as quickly as possible where I could think became my focus. It was the conversation I'd listened to after they'd found out he'd married Helene.

With my back pressed against the wall, I listened to the deep voice of my father. I liked it when he came home. It made me feel more at ease, more relaxed. Like a shield against my mother. When he came home, he always brought a letter from Anthony with him. It remained my only connection to my brother.

"I meant to tell you," he said.

"When did you receive it?" I heard my mother's biting voice.

"Only a few days ago. I sent a response along with a great deal of money. Anthony may no longer be my heir, but I will not allow my son to be destitute, even though he did not indicate he was in such a state."

"He chose to leave us, Edward. We didn't send him away. That you'd send him money, any amount, only speaks to your weakness."

Holding my breath, I waited for his response, but only heard him sigh deeply. There were times he bit his tongue, too. That must have been where I learned to do it. Sometimes my teeth weren't strong enough and words slipped out.

"Does he say where he is?" she continued.

"Only that he and Chester are considering settling in a county known as Bastrop near the city of Austin. That's in Texas."

"I know where that is," she snapped.

"He explains he is in good health, but there is much unrest in the country. He asks that we share this with Georgie."

"I disagree. Giving her updates on Anthony and his whereabouts will only cause her to want to follow in his footsteps, I fear. Edward, we've discussed this at length already. We agreed not to allow her to know about him."

I gasped softly, covering my mouth with both my hands.

Of course, Father would agree with Mother. She would see me married to a wealthy gentleman, preferably royalty. If she could wed me off to one of Queen Victoria's sons, she wouldn't hesitate to do so. But Father had agreed with her? I couldn't believe it.

"I never thought that was a good idea, Abigail. Anthony and Georgie were so close. It broke her heart when he left, and not receiving his letters is hurting her even more so." My father's voice lightened. "What will we do when she continues to ask? What if she asks if we know where he is?"

"We shall lie."

Summoning the courage, I peeked into the room and saw her feeding the letter into the fire in the hearth. I never thought I could dislike my mother more. Until that moment. I hated her. I rebelled when I could, but Anthony would always talk me around to behaving again. At least to appease my mother. Once she finally allowed me to officially come out in society, I'd been bent into the gracious and poised lady she'd wanted. But I'd never lost sight of the real Georgie. She was held deep down inside, but not gone.

They may have lied to me about Anthony's whereabouts, but it didn't stop me from wondering where he was and what he was doing. He had to be out there somewhere. My mother had only disposed of the written evidence at that time. Seeing the daily newspaper only drudged up more feelings about how much I missed him.

Sybil appeared when I sat at my writing table, curious about what my activity for the day would be. Poised to write a letter to my grandfather, I changed my mind a moment later. It would do no good. It may not reach him in enough time. But I would not be the next woman admitted into that institution for doing nothing wrong.

"Miss Georgie?" Sybil asked.

I stood up and paced the length of the room, my finger tapping at my lips while I tried to think of what to do. Catching a ship home would be my best option if there was one setting sail soon enough. My only other option would be to find Anthony. I only knew that he had been *thinking* about settling in Bastrop County, Texas. I never found out if that had been where he'd settled with Helene.

"Is there something I ought to do for you?"

"I need to find my brother, Sybil." My open admission had me looking around, just to make sure no one else listened. "But no one can know. I need to do so without Charles knowing. Somehow. I'm not sure how, but I need to find out."

"I know how."

My head snapped up, my pacing stopping abruptly. "How?"

"I know how you can sneak out. Where do you need to go?"

Hopes sunk as quickly as they'd risen. I continued to pace.

"The only solid information I have is that he married a girl from Charlotte, North Carolina. They could still be there or could have moved on to settle in Texas."

I stopped in front of her, fearing I would put her in a dangerous position. Or no position when I left. If I left abruptly, they might suspect she told me about her position as Violet's maid.

"I can return home. But Charles will expect me to do that and could follow me."

I looked at her. "I overheard Charles last night. He intends to commit me. I need to leave here before that happens."

Horror filled her eyes as she took a step back. "No," she whispered. "Miss Georgie, you can't let him do such a thing. You need to leave here."

I continued to pace. "Wouldn't it be dangerous for me to travel alone? Especially as far as Texas, without even knowing he's there? How can I go anywhere with no one following me, and safely?"

"I know how, but you must trust me."

"You are the only one I can trust, Sybil." I whirled. "Tell me."

She moved toward me, laying her hands on my arm. "It will still be dangerous for you."

I nodded. "I'm stronger than you think. But I fear it will leave you in a dangerous place here. I have money of my own to give you, so you may start anew and I'll provide you with a letter of reference."

Sybil shook her head. "I'll be fine." She hurried to the door, opening it before looking back at me. "It may take me some time, but I will return. I promise."

After Sybil left, I sat back down at my writing desk to write letters. It took me some time to write the letters, but when finished, I had a sense of satisfaction with my decision to leave.

It was growing dark by the time Sybil returned, my restlessness increasing as the minutes ticked by. She hurried into the room with her arms full of clothing, dumping the load on the bed. When I wandered over, I picked up a pair of trousers and matching vest, followed by a flat cap and pair of short boots, along with a white shirt that had three buttons near the neck.

She looked at me, a smile curving her lips.

"I'm going to become a . . ."

"Man."

Chapter Nine

"This will work," she insisted.

I wondered if Sybil said it to convince me or herself. The rhythmic snip of the scissors hypnotized me while I stared at my reflection in the mirror. It took all my courage to ignore the chunks of my dark brown hair falling listlessly to the floor, as though only feathers were floating away. All my life I wore my hair long, past my shoulders. My beautiful hair.

Once she'd cut most of the length off, I pressed my eyes closed and kept them that way. Focusing only on the scraping sound of the metal blades, once in a while feeling her fingers brush against my neck. At the touch of coolness on my neck, I knew the deed was done.

"Open your eyes," she whispered.

It scared me. I didn't want to face my new self. But the courage it took to not watch my hair fall carelessly away, I drew from now and forced my eyelids open. My lips parted, but I didn't gasp or cry. I stared. Stared at my hopes and dreams dash away along with my long hair.

Tentatively, I reached up and touched the short ends of my hair that curled behind my ear. My hair appeared darker, my eyes larger than normal. I brought my other hand up, touching the other side. How different I looked now. I almost didn't recognize myself in the reflection.

"What do you have next for me?" I asked abruptly, rising and stepping over the hair pooled around the chair.

Sybil led the way toward the bed, where she had placed several items earlier. I knew most of what she had gathered was clothing for a man, but I picked up a long white sheath of fabric with raised eyebrows.

"We need to bind your breasts," she explained. "It won't be terribly comfortable, but you are much too endowed to have anyone believe you as a man. Not as thin as you are. If you were plump, perhaps."

I nodded. "We'd best get started."

She helped me remove my dress, corset, and chemise. When I stood in only my stockings, she wound the fabric tightly around my chest until I gasped. Like a corset. No more challenging to breathe than wearing a corset, however, I wouldn't be able to remove it at night. I'd need to wear it until it would be safe not to.

"What shall I do if the binding comes loose?"

Sybil pursed her lips, standing back once she tucked the end of the fabric into the front. "I've tied it pretty tight. But if it should, you will need to bind yourself again the best you can. You shouldn't have to wear this long, I should think."

I grimaced, but we continued on with the trousers and the shirt. The reflection in the mirror made me stop for a moment. With my shortened hair and the trousers, my reflection revealed my transformation. This would work. I couldn't recognize myself. While Sybil set to unlacing the boots, I buttoned up the few buttons of the shirt and shrugged into the vest. Gone were the vivid colors of my gowns, replaced by the drab colors of a man. A modest man.

As soon as I sat down on the bed to pull on the scuffed boots, there came a knock at my door, followed by the jiggle of the doorknob. Sybil looked at me with wide eyes, while I looked at her back with equal surprise. Boots forgotten, I went to the door.

"Georgiana, let me in," Charles said.

My eyes widened further. "I'd rather you didn't. I . . . I'm not feeling well. What is it you need at this hour?"

The door knob jiggled again. Locking him out of my bedroom might have been a good idea for me to protect myself, but it certainly did not make Charles happy about it. "Why have you locked me out? Open this door at once."

"No, Charles. I told you, I'm not feeling well. What is it you want?" I forced myself to stay calm, keep my voice from shaking and betraying my fear.

"We need to talk."

"We can do so tomorrow."

Silence greeted me on the other side of the door, and I thought he had left for a moment. "I would prefer to speak now."

I pressed my hand against the wall to hold myself steady. "Are you saying you believe me now?"

Again, silence.

"Charles?"

"I can't tell you what you would like to hear, Georgiana. That someone saw you is enough for me to know it's true. How did you . . . how did it happen?"

So that was the way of it. Charles did not come to speak to me about his believing in me. He came to find out the sordid details of something that never happened. I pushed away from the wall, drawing my spine straight.

"I cannot tell you about something that never happened." I stepped back from the door. "Please go away. My head aches."

When his fist met with the door, thumping violently upon it, I jumped back with a gasp. "Open this door, Georgiana!"

"Charles, please! We will talk tomorrow."

"I swear to you . . . " I could hear his heavy breathing behind the door, my hands trembling in fear that he would break through the door and he would find out my plan to leave. "If I find out that you are not alone in there. That you've perhaps taken a gentleman caller into our home, into your bed, there will be dire consequences. Dire."

I jumped again. "There is no one here but me! I have brought no one to our home. Ever. Why can you not believe me?" The urge to bury my face in my hands and sob out my frustrations washed through me.

"For your sake, pray that I find out the truth soon."

I hoped only to be gone by that time. The damage was already done. Our marriage, already teetering on the line of aloofness, was now disrupted with a betrayal I would never forgive him for. I heard a growl come from the other side of the door, followed by his footsteps fading away.

I let out a deep breath. If I hadn't locked my door, I might have found myself in a locked cell before the night was over. I couldn't allow my plan to be discovered until I was well away from the city. When I turned back to Sybil, she looked fearful.

"He's gone."

"The sooner you are on a train, the better."

"You are quite right."

"Before you put your boots on, put some of your money into one of them. You'll not want to carry all your money in your pockets or in your sack."

We continued to dress me, finishing the ensemble with a flat cap that hid most of my hair except for the shortened back and around my ears. It pleased me to see it partially shaded my face. That would benefit me when I needed it to.

"What's this?" I asked, pointing at the knapsack.

Sybil upended the contents of the knapsack on the bed. It didn't amount to much, but I wouldn't need a lot. There wouldn't be a need, or even a safe way, to change my clothing during the journey. It would be short enough to get to North Carolina, and if they could direct me to where Anthony had settled in Texas, I could get there within a matter of days. It wasn't safe enough to bring any of my belongings with me.

She picked up a few things. "A ferry ticket across the river and your train tickets. I purchased you enough train tickets to get to North Carolina. You'll need to change trains in Washington. They are still repairing many destroyed train tracks in the south."

I nodded, quickly feeling overwhelmed by what I was about to do. This journey could be life or death. I would have to be diligent. What I found in North Carolina would set the rest of my course.

"Stay the course, Miss Georgie. I've given you a map in case you get lost, although if you stay the course, you should not need it."

Picking up the comb, I drew my thumb along the teeth. "I suppose I won't need a brush anymore," I whispered and set it back down on the bed.

"No, but you'll want to comb your hair. And this." She pulled something out of her apron pocket and pressed it into my palm.

I stared at my hand. "What is this?"

"It's a folding knife. It isn't much, but should you get into trouble, use it." She curled my fingers around it. "Stick to the trains, Miss Georgie. I couldn't get you first-class tickets. Don't stray from the depots. Especially not in the south."

"I will."

There was a smaller bundle that looked like a cloth tied at the top. "This is a bundle of fruit, biscuits and dried meat." She pulled a flask out of her apron, making me wonder what else she had in her apron. "Don't drink this all at once."

Together, we gathered everything back up and put it back into the knapsack.

I took the rest of my money, tucking it into the pocket in the vest before shrugging into the jacket. I had time to wait until the household had gone to sleep before I could make my escape. After Charles had come to my room, I couldn't take any chances. I had to be sure he wasn't lingering in the parlor with his port or whiskey.

I hugged Sybil. "You have been the very best maid. This isn't something you had to help me in, and you did. For that, I can never thank you enough."

She nodded. "Perhaps someday our paths will cross again."

"Go to bed. I'll be fine."

Sybil slipped out of the room through the dressing room and I locked that door behind her, prepared to wait out the next few hours until I could be certain no one would be awake. It would be hours before the ferry left for New Jersey, but there were at least thirty blocks I needed to walk and it would take me a long time, especially in the dark.

Hours ticked by while I waited until I silently cracked open my door and found the hallway dark. I hurried to make sure the note I left Charles sat on my writing table for him to find, pulling off my wedding ring and laying it next to it. I had made it very simple for him. *I never broke my vows to you. While a small part of me hopes you will find someone who won't mind being controlled, mistreated and dismissed, I pray to the Lord that no one else shall fall into your clutches. If you happen to find another to wear this, I pray you treat her better than you did me. And God bless her.*

Swinging the knapsack over my shoulder, I slipped out of the room as quiet as a thief.

Chapter Ten

It didn't take me much longer than an hour to get to the ferry. The streets, enclosed in darkness, made it impossible to see anything but shadows, and I kept my walk brisk while counting each block that I passed. Half way, I'd nearly turned back, wondering what I'd been thinking of leaving my life behind me. But what would I return to? A life worse than it already was? Not a single friend to speak with, a husband who didn't trust me. No. I needed to continue with the plan.

I'd never been so frightened before, voices in the shadows and things rustling in the trees and brush while I passed. There could be no pleasant activities at this time of night. But I'd kept my cap low and continued walking with a firm grip on my knapsack.

By halfway, I had blisters on my feet from the boots and legs aching with exhaustion. Somehow, I'd continued on. I'd made it to the park near the ferry while it was still dark and rested near a tree until the sound of the ferry horn blaring roused me the next morning. Nervous that Charles, or someone, followed me every step of the way didn't help. Even when I boarded the ferry, the unease stayed with me. The ferry ride, unlike a ship sailing across the sea, did a number on my turning stomach and I'd nearly been sick over the railing.

While the seagulls soared overhead, squawking in search of a meal, my thoughts had drifted, wondering when Charles would find my note. He'd be having his breakfast and reading his newspaper before he would think anything was wrong. I tried to imagine what his reaction might be, but it didn't matter.

I caught the train from New Jersey to Washington, but with it being a freight train, it had frequent stops and many travelers who didn't speak the same language. Lack of comfort aside, I'd reached Washington by midday in time to change trains on my way further south. Even though I reached Charlotte the same day, I'd been riding trains so long that by that time, I could only hear the clickity-clack of the train wheels in my ears and the acrid smell of iron ore assaulting my nose.

As late afternoon approached, I stepped onto the platform in North Carolina. Arrival in North Carolina was like stepping into another country. Far from the posh society of Fifth Avenue New York, there was an air of despondency when I stepped onto the streets.

Gone were men in suits with top hats and walking sticks or ladies dressed in the finest day dresses. Working-class people filled the streets, many of them children wearing dirty clothes and carrying buckets or baskets. As I walked, I had a feeling of dread at finding a suitable place to sleep for the night.

Buildings and homes dotted the streets, but many seemed patched together. One could still see remnants of the war in the buildings and in the people. When the war ended, which hadn't been that long ago, rebuilding began with the south needing much help. Lack of money made the rebuilding process slow.

Keeping my head low, I walked the dusty street close to the line of trees, hoping to find a room to rent for the night near the train station before venturing to find the home of the Ward family. There were homes, and some more like hovels, set up with little more than canvas for walls. People raised their curious eyes to me while I walked past, as though they sensed I didn't belong here.

While I passed between two run-down buildings, I spotted a trio of boys in a circle that looked like they were up to no good and quickened my steps. With the strap of my knapsack firm in my grip, my eyes swept each side of the street for a place I could inquire about the Ward family. I didn't know the boys had followed me until I passed another few buildings.

Bumped from behind, I tried to pull the knapsack around me but found my arms immobilized while propelled between two shacks. My back hit the wall of the building with a thump, stealing my breath from me until I wheezed and my eyes watered.

Surrounded by them, the tallest of them quickly divested me of my bag and upended the contents onto the ground while one held me from behind by the arms and the other one patted me down.

The feel of his grimy hands on my body renewed my struggles, my bindings making it difficult for me to catch my breath fully. I couldn't let him feel my bindings. I struggled against them, but they were stronger and bigger than I was. In the end, all he found on my body was my little knife and flask. He grinned at me with partially blackened teeth and tucked it into his pocket, giving it a pat.

All three were filthy, reeking of what I could only imagine was some type of liquor. I closed my eyes, feeling the burn of vomit rising into my throat.

"Jackpot, boys," the taller boy said, finding my money and holding it up. "Let him go. Nothin' else here for us."

As soon as they released me, I fell to the ground amongst the remains of my belongings. It took me a moment, kneeling on my hands in the knees in the dirt while I fought for breath. With shaking hands, I gathered up what remained of my food; a badly bruised apple and a dirt-encrusted biscuit, my comb, and the map. I thrust them back into the knapsack, scalding tears burning my eyelids.

With the boys gone, I sat down with my back against a tree to catch my breath and get my bearings. While I knew the dangers I faced being alone out in the world, encountering them was a different experience. My heart still raced. It took several minutes to get myself under control enough to continue on.

When I stepped out into the street, the heat immediately caught me by surprise. At that time of the day, the temperature smothered me. I would need to remove my jacket until I found the Ward family. Slowly, I took it off, looping it over my arm while I walked.

The further I walked the more the town looked more middle to upper-class. People lived along the streets, with houses that weren't as run down as the rougher side of town. I noticed they were more apt to stare at me while I walked, though I wasn't causing trouble.

I'm feeling a bit out of place, I couldn't help but to tell myself while I crossed the street, dodging horse-drawn carriages to get to the corner. By approaching a man sweeping in front of a market, I was able to find the information on the Ward family that I had been searching for. I only had a few more blocks to walk.

Sweat dripped down my neck and disappeared beneath my shirt as I stood in front of their charming two-story home with a front porch. Shivering, I wiped my brow with my shirt sleeve before ringing the front bell.

Moments later, a young girl opened the door, dark-haired and olive skinned. She was exotically beautiful and looked to be about my age, or possibly a year or two younger.

"May I help you?"

"Is this the Ward residence?" My voice came out like a squeak.

She eyed me with caution, her eye color a mixture of green and blue. "It is. Who are you?"

"My name is Georgie Rutherford." I drew up my shoulders.

"My brother is Anthony Rutherford. I'd heard he married Helene, and I'm trying to find him."

Her hand flew to her heart as she took an involuntary step
back, her other hand clutching the edge of the door. "Hel . . .
Helene."

"Who is at the door, Ginny?" I heard another woman call out
behind her.

A second later, another woman appeared with a young boy
of perhaps two years old propped up against her hip. She looked
like the woman who opened the door, apparently named Ginny,
but older. She looked at me, eyes narrowed. "Amelia, this
is Georgie. Rutherford."

Amelia gasped. The boy looked at me, curious.

I sighed. "I'm only looking for my brother. Or Helene. Is
Helene here?"

The two women looked at each other in panic. "You need to
wait here a moment," the one named Ginny told me, closing the
door in my face.

I stared at the door, hearing raised voices from within, then
shouting. Calm, I reminded myself. I've come a long way to turn
tail and run now. I only needed to remain calm and wait for them
to return, hoping they would invite me inside and tell me where
I could find Helene and Anthony. Or at least Anthony.

The door opened, this time to a much older woman with
black hair and striking green eyes. The two girls hovered behind
her. Her lips looked pinched. "I understand you are looking for
Helene," she whispered, her tone accusing.

"I'm looking for my brother. But I know he met Helene here,
and that they were married." She stared at me while I rushed on.
"Do you know where I can find Anthony?"

Her eyes softened, her lips parting. "I'm afraid I don't know
where you can find your brother."

My heart sank. I'd come all this way and found nothing.

"The man who brought Helene home settled in Abilene,

Kansas," Ginny said, a blush rising high on her cheeks. "His name was Rooke Preston."

The two girls dissolved into giggles at the mention of him, shushed by the mother, but I heard Ginny whisper to Amelia how handsome he was.

"Helene is no longer with us. She died in childbirth, her and the child, about a year ago after returning to us with this man. She wouldn't tell us what happened."

I gasped, my hand covering my mouth. "I'm sorry for your loss, truly I am. I'm only trying to find my brother."

The older woman looked at me, no hint of emotion in her eyes. "You might start with the man who brought her here. As Ginny said, he settled in Abilene."

I sensed she would shut the door in my face and said my goodbye before she could do such a thing, offering her a smile first. I continued down the walk without looking back. It didn't escape my notice that while they had given me information; they hadn't offered me to come in while I was there. Whatever Anthony had done, they were angry about it. The little boy made me wonder, especially after they'd said Helene and the child had died. I could be entirely mistaken. The boy could have been Ginny's or Amelia's. They didn't want me to stay around, that much I knew. If they knew more, they weren't in a hurry to share.

Part Two

Be careful who you pretend to be.
You may forget who you are.

Chapter Eleven

I kept to the shadows as much as I could. Keeping out of sight meant I would go unnoticed by most people coming and going. No one would pay mind to a poorly dressed, scrawny boy with scuffed boots and a knapsack.

The blast of the train whistle reminded me of the need to move on, shuffling from the platform to the dirt-covered streets of Abilene.

When I'd reached Chattanooga, I found out that I'd missed the next train. No matter how much I'd argued with the train cashier, he would not allow me on the next one without purchasing another ticket. I'd had no choice but to buy another one, which took all the rest of my money aside from a five-dollar bill. That wouldn't get me another train ticket to get further than Abilene.

I wracked my brain during the ride to Abilene to figure out what I could do to earn more money if I needed to.

I sidled along the streets, keeping my meager knapsack close. Anthony had to be in Texas, and I hoped if I found Rooke Preston, he could confirm. If I had any chance of making it to Texas, I needed to keep my wits about me and what little money I had in a safe place. Tucked in my boot seemed the only safe place remaining.

Taking advantage of the fact I didn't have to act prim and

proper, I hopped down from the platform and walked along the dirt-packed streets of Abilene. The city, being the farthest I'd been to the west, looked much different from New York and the other cities I'd been through. Empty didn't aptly describe the town. It had buildings and streets, but not a great many of either. I'd heard the town had grown substantially after the war, with thousands and thousands of people. Yet, the town still held no torch to the bustling life of New York or Charlotte.

I passed by some men standing out near the saloon, summoning enough courage to ask if they knew of a man who went by the name of Rooke. All three, dressed mostly the same in cowboy gear, shook their heads. With an odd name like that, I had to think someone knew of him. A few doors down, I ducked into a hotel and asked the front clerk who didn't know him, either.

This would be harder than I thought. After stopping a few more places, asking again about a man who went by the name of Rooke, I still had no luck. Someone would have to know him if he lived and worked here.

Daring a glance behind me while I walked along the street, I watched the sun descend from the sky for the night. The need to find him spurred me forward. Filled with nervous energy, I stepped directly into a gentleman who turned and bumped me back, sending me sprawling. My knapsack landed with a small thump.

Strong hands caught me under my arms, long fingers splayed against my back just above my bindings, holding me from landing on my backside in the dirt. I looked up into deep hazel-blue eyes shaded by the wide brim of a cowboy hat.

My feet found solid ground while he released me, swooping down to retrieve my bag. "Heard you've been looking for me," he drawled.

For a moment, I stared at him, dumbfounded still.

He held out his hand. His cowboy hat, pulled down low, still shaded his eyes. But I had already seen his eyes. It was too late to shield them. They were eyes that went deep, drawing you in. "Rooke Preston."

My hand trembled when I slipped it into his. The strength of his hand, I thought, would break the delicate bones of my fingers. "George," I whispered.

"It's nice to meet you," he said. And after a moment, he added: "George."

He eyed my scuffed-up boots, wide-legged trousers and simple button-up shirt covered by a dark vest. They were the only clothes I owned aside from the jacket stuffed in my knapsack.

"You got a last name, George?"

"Yes," I said.

"And?"

"Rutherford."

His eyes snapped up in surprise, disappearing quickly. "You hungry, George Rutherford?"

Not trusting my voice, I nodded enthusiastically.

"Now'd be a good time to tell me why you've been asking all around town about me."

As he began walking back down the street, I fell into pace with him like we were old companions, taking a stroll while the night closed in around us. I wasn't sure what it was about this man named Rooke, which was a peculiar name, but I felt comfortable around him. In my naivety, I knew I should not be so trusting of any man, especially after the things I had been through in the few days I had been traveling.

When I didn't answer, he asked: "What brings you to Abilene?"

"I'm looking for my brother Anthony. You brought his wife home to Charlotte."

"Anthony Rutherford? Sure, I know him."

I felt like I'd been lifted in the air, soaring on euphoria. "Is he in Texas?"

"Sure is. Been there running his cattle ranch for quite some time now. So, you're his long-lost brother looking to find him. Anything else?"

The huskiness of his voice fascinated me. Combined with his southern drawl, it created a cascade of shivers along my skin. I shook them away, blaming the coolness settling in with the night.

"I need to earn some money."

He stopped, looking at me with his head cocked to the side. I caught the glint of his eyes, momentarily struck that I'd never seen quite that color on anyone else. "You got a place to stay tonight, George?"

Instead of immediately answering, I slowly shook my head. Not sure what he was asking with that question, I didn't want to seem eager for a place to stay. Of course, we were talking in the street man-to-man. Nothing to be frightened of.

"Might have to bunk down in the stables with the horses." His eyes remained on mine, waiting for my reaction.

"That would be fine."

"Won't be terribly comfortable."

Again, he waited for my reaction. I wondered if he thought I'd pitch a fit over having to sleep on a pallet of hay.

"It's like I said." Careful with my words, I drew them out slowly with precise pronunciation. "I'm fine with that."

He resumed walking; me following quickly to keep up with the long length of his legs, eating up the distance of wherever he led me. "What kind of work are you looking for to earn money?"

That was a good question. I didn't have the skills needed to find the type of work befitting a young boy. Only luck would get me a job. I could learn and do well enough to earn some money to move on. I knew he was waiting for an answer, but I couldn't respond.

"Well?" he prompted.

I shrugged. If he'd have paid any attention, he would have noticed my hands didn't bear any resemblance to having worked a day in my life.

"If you're heading to Texas, ever think of ranching?"

"Ranching?"

"Cattle ranching. Your brother owns a cattle ranch. Think you can do it?"

I glanced over at my newfound companion. "When can I start?"

He laughed, this man with a strange name, his laugh a deep and throaty sound. "I think your luck may have turned. His men brought up some cattle for the market a day or two ago. I'd have to find out if they've headed back yet. You might've missed them." My heart sank to my boots while he rubbed his chin. "I'll ask around. In the meantime, you'll come with me to the stables and I'll get you some grub."

"Thank you."

While we walked further, I stayed silent even when we reached the end of the last block, where a stable stood away from the main buildings of the street. It looked like a normal stable with a housing unit attached to the side and a small front porch covered with an overhang.

The light within the stables illuminated outside a partially ajar barn door, as dark closed over. Rooke pushed open the large door enough for both of us to enter before he turned to close it completely behind us.

"Is this . . . uh, where you sleep?" I asked, following him down the wide aisle between each side of the barn.

"Mm-hmm," was all he said.

My head darted left to right, looking at each stall to see the horses. Black stallions, spotted appaloosas, mustangs, quarter horses. The horses here were beautiful. One caught my eye, holding my gaze and tossing its gigantic head back. Dark, sleek and beautiful. A stallion, I thought.

So engrossed in the horse, I slammed right into the back of Rooke, who grunted in return but said nothing. A low laugh slipped out, even though I admonished myself silently for not watching where I'd been going. When I'd run into him, it had been like running into a wall. The entire length of him was like a solid muscle, firm and unyielding. My face warmed.

"George?"

I blinked, then looked at him. He swept out his arm to a room in the back. Tentatively walking in ahead of him, I slipped into a type of living quarters. Small, and only one room, but unmistakably living quarters. I could only assume they were his.

A narrow bed shoved against the far corner with a chair beside it that looked like it served as a table rather than a place to sit, a table with two chairs and in the other corner to the right of the bed a cooking station with a cupboard over it. He opened the cupboard and pulled out a plate, setting it on the small countertop next to the stove.

When he noticed me still standing at the doorway, he motioned to the chair and I slid into it. With his back turned to me, he chuckled.

"I don't bite."

I relaxed my hold on the knapsack and waited for him to fix whatever food he thought to feed me. After not having eaten much, I didn't care if he served me cold chicken. At that exact moment, my stomach growled. Painfully.

When he set the plate in front of me a few minutes later, I saw it contained two pieces of cornbread slathered with butter. No sooner did he sit down across from me and I'd picked up one piece and scarfed it down.

"When's the last time you ate?"

"This morning," I answered, although it came out muffled because of the cornbread in my mouth.

I would have thought he'd laugh at me again, but the look in his eyes was nothing but serious. I swallowed thickly. He took off his hat, setting it down on the table between us while I studied the color of his hair between bites. Between the brown color of his hair and the color of his eyes, there was a vast contrast. The color of his hair brought out the lightness of his eyes, I'd determined.

"Tell me something, George." He leaned back in the chair, crossing his arms over his chest.

The sleeves of his shirt stretched taut when he did so, as though the muscles in his arms threatened to rip the fine fabric to pieces. I shoved the last bit of cornbread into my mouth, dusting off my fingertips over the plate.

"If you're planning on traveling to Texas, do you have anything to get there?"

I frowned. "I'm not . . . what do I need to get there? Can't I take a train?"

"Thought you didn't have any money."

Oh, that. Bugger it. "That's why I'm looking for work."

"If them boys are still here and they allow you to travel with them, do you have anything?" I must have still looked confused. He jerked his chin toward my little knapsack. "That all you've got?"

"Yes."

"Do you have *any* money?"

I gaped at him. "Would I be looking for work if I did?"

The soft lilt of my English accent slipped out, earning me a curious look. I looked down, shamed at allowing my façade to escape. It was something I had to work hard at. If we found those men and they allowed me to travel with them, I'd need to prevent it from happening again. Traveling from city to city on trains and keeping to myself was one thing. Staying with men and having to converse with them was something I would need to get used to. This would not be as easy as the last time I had pretended to be someone I wasn't. And then there were the bindings to deal with.

He chuckled. "I'll get you what you'll need."

When he stood, I jumped up. My bag fell heedlessly to the floor. "Why would you do that? What if they left already?"

"You're going to need things anyway, if you're heading to a cattle ranch in Texas."

"What will I need?" I asked, slowly.

"Do you have a bedroll?" I shook my head. "Saddle? Gun?" He released an exasperated sigh. "Knife?"

Again, I shook my head. I presumed that the knife he was talking about wasn't the same knife I used to have. The puny contraption wouldn't have done a damn thing against those boys that took my money. I didn't quite understand why they'd taken the useless knife.

Several moments passed as a heavy silence surrounded us. I assumed he was curious why I was traveling without the most necessary necessities. It surprised me he hadn't asked me about what I was doing, or where I had come from. If it were me, I would want to ask questions.

"You'll need a bandana."

"Why would I need that?"

"You'll need it to protect yourself from the sun, dust, and dirt. Trust me, you'll thank me for it. A new hat, too."

Absently, I reached up to touch the flat cap covering my coarsely chopped hair. My fingertips brushed the ragged edges of the shortened brown tresses, missing the long curls Sybil had cut so easily.

Rooke noticed my subtle action, one eyebrow raising. But he remained silent, lips pressed into a tight line. "Come on. I'll show you a place where you can sleep. I want you to stay here while I go out. This town gets rowdy. Best to stay in at night."

I followed him back into the stables and to an empty stall, cleaned out except for some bales of hay. He grabbed some blankets from a shelf in the aisle, blankets that were used under the saddle to protect the horse from chafing, but they would do fine.

I watched him move around bales of hay to form a makeshift bed and throw down the blankets. If he tried to conceal the frown when he looked up from his creation, he was too late. I'd caught it anyway, as though he felt bad to make me sleep out here.

"I mean it, George. Stay here."

I nodded. "I'm so tired, I don't think I could go wandering."

Following him to the entryway of the stall, I watched him settle the cowboy hat back on his head and stride down the aisle. When he pulled open the heavy barn door, I noticed it had fallen completely dark outside. It was impossible not to hear the drunken leers and cheers of inhabitants along the streets louder as they passed by. I had no intention of going out there.

Chapter Twelve

When I woke the next morning, sunlight streamed through the small window in the stall. Sleep last night had come quickly, deep and dreamless. Despite sleeping on hay bales that felt as lumpy and uncomfortable as the ground, I felt refreshed. I'd used my knapsack for a pillow again, slept in my clothes in case I needed to bolt, but removed my shoes.

The first thing I noticed after sitting up was a pair of boots, a cowboy hat and several other items set on a hay bale near the entrance of the stall. Jumping to my feet, heedless of my stockings, I hurried over to sift through the things. A bedroll, tied together with two fastenings that looked like belts, a square red cloth made of thin fabric, a tin cup along with plate, knife, and strange looking fork and spoon combination, and I presumed a knife.

Carefully, I picked up the knife and pulled it out of the black sheath. The blade had to be at least five inches long, with a serrated edge. No sooner had I pulled it partially out that I slid it right back in. It looked lethal.

The boots were so much nicer than the ones I'd been wearing, tall enough to reach mid-calf and when I touched them, had a tougher exterior. Sybil had done her best to get me what I needed on short notice but they didn't compare to the ones Rooke had sent. They didn't look new, but when I slipped my foot into them, I found they'd fit perfectly.

After I had the other boot on, my fingertips brushed the fine fabric of the cowboy hat. It curled on the sides like I'd seen on all the other cowboys, including Rooke. The center indented a fraction, and it wasn't tall like I'd seen some. The color crossed between white and brown.

"Put it on."

I nearly dropped it when I heard the deep rumble of Rooke's voice in the doorway. The wild thumping of my heart threatened to beat right out of my chest. "I . . . don't know how I can ever repay you for these things."

"I'm not asking for repayment. Now, put on the damn hat."

The roughness of his voice may have scared me had it not been the hint of tease in the tone. I tucked my hair behind my ears and settled the hat on my head, surprised that it fit perfectly. Far different from the flat cap I'd been wearing, the brim covered a much larger expanse and would shade my eyes from the scorching sun.

"That'll do."

A gleam in his eyes and the smile on his lips had me flustered. "Thank you. I will pay you for these things when I can. You don't know me. You shouldn't have to purchase things for me."

"I won't accept any money from you. But I want to talk to you about getting to Texas."

Judging from the sound of his voice, it didn't sound promising. I could only imagine what he'd found out didn't bode well for me. To brace myself, I leaned against the nearest bale of hay.

"Tell me."

"Anthony's group has already left on their way back to Texas." My breath caught in my throat. "Hold on. There's some things we need to talk about."

I stood straight up.

"Come on with me. Least we can eat while we talk. Leave

your things. We'll be back out here soon enough."

All he did was confuse me, but I trailed after him and into his living quarters. Strange that he'd been sleeping only about thirty paces from me last night and I'd been oblivious to anything. I'd been in such a deep sleep. This time, when he plated up more cornbread, he gave me a few slices of thick bacon and a cup of dark coffee. He must have heard me waking up and left the coffee brewing.

Once I sat down, I gave the coffee a tentative sip and grimaced. Bitter met my tongue, and it didn't like it. Rooke didn't see it, having his back turned to pour his own cup.

"What do we need to talk about?"

"We're going to have to set out on our way to Texas after them," he said, easing himself into the chair across from me and taking a drink from his mug.

"We?"

"Us. You and I. Me and you. We."

"Why would you do that? Don't you have a job to do here?"

I watched him pick up a slice of bacon, taking a bite and chewing it some before putting it down. Then he picked up his coffee and drank more. He purposely made me wait. I knew he did.

"I do, but I've been here a while, and it's about time I moved on. I haven't been back in Texas for a minute. Maybe it's time to head back there."

I raised an eyebrow. He didn't think I believed that, did he? No one up and quits their job just to accompany a boy to Texas to find their long-lost brother.

Finally, I could see Anthony! Talk with him, ask him why he never wrote to me as he'd promised, beg him to help me with this situation I now found myself in. I only needed to get there first. Rooke proposed to bring me himself. Not knowing my gender, I shouldn't have anything to worry about.

I nodded. "When do we leave?"

"As soon as you're ready."

I couldn't shovel the bacon and cornbread into my mouth fast enough, washing all of it down with the bitterness of the black coffee. This would appall my late mother if she'd witnessed it. During our conversation, I hadn't noticed he'd packed his own bedroll and the things that laid on his narrow bed.

"Our horses are saddled and ready to go. Go on and gather your things. I'll be out in a minute."

Bolting from his living quarters, I rushed into the aisle of the stables to see two horses saddled and ready to go. I hurried into the stall I'd slept in to retrieve my things before slowly approaching the horses.

I reached out, allowing a brown quarter horse to sniff at the palm of my hand and get to know me. The other horse, the black one that still eyed me, had to be Rooke's horse. Beauty didn't aptly describe the horse. Powerfully muscled with a thick mane and tail, his eyes stared into mine while I held out my hand. Ears perked up, he nudged my hand like the other horse did.

"He likes you."

Rooke apparently liked to sneak up behind me. I knew horses enough to know you didn't approach them from behind. My eyes caught him when he came around to the side, finally stopping in front of us.

He tucked the knife into my waistband for me. "That should hold you until we get you a belt. I couldn't find one here worthy. Or a gun. Have to look in Wichita."

I watched him take the bedroll from me to secure on the quarter horse before taking my knapsack and dishes to strap up along with the bedroll.

"Sleep all right?"

"I slept fine. Are you going to tell me your horse's name? Or the name of whichever one I'm riding?"

"Your horse's name is Dusty. And this is Fury." He put his

broad hand on Fury's neck, causing the horse to shudder. "His name rings true, so watch out. When he's having a fit, you'll know it."

Rooke and I led them out into the bright morning sun and mounted. It had been over a year since I had been on a horse, and riding had been nothing but leisurely. My entire life had been nothing but learning, but riding was one of the few things that did not need to be done under the supervision of my mother. Playing the pianoforte, painting, embroidery, and social gatherings. That was what I knew. How far between Kansas and Texas, I didn't know, but it couldn't be a quick ride. It would be a lot of riding. I didn't need Rooke to tell me that.

A half hour later, we were riding across Kansas toward Indian Territory. With the hundreds of miles we would cover, we wouldn't be able to ride fast the entire way and would need to give the horses breaks now and then. Rooke had packed enough food to get us to Wichita, which would be over a hundred miles. His confidence that we'd find the group within a day or two helped my optimism.

Riding well into the day, I couldn't help but to admire the way Rooke rode with such ease. I knew I looked like I clutched the reins tightly, not used to riding a horse this way. I should wear a gown, laid out around me with my legs on one side instead of astride. After an hour, my backside grew numb from the bounce against the saddle and my inner thighs felt chafed raw.

When we stopped at a creek to allow the horses to graze and drink from the stream, I stumbled when I dismounted and fell with a plop on my backside. I couldn't tell if Rooke wanted to laugh at me, but he didn't. Instead, he busied himself with digging in his saddlebags to produce some biscuits and jerky.

"Do you think we'll catch up with them?"

"Sooner or later, we will."

The sunlight bounced from the water, shimmering lights on the ripples of water where the horses dipped their heads to drink. Rooke and I stood side-by-side watching them, nibbling our midday meal slowly. He withdrew a silver flask from his boot, uncapping it and offering it to me.

I knew what he offered, but with the lack of anything else to drink, I accepted it. When the searing liquid hit the back of my throat, I refused to sputter, even though my eyes watered. The corner of his mouth quirked up.

"Going to tell me your story?" he asked, tipping the flask back and gulping it down with no reaction at all.

"Going to tell me yours?"

His eyes shot to mine, staying for a moment before he leaned down to put the flask back into his boot and cover it with his pants. Alone, in the middle of nowhere, with a man I didn't know, I shouldn't anger him. I had a mean-looking knife, but that didn't mean I'd use it. Had Charles not taken my Derringer, I might have had a gun. I might not have gotten robbed in North Carolina if I'd had it.

Charles had taken it to maintain control over me. I knew he did. He had to know that with the money I had, I could purchase another one. Truly, he didn't know me as well as he thought he did. Taking it had rattled me, but it didn't deter me.

"What do you want to know?" I finally asked, after realizing he wouldn't answer me.

"Where're you from?"

"How did I get here, or where was I born?"

"You choose."

If I told him about my life, leaving out quite a few details, he'd need to give me something in return. There wasn't a way to be sure how long we'd be together. We may be together the entire way to Texas without another person, just the two of us. I might need to trust him.

"If you know my brother, you know I was born in South Lancashire, northern Britain." That would be all I'd tell him. If I admitted to having come from New York, he'd have more questions I didn't want to answer.

"And how did you get here?"

"By train. From North Carolina." He nodded, accepting my answer. "And you?"

"My history is much harder to explain. I've moved often. I was born in Nashville. That's in—"

"I know where Nashville is. I may be from Britain, but I am educated in American history and geography."

If interrupting him had bothered him, he didn't show it and continued. "While I was born in Tennessee, we moved often and ended up in Texas. I spent the better part of my youth in Texas. Guess it stuck because I spent most of my adulthood there, too."

I studied him for a moment. "You don't appear to be that old to have most of an adulthood."

"Coming up on thirty. You?"

A woman didn't divulge her age, but I didn't think I had much choice at the moment. "Twenty-four. Shouldn't we be getting back on the trail soon?"

Rooke whistled, and the horses lifted their heads, reluctantly returning to us. We stuffed the rest of the food into our mouths, ready to be on our way again. Rooke swung up into his saddle with little effort. It took me several tries to get back up, my legs and lower back were so sore I could hardly use the scant muscles I had to do it. He patiently waited.

Biting back the groan that threatened to tear from my throat once my backside hit the saddle, I winced instead. Rooke clucked the horses into motion and we were once again on our way. He gave me fair warning that we'd want to ride well into the night and even then stop for only a brief rest, or we'd have little chance of catching up with them.

Chapter Thirteen

Rooke hadn't been lying when he said we'd rest briefly. It felt like we'd barely closed our eyes before his boot nudged me awake again. At this rate, I didn't think I'd make it another full day in the saddle. Every muscle groaned in protest when I tried to stand up, walking around like I'd sat on a hot poker. He tossed me a biscuit, which I nibbled while I walked out the kinks in my back.

While I thought he would have mounted and waited for me, he did the opposite. He stood by while I attempted to get into the saddle. Dusty, more patient than a saint, stood still while I tried again and again. When I felt Rooke's firm hands on my hips, pushing me until I could get my leg over the saddle, a breathy gasp released from my throat.

Thankfully, he'd turned to get on Fury before he could see the redness hit my face from the feel of his hands on my hips. Dear Lord, but I didn't know if a man had ever been so bold as to touch me that way before. I remembered Ginny and Amelia Ward giggling at the mention of Rooke, and the one saying how handsome he is.

"Walk on." I heard him say, assuming he talked to the horses and not me when they both moved toward the trail.

Although we stopped several more times for the horses, night had closed in by the time Rooke slowed on the trail. He scanned each side. While part of me hoped that we'd find the rest of the group from Anthony's ranch soon, my nerves said differently. I didn't know how I felt about being around more men.

I'd just about asked Rooke how many there would be when he told me to follow him, deviating from the trail. We walked the horses through tall grass, meeting with another trail that wound around for a while until we met with a creek. Following that for a time, I saw the telltale rise of smoke from a campfire ahead.

"Cade!" Rooke called out before we reached the campfire.

I heard a deep voice from across the left. "Rooke?"

Following Rooke toward the voice, we came across a man sitting on a fallen log with his cowboy hat pulled down low over his face while he worked on a bridle. I noticed a pair of toggles at the front of his hat, secured by a fine piece of brown satin. When he looked up, my eyes widened at his piercing amber eyes. Rooke jumped down from Fury, and while I followed his actions, mine were painfully slower.

"What are you doing out here?"

"Cade, this here's George. He's fixing to get to Texas. Thought it might be about time I return."

The height of the man was to be admired when he stood and ambled toward us, thrusting out his hand toward me. Behind him, several horses grazed. "George, it's a pleasure to meet you."

Not to be intimidated, I slid my hand into his. "Nice to meet you," I murmured.

The grin that spread on his face lit his eyes, making me smile. No need to give any more than necessary. "It'll be good to have you back at the ranch, Rooke. Hasn't been the same since you left."

"Yeah, yeah . . . you just mind the remuda. You'll have two more to take care of." Rooke whistled, both Fury and Dusty moving toward Cade.

With a jerk of my head, I felt Rooke's hand at my elbow leading me away, with Cade calling out goodbye to our backs. Stars twinkled overhead, my stomach letting out a painful growl

I hoped Rooke hadn't heard.

"Remuda?" I asked.

"Extra horses. Horses can only be ridden for so long before needing rest, so they bring along extra horses. We'll still have some days of rest on the way back, not traveling at such a slow speed with a herd of cattle, but we need to switch up our mounts from time to time. Cade's the wrangler, keeping track of the horses."

When we reached the camp, I could hear the rush of the creek and smell the tang of sweet grass mixed with the acrid smell of a campfire in the air. It was full dark now, stars twinkling overhead in the clear sky and the glow of the campfire drawing nearer as we stepped down a path toward the creek. There was a group of men around the fire and bedrolls already rolled out close by.

Alarm hit me while I scanned the area. By the count of the horses in Cade's remuda and the number of bedrolls, there were quite a few men.

"How . . . how many are there? I mean, how many men are traveling to Texas?"

Rooke chuckled. "Four of them, and that's a small crew. Usually there's ten to fifteen men driving a herd. Probably why they waited a few days in Abilene before leaving again."

I choked. "Four?"

"A thousand heads of cattle take a lot of men to keep in check. They've got riders in the front, on the sides and in the rear. They usually have a wagon and a cook, too, but I see Anthony didn't send Mack along." He shook his head, as though disappointed. "No cook means the men have to cook for themselves every night and morning."

I studied the men while we walked toward the creek. These men would soon be my only company for an unknown amount of time. There looked to be a younger man closer to my age with his back to me, who turned at our approach. Another, long legs stretched out in front of himself with his booted feet crossed at the ankle, leaned against his saddle with a horseshoe mustache and piercing blue eyes. It was the third man who caught my full attention.

He was immediately on his feet and coming toward us, his hair already gone gray along with the bushy mustache above his lip that curled up at the ends. The cowboy hat he wore looked like it had seen better days, and he wore leather coverings over his pants that slapped against his legs with each step. The set of his jaw spoke volumes even before he opened his mouth.

"Dammit, Rooke, what the hell are you doing here?"

Rooke cocked his hip out casually as though making a statement to the older man coming toward us. "Geezer, you old son of a bitch. I'm headed to Texas. Mind if I join you?"

Geezer looked at him without saying a word, but then looked at me. "We've got enough mouths to feed. Don't need another."

I looked over at Rooke, who merely shrugged his broad shoulders. The older man had purpose in his stride. The closer he came, the more noticeable the glower in his eyes became.

Stopping abruptly in front of us, he set his hands on his hips. "We've already got enough hands back at the ranch."

Rooke shrugged again. "This is George, Anthony's brother. I'm bringing him there. If Anthony doesn't have a need for me, he'll let me know."

The old man turned his hostile gaze on me. "Coulda done better by sending him on a train. Has no height, and no muscles to speak of." His crystal blue eyes traveled the length of me, from my new cowboy hat to the scruff of my boots. "He's about as puny as they come. What good is he gonna do?"

"I'll do fine," I snapped, earning myself a glare.

I felt Rooke step closer behind me, while the other man stepped closer in front of me until they had me sandwiched between them. Both of them were a head taller than me, and I was defenseless between them, but I didn't think Rooke would hurt me. The other man would if he had the chance. Somehow. Even after Rooke told him Anthony was my brother.

"He'll do fine, Geezer."

Geezer gave me one last look of disdain. "Anthony ain't said nothing about having a brother. We'll see if he lasts the ride back. I doubt he will."

Rooke gave a nod and the old man strode away without saying another word. I had a feeling this would not be the last time I would hear him complain about me or have words with me. He was right. I wasn't tall, and I had no muscles to speak of. As a woman, I wouldn't. I would have to do my absolute best and watch my back. Anything less could get me hurt, and it wasn't up to Rooke to protect me.

My eyes followed Geezer, leaving him when I felt Rooke's hand giving me a slight shove forward. Halfway turning, I gave him a mean look before turning back to walk toward the campfire. I kept my gaze away from the man with his legs stretched out in front of the fire, looking over to the one that was more my age. He gave me a lopsided grin, a showing of respect for having endured my first encounter with the old man.

"This is George," Rooke told the group of men.

"Come on and sit down," the one with the horseshoe mustache said, his eyes roaming over me. I noticed he had a dimple in the center of his chin and eyes the color of coffee.

I perched on a log, clutching my knapsack to my stomach as though I was protecting the last of my possessions from the devil himself. As though anyone would want a map that would do no good and a comb. I didn't want to admit how badly I didn't want to lose my comb. The comb was my last claim to womanhood, for there was nothing else I had that made me feel womanly. I could drag the comb through what I had left of my hair, knowing that someday it would grow back.

"Name's Billy," he said, his drawl thick and his voice low.

The other one leaned up, holding his hand out. Up closer, I

saw he had golden hair and a twinkle in his eyes. His hat wasn't like any other cowboy hat I'd seen. It had a round rim unlike the rest of us, which were more oval. Even the top of his hat was round and not indented.

"I'm Matthew," he said. "Don't mind Geezer. He's all bark, no bite."

A grin nearly lifted my mouth, but I wasn't sure I believed that.

"I'll be back," Rooke announced.

He was striding away from our camp before I could stop him, an inkling he was going to find a place for privacy. Looking around, I knew I could sleep anywhere after having spent the last night in an uncomfortable place. This time I would sleep on the hard ground. Tired enough, I'd sleep anywhere. My thoughts turned to when I might have the luxury of a bed again.

"How many days until we reach Texas?"

Billy chuckled. "Lots of variables. Had to guess, I'd say a month. Maybe more, depending on the weather."

A month? My mouth popped open. Enduring a month in the company of five men, sleeping outside and riding for days on end would be an adventure. Once we reached Texas, I didn't know what to expect. It was possible I wouldn't be sleeping in a comfortable bed even then. I was a woman at the mercy of men.

A laugh burst from Billy and Matthew, although Matthew seemed more reserved than Billy. "Don't look so surprised," Billy said. "You should know what you're signed up for. Where're you from, George?"

I shrugged, trying to think of a response other than the truth. "Here and there. Nowhere really. I move around, trying to find work."

"The war was hard on a lotta people. Lots of people moving around trying to find work." Matthew winked. "You aren't alone."

That I knew. I had seen it first-hand.

"Find any work?" Billy asked.

My gaze stuck on Billy's mustache. I wasn't sure I'd ever seen a man wear a mustache that went all the way down each side to his chin. Like an upside down horseshoe.

I gave him a timid smile, shaking my head. Giving up all my secrets wasn't on my list of things to do. I needed to tell my companions something to avoid suspicion while trying to get to Anthony.

Matthew was about to say something when Geezer returned, causing an uncomfortable silence to settle among us. I held my breath as he stretched out. Beneath the shadows of his cowboy hat, I felt the heat of his gaze on me.

"What makes you think you can handle keeping up with us?" he asked, his voice deadly quiet and meant for me. "Traveling like this ain't meant for a scrawny runt like you."

Hatred burned its way through my veins, but that wasn't who I was. I wasn't a person who hated anyone. Not even Benjamin, as mad at him as I was. Geezer didn't know me, and he didn't know what I could do. He could at least give me a chance to prove myself. I deserved at least that.

My chin raised as I prepared to respond, but Billy beat me to it. "Aw, leave him be. You've gotta give him a chance. Might surprise you, Geezer."

"Why do they call you Geezer?" I blurted.

His quick gaze could have knocked me off my log, as if it had been a gust of wind. "That's my name," he snapped.

Stunned, I closed my mouth. Jumping to conclusions about this man and getting further on his bad side would only get me into more trouble. Better to stay as clear of him if I could, if that would be possible. With six of us, it might not be so hard.

Refusing to meet his eyes, I could still feel him staring at me as I turned my attention to the angry glow of the fire. The night cooled, the coldness seeping into my back, yet I couldn't bring myself to move closer to the fire. I wanted nothing more than to melt into the shadows and pretend this was over.

Rooke eventually came back, carrying our bedrolls that he set behind me. With a grunt, he eased himself down to warm himself by the fire without so much as a word to me. It had been a long day, one I wanted to end by closing my eyes somewhere other than where I was.

"You're going to fall right over," Rooke murmured.

I perked up. My eyes had grown heavy, but I was too stubborn to be the first one to turn in with my newfound companions. I had no choice but to trust them. I didn't trust Geezer, but I had no possessions other than what Rooke had bought me, so I wouldn't get mugged again.

Rooke tipped his hat and I could see the color of his eyes clearly for the second time. They were deep, but it wasn't the color that struck me. It was the way he was looking at me. It was as though he was looking right at me. Not at me, but deep within.

The corner of his mouth lifted a fraction. "We had a long day today and I bet you could use some shuteye."

I couldn't disagree, but I couldn't respond. His eyes captivated me in the way he looked at me. For a moment, I thought perhaps he might be onto my lie, but it wasn't possible for him to know. Other than the few slips in my speech, nothing else could give me away. The button-up shirt and vest covered my bound chest, and having my jacket on disguised it even more so. My new cowboy hat hid most of my shortened hair. With a fair amount of spit, I could easily smooth down the short ends around my ears.

I had taken precautions for my safety with the help of Sybil. She told me about women who had joined armies to fight in the war between the north and the south. Some had gotten away with it. They had found some out, but they only returned. But this wasn't a war I fought. It was a battle for survival. No one could know who I was.

Rooke jerked his chin behind the log I sat on. "You can bed

down over there. We ride out at first light."

Slowly rising to my feet, I gave him a nod. I wouldn't be far from the fire, but I wondered how far I would be from him. I didn't know the others, and I didn't know him much either, but I felt more comfortable around him. As I settled down on the ground, my eyes grew heavy before I even got comfortable. This would be my bed for the next month. I should get used to it. The last thought I had before my eyes fluttered closed was in hopes I would wake up and not get left behind.

Chapter Fourteen

At the nudge against my thigh, my eyes popped open to the bright light of a new day beginning. It took me a moment to realize where I was. Matthew leaned down over me with a tilt to his lips.

"We'll be on our way soon." He cast a look around. "Geezer will make darn sure you're left behind if you ain't ready."

Matthew straightened and looked around once more, making sure he didn't get caught waking me. As soon as he did, I sat up and struggled to my feet because of the tightness in my lower back. Cade, with Billy's help, was readying the horses, but I didn't see Geezer or Rooke around. I thanked Matthew with a quick nod before I bent to pack up my bedroll.

Rooke's purposeful stride across camp was hard to mistake while I was finishing rolling up my temporary bed. As I tied it, he took it from my grasp. I hoped I looked as well-rested as he did. The sun was brightly shining, promising a good day of weather. It was cool, but I sensed the sun would warm throughout the day.

"When I got up, it didn't look like you were going to make it this morning." His voice sounded rough, as though still laced with sleep. I raised a brow. "You looked to be dreaming so deeply."

It was a rather vivid memory, as though it had happened yesterday rather than two weeks ago. The shudder that shook my shoulders went unnoticed.

Rooke cocked his head to the side, and I could see his eyes again. He held out his hand and when I looked down, I saw he held a biscuit and some jerky. It seemed this is what we ate day in and day out. I wouldn't complain.

"We'll be riding hard. Geezer won't make it easy on you."

"I won't let you down, Rooke."

His name on my lips was foreign. Quickly, I looked away until I felt his hand on my shoulder. "I know you won't. George."

I watched him saunter toward Billy and Cade. Saying my name like that made me suspicious again. Suspicious that he knew what I was up to.

Billy gave me a quick nod when I approached but continued on with saddling the horse. The sooner we were on the road, the sooner we could stop for the night. They kept me in the dark on the route we were taking, but it wouldn't matter. I would be lost without them. I wasn't a world traveler by any means. Not now, and I would never be.

I had my bandana secured around my neck, knife tucked into my waistband, and hat on when Geezer roared for us to leave. It was time to get this journey started. Again.

Wedging my foot into the stirrup, I grasped the pommel on the saddle and waited while the horse took an unsure step away. Painfully sore this morning following a full night of rest, I thought I might be worse off than before. My entire body felt on fire. Every muscle pulled with the effort to get on Dusty.

"Get on the horse, George." I heard Rooke say, patience testing his tone.

With a huge deep breath, I gripped the saddle and threw my body against the horse while swinging my leg up and over. Finally, victory, albeit one I wasn't about to gloat over. It was the first time of many I would have to mount.

Fascinated, I watched Cade to the left of us with his remuda of horses. Four horses without saddles, free to go where they wanted, gracefully trotted around him and his horse.

It was a grueling ride further south that day, and we made it about thirty miles. I knew this only because Billy told me when we stopped briefly to rest the horses and stretch our legs. He also told me we were aiming for about forty miles of travel that day. It wouldn't put us anywhere near Indian Territory yet, not by a long shot. It would be several days of riding hard to get even close to the edge of Kansas. My body ached from the long ride, but I had to get back into the saddle or risk being left behind. After three times, I finally got onto my horse.

Even during my futile attempts to get back into the saddle, Dusty remained still and calm until I was successful. Geezer watched but did nothing to assist me. I thought he would leave me behind. But he didn't. He waited me out until I was back in the saddle and we continued.

Geezer rode ahead as night was closing in around us and returned to announce he found a place to make camp. The movement of my horse beneath me was renewing the aches in my muscles when we slowed down. By the time we arrived in the clearing near a patch of woods, my backside was numb again. I jumped down and promptly fell onto my backside, earning a blast of guffaws from my companions. Frowning, I pushed to my feet and swiped the dust from my pants.

"Boy, gather firewood and get a fire started," Geezer snapped at me.

The grimace and unladylike words under my breath were for my ears only as I hobbled into the woods to gather firewood. As much as every muscle ached while I walked, I wasn't about to give him a reason to abandon me. I grabbed as many fallen branches as I could before returning to camp. My inner thighs felt like they were on fire, my lower back aching with a ferocity I'd never experienced before, and my backside hurt with each step I took.

Finding firewood had been easy. Starting a fire was not. I

arranged the logs in what I thought was a good enough assembly to start and maintain a pleasant fire, but I didn't know how to get it started.

"You need kindling," Billy called to me from where he helped Cade tend to the horses. "Go find some dried grass or tumbleweeds to stick in there."

Shoving back to my feet, I hurried to the edge of the woods to find something to put in the fire that would spark. I collected more firewood while I was there before hurrying back to the fire.

"We're hungry, boy," Geezer growled. "Get that fire started or give up and have a man do it for you. If you can't do it."

I stabbed him with my eyes. "I can do it."

Billy threw me his matches, and I struck one, nearly burning the tips of my fingers trying to get the kindling lit. After the third match, I was successful and fed more dried grass into the small flames. Grinning, I sat back on my heels and watched my fire build momentum.

Satisfied the fire wouldn't go out, I stood up with a painful wince and brought Billy back his matches. While he stuck them in his pocket, I reached out to pet one horse.

"Thank you," I whispered.

The look he gave me was full of curiosity. His eyes were kind, despite his scruffy face that badly needed a shave. Like most of the men surrounding me, I thought. I looked back at Billy. His hair was dark brown and flopped into his eyes, causing him to remove his cowboy hat and smooth it back.

"Don't say much, do you?"

"I . . . don't need to."

"You hidin' something?" The shock on my face caused him to chuckle. "Relax, kid. We're all hidin' something."

I didn't want him to think I was hiding something. "What are you hiding?"

When he grinned, I could tell that his teeth were fairly straight but had a yellowish tint. "I'm not giving up my secrets if you aren't giving up yours. You want to tell me what you're hidin', we'll talk."

Every time I talked to Billy, I liked him more. My curiosity about him grew, but I wouldn't ask. How could I ask him about his life when I wouldn't share mine? I wondered if he would act the same, knowing I was a woman. I offered him a small smile before turning around, running right into Geezer. He stood directly behind me with his hands firmly on his hips.

"Fire went out. Start again," he snapped and walked away. "I'm paid to do one job. Babysitting ain't it."

The sight of the smoking billowing from the campfire I had only a moment ago was so proud to have started deflated me. Billy held the matches out to me when I turned back to him, and I trudged back to the woods for more kindling, like my feet had two cannonballs attached. I wouldn't make the mistake of leaving the fire unattended again.

I had it going again soon, staying near until it was roaring, and I couldn't take the heat of it. Only then, I stepped away to get my bedroll out and place it close to the fire next to my saddle.

Geezer was still sneering at me while Matthew cooked some kind of meat and a pan of beans over the fire. I wondered why he had made me start the fire when there had been so many others who could have done it.

I sat down on my bedroll, leaning against my saddle while I patiently waited for supper. My stomach rumbled so loudly I thought Matthew could hear it sitting across from me. I hadn't seen Rooke since we had stopped, wondering what task Geezer had set him out to do. Whatever it was, it was fully dark and growing colder by the minute, yet there was no sign of Rooke.

Gloating about the fire had crossed my mind, but the scowl never seemed to leave Geezer's face. I was reluctant to continue on his bad side. None of the others appeared to be at the mercy of his nastiness. Only me. I was sure it was because Rooke had squeezed me into an already full team, and Geezer didn't like it.

Before too long, they gave me a plate and a cup. Crossing my legs, even though it created a fire in my muscles, I balanced the plate of beans and meat in my lap while I set the cup down next to me. Grateful for a warm meal and something other than a chalk-hard biscuit, I washed it down with the bitter cup of coffee.

Struggling to my feet, I brought my plate and cup over to where Matthew leaned up against a tree. He raised a golden eyebrow at my approach.

"Er, my plate? What should I wash it with?"

He grinned, setting his cup of coffee down on a fallen log. "You've gotta lick your plate clean, then put it away."

My eyes widened. He couldn't be serious. Was he?

"Go on," he said.

I looked down at the brown gravy on my plate. What the hell, I thought, bringing the plate to my tongue and licking it clean. It earned laughs from Billy and Matthew, but when I turned around I had the odd feeling that the action had made me one of them.

Leaning down, Billy pulled a flask out of his boot and took a swig from it before offering it to me. Did they all keep a flask in their boots? I wondered. Another way to ensure I was one of them. I accepted it and took a small drink. Fighting the urge to cough at the burning trail of liquid down my throat, my eyes watered when I handed it back to him. He laughed again, then tucked it back into his boot before ambling away from me. I saw him spit a string of brown liquid, wrinkling my nose. Chewing tobacco, I thought with disgust.

Once the burning down my chest ceased, I settled down by the fire and stretched out my legs until I could feel the heat against the soles of my boots. Looking at the other men, they had done the same.

While I studied my shoes, Rooke slipped quietly back into camp. My eyes stayed with him despite trying not to stare at him while he spoke in hushed tones to Geezer before getting a plate of supper. He was handsome, with strong cheekbones and brown hair that curled at his nape. Skin darkened from being out in the sun, and strong, weathered hands from hard work.

As though he sensed it, he caught me staring at him and I realized what I was doing, looking away quickly. But it was too late. He'd already seen me watching him. I groaned. It was best to avoid everyone, including Rooke. Stay to myself, do what Geezer told me to do, and make it to Texas unscathed.

The temperature had dropped, and although I was reluctant to leave the heat of the fire, I knew tomorrow would be another grueling day on the road. I would need my rest. Feeling sluggish, I staggered to my feet and slid into my bedroll as quickly as I could to keep in as much warmth as possible. I hadn't so much as bid goodnight to the men before my eyes grew heavy. Right before I drifted off to sleep, I saw Rooke shake out his own bedroll not so far from me.

Dreams of my past assaulted me, drawing me in as though I was still living in the height of aristocracy in New York City. My life hadn't been perfect with Charles, far from it, but the pain was still fresh from having to defend myself against lies and Charles' mistrust.

Abruptly, my eyes popped fully open. I was lying on the hard ground, the coldness of the black night seeping through my coverings and clothes. This was freedom. My bonds had been broken. I should feel joy sweeping through me, yet sadness settled in.

Tears sprung from my eyes without warning and I pushed my face into the coarseness of the blanket to muffle my cries. I wondered what I was doing here in this untamed land with these men, who could be more dangerous than Charles. Had I gone around the bend? The thought only made me cry more until I felt a kick to the bottom of my boot. I looked up to find Rooke staring at me, his eyes hard.

"Stop that," he snapped, his tone hushed.

It was the first time I had heard him speak to me any other way but kindly. The edge in his voice demanded respect, and I didn't dare question his authority. He was the only one I could trust. The others seemed trustworthy, but there was something about Rooke that gave me a sense of protection.

Angry at myself, I swiped the wetness from my cheeks with my palm, my eyes staying on his. He watched me, not taking his eyes from me either. *Does he know? Does he know I'm not the boy I'm pretending to be? Will he tell the others if he does?*

"You'll bring attention to yourself if you keep that up."

He returned to his back, covering his face with his hat. I continued to stare at him, watching him until I could hear the deepness of his breathing. He hadn't been wrong. Crying was a sure way to get the others to think me soft. Like a woman. This was a time I would need to be tough. But even as I lay down, I looked up at the stars sparkling over the dark sky and I could not help but think of my life as it had been.

Charles had treated me horribly. It shouldn't be a surprise he'd believed the lies so easily. When Benjamin wanted something, he would do whatever it took to get it. For whatever reason, it was me he wanted. Except I was the variable he hadn't intended on. He would never have me. Even if it meant that Charles would not have me, either.

Chapter Fifteen

We didn't linger the next morning. I barely had time to swallow another hard biscuit washed down with lukewarm coffee before we continued on our journey south. Billy warned me it would be a lengthy ride, wanting to get past Wichita. Clouds with colors varying from light gray to a dark, tumultuous bluish-gray churned overhead. Riding in the rain wasn't something I had expected when I'd accepted the challenge of riding a horse all the way to Texas.

My thoughts drifted while we plodded along, nothing but sparse trees and land all around us, wondering what happened if it rained hard. Would we seek shelter or keep riding through it? I shuddered. Drying out by the heat of the fire seemed easy enough to do. I could escape having to remove any clothing. If I got drenched, would I be able to get away with it?

These were things I didn't consider when I left New York behind. Although I didn't envision traveling as a man for the entire journey, I should have had the foresight that being disguised would have its drawbacks. I should be on a train, not in the saddle from sunup to sundown. The movements of all my muscles alone still took getting used to. The burn of my inner thighs persisted from rocking back and forth in the saddle. My tailbone felt rubbed raw. Everything about this journey brought an unfamiliar experience into my life.

As evening closed in behind us, the landscape changed from forests to more prairie. The landscape flattened, dotted with farms and smaller clusters of trees. I remained silent while men chattered around me. Billy brought up the rear and I could hear him singing songs I didn't recognize. Something about a man named Joe who was cotton eyed. I didn't know what cotton eyed meant, but it couldn't be good.

If Billy told me the truth, we had a lot more days of travel to know my companions better. I'm a newcomer, I thought. If Geezer thought so little of me, I was sure the others did as well. Only Rooke, Billy, and Matthew paid me any attention. Cade kept mostly to himself, I'd noticed. Shrugging, I looked around to see if anyone had noticed my lips moving silently. Talking to myself, sane enough to do, but answering could be a sign of madness.

Movement out of the corner of my eye had me swiveling in my saddle to see a group of deer gracefully loping across the fields, their legs making them look like they were bouncing instead of running. I envied their freedom, watching them run.

"But I am free," I whispered.

Rooke pulled his horse up beside me. "You say something?"

I didn't realize I spoke aloud. Rooke stared at me, waiting. In my gut, I knew I could trust him. He had done nothing but help me along, giving me no reason to think he had anything but my best interest in hand. Yet I couldn't trust him with this.

"Spit it out."

"I was watching the deer, thinking how lovely to be free."

My lips immediately snapped shut as the words left my mouth. When we rode for long stretches with little talking, I got used to not having to watch how I spoke. So much that by the time we stopped, I had to watch my language.

"Lovely," he said, like he agreed with me.

Dropping my hand, I glanced at him. His natural ease and self-assurance made him seem born to be in a saddle. The deer had my envy, but Rooke had my admiration. The deep hazel-blue of his eyes caught mine, holding firm until I was drowning in them. There was a fine stubble along the firm line of his jaw, chin and upper lip. I tore my gaze away, feeling my lungs working hard to breathe. What was wrong with me?

"George?"

I didn't answer, keeping my eyes averted. Looking back at him now would ask for trouble I couldn't afford. There was enough trouble with Geezer.

"You can trust me."

His voice was low, like it should reach no further than my ears, even though I knew others trusted him. Why wouldn't they? I liked Rooke immediately, though he was elusive enough that I knew nothing about him. He had a way about him.

All I could do was nod. He made no move to ride on, staying beside me but keeping his eyes on the trail and our companions ahead. Out of the corner of my eye, I watched the way he moved with his horse. I'd need to watch my admiration of him, feeling it grow with each passing day.

"I see you watchin' me."

My head whipped around to stare at him. How could he possibly know I watched him? And how rude to point it out! He continued to stare straight ahead, but I noticed the tilt of the corner of his mouth.

"Why?" he prompted.

My mind raced to think of something to tell him, something to appease his question, that didn't question my gender. Opening my mouth, I breathed in and out calmly, but all that came to me was emptiness. Think, Georgiana Victoria St. John! I couldn't help but scold myself.

"How long have you been a cowboy?"

"Who said I'm a cowboy?"

I shifted in the saddle, trusting my horse to stay on course while I watched Rooke. The men seemed to know him well, even asked if he meant to come back. Wouldn't that make him a cowboy? I couldn't rightly say I'd met a cowboy in my travels until I met Rooke and the rest of them. Heat crept up my neck, warming my cheeks.

"You said you knew my brother, and since you were the one who brought Helene back to her family, I assumed you worked for him."

"I did work for him."

"On a cattle ranch. Isn't that where cowboys work?" I tilted my head, waiting for his explanation with eager but masked anticipation.

I'd spoken with the others, and was constantly yelled at by Geezer, but Rooke and I hadn't said so much as a few words to one another in the last few days. To learn more about him piqued my interest.

"I'm not a cowboy. Not anymore. Not since before the war."

The words died on my lips, watching sorrow crease his brows. I didn't know if I wanted to continue with my questioning. Rooke was one of my few allies on this trek. We still had a great number of days left of the journey.

"I did a little of everything on the ranch," he finally said.

"Like cattle drives?"

This time, he smiled. "It's your turn to answer questions."

Bugger it! I didn't know he would turn it around on me and not be prepared to answer questions honestly. Nothing he told me seemed dishonest. I could only give him the same respect and answer his questions truthfully.

"Is your name really George?"

I smiled. "Yes."

"And you're coming from North Carolina?"

My mouth flattened. "I told you I wasn't lying."

I pressed my lips together.

He chuckled. "Your secret, whatever it may be, is safe with me."

"Who said I have a secret?"

When his gaze met mine, his hazel-blue eyes looking so deeply into mine it felt like he was looking into my soul. I regretted asking such a question. My intention was for him not to mention his suspicion about me having a secret. "I know you have secrets. We all do."

We fell into silence. I didn't know what to say after that. I shifted my focus back to the landscape and the growing darkness looming. We passed through Wichita, past the trading post built by trading pioneer Jesse Chisholm. It was his trail we followed, Jesse having built several trading posts along the cattle trail from Texas up through Kansas.

We were heading into Indian Territory, where there wasn't much civilization. I shuddered, wondering if we would encounter any Indians along the way. I'd heard a mixture of tales about them, some bad and some good.

As we continued on the road, I thought it would be full dark by the time we stopped to set up camp. The sky was opening to let out a fine drizzle, creating a sense of dread that I couldn't start a fire with wet wood and kindling. My luck would run out, eventually. Wet materials, wet clothing, and darkness. This day wouldn't end well for me if we continued much farther.

As soon as the thoughts entered my mind, Geezer threw up his hand and motioned the group toward a farm set out in the middle of a field. We halted while he spoke with the farmer, then motioned us on. The farmer would allow us and our horses to sleep under the cover of his barn that night, out of the rain. The barn was bigger than the house. Big enough for all of us and the remuda.

"No fire tonight," Rooke said as we dismounted and led our horses toward the big barn. "We're lucky enough to get shelter instead."

I counted my blessings not to have to deal with Geezer yelling at me to hurry with the fire that night. The air had grown cool along with the rain, beginning a heavier descent as we neared the barn. As I ducked into the building, leading my horse in by the reins, the skies opened and unleashed a torrent of rain that would have soaked me through had I been but a minute later.

Since I didn't have a chore, I helped Matthew and Cade settle the horses at the far side of the barn. Removing saddles to set in a wide circle where we'd seek rest while Matthew gathered hay. I ran my hand along my horse's flanks and giggled when he pressed his wet nose at the crook of my neck. My eyes widened when Rooke stood staring at me. Bugger it!

"Billy's got tack ready. Isn't much, but it'll have to do without a fire. And you'll have to make do with whiskey, not coffee."

I shrugged. I didn't think I would miss having hot coffee that night. It was foul-tasting and after this journey, I would gladly never drink it again. Giving my horse more of my attention, I left him to rest and made my way back to the group. The best place for my bedroll was closest to the barn doors without getting wet, which was close enough to the group that I could sit on it to eat and lean against my saddle.

Billy handed me a plate of cold beans with a biscuit balancing on the edge with a cup. When I reached out to grab it from him, he held it firm and looked at me curiously.

I stared at him. "You going to give me my supper?"

He chuckled, releasing the plate to me. I sat on my bedroll, balancing them while I eased down carefully without spilling. I scooped up a mouthful of beans, immediately pulling a face at the taste of cold beans.

Gulping down the thick lump, I chased it with whiskey from my tin cup. The burn of the whiskey down my throat made me close my eyes before water could run down my cheeks.

"Sumpthin' wrong with your food, boy?"

I glanced up at Geezer, realizing he was talking to me from across the way. Nothing good could come from this, and though

I tried not to talk much, I knew if I didn't answer, it would only be worse. Hastily, I took another gulp of whiskey and swiped my sleeve across my mouth. Everyone looked at me.

"No."

"Looks like you don't like it."

Of course I didn't like it. None of the food I'd consumed so far on this trip had been good, but I wouldn't complain. I wouldn't dare complain about anyone's cooking so long as I didn't have to do it. At least I had food to eat.

The whiskey still burned a path down to my belly, but my throat had cleared enough for me to respond. "I like it fine, Geezer."

Everyone laughed. I held my breath until everyone resumed the surrounding conversation, aware that Geezer glared at me from afar. It would be good to know why he disliked me so much, but I wasn't about to ask him. Not here, and not now. Eventually, I would find out.

With my plate licked clean, I swirled the dark liquid left in my cup around. The amount of whiskey consumed made me feel as though my body was humming. When I stood, I swayed and earned several guffaws from the men. My vision was swimming, but even Cade was belly-laughing. Befuddled, I tucked my plate into my bag, then looked at the contents in my cup.

"I think George's drunk," Matthew announced, bringing out more laughter.

Bugger it, I am, I thought. I needed to drain the rest of the whiskey to put away my cup, but I knew I shouldn't drink any more of it. Being drunk meant I could get into trouble I didn't need. Too late for that. I tipped the cup back and drained the rest of the contents before putting the cup in with my plate.

I could hardly walk straight over to my bedroll, falling onto my knees painfully and rolling to my back. The roof of the barn moved. Or my head moved. Either way, the world was moving around me and I didn't like it.

Hours later, I still didn't like it and crawled out to the edge of the barn to vomit. The rain had stopped, but the ground remained damp. I paid no mind to the dirt on my hands and crawled back to my bedroll. When I climbed back in, I noticed Rooke had his bedroll close to mine and his eyes were open, looking at me. I gave him a nod, hoping he knew I'd be fine.

Chapter Sixteen

"Take this."

Unpacking my bedroll the next night, I looked up at Rooke. Cradled in the palm of his hand, lay a pistol much larger than my Derringer. My eyes widened. When he had mentioned securing me with a gun, part of me didn't know if he had been telling me the truth. Other than the Derringer, I'd never handled a firearm before. I'd certainly never fired one.

I stood, eyeing the long-barreled pistol and brown handle. Tentatively, I reached out but I couldn't touch it. Something stopped me from doing so, and I knew it was fear. What if I shot someone? What if I accidentally shot myself? Thinking back to that night, I don't think I would have ever pulled the trigger.

"George?" Rooke asked. "Have you ever handled a gun before?"

Wanting to laugh and tell him I had, I merely shook my head. His curse followed immediately after my answer. He took my hand, putting the gun into it regardless if I liked it, and forced my fingers around the handle.

"It's already loaded with six shots." He looked up and around. "You're going to have to learn how to shoot it without being obvious about it. Dammit."

We'd ridden hard that day after crossing the Arkansas River, and Billy hadn't been lying when he'd told me it was big. While it hadn't been deep, it had been wide and difficult to cross. Wet up to my thighs, the sun and the wind dried most of me. My stomach still rolled from the whiskey I'd had, but after vomiting a few more times and skipping breakfast, I felt better.

The area we stopped for the night and everywhere around us was flat, open land. There wouldn't be a suitable spot to shoot at anything without calling attention to ourselves. I watched Rooke stomp away, puzzled at what to do with this gun in my hand. It paralyzed me to have it and not know what to do.

A few minutes later, Rooke returned with two biscuits in one hand and a belt draped over his arm. He grabbed me by the elbow and led me away from the camp. I looked up at the sky, twilight fast approaching, glad the rain had cleared.

"Where are you taking me?"

"Shush," he said. "Just don't shoot it yet."

The trigger wasn't near my fingers. Certain that I wouldn't shoot it on purpose, I only gripped it more firmly. "I won't shoot it," I said, a low rumble in my voice.

"Did you tell them we were leaving?"

His jaw clenched, but he didn't answer me.

"Isn't it going to be loud if we shoot right now? And it's getting dark."

"We aren't shooting it. I'm going to show you how, but you are not pulling the trigger. Do you hear me? George? You will not pull the trigger."

The way he said my name sounded strange, like it was a point to be made. Did he know? Rooke questioning everything had my suspicion piqued. He knew something was off with me. I needed to be better at my sham.

"Did you hear me?"

"Yes." I tried to pull my arm out of his hand, but he held firm. "You can let go."

"I'm not losing you out here."

A sound escaped from my throat between a scoff and a laugh.

"There is nothing but flat land and fields out here. I won't get lost, Rooke."

His name on my lips sounded intimate. I'd called him by his name before. And what kind of name was that, anyway? Before I could ask him where he got such an odd name, he spoke.

"I'm not taking the chance. We don't need anyone knowing we're out here. There are still Indians and a hell of a lot of thieves, too. We don't need the trouble."

"Where'd you get the gun?"

"Wichita," was all he said.

Resigned to be propelled across the grassy fields away from the rest of the group, I sighed. For every step he took, I had to take at least two to keep up. I needed to trust him. Soon, I could barely catch my breath and we stopped.

Rooke snatched the gun from my hand while I doubled over to catch my breath. With these bindings, walking at such a fast pace wasn't a good idea. I was gasping for breath, concentrating on him while he watched and waited for me to compose myself. When I stood up, he motioned me over. It was impossible to tell how far we were from camp.

There was a small group of trees in the middle of the field, surrounded by nothing else like God put them there by accident. I walked over, one foot in front of the other with slow purpose, until I stopped in front of him. He put his hand on my hip and twirled me around. The feel of his hand on my waist burned through the thin fabric of my trousers and shirt. If his hand slid against my bare skin, I swore it would feel the same. Shivers danced through me.

His other hand came around me and skated up my arm. He pressed the gun into my hand, but my attention was not on the gun but on the way he pressed his body against mine from behind, his chest against my back. He made my breath hitch, every inch of my body aware of his presence. No one, no man, had ever handled me this way. Touched me. Been so patient with me.

"Now," he said, his tone serious. "When you fire this, make sure you're aiming. You see the hammer at the top?"

I nodded, weakly.

"Use that to focus your aim. See those trees? Try to find a spot on the tree and aim, but do not pull this trigger. Do you hear me?" I nodded again. He pulled our hands until the gun was level with my line of sight, allowing me to bring it the rest of the way until I squinted and looked at the hammer.

There was a notch on the bigger tree. I tried to focus on it, but the gun wavered in my hand. He increased the pressure of his hands on mine. Flames were ricocheting throughout my body like lightning strikes, making it impossible to concentrate.

"Focus." His whisper against the shell of my ear only made my hands shake more. "Control it. You can do this."

Concentrating on our hands, I straightened my arms, and he moved even closer behind me. Bugger it. I couldn't see straight with his body behind me like that. I could feel his muscles through the thin layer of my clothing. He was everywhere. Surely, this wasn't proper. Would he do this if he knew I was a woman? When my eyes closed, my finger twitched.

"Take your finger away from the trigger." His voice consumed me.

My eyes sprang open.

When he moved back, I took in a full breath. My entire body felt overheated. I couldn't turn around in fear that my face would betray my feelings. Slowly, I withdrew my finger from the space to remove the threat of accidentally pulling the trigger. He was behind me again, and I felt his hands at my waist. If he moved his hands any higher, he'd feel my bindings. I looked down. He was securing the gun belt around my hips.

"Don't pull the gun out unless you intend to use it," he said, the stir of his breath moving the ragged edges of my hair behind my ear. "You'll wear this at all times except at night. Then you'll keep it next to you. I'll teach you how to shoot it when it's safe to, and how to load and clean it."

"Won't the men think something is wrong with me?" I asked.

He chuckled. "There's something wrong with all of us."

I smiled when he reached out to bring my hand and the gun safely into the holster, like he knew I didn't trust myself to do it. Finally, I sucked in a deep breath, earning another chuckle from him.

"Do you know why you're named Rooke?" I blurted.

"Of course I do. Do you know why you're named George?"

"George is a normal name. I don't know that I've ever met anyone named Rooke."

"Probably because you haven't. I was named after a chess piece."

I followed when he walked, I assumed, back to camp. "Chess?"

"My old man was a gambler. There wasn't a game he wouldn't play, but when he was a boy, he played chess. He won a chess game and his opponent accused him of cheating, threw a rook at him and nearly took out his eye. Tucked that very piece in his pocket and it seemed to bring him luck. So when I was born, he named me Rooke."

It wasn't a story I expected, rendering me speechless. "What happened to him?"

"Don't know. Haven't heard from him since I was young. Went off to chase the gold in California." He looked at me. "Why were you named George?"

"After my grandfather."

I didn't lie. It was true, but usually people called me Georgie, not George. If he never discovered the complete truth, my omission couldn't be a lie.

"You got a middle name?"

I sucked in my breath. "I can't tell you that."

"Why not?"

"Some things are better left unsaid."

"We all have things to hide," he said. "You, I think, have more than most. I'm telling you that you can trust me, and you still won't. Maybe in the days ahead you will. Promise me you'll stay close to me."

"Why?"

"There are more dangers out in the wilds of the land. Shooting aside, you're more vulnerable than you think you are."

"You mean weak."

"Innocent."

"I'm stronger than you think," I snapped. "I'll shoot this gun if I need to."

He chuckled. "You may be stronger than I think, but that doesn't mean I'll worry any less about what trouble you might find yourself in."

Chapter Seventeen

The next day of travel passed much like the others, long hours in the saddle with several breaks along the way and crossing more rivers. I always breathed a sigh of relief when the river appeared small. The big rivers, like the Arkansas River, with rippling, flowing water, scared me. There had been no more signs of rain since the night we spent in the barn, though clouds were visible in the sky giving some reprieve from the heat of the sun. The heat was increasing as each day passed; the nights stayed somewhat cooler. I'd switched horses that day and missed my sweet horse, but this thoroughbred was still gentle. I was getting better at mounting, and my muscles had eased somewhat, although I still felt queasy from the whiskey in the barn.

Camp that night started a more organized effort to get the horses secured, the fire started, and supper underway. The sun was setting, giving a vibrant swath of orangish-red color toward the west like an artist slapped a paintbrush over the horizon. The sunset was a spectacular sight to behold, and as soon as Matthew and I got the fire started, I slipped away to watch it as Billy came through the trees, holding several dead rabbits by the feet, and my eyes widened.

As soon as he walked past me, I stumbled closer to the nearby stream and vomited. There had been little to throw up, but I sat on my haunches and wretched until sweat beaded on my forehead. I'd seen animals slaughtered for food before and never lost the contents of my stomach.

I unwound the bandana from around my neck and pressed it to my forehead, finding no solace in the dirt-packed garment. A horrible thought snuck into my head while I walked to the stream and dipped it in the water, rinsing out the dirt and wringing the water out before pressing it to my forehead again. I ticked off the dates in my head from the last time I'd had my courses.

It couldn't possibly be true. Not now. Hundreds of miles from New York, in the middle of nowhere, traveling with a group of men I barely knew. The rough bark of the tree trunk pressed against my back while terror of this predicament skittered down my spine. Without realizing it, I unbuttoned part of my shirt and pressed the bandana against my neck where sweat trickled down into my bindings. The hotter the weather became, the more uncomfortable I felt.

It hadn't been the whiskey making me ill today. If I wasn't mistaken, I'd gotten pregnant within the last month. My heart skittered at the thought. I'd wanted a baby of my own for so long. Still wanted one. But now? This couldn't have happened at a worse time.

"What am I going to do?" I whispered to no one in particular, pressing my hand to my stomach.

I craned my neck, looking back toward the camp. Everyone still worked around the camp, paying no attention to me. Just as well, I had enough to figure out. I could only pray that my brother would help me with this situation because I knew I would never return to New York. I'd be out here. Alone. With a baby.

The fatigue I'd felt lately, I assumed, was from the stress of my situation. But the more I thought of it now, and the more I thought back to the last time my monthlies came, the realization that I was pregnant hit me. I was very newly pregnant.

Slumping against the tree, I felt a mixture of happiness and anxiety. From the moment Charles and I had been married, I wanted nothing more than to become pregnant in hopes we would be a happy family. I knew we would be happy. But this couldn't possibly get any worse for me.

I found a boulder near the creek and sat on it, pulling off my boots first, then my stockings, the air cool against my bare feet and my body temperature slowly coming down. I pulled my leg up and rested my chin on my knee, letting my other leg dangle.

Instead of thinking about what could have been, and the predicament I'd found myself in, I concentrated on the gurgle of the stream and the dazzling display of twilight falling. I couldn't remember the last time I enjoyed a sunset. In the city, life was busy and the small things in life, like sunsets, seemed to have slipped away.

"You look deep in thought." Rooke's voice, deep and soothing, washed over me from behind. "Mind if I join you?"

I shrugged as he stepped up beside me, thumbs tucked casually in the pockets of his vest. The cowboy hat was low over his eyes, but from where I sat I could see their color and they were glorious. Gaze darting forward, I settled on watching the ripples of whitecaps in the rushing water. I couldn't swim, even though the stream near our house was my favorite place as a girl.

"You holding up, George?"

I swallowed a gulp and whispered: "Why?"

He laughed, deep and throaty. "It doesn't take a smart man to see you've got no experience out here in the wilds. Funny how Anthony never mentioned a brother."

I nearly leapt off the boulder, but Rooke's arm swept out and I stayed put. Not sure what he was aiming for, I couldn't help but be defensive by where this conversation might lead.

"Don't get all wary."

I smothered my laugh by stuffing my face into the crook of

my arm. If everything came to light, I could be sure none of them would look at me the same. Especially Rooke.

"You can trust me."

I lifted my head, my eyes slowly meeting his and my breath hitching in my throat. Rooke had the eyes of someone to be trusted. Yet I couldn't, I wouldn't, spill my secrets to anyone. Now more than ever, it would be safer that no one knew. I'd do everything possible to make sure no one suspected. Redoubling my efforts if I needed to, I'd make sure no one found out.

"George," he whispered, his voice softening. "Snakes out here. Best not to be wandering around barefoot when dark falls."

I watched Rooke walk away, admiring his confident stride. Then I looked down at my bare feet and rolled-up trousers. Snakes? Thoughts of snakes had me swiping up my boots and stockings before running past him a second later, regardless of how much my muscles still ached. I heard the deep rumble of his laugh trailing behind me.

By the time the sun disappeared over the horizon, I'd eaten my roasted rabbit with coffee instead of whiskey and waited for the rest of them to seek their bedrolls. Laying on my blanket, staring up at the twinkling lights in the sky, I thought about my situation. If any of these men found out that not only had they been toting a woman along with them, but a pregnant one at that, they might drop me at the nearest trading post. If that happened, I'd have to figure out a way to get back to my grandfather.

The circle of snores around me only made it harder to think, Billy being the worst snorer I'd ever heard. The only one I never heard a peep from was Rooke, which made it impossible to know if he had fallen asleep. I needed to get up without having any question why I was sneaking off, and this would be the best time to do it.

I tiptoed out of the camp to find a tree and some privacy, remembering Rooke's warning from earlier about the snakes.

Maybe they were all sleeping. I quickened my pace, hoping to find a tree. They were sparse in these parts.

No sooner than fifty paces from camp, I heard the rustling of grass behind me and whirled to see Rooke standing there. The beat of my heart pounded so hard, I put my hand to my chest to slow it.

"What are you doing?" I hissed.

Rooke wasted no time in striding up to me until I needed to tilt my head to look up at him. He left his hat behind. "What are *you* doing?" he countered. "You've got to be some kind of crazy to think of leaving, and on foot, no less."

I lowered my eyes, staring headlong into his chest, where his shirt had a few buttons unbuttoned. In the dark, I could still see the glow of his skin. "I need to go."

"Need to?" Repeating my words only aggravated me. "Now? Why now?"

"You won't understand."

He hooked his thumbs in the pocket of his vest. Even in the dark, I could see the ruffle of his brown hair in the moon's light. The breeze blew against it, teasing the slight curl at his nape. He'd need a haircut before long.

"Make me," came his husky reply.

"I have to pee."

The darkness hid the redness in my face from having to admit such a thing to him. How had he heard me leave? Why had he followed me? That he thought I would leave in the middle of the night with nothing with me, made my veins come alive.

"You thought I meant to leave out of here in the dead of night? On foot?"

I didn't think he would answer me. When I moved to get around him, he stopped me by curling his fingers around my wrist ever so lightly. Surprise washed over me at being stopped without brute force. His entire hand swallowed my delicate wrist. I looked at him, our eyes colliding in the night's darkness.

My breath caught in my lungs, heart picking up speed beneath my bindings. He didn't need to hold me hard. I wouldn't attempt to get around him with his hand on me.

He let out a low laugh. "I didn't know what to think."

I knew he watched me when he didn't think I noticed. His suspicion without making it seem obvious had become clearer each day. I could only continue to play my part. And well.

His hand dropped away. "But there are things more dangerous out there than the men in this camp. Wild animals, weather, Indians, and that doesn't even cover criminals that would do you harm."

His words sunk in, stunning me into a breathless gasp. Should I assume there was more in his warning than there meant to be? It was awfully hard not to. I moved away from him, not waiting for him to follow, but I knew he did.

"I told you before you could trust me," his voice said behind me.

"You did."

"When are you going to?"

I turned around, fury taking hold of me. "What makes you think I don't?"

When he folded his arms in front of his chest, I thought I'd angered him. I mimicked the movement, more out of tenacity than anger. He shook his head with a low laugh. We stood close enough to camp to wake others if we were too loud.

"Seems there's something you aren't telling me. Why?"

"I'll share it when I'm ready."

For several minutes, he stared at me. I felt like he looked into my soul, peeled back the layers and took the time to study the inside when he looked at me like he did. Waiting for him to respond, slowly melted away my doubts in going on. I believed him. Believed in him.

"Will you?" he whispered.

"I will," came my promise. I didn't know when I could share

it, but I hoped one day I could honor it. After all that he'd done for me, I owed him that much.

Chapter Eighteen

Turns out, we would stay in this camp for another night to allow the horses and cattle proper rest near a river with fresh water and fields for grazing.

The first thing I did when I woke up was feel around for the pistol. Sure enough, I had it tucked up next to me within the gun belt. Along with the Bowie knife, the knowledge that if I had to use either of them, I was positive I'd be able to. Out here, the dangers were much more real than a mere robbery. It was life or death. By God, I would use one of them without pause. After the lesson Rooke so kindly gave me, never again would I be defenseless like I'd been in North Carolina, held hostage while my belongings were gone through with filthy, unwanted hands pressing against my body.

Lifting my head, I looked around to see the camp slowly coming to life. Birds were singing, scattering in flight across the wide expanse of sky that fairly glittered with the light of the sun coming up. It felt like several moments that I lay on my bedroll, watching the birds and the sky. The world was different here. Calmer, not as fast paced as New York life. My childhood eased into my mind. The fearless girl who ran across fields and dipped her toes in the creek slowly returned to the woman who spoke in hushed tones and never argued.

A laugh erupted from my throat. If my mother were still alive and could see me now, she'd be shocked and ashamed. Rising on my elbow, I looked down at my hand. Dirt beneath my fingernails and smudged on my palms. I turned them over to see my roughened knuckles having scraped them against the wood last night.

Billy rose, stretching his arms above his lanky body before heading toward the small copse of trees. I looked away, having to wait until the rest of them went into the woods before I could go. With the creek beyond, I yearned to bathe. I'd never gone so long without bathing, and the further south we went, the more the heat rose.

Rolling to my feet, I stilled for a moment to let the wave of nausea pass before coming to my feet. The small of my back ached, and I rotated my hips to work out the kinks while Matthew knocked around pots and pans.

The thunder of hooves stole my attention as I spotted Cade racing across the fields with his remuda around him, their wild manes and tails flying with the wind. He looked so natural, so free. Envy shook me for a moment.

"Alright there?"

I glanced up at Rooke and nodded. The ease of his movements, deliberate and confident, was to be admired. Here stood a man comfortable with his surroundings. How I wished I could get to be as comfortable as him. Resisting the urge to smooth my hand over my flat stomach, my heart lurched at the thought of my dilemma. Finally, nestled within, my child grew. A part of Charles, yes. But mine. Charles, although it would be sinful for me to never tell him, did not have to be told of this child. Selfishly, I could live in Texas with Anthony and this child and never see Charles again. He would never know.

Ordinarily, I didn't consider myself selfish. Not sure I could keep something like this from Charles, despite our difficult marriage, it put a pressure on me. I wouldn't think about it yet. Pushing it from my mind, I focused on the day ahead and preventing anyone from finding out my lies.

Queasiness aside, this could be a more dangerous situation than any other problem we may encounter. Scared they'd discover a woman traveled among them, terrified they'd find out I carried a child.

"George."

"Rooke."

He hooked his thumbs into his vest, which looked like it needed a good washing, and rocked back on his heels. "You want to take a walk?"

A walk? I looked around, nothing but fields and a creek with an insignificant wooded area around us. "Where?"

"Try to find some kindling. What else are we going to do? Cade's got the horses under control, Matthew's getting breakfast underway, and Billy went into the woods to do his business. Geezer, well, he's busy."

I could think of a few things to do, like settle in with a cup of the bitter coffee and some bacon. With my stomach empty, it only made me feel sicker. Eating would be essential. My stomach rolled at the thought.

Rooke watched me expectantly.

I shrugged. "Lead the way."

Our walk started at a slow pace, picking our way through the fields while the morning sun warmed the air. We didn't talk. We didn't need to. My comfort with him surprised me. He appeared to be as comfortable with me, making me wonder if he'd be this comfortable with me, knowing he walked with Anthony's sister, not his brother.

"We'll be on our way again tomorrow," he said after a while. "Reach Indian Territory before sundown."

"That's good?"

"We're making good time. That's expected. The way back is usually much quicker than the way there. Cattle need time to graze along the way or they lose too much weight before reaching the market. We travel double the miles each day, sometimes more, without cattle."

I tried not to look at him too much, not wanting him to think I watched him again. Covered with a shade of stubble darker than his hair, his jaw cut a firm line. He had high cheekbones to go with his jawline. Aristocratic men in New York had thick sideburns, but Rooke didn't and it made him looked rugged. Untamed. An adventure I didn't know I'd been looking for. My lips curved upward without meaning to.

"You're watching me again."

The softness of his deep burr made my smile widen. "I admire you."

Suddenly, he stopped and swept his arm out to stop me from stepping any further. Perhaps I should have not been so blatant. He pointed to where the grass thinned, and I watched a snake slithering across our path, paying us no mind.

"Rattlesnakes out here don't usually bother with us but I would hate for you to get bitten. There isn't a town or post for miles yet." His arm lowered, but his eyes remained on the path the snake took to ensure it was gone.

"I'd rather not get bitten. Have you ever?"

"No, and I'm with you. I'd rather not, either."

Traipsing across the plains hadn't been the plan. I should have been on a train, third-class ticket passenger or not. Not that Sybil could have found me the gear Rooke had. Not in New York, but I'd have never thought to look for cowboy boots and hats, or Bowie knives.

Rooke continued walking, and if he thought it would be safe enough, it must be. He would know more than I did when it was safe to move along.

"Don't you want to know why I admire you?" I asked.

"No."

"Why not?"

My accent slipped again, and I saw the corner of his mouth

lift. He knew where I came from having already been acquainted with Anthony, but I thought I sounded more like a girl with my English lilt. Stepping carefully, I followed closely next to him while fully expecting a snake to lash out. We were so close I could feel the laugh rumble through him.

"I'm not a good man. You shouldn't admire me."

I doubted it, but I didn't say it. We walked on, stopping to see a herd of buffalo in the distance. In awe, I watched these massive animals with shaggy brown fur and enormous heads while they lumbered across the land. Slow in pace, with no particular place to be just as Rooke and I.

"Beautiful," I whispered.

I could feel his eyes on me instead of watching the buffalo, but he didn't utter a word. He let me watch the buffalo roam across the plains in silence, keeping to my own thoughts. We stayed for a few more minutes before deciding to head back to camp for breakfast. He allowed me some privacy when we passed by a small copse of trees, which surprised me, before we continued on to find the camp in full swing.

Matthew had bacon sizzling in the pan and, surprisingly, warm biscuits. Rooke and I parted ways without another word, and I accepted a cup of steaming black coffee from Billy. That familiar twinkle in his eyes had become a sense of home to me. Anthony had always had a sparkle in his eyes when we were young. I missed it.

Billy and I leaned up against a couple of trees, drinking our coffee and eating biscuits while Geezer stomped around. That made me smile. As soon as his gaze found mine, my smile vanished.

"Good Lord, what's got his suspenders in a tangle now?" Billy grumbled, then took a gulp of his coffee. After a minute, he spit and I grimaced. I'd never get used to him spitting.

Waiting with my breath held, I kept a firm grip on my cup until Geezer turned and strode in the opposite direction. Only then did the air leave my lungs in a whoosh. We dissolved into quiet laughter.

"Why is he so mean?"

Billy shrugged. "I've only known him a short while. He's been like that since I got to the ranch. He left for a time, I know that much, then came back asking for his job back."

"Did he get it?"

He shook his head. "He got a job, and he was lucky. Him and the ranch owner don't get on. Geezer don't do half of what Rooke did while he ran the ranch."

That didn't surprise me, as ornery as Geezer was. "Anthony gets along with everyone. He must be terrible. Do you know his real name or is it really Geezer?"

I heard Matthew's laugh nearby. I declared then I would never tire of that sound. It was light and jovial. I couldn't blame him for listening to the conversation Billy and I were having.

Billy sighed. "I can't give away the man's secrets. But I will tell you that Geezer is not his real name." He shoved away from his tree, tossing the rest of his coffee into the dirt and setting his cup on a log. "Time's wasting. Might as well take a bath in the river while we're here for the day."

I watched him walk away, taking a sip from the cooling liquid while I longed for a bath. Even with short hair, a wash would feel like heaven.

He turned back. "You coming?"

Quickly, I shook my head, causing him to laugh again. "Maybe later."

"You're going to have to bathe, George. You might be the smallest in the bunch of us, but you're going to have to get used to teasing. It's what we do."

I'd have to slip into the creek after everyone had gone to sleep and be very careful not to undo my bindings. The days were growing hotter; the bindings itching like the devil had come after me. That and the bindings hurt like they hadn't before. I resisted and ignored as much as I could, hoping I would get a reprieve soon.

Matthew and Billy went down to the river, close enough to camp to hear them whooping and hollering in the water. I sat down on a log, watching Rooke and Cade play poker. They'd been down to the river already, I could tell by their wet hair.

Cade looked up. "You play?" I shook my head. "We can teach you."

I slid closer to them. "I don't have any money."

They laughed. Cade said: "We'll teach you. What you do when you get wages is up to you, kid."

"Blackjack's the name of the game," Rooke explained. "I'll deal you two cards. You get a face card and an ace, that's black-jack and you win. I'm the dealer. If I get blackjack, I win."

"You get whatever's the bet?" I asked.

Cade cracked a grin. "You're catchin' on. If you don't get blackjack, you want to get as close to it as you can without going over–or bust. If the dealer has a higher hand, he'll win."

Geezer strolled over, hovering over Rooke's shoulder. I could tell by the grimace on Rooke's usually passive face that Geezer hanging over his shoulder irritated him. After a few more minutes, Rooke shifted and looked over his shoulder.

"Mind not hovering?" he asked, his voice calm. "George's got room next to him. Or maybe you want in on the next hand?"

Geezer snickered. "Maybe I like hoverin'."

"Not everyone appreciates it." Rooke's voice sounded dead calm.

"Maybe I don't give a damn."

Rooke stood, then Cade. Feeling like a mouse among giants, I also stood, stepping to the other side of the log and out of the way. Rooke still looked calm, but Cade looked agitated now.

"Something you want to say?" Cade asked. "Say it now."

My eyes widened when Cade's hand moved, hovering over his pistol, still snapped within his gun belt. I scanned the camp to see if the boys were returning from the river to stop this.

"Nothing needs saying. Now." Geezer gave one last look to Rooke, then Cade, and swung around to saunter away.

Of the few conversations I'd had with Cade, he seemed civil, though his eyes sometimes said differently. This had been a different side, and one I'd be wary of. We all had guns. It wouldn't be anything for someone to get angry and pull a gun out to shoot.

When Rooke and Cade sat to resume their game, I joined them again and eventually relaxed while I watched them play a few rounds. They played for money, but they weren't playing for much. While I was walking away, I saw Rooke give Cade back the money he'd won from him and smiled.

◆

The rest of the day passed quicker than I thought it would have, with not much to do but sit around playing poker. I helped Matthew with taking counts of the remaining supplies, mostly in silence. After that, I helped Billy collect more firewood to ensure we had enough flames and heat for supper and after. By that time, it was nearly dusk, so I helped Cade brush down the horses. With all the men plus the extra horses, it was many horses to tend to. Cade appreciated any extra help any of us gave.

While I ran the brush over Fury, I smoothed my hand over his muscular flank and he nudged my shoulder with his muzzle. I laughed, sliding my hand up his forehead as Geezer strode toward me with purpose in his gait.

"Boy," I heard Geezer grumble, "take them buckets and get

some water from the creek."

While he strode away from me, I glanced around, not seeing any buckets. Even moving around the horses in search of them, I couldn't find them. Was he testing me? Without warning, he reached out and grabbed hold of my shirt at the shoulder and gave me a shove toward the back of the herd.

"If I have to tell you again, you ain't gonna like it."

I stared at him, with his white mustache tipped up at the ends and hard blue eyes, wondering what it was about me he found to be angry at. Since Rooke and I had joined the group, I'd done everything asked of me without complaint. Instead of standing there thinking about it further, I moved around the horses to find the two buckets and picked them up on my way toward the creek.

Mumbling every curse word I could think of, I headed toward the creek to do what I was told. It seemed a good time to swing the buckets while I walked, enjoying the fading warmth of the day. Tipping up my face to the evening sun, I welcomed the freedom of walking unhindered by a dress. Although a dress would be more comfortable than these bindings, it would only enhance my bosom instead of hiding it.

The color of the water in the creek looked refreshing, flowing with gentle ripples, unlike a river with rushing currents. I carefully stepped closer, mindful of my footing, and setting one bucket down before squatting next to the water.

I pulled the bucket around, leaning forward to tilt it into the water and let it fill to the brim. When I pulled it out, the heaviness compared to the lack of muscles in my arms started a battle. The winner would get the bucket of water. The loser would end up in the water.

Pressing my lips together with determination, I gave it a hard yank. And pitched forward into the creek with a splash. Water rushed into my mouth as soon as I went under, legs kicking for solid ground while my arms fought to pull my head to the surface.

When I broke the surface, sputtering and trying to grab onto something to get back to the grass, my hands met nothing but more water. It swirled around me, pulling at my clothes.

Coughing, kicking and trying to save my own life, I jerked when something wrapped around my chest. I opened my mouth to scream, only to have it fill with more water. Choking, I squirmed against my sudden captivity.

"Stop struggling," came a deep voice right next to my ear.

Someone's arm banded around my chest, tucked beneath my breasts, pulling me to the grass. Once we neared the edge of the creek, I noticed that I'd been dragged to nearly to the other side of the creek when I'd fallen in. In horror, I looked down to see the bindings had loosened enough to ensure anyone that saw me would see I had the chest of a woman. Solid ground met the bottom of my boots and I stood, water washing down my body. My hand flew to my head.

"Holy hell." I heard Rooke mutter.

My arms clamped across my chest, hoping he couldn't see what he shouldn't see. There didn't seem like much else I could do to shield myself. The attempt was futile. I spilled out anyway, despite the vest and shirt in the way. It felt like heaven to be free of the constraints.

"Here."

Rooke stood in the water next to me, his clothing molded to his sinewy body and the white of his shirt translucent to every line of his chest. I could even see a swirl of dark hair at the center of his chest. My mouth, with a mind of its own, popped open.

"You gonna take it?"

He held my cowboy hat in his hand. I had to move one of my arms to grab it. Quickly, I accepted the sopping wet hat from him in grateful silence. When he cocked his head to the side at my lack of voice, his eyes remained locked with mine. Waiting.

After a moment, he finally broke the silence. "Nothing to

say?"

Quietly, I murmured, "Thank you."

It took effort, as water filled my boots to the brim, but I walked up the grass and sank down next to the empty bucket. The other bucket bobbed up and down in the water, mocking me, until Rooke walked out into the water to grab it.

Shamed, I realized the water level in the creek only reached mid-chest on him, which meant I could have stood up at any point. It still would have been deep for me, but I might have been able to touch bottom. Instead, I panicked.

I watched him wade through the water, the muscles beneath his shirt rippling. When he reached the grass and threw the bucket next to the other one, I glanced away. My bindings undone, I could draw full air into my lungs. I knew they were going to remain undone until I fixed it. With Rooke next to me, I couldn't do anything.

After a few more minutes of silence, I looked over at him. "Why did you jump in after me?"

"Couldn't let you drown, could I?"

I sneered. "I wasn't going to drown."

"No? Then why were you flailing around like you were going to?"

He had me. "I . . . didn't know it was shallow." I cleared the lump in my throat with a quick swallow. "You don't need to stay. I'll be fine now."

The way he looked at me made me uneasy. Was he looking into my soul? And could he see it? I'd not experienced such unease with him before, whether alone or with others. We seemed well suited together.

He sighed, heavily. "No denying it now. I know your secret."

Every muscle in my body tensed. Air locked in my lungs while my eyes burned into his. His eyes didn't waver. "You know?" The words came out slowly. "My secret?"

"I know you're a woman, Georgiana Rutherford."

I gasped. Bugger it! If Rooke knew, how many of the others knew or suspected it? Then I gulped. Cade came to mind. Even in the short time I knew him, no one could get anything past Cade.

"Relax," he whispered. "I'm not about to tell anyone. And you'd best hope no one else figures it out. I doubt any of them boys would hurt you, but we've got enough dangers out here without having to worry about you, too."

"Everyone calls me Georgie."

I took the time we sat there, since the sun was still out, to unlace and tug off my boots, followed by my socks. Setting them aside to dry, I hoped they would dry off enough before heading back to camp to dry the rest by the fire. I slid another glance toward Rooke.

"How did you know?" I asked, recalling all too well his body pressed against mine when he showed me how to aim the pistol. My face grew warm, wondering if he had known.

"You don't think your brother never talked about you? All them nights during the war, when we had nothing to do out there in the cold to keep our minds off anything else but talk about our lives as they were. He missed you. Often told me regretted leaving you behind. When you came to Abilene, it was clear you were in trouble."

I gasped. So he had known. The heat in my cheeks grew hotter. "And you didn't tell me you knew?" He didn't answer. "Why?"

He wouldn't meet my eyes, not even to turn to look at me. "Because I wanted you to trust me enough to tell me."

When he moved to stand up and leave, my anxiety got the better of me. I struggled to my feet as he turned his back to leave me alone by the creek. Bugger it!

"I . . . need your help."

He turned halfway around, finally looking at me. "Is that so?"

I nodded my head with a jerk, unable to find my voice.

"With?"

My face burned hotter. "My bindings came loose in the water. I can't bind myself."

When he tossed a look toward camp, I thought I had gone around the bend in asking him to do this, of all things. If anyone came upon us while he helped me, there would be no question as to my gender. But I had no choice. If he didn't help me do this, there would be no chance the others wouldn't find out. They would all know immediately, without my bindings.

A grumble burst from deep in his throat before he turned back around and came toward me, taking me by the arm before guiding me over to a small group of trees. The cover was hardly enough, but it would have to do.

I slipped out of the vest, tossing it down and darting a cautious look behind him before unbuttoning my shirt. His hands fell to mine, stopping me from sweeping the garment over my head.

"Let's try to do this without taking it off." His voice sounded ragged. I felt guilty asking him to do this. "Lift it and hold it there while I do the fixing."

With a shaky nod, I pulled the edge of the sopping wet shirt free from my trousers and lifted it until the bindings came into his view.

He grasped the end of the bindings and pulled the rest free. "Holy hell," came his hoarse whisper.

When the bindings fell free, I took the deepest breath I had taken in a week. It felt like my lungs were finally free to take in as much air as possible. Rooke allowed me a few minutes to get my breathing under control, averting his gaze while he did so, before he reached around and began winding the strip of fabric around my torso.

"It has to be tight. As tight as you can get it."

My face remained red until my breasts were once again covered, painfully so when I drew in a sharp breath. No one had seen me like this other than Charles. And my maids. Yet, it didn't feel odd that Rooke did now.

"How can you stand being trussed up like this?" he asked, about halfway done.

"I don't have a choice."

"Looks painful."

"Don't make me walk fast again. I'll likely pass out."

That made him smile. "I'm not sure I like the thought of you having to do this."

Warmth spread through my lower extremities. "Shall I leave myself unbound?"

He made a choking sound. "Good God, no."

Chapter Nineteen

The next morning dawned bright, hot, and humid. If not for sitting by the campfire last night, my clothes would still be damp because of the humidity. The air seemed saturated with it. I sat up, struggling to breathe. Quickly grabbing my hat, I slapped it onto my head before reaching for my boots. After taking a quick look inside for snakes, I tugged them on and bounded over to Matthew for coffee and whatever he had available to eat before we mounted up for the trail.

"Fell in the creek, I heard," Matthew said, handing me a cup.

"Much to my regret."

"D'ya take a bath while you was in there?"

My gaze lifted to his twinkling eyes. He made it impossible not to smile. "Forgot my soap, but I believe I got washed up enough while I was swimming." I leaned closer to him. "You think so?"

That brought out his cheerful laugh. He fell back on his heels in laughter. I pulled at my shirt, taking a sniff. Seemed clean enough. My vest! I thought. I forgot it by the creek last night.

Downing the coffee, I dropped my cup next to my bedroll and took my dried beef with me toward the creek. I never knew when Geezer would yell at everyone to get on the way, so I hustled my way as quick as my bindings would allow, which wasn't fast. The last thing I needed was to be left behind, although after last night, I thought Rooke wouldn't allow that to happen.

Rounding the corner of a small batch of trees, my boots skidded to a halt at the sight of the man, waist-deep in the creek. All the moisture in my mouth dried up at the vision before me. Rooke, in all his naked glory, stood in the creek. Thankfully, his hips were below the water but what his wet shirt hid last night was now fully open to my gaze. tapered waist, flat stomach with heavily coiled muscles that led up to sloped muscles in his chest and arms.

Every single ridge and crevice of his defined muscles. A dusting of light brown hair covered the center of his chest, trailing down toward the line of the water, bringing my gaze quickly back up to meet his.

I gasped, taking a step back at the intensity in his eyes. His hair slicked back away from his face, darker wet, and the edges gracing his neck. Every inch of him was sun-kissed golden brown.

I'm not a boy, I thought. Absolutely not a boy.

Rooke still watched me as I watched him. If anyone else came upon us, this would be awkward. Turning, I fled. It took everything I had not to run back to camp, even though I couldn't catch my breath when I reached Cade. He laughed, continuing to saddle up horses along with Billy.

"Something after you, George?"

I shook my head, unable to speak. Bending at the waist, I focused on breathing until I could get myself under control. When Rooke came back to camp, I didn't know if I'd be able to look at him the same way. Now that he knew about my womanhood, I felt a freedom I hadn't felt since leaving Abilene. But seeing him in the creek made me feel things I hadn't felt before. Dear Lord, but I felt an ache at the very center of my body. A pulsating thunder nearly as bad as my head since I'd bent over to catch my breath.

"George, you alright?" Billy came around, carrying a bucket.

I straightened. "Yes."

"Good." He thrust the bucket at me. "Go get some water."

Oh no, I inwardly groaned. Unsure if I could go back to the creek and see something I shouldn't, I didn't want to let Billy down with his demand. Perhaps if I strolled, I wouldn't see anything else other than a fully dressed man.

"Faster, George," Billy called after me. "We need to get on the trail soon."

My pace picked up, but only just so. To my delight, I hadn't reached the creek yet when Rooke appeared. And fully dressed. His hair still wet, and shirtsleeves rolled up, he looked clean.

My face must have betrayed my shame at having spied him in his state of undress because he spoke first. "Georgie," he whispered.

My name on his lips, my real name, didn't make breathing any easier. I held up my hand. "Please don't say anything."

Reaching out, he took the bucket out of my hand and turned back toward the creek. I gaped after him. After sensing my discomfort, he avoided it and took the chore from me. How gentlemanly, I thought, watching him walk away.

It took a few minutes before I collected myself enough to return to camp. I bypassed Cade, Billy and the horses on my way to roll up my bed and pack my belongings. No one said a word, quietly dismantling our temporary home over the last couple of nights. Rooke returned with the water, and surprisingly, my vest. After a few more chores, we were all ready to begin the day of riding.

Geezer yelled at the group and we lurched into motion, with Billy following behind him and Rooke bringing up the rear on Fury. My horse fell into step beside Matthew, who allowed me some comfortable silence for the duration of the first portion of our ride.

After we stopped midmorning to rest and drink some water, I rode by Rooke for the next portion of the ride. We rode into

Indian Territory; the terrain flattening with open views of buffalo herds roaming. We alternated between a gentle amble and brisk runs, trying to cover as many miles as we could before stopping for another night.

Riding next to Rooke put me at ease.

"You still need to learn to fire that gun," he said. "We'll find a place suitable enough for it."

I looked around at the flatlands, certain there would be no place to find. "I'll be able to shoot it if the need arises."

The corner of his mouth quirked up, making him look charming. I looked away quickly, scolding myself for such thoughts. I hadn't been gone from Charles long, carrying his child, and had no business allowing my eyes to wander to another man. All the same, it warmed me he'd not mentioned the creek incidents. Either of them.

"If it's all the same to you, I'd like to make sure of that."

I looked back at him. But Rooke knew about me, and others still thought I was a boy, and a boy I would remain as long as it took to get to where and whom I needed. "Very well. I'll allow it."

Rooke chuckled. "Sometimes you talk like . . . "

Shifting in the saddle, I rested my wrists against the pommel. "Like?"

"Nah," he whispered. "Forget it."

I scoffed, not about to let it go. "You talk like you're educated."

"I am."

My eyebrows raised. "Schooled?"

"I taught myself. And my brothers. After my old man abandoned us." He wouldn't look at me, keeping his eyes on the trail ahead of us. "It was enough for us."

My lips flattened into a thin line, unsure of what to say to that. Me with my fine education and pampered life when Rooke had grown up without a father. He had to teach himself and his brothers.

"Your mother?"

"Stuck around longer than he did. But not by much."

My heart sank.

"Haven't told me much about your upbringing."

"I thought you're well acquainted with my brother."

"I am. I'm asking about you."

"I'm educated. I'd rather not talk about my upbringing, if you don't mind." Mindful to keep my voice low, unsure of who might be listening to our conversation. "There is quite a difference between my upbringing and yours."

At the incline of his head, I knew he understood. How, I didn't know. But he did. When he didn't push me to explain, it made me realize the genuineness of the man that rode beside me. Looking over at him, I craved to learn more. But the set of his jaw told me to stay quiet.

"I grew up with Billy, so to speak. The others I met when I worked at the ranch. Surprised they're all still working for Anthony."

A soft laugh escaped. "Why?"

"He's not the same brother you might remember. Anyhow, I spent a lot of my youth with Billy. He and his brothers. Me and mine."

The jerk of his chin toward Billy had my eyes following, landing on Billy, who seemed to have perked up at the mention of his name. Rooke waved at him nonchalantly until he turned back around, resuming his conversation with Matthew. These men intrigued me with who they were, where they were from. Even Geezer, with his set jaw and habit of being mean.

"We grew up near one another in Georgetown, north of Austin. What're you smiling at?"

I hadn't realized a smile touched my lips. "You as a boy. I can't imagine it."

He threw his head back with a laugh then, the sound deep and rippling. "We were all young and rowdy. Stupid." He shook his head. "Suppose we all were at one time in our lives."

"Me as well."

Surprise lit his eyes, meeting mine at the same time. My smile deepened. "Somehow, I can't picture that. George."

The way he said my name had laughter peeling from me, except the more I laughed, the more the bindings hurt and I struggled for breath. I ended up coughing more than laughing, my eyes watering. A few heads turned back to look at us, but not much to see other than me carrying on had them turning back around. I saw Matthew smile before he turned back around. Cade, off to the side, narrowed his eyes.

"Foolish, I was," I whispered once my coughing subsided. "That's all I can tell you, Rooke. Foolish. I suppose I still am."

"I couldn't agree more."

"You don't need to sound so sure of yourself." It came out snappy, though my smile still lingered. "I think I've done well thus far."

"Other than falling into the creek and nearly drowning."

Turning, I stuck my tongue out at him. "The bucket was heavier than I thought."

"Mm-hmm," was all he said.

I laughed again, though softly this time. We'd get along fine, Rooke and I. Like old friends. It helped that I could trust him to not share my secret. If not for the others, I could relax more. The baby would be another secret to divulge to Rooke, but that would need to wait until I could be sure he wouldn't dump me off at the nearest town.

Chapter Twenty

The next two days passed much the same as the others, riding all day with rests every so often and making camp at night. We were nearly halfway through Indian Territory, the flat of the plains looking the same one day as it was the next, and the nights as hot as the days. The bandana did little to soak up perspiration, but it kept the dust out of my mouth when it stirred up unexpectedly.

After nine days in the saddle, I'd grown used to riding all day. I didn't struggle to mount and dismount any longer, no matter which horse I rode. When I woke in the mornings, I didn't struggle to my feet from the agony of stiff muscles. My only issue, other than Geezer's calculated stare and barking orders, was feeling ill every morning.

I drank my coffee that morning but couldn't stomach the biscuit until we were well on our way. Instead, I tucked it into my knapsack for safekeeping until I felt safe enough to eat it. Too many times during the last few days, I'd felt like leaning over to the side of my horse and vomiting. That would draw stares and questions I couldn't answer. I wouldn't risk being left in the dust in a land I had no familiarity with.

The landscape changed little. Nothing but flat lands as far as I could see, with rock formations that could pass as mountains in the distance. Cade told me it would be a few more days until we reached the treacherous Red River. The men were hoping the spring rains had subsided enough to allow the river to mel low, but the river had a reputation of being wide and dangerous. More so than the Arkansas River, he'd said.

We stopped for the night near another creek, this one less deep with light rippling water. Camp came together quickly, and I had the fire started in record time. Sitting back on my haunches, I surveyed my handiwork with pride. Trail life seemed to grow on me. I met Rooke's twinkling eyes over the tops of the licking flames, respect in his hazel-blue eyes.

With the fire underway, I confidently wandered away. Matthew quickly stepped in to cook, filling the space where I'd just been. The ride that day had been hard, darkness quickly filling the sky. At my right, the horizon displayed a peek of reds, oranges, and blues all splashed together. Tomorrow, the weather would be good for riding. Since the day we rode in the rain and slept in the farmer's barn, there had been none. It lent to the dust on the road, making the bandanas a necessity, as Rooke had told me.

The boys, exhausted from riding, had gathered around the fire where Matthew worked at cooking supper. I thought this might be the best time to bathe, with no one stumbling upon me, but I had to make certain. I caught Rooke's gaze, giving him a discreet jerk of my head. He wasted no time sauntering toward me, the length of his legs eating up the distance between us in only a few strides.

"Something wrong, darlin'?" came his husky voice, sliding over my skin like silk.

Hearing him call me something other than my name, even under his breath, felt oddly titillating. Especially something such as that. Although warmth didn't rise to my face, I felt it elsewhere. Filled with sensuality, it rolled through me.

"I need to bathe."

The rise of his eyebrow brought warmth to my face. "And you

need my help?" I nodded, trying not to seem too eager. He glanced back at the group, paying no attention to us. "Lead the way."

Turning from the setting sun, I drifted toward a bank of trees. Surely, I'd gone around the bend this time, I thought as I led Rooke away from camp. There were few trees since we'd left Kansas, but as we'd traveled closer to Texas, they were thick enough for coverage. I followed the sound of the creek, the idea of washing the dust and grime from my face, hands and arms exciting me beyond words.

"I'll be over here," Rooke said roughly. "Call when you need me. I'll stop anyone who tries to come this way."

Words wouldn't be enough to thank him for this. Moments later, my clothing lay in a heap next to the creek and, as naked as the day I'd been born, I waded out into the water until it covered all of my private areas. Not being able to swim, I didn't dare go out further. Instead, I used the bar of soap Billy had left by the creek to scrub down. While I wanted to linger, reveling in the feel of the cool water against my skin, I didn't dare.

I rinsed my hair, easy to do since it was short, and smoothed it back from my face. When I opened my eyes, I let out a sound halfway between a scream and a squeak.

There was a man across the creek, staring at me. A Native American man. He sat on his heels, watching me. And I didn't have a stitch of clothing on. How long had he been watching me? While he stared at me, I stared back at him. His hair, as long as mine had once been, hung down and red paint marked his face in three lines on each cheek. His chest, rivaling Rooke's, was bare, as were his feet, but he wore buckskin pants. In his hand, he clutched a bow.

I could only assume the man had been out hunting when he'd stumbled upon me, a woman bathing in the creek. Other than Charles, no other man had been privy to seeing me like this and I wondered if Rooke was by chance watching me too. The way the man across the creek stared at me, his eyes locked on me, sent ripples of desire through me. Except I wasn't imagining him watching me. I wanted Rooke to be there instead. I couldn't recall a time when I'd felt my body react this way.

I couldn't get out of the creek without him seeing every part of my body, something I didn't even want my traveling companions to see. This situation could be dire. Until I heard the rustling of trees behind me, closing my eyes in hopes Rooke was coming.

"Georgie." I heard Rooke's urgent but hushed tone behind me. "You're going to have to get out of there, darlin'."

I would have laughed, but his tone didn't sound like a joke. Mortified, I scooted closer to the edge of the creek where my clothes were. Getting dressed while being watched, rather intensely, by this man wouldn't be easy. I gritted my teeth and pushed out of the creek. I felt Rooke's hand when I darted behind him, blessing him for standing in front of my clothing so he could shield me further from this man's gaze.

Pulling on my clothes while wet proved to be more difficult than I thought it would be, but I managed to get my trousers on. The issue would be to get the bindings on before I could shrug into my shirt.

"Rooke," I said, my voice coming out in a squeak. "My bindings."

Not taking his eyes off the man across the creek, Rooke reached around and grasped my arm to pull me to the side of him. I couldn't help but to be amazed that he grasped the bindings and wound them around me while barely taking his eyes away from the man. Time slowed while I sucked in my breath for Rooke, but he tucked in the end of the binding in record time and I threw on my shirt.

When I turned to look at the Indian, my breath held. He stood, his obsidian eyes locked on me. Dear God, I thought, please don't draw an arrow and shoot me with that bow. Or Rooke.

But he simply turned and walked away, eventually disappearing.

Slowly, Rooke's hand slid up my side and rested on my lower back, over my bindings. "You okay?"

I nodded, not trusting myself to speak coherently.

"Tell me the truth, darlin'."

Violent trembling conquered, causing him to pull me closer even though I stood nearly on the side of him. His hand pressed full against my back and I laid my head on his arm. Adrenaline from the encounter blasted through me, leaving a quaking mess behind. It took me several minutes of standing there while Rooke held me to calm down enough to pull away. But he wouldn't allow me, tightening his arms and keeping me prisoner in his powerful embrace.

"Georgie . . ."

"I will be."

"Honest?"

"Honest. You can release me now. This won't look good if anyone comes along."

It wouldn't look good if anyone happened upon us, but the feel of his arms around me had struck something deep. And by God, I didn't want him to let me go. His hold eased enough for me to put space between us, but he still kept his hand on my back while he looked into my eyes. My lips parted.

His eyes roamed over my features, leisurely. "There's a color to your cheeks that rises when someone puts you on the spot."

I watched the corner of his mouth curve up. "What?"

"Like now. You've got this pinkish color." He reached out, the tips of his fingers brushing against my cheekbone. "Just there."

His fingertips felt soft, even though his hands were rough from work. My eyes closed when his hand stayed where it was, fingertips against my cheekbone, opening only when his hand dropped away.

With a rough clearing of his voice, Rooke released me and stepped away. I stayed still for a moment, gathering my wits before I realized I stood with my feet bare. He waited while I tugged on my stockings and boots, slipping into my vest while walking toward camp. I couldn't speak. I didn't know what to say.

The fire had burned low. All the men in their bedrolls with Billy snoring so loud every wild animal near camp would stay away. Rooke grabbed my hand, stopping me from stepping back into the camp.

"You sure you're good?" I nodded. "You wake me if you aren't."

Without another word, we crept back into camp and found our beds. I yanked off my boots, setting them aside before slipping into my bedroll. When I stretched out on my back, I stared up at the twinkling sky and thought about our adventure that night. The thought of waking him, laying with him on his bedroll while his arms circled me, had me nearly groaning aloud. Thoughts I had no business having flooded my mind until I pushed them away.

Chapter Twenty One

We made it to the southern part of the Indian Territory the next day, stopping for the night near an abundance of trees. For the last few days, it seemed like there had been nothing but flat fields surrounding us. I welcomed the sight of full trees with wildlife hiding from our presence. It meant we were getting closer to Texas.

"Gettin' some muscle."

I turned to look at Matthew, pulling up his horse beside me, a grin curving my lips. "Am I?"

"Didn't think you'd ever put on any. Don't eat much, do you?"

He spoke the truth. I hadn't been eating much. None of us did except in the morning before heading out, and in the evening after setting up camp. Holding out my arms, I studied the slender limbs. When he reached out, curling his hand around my biceps, my eyes darted to him. Rooke, watching from the side, narrowed his eyes.

"Right here," he said, giving my upper arm a squeeze.

How he could tell I'd put on muscles, when I never divested myself of anything other than my vest, socks and boots, I didn't know. When his hand fell away, I looked down at my arm where his hand had been. The urge to feel my arm with my own hand gave me a laugh.

He had certainly been right. Muscles were in places I thought they never would be. I'd been riding for days, sleeping on the hard ground, and keeping up with a group of men doing things men, not women, did. I smiled in triumph.

"How many more days do you think we have until we reach the ranch?"

"Oooooh, we got a ways yet. More'n a half a month, at least." He chuckled at my dejected look. "You gonna make it?"

"I'll make it. I will."

Rooke pulled back, giving Matthew no choice but to move the position of his horse. I frowned at the rudeness. How I longed for another bath. A long, warm bath where I could lather a bar of soap and wash every inch of my body. The bath in the creek had done well enough, but the heat, the sweat, I never felt clean enough.

"You're deep in thought."

I turned. "Daydreaming."

"About?"

"Bathing."

"We won't be stopping for a long while yet. Although we'll be at the Red River in probably four, maybe five days."

"Matthew said we have at least a half a month left of travel."

"He's right. The Red River, if you don't know, borders northern Texas and Indian Territory. Once we cross it, we'll be on Texas soil."

"I can bathe in the Red River?"

He chuckled. "That river is about as deadly as they come. It's deep, and it's wide. I wouldn't recommend stopping to take a bath in it. But you'll get wet, and that might be enough to tide you over some."

Good enough for me, I thought. It would need to be. "You said you grew up in Texas?"

"Mm-hmm," he murmured, turning to ride away.

I moved with him, urging Dusty to follow him and Fury. "Anywhere else?"

"Mostly Texas. My old man was away a lot gambling, so we stayed in Georgetown for the longest. Why?"

"I'm curious. We've spent several days together, but I can't say I know you very well. I know nothing about your upbringing."

"I could say the same about you."

"You know I grew up in northern Britain." I cast a brief look at our surroundings, ensuring no one else could overhear anything. "My family is in the mercantile business."

"I noticed there's no ring on your finger. Can't help but wonder why a young lady is traveling alone, even dressed as you are. You don't have a husband somewhere?" he asked, his voice low.

I gritted my teeth, unsure if I should admit it. To me, it ended the moment I stepped out of that house. "I do."

"You don't need to say anything else, but I need to ask you one thing." I looked over at him, the seriousness in voice giving me doubts I should say anything else. "Does he know where you are?"

"No," I whispered. "And it's better this way. Please trust me with that."

He nodded curtly. "I trust you."

That made me laugh. "You don't know me. How can you trust me?"

"You don't know me, yet you trust me."

He had a fair point. How could I explain to him that it was the way he made me feel that allowed me to put my trust in him? That and his incessant badgering for me to trust him. There were only two other men in my life I trusted, and one of them was not my husband. I didn't know if I'd ever truly trusted Charles.

"You've given me no reason not to trust you," I said. "You could have outed me to every man here, and you haven't."

"That's not for trust. That's for your safety."

"Why are you arguing with me about this?"

"Why can't you tell me why you really trust me?"

I huffed out a frustrated sigh, looking away from him. "You could have left me in the creek for that Indian," I pointed out. "You could have let the creek take me away."

"It wasn't that deep."

"Bugger it!"

This time he laughed, deep and sinful. "I don't think I've heard you curse before."

"That wasn't a curse. You'll know it when I do."

Sweat trickled down his temple, and he swiped it away with the sleeve of his shirt before settling his hand back on the reins. "I've known no one like you before."

"Of course you haven't. How many women do you know going around dressed like men?" He smiled at that. "I would not have done this had I thought it safe enough to travel alone."

"When was the last time you spoke with your brother?"

"Before the war here."

"And he never told you where he ended up?"

I sighed. "When he left, he said he'd write. He never did. I only know things because I listened at doors, found things out my parents didn't want me to know."

Rooke scratched his chin, where his lack of shaving recently showed. The roughness of his face made him look rogue, dangerous, and unpredictable. But I knew differently. The man I knew couldn't be safer.

◆

The next morning, it was raining when we set out, soaking us through before the sun broke its way through the clouds. We dried out after that, but when the sun returned, it returned with a vengeance of heat and sweat.

Not so much as a breeze stirred the stagnant air, and although we moved at a good pace, it created nothing that would take the perspiration away. We weaved in and out of forests the closer we came to the Texan border, the bandana around my neck used to mop the wet from my face instead of shielding it from dust.

The trail made for an easy canter for a good portion of the morning. By late afternoon, we stopped to swap horses with the remuda and continued our way south. Each time we rode under the cover of thick trees, the air thickened. Sweat dripped down my spine, dotted my temples below my hat and made every inch covered by my bindings itch terribly. I ached fiercely.

Late afternoon I sensed an alertness in the men. Talking had come to a stop. I could see them looking around cautiously through the trees, as though searching for something. I squirmed in my saddle, uneasiness spreading through me.

Rooke pushed his horse up beside mine, settling close to me. "Stay alert," he said, voice low and steady.

"Is something out there?"

"We're being followed."

I looked behind us, seeing nothing but trees and the empty trail. "Who would follow us? And why?"

"Your guess is as good as mine. Keep your pistol close."

Instinct had me putting my hand against the pistol tucked in the holster on my belt. I unsnapped it for good measure, earning myself a wink from Rooke. Knowing that someone followed us increased the beating of my heart, the adrenaline pumping through my veins at the thought of more danger.

When the trees thinned, we continued riding, and I spotted the riders to the left. There had to be at least four of them, but we outnumbered them. If they were there to rob us, we'd put up a fight. I didn't have money left, but having anyone's hands on me again was out of the question. I vowed to use the pistol hovering beneath my palm.

I looked back over at Rooke, gasping, when I noticed another four riders to the right. Fighting would do us no good against that many riders. Sweat slicked my back. As I swiped my sleeve over my forehead, I saw Geezer hold up his hand and motion forward with two fingers to pick up our pace. Not at top speed, but faster.

Another batch of trees loomed ahead, making me curious if he hoped to reach the trees and lose them there. How long had they been following us? I wondered. Rooke stayed beside me, even when the trail narrowed. The riders still followed us, picking their way in and out of trees at an evenly matched pace.

These woods had more openings than the others we had passed through, making it easier to ride faster. Yet the riders stayed with us. Geezer held up his hand, waving us on. Faster, we galloped on. Faster, until the sounds of the horses' hooves digging into the ground thundered around me. My heartbeat picked up, as did my breathing, and it did nothing to help my situation with the bindings. But I couldn't think about that right now.

A shot rang out, the sound deafening in the woods. It felt like lightning had struck my veins, a shock of fear like I'd never known before. Riding so hard, fear had a choke hold on me.

"Move!" Rooke roared from behind me.

Kicking my heels into the horse's flanks, we bolted through the forest. At one point, I thought my hat would fly off. More shots were being fired at us. Matthew rode in front of me, Rooke behind me. Dread forced me not to look back, praying a bullet wouldn't hit Rooke. Wouldn't hit any of us. Dirt and clumps of grass sprayed up at us, some branches dangerously low in the path.

I pressed forward, feeling the horse beneath me move with great agility, as though we were flying. The thundering of the hooves surrounding us was all I could hear.

When we reached another clearing, it appeared as though we had lost the men and slowed when we entered the next group of trees. My horse snorted, nostrils flaring while we pressed forward. One by one, I watched the men look around while we slowed. I couldn't help but doubt we'd lost them so easily. Not when there were so many of them.

Another shot ringing out shattered my focus. "Move!" Rooke roared in my ear.

My horse bolted. This time, I had to grab my hat before it flew off. If I thought for a moment we rode as fast as we could before, we were riding faster now. Trees came at me, my horse darting between them directly behind Matthew until the trees thinned out. A scream wrenched from my throat when I saw men boxed us in on both sides with pistols out.

The jarring of my horse beneath me made it difficult to grab my gun out of my holster, but when my fingers slid around it, I made sure it was firm in my grip. At this speed, I couldn't be sure I could aim straight, but I'd try. More shots rang out. I resisted the urge to squeeze my eyes shut, not wishing to see anyone hurt in this fray.

My horse pulled alongside Matthew, about to reach him, when a single blast of a shotgun resounded. Another scream pushed from deep within my lungs when I saw Matthew jerk. Even riding this fast, I could see red seeping from his shoulder.

Dear God, if that hadn't hit him, it would have hit me, I thought. More shots fired, my horse skidding to a halt. The reins slipped through my hand, my pistol gripped in my other as the horse reared again. I felt my backside slipping from the saddle, my boots sliding out from the stirrups, and then I felt nothing but air around me while I looked up at the sky filtering through between leafy tree branches.

I hit the ground with such force that it should have knocked the wind from me had it not been for the branches I'd landed on to break my fall. I was still winded, but not so much that I couldn't roll to the side.

As I knelt on my heels, tears, bile, and sweat flowed uncontrollably from me. This can't be happening, I thought and swiped my sleeve across my mouth. How did I end up like this?

I felt a hand on my arm, helping me to stand. Bile rose again, but I fought it down with determination not to vomit again.

I looked up at Billy, who released my arm after making sure I didn't fall over. He earned a nod from me.

"Get him up," Geezer snapped. "Let's get out of here before they come back."

Rooke reached out, but I swatted his hand away and threw myself onto the horse. Yet, I wouldn't argue with Geezer. It didn't look like anyone would as we rode on.

No one spoke until the sun went down, and I could hear the hushed voices up in front. Rooke pulled up next to me. It took me another minute to look at him.

"All right?"

I nodded. "Sorry I vomited."

The corner of his mouth quirked up. "That was some pretty hard riding."

"Is Matthew . . ?"

"Just a graze. Those bastards were after the remuda. They outnumbered us."

His eyebrows drew together, but he said nothing. Would he yell at me for being in the way?

"You did good."

My gaze snapped up to meet his eyes. Of all the things he could say to me, that would have been the last thing I'd have thought. "I did . . . good?"

"You kept up with us." He smiled, the curve of his mouth widening until he grinned. "I'd have thought you were one of us the way you rode like hell."

We smiled at each other. Me with euphoria, him with pride. Finally, I'd settled in with this lot of men after two weeks on the trail. The adventure had pulled me into a world of my own, and I thrived in it. I'd survived nearly drowning, although I wouldn't admit that openly, and now narrowly escaping being shot and killed by outlaws out to steal horses. Nothing could bring me down now.

Chapter Twenty Two

Another half hour passed before we were on the trail headed back south. My body, although still humming with adrenaline from such an adventure, felt heavy with exhaustion. Eyes scratchy, stomach pained with hunger and back sore from riding, I only hoped to stop soon. The longer we rode, the worse I felt.

A short time later, the sound of rippling water had me sitting up straighter in my saddle, anticipating making camp for the night. The sun was getting lower on the horizon and the horses were tiring. If we didn't stop soon, the heat would make setting up camp miserable.

They didn't have to tell me twice to get a fire going as soon as we stopped. I scrambled from my horse, handing the reins over to Cade before making haste toward the river. I had never seen a man so filled with despair before. Losing those horses was a devastating blow for him. Thankfully the thieves didn't take Fury and Dusty.

I carried on toward the river and noticed that it seemed shallow, which would allow me to jump in without being swept away. That was if I could sneak away. I gathered firewood and kindling as quickly as I could, returning to find everyone getting camp set up. I bent to get the fire started where Matthew laid a circle of rocks.

It took me a few minutes to get the fire started, sitting by and watching it smoke and spark until the flames grew. My stomach ached. I was hungry. When Matthew set a pot down near me, beans already swimming in it, with some meat wound on sticks, I looked up at him.

"Do we have any dried meat, Matthew? I'm starving."

He chuckled. "No. It'll be a few days yet before we get to a town big enough to resupply."

I groaned.

"Won't take no time at all. Go on, get your bed set up. The fire's good enough now."

I stood, turning to get my bedroll from my horse and finding a decent place to lay it. While I was curious about where Geezer and Rooke had gone, I was more interested in jumping into the river. Every day that passed, the closer we got to July, the heat became more unbearable.

While I walked toward the river, my eyes swept the camp to note where everyone stood. What I would attempt could be dangerous. I'd need to stay above the waist to not get my bindings wet again. Rooke wouldn't be so easy to find this time.

"Where're you off to?"

I stopped, frozen in place, at Billy's voice behind me. "Uh, I'm taking a walk."

"You going to the river to bathe?" He didn't wait for an answer. "I'll join you. Hey, Cade! George's going to the river. Let's go!"

And so I had company. Together, the three of us walked to the river. I removed my boots, then my stockings while the two of them shed their clothing so fast they could have been on fire. I avoided looking in their direction, seeing only a blur of two pale white bodies jump into the river.

"Come on, George!" Billy called out, coming up out of the water like a fish, water dripping from his mustache on both sides.

Laughing softly, I took my time rolling up the legs of my

pants and slowly stepped into the cool water while the two men splashed about.

"Christ, George! Are you afraid of water?" Billy laughed.

"I'm tired."

After splashing water up my arms and face, I let my bandana soak up water to get clean enough to wash whatever visible skin I could find before wading back up to the river bank and sitting down to dry. As though I would ever get dry in this humidity.

There would be no chance again. As soon as Cade and Billy decided they were done, I picked up my boots and hurried away from the river. Matthew had the food done, and I shoveled beans into my mouth faster than I ever had before, but I'd done so too fast and my stomach ached from it. I laid down on my bedroll soon after.

Geezer and Rooke still hadn't returned to camp when I closed my eyes and let the lull of sleep pull me in. Dreams were fitful, and I tossed and turned in my bedroll. The cramps in my stomach grew worse, the deeper into the night we plunged.

When I thought I finally found a comfortable position, I sank into sleep once again only to be woken up by a sharp pain low in my stomach followed by wetness between my legs that I knew couldn't be right. Shoving away from my bedroll, I smothered my sharp cry with my hands from the tremendous pain ripping through me.

Stumbling, I tried to find my way to the river as quickly as I could while pain tore through my lower extremities. Never in my life had I experienced an agony of this extent before. I needed to get to the river with no one waking up because I'd need to remove my trousers under the cloak of darkness.

Using sound to guide the way toward the river through the dark night, I'd given no thought to putting on boots and stockings. The threat of losing this baby outweighed the threat of any wild animals, or worse, snakes. The burn of hot tears streaking down my face did little to help to find my way, but the sound of the river had been thankfully enough. Falling to my knees, I wrapped my arms around my midsection as pain gripped me and whimpers mixed with groans tore from deep in my throat. I rolled over, pulling my legs up, attempting to stop the pain while I sobbed out the agony. Hoping I was far enough from camp so no one could hear me, I let out a groan. It was so loud I thought the trees would shake from it.

Though the trousers would need to come off, the agony kept me where I was for a few more minutes until I could catch my breath enough to rise. Amidst unbuttoning the flap, I'd barely got them down past my hips when something in the brush behind me gave me pause. I needed to get them off before I ruined my only pair of pants.

"What're you doing?" I heard Rooke, sleep still thick in his voice.

"I . . . have a stomach-ache," I whispered. "Go away."

The light of the moon must have given him light enough to see me. He stepped around me. Positive my face had no color left, I couldn't tell by the look on his face what he might be thinking.

"Dear God," he said. "Sit down."

"No, I need to . . . " My voice shook.

"When I agreed to bring you along—"

"Offered."

His eyebrows drew together while he helped me sit down, dragging my trousers down to reveal my pale white legs. I didn't have it in me to stop him. "When I offered to bring you along, I wasn't expecting you to get your courses."

There was a tremble in my laugh, cut off by a sharp pain that stole my breath right out of my lungs. "This isn't that," I finally said.

His head snapped up, his hazel-blue eyes meeting mine while his mouth fell open. Shock intensified his gaze at my revelation and he muttered a curse as another person stumbled out of the brush.

I gasped, seeing Matthew burst into the open and come to a skidding halt when he saw Rooke kneeling before me with my trousers down around my ankles. His eyes widened, then dropped to my trousers where red had stained the inside.

"Is that? . . . is he?"

"Quiet," Rooke snapped, sweeping the trousers away from me the rest of the way.

Matthew dropped to his knees beside me. "Did something get you? Did . . ." He rubbed his eyes, as though he doubted his lucidity.

Rooke bent into the river, trying to rinse out my trousers. He so easily handled trying to clean my pants when most men would revolt at the sight, it stole my breath as much as the pains. Another pain gripped me so rapidly that I cried out before I could smother it, rolling toward my side.

When Rooke whipped around to look at me, concern locked in his eyes, I felt it in my heart. "Can you walk? You might sit in the water, and it will help."

I wasn't sure I could walk, but I needed to do something or bring the entire camp to see my future dying out. Tears sprung to my eyes, hot and blurring my vision. Anything but this, I thought. Please. I couldn't lose this child. My heart pitched, sinking low at the thought.

"Matthew, help her up."

"Her?" he whispered, then looked over at me. "You're . . . oh, Jesus."

I extended my arm, quickly pulled into him and his support while he helped me to my feet. Getting into the river might mean the shirt would get wet too, and I couldn't help but to think I'd need to stay away the rest of the night or go back to bed in wet clothes. I didn't care. I needed something to take this pain away before I screamed the forest down.

The next pain felt much tamer than the others had while

we walked toward Rooke and the river. He stood up, holding my other arm while I stepped into the coolness of the river water.

"Matthew, turn around," Rooke snapped. "Georgie, you can pull up your shirt a little so it doesn't get so wet."

If I pulled my shirt up, Rooke could see the entire lower half of my body. Although it wasn't so long ago, he'd seen me clamor out of the river when an Indian had been watching me. My face flamed while I slowly inched the shirt up past my waist.

"Georgie?" Matthew asked, putting his back to us.

"That's my name." I kept hold of Rooke's arm while I lowered myself into the river. "I didn't lie."

Matthew laughed softly, then sobered after remembering this wasn't a time for laughter. "I would have never guessed it."

Rooke bent over the river, washing out my trousers. "Better?"

I nodded. The water soothed, the pains subsiding while I sat there with my shirt fisted in my hand. Water brushed the edges of the bindings, but not enough to loosen them again. If it wasn't from the light of the moon, we wouldn't be able to see each other. Matthew had turned around, sitting behind me on the bank of the river while Rooke squeezed the water out of my trousers and inspected them. He draped them over a low branch to dry.

"D'ya get bit by something?" The worry in Matthew's voice only made me like him more. The concern for me they each had displayed was something that would stay with me forever.

"Matthew," Rooke said with a hint of annoyance in his voice, sitting down on the other side of him so I could see them both. He passed a hand over his face, looking at me. "Did you lose it?"

I choked on the sob, more tears falling when I looked away with a nod. Suddenly, I couldn't stop it and the dam of tears broke. Cries shook my shoulders, and I heard Rooke curse before I felt him pull me up out of the water and against him. My head was against his chest, his hand on my head while I wept into his shirt. He let me cry, even though no amount of tears would bring my child back.

I knew it was just as well, and this happened to women all the time. There were hardships all around, and I was young enough to still have enough time. But it still made me sad.

When my crying slowed, Rooke helped me to sit back in the water. Matthew stared at me, frozen in shock, even when Rooke sat down beside him again.

"We don't know how the others will react to having a woman among us. You can't tell anyone about this, Matthew."

"I would never."

My gaze swept over the river, looking away from the pair of them. I no longer had any connection to Charles, and that brought me great joy. If there could have been any relief that I wouldn't need to worry about the predicament I'd be in, it was gone because I'd been pregnant and lost it. Tears pricked my eyes. A baby had been all I'd wanted for the last six months, but there would be other chances.

"Georgie?" Rooke asked, his voice soft.

I looked back at him. "I didn't know I was pregnant. Not until we'd already been on the road a few days." He looked so concerned. It was commendable. All that I'd put him through, and he was still concerned with my well-being.

Matthew looked between us, back and forth, as though watching a poker game. He had to have so many questions running through his mind, he couldn't decide what to ask me.

"Please don't tell anyone," I whispered.

When he looked back at me, the look in his eyes was nothing but serious. "I would never tell a soul."

And I believed him.

Chapter Twenty Three

We stayed in the same camp for another night, although Geezer made it known that he was not happy to be stalling for a day. Rooke and Cade convinced him the horses needed to rest, especially now that we didn't have extras to rely on. I didn't move around much, irritating Geezer even more, but Rooke told him that if he wanted to move along, he had the option. But leave me alone.

The pregnancy had not been so far along. A yearning that would never come to pass. Not now. I knew I'd never return to Charles, no matter what I found in Texas. I'd return to my grandfather, if anything.

Camp broke the next morning, and we rode all day, stopping again for the night. It would be another day before we reached the Red River. Geezer stayed silent for those two days, not saying a word to me or anyone else. He took the lead on the trail, as he usually did, but not a word sprung from his lips.

The following day, we resumed riding until we reached the Red River. When we made camp that night, close to the massive, red-colored river, I could hear the rush of the water. Like no other, the sound of the rippling water all night was enough to keep me paralyzed in fear of crossing it the next day. Crossing it had been an adventure I'd never thought to do, with the river water over the entire saddle and up over my thighs. But we'd all made it to the other side safely, reaching Texas soil with no one being swept downriver.

In Texas, I couldn't help but to be excited to be closer to our destination. To see Anthony again after so many years, my nerves were mixed with emotions. Some of my emotions were still in turmoil over my loss, I knew.

After we had recovered from crossing the Red River and thoroughly rested ourselves, we proceeded the following morning and arrived at the next town by evening. We restocked supplies for the rest of the journey, which Rooke said would be about another nine or ten days. It would depend on weather, conditions of the trail, and barring anything detrimental from happening along the way.

I couldn't help but to wonder if he meant something caused by me. Were we delayed an entire day because of me? Although the fault hadn't been my own. I'd replayed the days leading up to the fateful night and nothing I could have done would have prevented the miscarriage. Perhaps Charles has been right that it had been my fault we'd had no children.

We rode slowly, taking breaks when possible. I'd finally recovered enough to walk steadily and not be tempted to wander off to cry alone. Rather than get myself into trouble, I walked toward Cade and the horses.

"You look like you're up to no good, George," Cade drawled when I stopped near him. "Come to help me with the horses?"

I shrugged. "If you'll let me."

He smiled, but I could tell that sorrow still gripped him. "Start getting saddles off. We'll get water later. I'm sure they've had their fill of water for the time bein' after that river crossin'." I laughed. "We'll brush 'em out and set them on their way to graze and calm down some."

"How did you become so good with horses?"

"I've always been good with them."

"Did you grow up with horses?"

Slipping the buckles loose, I lifted a heavy saddle from one horse and set it to the side before setting to work on the bridle. The horse stomped, having the burden lifted after such a workout. I smoothed my hand down her flanks, gently.

"Course, I did," Cade answered, working on a horse. "Grew up in the mountains."

My eyes widened. "The mountains?"

"My family are trappers in the Appalachians outside of Gatlinburg, Tennessee." He looked into the distance, his gaze softening with the onset of memories. "We had horses up there. Lots of 'em. Helped us with trapping, you see."

"Do you have a large family?"

"Eight brothers and sisters."

"Eight?" I cried. "When was the last time you saw them?"

"After the war," he said, his voice quiet. "Didn't figure it would do them no good, me stayin' there with such anger." My heart faltered. "I met Rooke during the war. Said there'd always be a place for me at the ranch in Texas, if I ever wanted a change."

"You don't enjoy trapping?"

His shoulders rolled. "Needed more. I need to be with horses." He gave the horse a pat once the horse was free of gear. It danced away, trotting toward a small field where the other horses had found grass to eat.

"I can see why. They like you."

"Had no problem with them coming back while on the trail. Some have stragglers wandering too far off. Not me. They stick close by."

It wasn't a mystery why. An unmistakable gentleness in the touch of his hand, the glimmer of trust deep in his eyes. I'd noticed he steered clear of the group when he could, spending most of his time with the herd of horses. It made me curious why.

"Is that what you do on the ranch?"

"Yup. I'm in charge of the horses. I've got help, but I'm the one Anthony relies on to make sure the horses get fed, bred, broken, birthed, the whole deal."

"Anthony relies on you?"

Cade's head tipped back and he let out a soft laugh. "He don't hardly come out of his house. When Rooke was working there, he'd run everything. But Geezer does now, and Anthony don't come out much. They don't agree like Anthony and Rooke did."

Interesting, I thought. And not surprising. I wondered why Rooke had left. Although I'd noticed that the men looked up to Rooke, I couldn't help but to think Geezer had an air of superiority to him.

I knew nothing of running a ranch or even working on one. But I couldn't imagine the lack of an owner taking an interest in the running of his own ranch. Charles, even though he did not own the St. John textile, would inherit it someday and took a vested interest in the running of it.

"You seem to have a knack for horses," he said, sidling closer to me. "Did you grow up around horses?"

My gaze slid into his, meeting his deep amber eyes. Cade was smart, and an excellent judge of character. If I wasn't careful, he'd find out I wasn't who I claimed to be quick. "We had horses."

"You come from money, you and Anthony."

"Wh ... why—"

"I can tell when someone has a better upbringing than I did. We were piss poor, living up there in the mountains. But we were happy. You have a way of speaking." I must have looked shocked. "You don't need to hide it."

"I'm not—"

"You don't gotta tell me."

When, and if, the time came that I needed to tell them they'd been traveling with a woman all along, I'd need them to forgive me. Forgiving me for that would be easier than forgiving me for outright lying to them. Or so I figured.

I sighed. "Anthony and I grew up in northern Britain. I traveled here less than a year ago. With my parents."

He whistled. "Never woulda thought that."

"Sarcasm does not suit you," I quipped with a smile. "You are right that I'm educated. My parents returned home, and I . . . well, I'd rather not say."

When his lips turned into a grin, I had a feeling there would be a less than tasteful reason. "Trifling with a girl that you ought not have?" he teased. The skin high on my cheeks warmed. "I knew it."

Better he think that I'd been trifling with a girl, than to know I'd been married off to an aristocratic fool who would commit his wife because of a lie. I glanced toward the horses, watching them grazing while wondering where I'd be if hadn't slipped away in the dead of night. Would Charles have changed his mind and taken my side? Or would he have gone through and had me committed? A shudder shook me. Would I be dead by now?

"You alright there?"

I nodded, quickly. "You said you didn't stay home because of the anger. Has that gone away now?"

At the distant look that glazed over his eyes, the hardening of his jaw, I regretted bringing it up again. But I needed to steer the conversation away from myself. Absently, he picked up a brush to run over the flanks of the horse.

"It comes and goes. War is hard. Lots of men died. Friends. Brothers. Uncles." He shook his head, stopping to look at me. "Too many. It was much worse after it ended than it is now."

"Is that why you prefer the company of the horses over others?"

That made a smile touch his lips and light his eyes. "Maybe the horses prefer my company more than the others."

"I doubt that."

◆

We continued on though dark clouds loomed overhead and threatened our otherwise calm journey. We'd escaped any wild storms and rain for several days.

While we rode, my thoughts lingered on whether I would ever have another chance to become pregnant again. Although I had no husband at my side, I was still legally married. I could never wed again unless Charles set aside our marriage, and to do that, I would need to notify him of my whereabouts. Would I ever do that? I didn't know.

It would depend on Anthony. Surely, he would allow me to stay with him. Then I could eventually write to Charles and petition him for a divorce. With me thousands of miles away, it shouldn't create any shame, and he could marry someone more suited to him and his family name. Unless he thought differently and came after me. For all I knew, he was after me now. I thought I'd covered my trail well enough.

I'd heard of people remarrying without the benefit of divorce because there was no money to be had for such a thing. Some towns had no recordings out here in the wilds of the west. Most people lived in houses where there weren't any towns. We'd passed hundreds of them along miles we'd covered, and those were only the ones we could see from the trail.

"You look deep in thought."

I raised my head to Rooke's voice beside me. Glancing up at the rolling clouds sweeping overhead, I shrugged. "Wondering if these clouds will break so I can have a bath while in the saddle."

He chuckled. "We're in for a nasty storm. Hang onto your

horse."

"Shouldn't my horse hang on to me?" I quipped.

"You would think, but these horses will not like the lightning, rain, or thunder. They're going to want to bolt for cover."

"Why don't we stop?"

"And do what?"

"Find shelter."

"Where?"

I sighed. "What will I do if my horse gets away from me?"

"Don't."

Was he purposely being exasperating? I wanted to beat my fist against my forehead. If the horses bolted, Cade would find them. Or they would find him. But what would I do?

"Hang on for dear life. If you get bucked off, try to get back on before your horse makes a run for it." He looked over at me. "We're trying to find shelter in the meantime."

That helped ease my anxiety, at least some. I nodded, hoping to convince him I understood.

"Cade said you used to oversee the ranch."

"I did."

"He also said Anthony doesn't come out much now that Geezer oversees it." Curiosity, I couldn't help. Prying I could.

"After returning from the war, I was in charge for a time." His jaw tensed, much like Cade's had at the mention of war. "He's had some issues since the war."

"Were you both in the war?"

"Georgie," came his soft voice. "I don't want to talk about the war. No good came of it, and definitely not after it. Not a single one of us here has anything good to share about that time, except the friends we made and didn't lose."

The bitterness in his voice made me wince. I might think twice before mentioning the war to any of them again if this would be the result, although Cade had been much more forthright than Rooke. Had Rooke lost many he was close to?

Curiosity threatened, but I pressed my lips together. I wouldn't ask.

"Don't worry about it," Rooke murmured. "None of us like to recant any tales from it, even after three years. Maybe someday, but not today."

"I hope you know you can tell me, should you need to."

"Thank you."

"What is it you did around the ranch?" I asked, hoping to guide the conversation toward something else.

He smiled. "Everything. I made sure everyone's doing what they ought to be doing, the animals are staying where they're supposed to be, and that everything is running as it should."

"That's an awful lot for one person to do."

"I had a dependable crew."

"The men here respect you."

"They damn well better," came his endearing growl.

The roll of thunder overhead interrupted us momentarily, pushing silence into the space between us, but not an uncomfortable quiet. My horse inched closer to Rooke, and although I noticed the corner of his lip curl up, he remained silent.

Lightning lit the skies moments later, followed by more thunder. Looping the reins around my hand once, determination made me clutch them tighter while we plowed our way along the trail at an easy pace.

The pace at which we rode was not nearly fast enough, and the first splatters of rain caught up a short time later, followed by a torrent of water coming from the sky like it had opened up to unleash wrath upon us. The weather agitated the horses, including my own, but we continued riding through the rain that came down. It came down so hard I could hardly see Billy in front of me.

At one point, he turned back to look at me or to ensure I still sat in the saddle. I'd have shouted at him if I thought he would hear me over the booms of the thunder and the deafening sounds of hard rain. I wished fervently that it would ease soon so I could remove my hat and feel the rain against my hair.

Though difficult to ride in the storm, we pressed on, barely keeping our seats through the rumbling storm until the skies grew lighter and the rains subsided to a steady thrum.

The urge to whoop in glee shot through me, so I settled for grinning. Rooke looked over at me, a grin splitting his face in return. No one perished, the horses didn't bolt, and although wet through, we had all survived.

By the time we stopped to make camp that night, my hat was the only dry thing on me. Only because the sun had broken through and dried it along with the heat. I knew the rest of the men would strip and hang up their clothing to dry, wondering why I wasn't doing the same.

Instead, I wandered away for a more private area and looked behind to make sure no one followed. I found a quiet place to sit near the creek that wound its way around trees like a snake. Removing my hat first, I combed my fingers through the tangle of tresses with a sigh. It had grown, but not enough to be concerning. Yet. I unlaced my boots and set them aside.

After I'd set out my stockings to dry next to my boots, I shrugged out of my wet vest and hung it on a nearby tree branch. Hanging my things near the fire would dry them out faster than the humid air that followed the storm, but it would have to do. Slowly, I unbuttoned the top buttons of my shirt when the rustling of tree branches had me whirling around from where I sat.

Seeing Rooke strolling around with his chest bare and his suspenders hanging down, I sighed. It felt different, seeing him only partially dressed. His muscular chest, lightly dusted with hair, was a sight to behold. I'd seen him without a shirt only one other time, and that was when I'd stumbled upon him bathing.

All moisture within my mouth dried instantly while I took in the sculpted slopes of his torso, sun-kissed by the sun with a distinct scar skidding over his right shoulder. The scar appeared to be a burn.

As though sensing where my gaze had fallen, his hand rose and fingertips brushed the scar. "Bullet," he murmured. "Had I been standing only slightly over, I would have taken the bullet instead of my good man, Timothy." He stopped beside me, dropping on his backside. "He died instantly."

I couldn't find my voice.

"That was my first battle. Eltham's Landing in Virginia. Patched me up and sent me on my way into the next battle, a month later." He closed his eyes. "So much death. Things you can never unsee."

My heart squeezed, hand inching toward his until our fingers joined. When his eyes opened, he looked down at our hands. Instinct had me pulling away, but with iron strength he held me there. As though he needed comfort. My comfort.

"Thank you," he whispered.

"It's the least I can do. After what you did for me when I . . . when I lost . . . " He squeezed my fingers. "I've been alone since my parents left me here, without realizing it. Even before I left."

"You aren't alone," he said. "You have me."

Chapter Twenty Four

Something changed between Rooke and me after that. We'd sat at the creek for a long time, words spoken only when they needed to be. Eventually we dried out enough and returned to camp, ate our supper and went to bed for the night. I lay awake thinking about him for a long time before sleep finally overtook me.

How different he was from when I first met him. Somewhere deep down inside of him, something needed to come out. I didn't know what it was, and I didn't know if I would ever know it or ever try to figure it out. Slowly, Rooke was letting me into his life. And while he did that, I had changed too. Was I the same woman who had left the aristocratic society behind me? I couldn't be. Trials and all, I had become hardened along the way. And I wasn't finished yet.

We rode hard the next day. It seemed like now that we were on Texas soil; the men were in a hurry to get home. I didn't blame them. We would reach Fort Worth that evening, and I could barely contain my excitement. It'd been some time since we'd been in a decent-sized town.

When we rode into town, a military camp before the war, the men were intent upon camping close within the confines of the town. I could instantly understand why, now that there was some resemblance to civilization. Although still smaller than the cities in the east, there was a general store, several saloons, department stores, a stage line with a mail stop, a flour mill, undertaker, school, church, and more houses surrounding. Above some saloons were hotels, and I longed to sleep in a bed with pillows and blankets. Passing by a storefront, I stared at the pretty dresses and bonnets through the windowpane. It had been so long since I'd worn a dress. These styles differed from what I used to wear.

Billy caught my eye, throwing his head back in laughter. "Looking to get yourself under a skirt while we're here, eh, George?"

Snapping my eyes forward, warmth rose to my face. I noticed we'd caught the attention of townsfolk while we rode through, stopping at the end of the street near the livery. Matthew stopped at the end of the road, hopping down and slapping his hands together in eagerness while the rest of them dismounted.

I looked toward Rooke for guidance, unsure of what they expected of me. He motioned me to dismount, which I did gracefully. Smoothing out my vest and adjusting my hat to shade my eyes, I prepared myself.

The lowering sun made it clear our visit in town would be brief. We'd need to get the camp set up before it went down entirely. I had no desire to search for firewood or start a fire in the darkness.

"We'll get camp set up soon," Rooke told me, inconspicuously taking my elbow to steer me toward either the saloon or the general store.

A sneaking suspicion told me we were bound for the saloon, a thrill of excitement shooting through me at the thought of seeing the inside of a notorious wild west saloon with men playing poker and swilling whiskey or beer, smoking cigars. After my bout with whiskey, I had no desire to drink, but I was curious about gambling. I blamed Rooke and Cade for that curiosity. Not to place money on any games, but to watch it fascinated me.

The group of us stepped onto the boardwalk, the wooden planks sounding hollow underneath our cowboy boots while they nodded silent greetings to men leaning against the outer walls of the buildings. I kept my eyes shaded by my hat, as Rooke warned me to keep a low profile while in towns.

"Aw, shit." I heard his low mumble when we stopped in front of the saloon.

At his curse, I looked around suspiciously. Swiftly forced through the door, we joined the other men, and he had no chance of uttering another word. Matthew and Billy were ahead of us, laughing loudly as Billy slapped him heartily on the back while shuffling in.

The saloon was spacious, with several tables strewn about the main floor. Benches and couches dotted the perimeter, and a bar made of dark wood pressed against the back wall. The barkeep behind it had his hands braced on the shining wood, as though waiting for more customers. The air was thick with smoke, and I waved my hand to clear it away when I froze.

Scantily clad girls lingered on the side staircase, the looks on their faces and in their eyes unmistakably flirtatious. Involuntarily, I took a step back, only to have my arm seized by Billy. He'd seen my hesitation and stopped to pull me in.

"Oh no, my young friend," he shouted over the booming laughter and the piano playing in the corner. "Let's get you a girl. You look like you need one."

Then I noticed the women sitting on the laps of men, their bosoms fairly hanging out from their corsets. Lips painted ruby red, cheeks touched with too much rouge, and stockings ending mid-thigh, showing far too much skin, was all I could see. My face reddened when Billy pulled me in.

"Gentleman! Come in, come in!" A woman's booming voice came from the back of the room near the bar.

I dug in my heels when a woman came into view, dark coiled hair tucked up into a neat coiffure wearing a modest dark green gown that had a high collar. She wore no cosmetics on her face and she didn't need to. Her eyes, as dark as her hair, swept across us newcomers.

"Order yourself a whiskey and find yourself a girl, gents," she said, coming into the room more fully.

Her height had me by at least two inches when she stepped up toward us, reaching around me for Rooke. My mouth slid open when she wrapped her arm around him, pulling him away with her.

My blood boiled at her familiarity with Rooke, her arm slung around his waist so possessively. He seemed so comfortable in this place, as though he'd been in this type of establishment dozens of times. I cursed him every which way to Sunday if he would be partaking in this type of activity.

I'd recognized my deepening feelings for him, not having felt like this for any other man before. Not even Charles. I still couldn't be sure I should feel such things, but while I was powerless to stop them, I also couldn't stop thinking about it.

I couldn't breathe. I never thought I would be in a house of ill repute. A saloon, yes, but never this. The backwards glance from Rooke only increased my anxiety, the girls coming down to pick each one of us to lead away, making my heart thunder. I couldn't do this. And then Rooke smiled. I wanted to scream at him not to leave me here.

"That's Madame Charlotte. She owns this establishment. Finest one in the area." Billy leaned down to whisper in my ear.

I wanted to ask where she was leading Rooke but saw them stop at the bar and her wave to the barkeep. She turned, snapping her fingers at the last pretty girl on the stairway, then pointed at me.

No! I wanted to shout. Not me. I didn't, I couldn't, do anything of the sort. Before I could turn and run out the door behind me, Billy propelled me forward. I wouldn't make it out of this mess without them knowing I'd fooled them all into believing I was a boy.

The girl stepped down, sliding over to me. She, like the others, wore very little clothing. The dress, if one could call it that, fell from her creamy white skin. Her light blue eyes caught mine at the same time she reached for my hands.

Oh dear Lord, I thought, willing myself not to faint. I couldn't recall a time in my life that I had ever fainted, and I'd be damned if I'd do so now. The barest of smiles tilted her lips while she pulled me to her.

"You come on with me," she said, her voice a slight whisper while she tugged at my hand. "I'll take care of you."

The stairway creaked and groaned under the weight of our footsteps, the railing well-worn from visitors coming and going. I managed a glance behind me, finding Billy highly amused and Matthew looking at me with wide eyes. When I looked down at Rooke, he saluted me with his glass of whiskey. Bastard, I mused before I disappeared upstairs with the girl.

I couldn't deny the pounding of my heart beneath the bindings or the sweating of my palms even though she held one of my hands firmly in hers while leading me down a hallway with walls covered with blue-flowered wallpaper.

Between each doorway a lit sconce flickered, but I didn't need to count to know my way back downstairs. The minute I could, I'd be escaping back downstairs so long as this girl didn't intend to block me in.

She stopped at the doorway at the end to the right, glancing at me coyly before opening it. I had to admit that she was pretty with her light hair and skin. The innocence in her eyes, I was certain, had earned her many coins. I couldn't understand why she would do this.

"This is my room," she whispered.

I nodded, unable to find my voice. The door opened with a slight squeak, revealing a dimly lit room with a small wooden tub in the far corner alcove close to the two windows and a wrought-iron bed against the wall. No other furniture adorned the room but for a tall dresser and a rocking chair with several garments strewn over the top.

With a tug of my hand, she pulled me in and closed the door behind us. I wanted to ask if I could make use of her tub, but still couldn't find my voice. The minute I spoke, would she know I wasn't a boy?

"What's your name?" She released my hand to wander into the room.

I stopped at the threshold, frozen in place. She giggled.

"I'm not going to hurt you, silly. Is this your first time?"

Dumbly, I nodded. I didn't lie. Never had I before been in the company of a prostitute, and never had I been in a whorehouse. And I was fairly certain there wouldn't be a first time, at least when she noticed I was the same gender as she.

Before I could wonder what she would do when she noticed my bindings, she grabbed my hands and pulled me further into her room. Wasting no time, she pushed the vest over my shoulders, but I stopped her.

"I can't do this."

Her hands dropped away, her head notching to the side while her front teeth sank into her bottom lip. "My name's Birdie." When she reached her hand toward my face, I whipped my head to the side out of her reach. "I'll take care of you."

"You don't understand."

"What's your name?"

"Georgie."

When she smiled, she looked pretty. "Well, Georgie, I can promise you I will take care of you. It's what I do."

"Why?" I asked, wincing at my abrupt question. "Why do you do what you do?"

Her smile slowly faded away. "If you want a conversation, you've come to the wrong place. You should at least bathe while you are here. You don't smell all that great."

I couldn't argue with her. "But . . . I need help. I'm not who the men who came in with me think I am. They cannot know who I am."

Her eyebrows arched delicately. "I'm not sure—"

"Can I trust you?"

I had no money. How could I trust her? She didn't know me, she owed me nothing. And yet I asked her to trust me. Shaking my head, I decided this wouldn't work out well if I stayed in this room with her.

Before I reached the door, I felt her take my hand again. "Don't go. Please. My mother will not take it well if I don't please you."

I whipped around. "Your mother?" She nodded. "Is that the dark-haired woman downstairs? Madame Charlotte?" Another nod. "Does she make you do this?"

Releasing my hand, she sat down on the edge of the bed with a bounce. "This is my life. It's always been my life." I watched her shake her head before standing up again. "Come on. You can at least bathe before she gets suspicious and comes knocking. I'm one of the few who has a tub in my room. It's rare, but since my mother owns this establishment, I get extra perks."

I nodded, hoping once I removed the bindings, I'd be able to get them back on. I might need to call for Rooke and hope that no one noticed. Stepping over to the tub, I saw it already contained water, although not steaming. Beside it, a table with soaps and bottles stood on a pedestal.

Shrugging out of the vest, I gasped when Birdie whisked it away from me. My fingers trembled when I unbuttoned my shirt, pulling it out of my trousers and over my head while still turning away from her.

I heard the sharp intake of her breath when she reached for my shirt. "What . . . did you hurt yourself?" she asked.

With the deepest breath I could muster, I began unwinding the bindings until they dropped to the floor. I folded my arms across my chest and turned toward her, shielding my breasts from her view only so she could understand what I hid.

Chapter Twenty Five

"Good golly!" She fell back onto the bed with another bounce, covering her mouth with wide eyes. "You're a woman!"

I nodded. "It's not safe to travel alone, so I disguised myself. And why I haven't been able to bathe often while only in the company of men. You understand?" She nodded. "Can I bathe now?"

"Yes! Please do!"

Making haste, I removed my boots, stockings and trousers before slipping into the tepid water. I didn't care that it had hardly any heat to it. It felt heavenly against my skin and limbs. Birdie made herself busy with laying out my discarded clothing while I dunked my head underwater, coming up and smoothing short strands back. She giggled, coming up to kneel beside me.

"Do you want me to wash your hair?"

"That would be wonderful."

While she set to work lathering up my hair, I rubbed the soap against my skin until it turned red. The smell was enough to brighten my outlook for many days ahead. It felt good to be clean after so long.

"Is Georgie really your name?" she asked, her fingertips massaging against my scalp.

"Georgiana, but I've always been called Georgie. The men downstairs know me only as George." She scoffed. "What?"

"That worked out well in your favor, having a name like that."

"It has helped a great deal. I don't like lying." I set the bar of soap back on the table. "Is Birdie your real name?"

"Yes," she murmured, filling a cup with water and pouring it over my hair while I tipped my head back. "We're originally from New Orleans. We moved here before the war when the town was building up fast."

"Have you . . . " I bit my lip, wondering how to ask her such a question. "Have you been doing this long?"

"Long enough. Madame Charlotte has been in the business for most of her life, so when she accidentally had me, she decided not to change her ways. What better way to do it than to have her daughter follow in her footsteps?" She set the cup down. "All done."

I wrung out the water left in my hair while she handed me a large towel. Water rushed down my body in rivulets when I rose, wrapping the soft towel around my torso and stepping out. She ushered me over to a chair, sitting me down to brush through my hair.

"Did you have long hair?"

"Yes. Nearly to my waist. Cutting it was the hardest thing I've ever done."

There were many things I could think of that were the hardest things I'd ever done. Cutting my hair had been only one of them. When it grew back to the length it had been, I vowed never to cut it again.

"But I had to. I can't take any chances."

"I won't betray your secret, Georgie. Where are you going?"

"To my brother. He's my only family here."

"You're from another country, aren't you? I can tell by how you talk."

My head jerked, tears sneaking into my eyes. "I haven't spoken with him for several years, but he's all I have. I need to get to him. And quickly."

"You can get dressed now." She set the brush down.

Casting a furtive gaze at my clothing, I was reluctant to put dirty clothing back on, besides binding my breasts again. But I didn't have a choice. There weren't many more days before we reached the ranch. I could manage for a few more days. The ache had gone since the fateful day by the river when I'd lost the baby, but it was still challenging to breathe.

A sharp knock on the door startled us both. "Birdie, you've been in there too long. Madame Charlotte sent me up to find out what's taking so long."

Birdie came around me, putting her finger to her lips. "It's his first time, Meg. Tell her we'll be down soon enough."

I used both hands to cover my laugh, fearing someone would hear us and discover that we weren't doing what everyone should think we were doing. Removing my hands from my mouth, I pressed them to my cheeks while Rooke came to mind and the sight of his bare chest.

"Have you ever been with a man before?" Birdie asked, once certain no one listened outside the door.

"I'm married," I admitted. "I ran away from my husband in New York. That's why I'm going to my brother."

"No!"

"It's the truth. He would have had me committed had I stayed."

"Oh! That's terrible. Makes me glad I've never burdened myself with marriage. To think a man can just say his wife is insane and send her away! It's unfair." I nodded, in complete agreement with her. "I wouldn't have stayed either."

Birdie turned out to be a delight to talk to after having spent the last two weeks in the company of men. Gracious enough to help me with the bindings, more knocking sounded at the door and we knew our time had ended.

Floorboards beneath our steps creaked while we walked down the hallway. The men would tease me mercilessly for this.

They would laugh, thinking I had done something I hadn't.

My face had turned a shade of pink before we reached the staircase. Trying to hide my face, I slapped my hat on my head and started down the stairs. The louder the jeers and cheers grew, the more I felt my heartbeat in my face. Bastards, I thought.

As we reached the bottom of the staircase, I felt Birdie grab my hand and tug me back and right into her. My hat fell off when she pressed her lips against mine, softly. When she pulled away, she looked into my eyes.

"I had to do something," she whispered, giving me a wink.

I stood in stunned silence while she ran back up the stairs, my eyes sweeping the men at the poker tables with girls on their laps, those at the bar with glasses of whiskey in their grasp. And there stood Rooke, leaning up against the bar with eyes wide in shock.

Slowly, a grin spread across my lips until my cheeks hurt. I bent down, sweeping my hat up from the floor and bounded down the rest of the stairs, not stopping until I was out in the street. Unsure of how I'd escaped the entire encounter, I breathed in deep.

When I stepped out into the street, I turned to look up at Birdie's window where she stood in the parted curtains. She gave me a wave, and I returned it before settling the hat on my head and heading down the road. I didn't know where I was going. I didn't know which way camp was.

"Wait."

I stopped in the middle of the street, Rooke's less-than-gentle command at my back. He hadn't stopped what had happened back there. He could have, but he didn't. That he thought he could command me caused me to laugh. I kept moving.

I promptly ignored his footsteps behind me until he grabbed my arm, forcing me to stop. "Darlin', I said wait." His jaw clenched, his eyes blazing. "What were you thinking back there?"

"What was I thinking?" I asked. "What were you doing while I was up in that room doing everything I could not to undress in front of that poor girl, Rooke?"

His face flushed. The moment the words rushed out of my mouth I wanted to take them back. I had no claim to Rooke. I acted like he owed it to me to not be in the company of another woman. Jealous of that other woman getting a second of his time, but not knowing why.

He released my arm, eyes softening. "My mother was a prostitute, Georgie. If there is anything in this world that I do not do, it's spending my money on that."

Blood drained from my face. "I didn't want to go in there."

"I didn't either. We've got more'n several days left on the ride. You've got to lie low." He sighed, a smile curving his lips and making him look devilish. "Damn it all, but you smell good."

Chapter Twenty Six

Four days after leaving Fort Worth behind us, the dirt and grime the bath had washed away came back with a vengeance as July pounced on us with a heat and humidity I couldn't recollect ever experiencing. While the hat provided shade, it also created a heat source for the sun to collect within. The result was a fine layer of sweat on the back of my neck, traveling down my spine and collecting around the bindings, which were proving to be more uncomfortable the higher the heat became.

I was not the only one suffering in the heat, although the rest of them were used to the Texas summers. I'd experienced plenty of hot summer days, but none as ferocious as this. This type of heat, I would have remembered being suffocated. This much perspiration. Not only that, but the bugs were vicious.

"We'll reach Austin in two days," Rooke told me as he brought his horse up alongside me.

While Indian Territory had been nothing but flat lands, Texas at least brought shady trees and river bends. The horses showed signs of slowing, having to stop more often to drink from creeks and streams when they could.

"At this pace?"

I couldn't help the bite of my tone, earning myself a stern look.

"Better get used to it. Welcome to Texas."

I scoffed.

"Have you given any thought to what you'll do if Anthony isn't happy that you're here? What will you do if he doesn't want you to stay?"

I shrugged. "I suppose I'll need to write to my grandfather and go back home."

His mouth opened like he had something else to say but closed it promptly. There were too many ears around us to have this conversation. We'd need to wait until we could find more privacy.

"You could stay."

My gaze shot to his. "What do you mean?"

He had the decency to look like he misspoke. "Forget I said anything."

I wanted to ask for further explanation, but the look in his eyes and the set of his jaw gave me pause. It might not be a good time to push it. I wouldn't last much longer in these bindings, hoping to shed them once we reached the ranch. My breathing had become more labored with the increase in the heat. I think Rooke knew I struggled and I wondered if he was trying to tell me something more.

We rode on in silence, stopping in the late afternoon to allow the horses to rest and drink. It seemed the perfect time to get Rooke alone to ask him what he had meant. I couldn't stop thinking about it. The only decision would be to write to my grandfather to send money for a ticket home. In disgrace.

I found Rooke with his hands on his hips next to the creek, staring into the glittering water. He looked deep in thought. So deep I didn't want to disturb him, but he and I had gotten close in these last weeks.

"Tell me what you meant," I whispered.

He stayed where he was, not turning to look at me. "You don't have to leave, even if Anthony isn't the same brother you once knew. You could make a life of your own here, if you chose to." He whipped off his hat, running his hands through his hair. When he turned toward me, I noticed the stubble along his jaw had grown as well as the bronze of his skin. Even though he shaved when he could, it didn't take long for it to regrow. His light eyes turned on me, the concern so deep it stunned me.

A feeling came over me. He wanted to add something else but hadn't asked. Did he mean for me to stay with him? At the ranch? Would Anthony allow me to? And could I do that as a married woman? I may have another society shun me, if anyone knew I was married.

"I'll consider it," came my reply before I turned.

"Georgie—"

A shout tore through the air, stopping him from saying anything else. Both of us rushed back toward the group when a gunshot resounded through the area. I couldn't move as quickly as he could, but I was only a few steps behind him. We found Billy clutching his arm, and a dead snake at his feet.

Billy howled in pain, his face going white despite the heat of the sun. Helpless, I watched Cade tear off his bandana and wind it into a long strip. He tied it around Billy's forearm, halfway between his wrist and his elbow.

"What happened?" I asked Matthew.

He gave me a wry look. "What's it look like? Snake got 'im."

"How? We've been on the road for days with snakes, sleeping on the ground even."

"Dropped his canteen. When he reached for it . . . " He made a snatching motion. "Didn't know a snake was hiding in there."

It could have happened to any of us, I thought. Billy had bad luck to have been the one to drop something right next to a snake, who clearly didn't want to be bothered.

"Is it venomous?" I asked, my voice coming out in a squeak.

"Sure is." Matthew looked up at me. "Cottonmouth. Them are nasty buggers."

"Someone give me a knife!" Cade yelled until Geezer stepped

up, slapping his Bowie knife, handle first, into his open palm with a curse.

It was the first time I had seen Geezer do anything for anyone. As soon as he did, he stepped away. Fascinated, I watched Cade cut a shallow line between the two fang marks in Billy's arm. The color in Billy's face returned to an angry red while he howled in more pain.

Matthew pressed a flask to Billy's lips, tipping it back so he could take in some whiskey for the pain. Seeing this, I never wanted to be bitten by a snake. I could only hope that what Cade did to his arm would help him because as he squeezed the cut, a gush of blood mixed with venom, oozed out. Billy screamed in agony.

Rooke stepped over to Geezer. "Someone's got to get him over to Salado, and quickly."

"Why's that?" I couldn't help myself from asking.

Rooke tossed his gaze my way. "There's a well-known doctor in Salado. If Cade doesn't get all that venom out, he's going to need him. You're going to have to ride at night and fast. And whoever goes will make it home before the rest of us."

When no one spoke up, it surprised me. I was fairly certain they wanted to be home faster than they wanted Billy to get to the physician.

Rooke pointed at Geezer. "You go. He's in your charge." Geezer gave him a snide look. "Anyone else?"

Looking at Cade, then Matthew, they looked like they wanted to go but were uncertain between wanting to get home and leaving Rooke and me alone on the road. If they wanted to get home so badly; they didn't care about riding hell bent at night.

Matthew looked at me, the reflection in his eyes torn between leaving me alone with Rooke and getting home maybe faster.

"Can you manage with no one else?"

Geezer didn't look convinced. "I'd sooner be home than

spend any more time on the trail."

"Is that safe?" I asked Rooke. Rooke nodded at me

I exchanged looks with Matthew while Rooke went to divide up enough food to last us a few days.

When I returned, my attention went immediately to Rooke when he bent down over Billy, whispered to him and earned himself a few nods from Billy. He grasped Billy around the neck, pulling him toward him until their foreheads touched.

Air filled my lungs, holding at such a touching display. They grew up near each other. Must be close enough like brothers, I thought. He must be terribly worried about him.

Not a half hour later, Geezer and Billy had left us. Billy, riding his own horse and cradling his arm, didn't look well but he sat upright. Rooke watched them leave, a frown creasing his forehead. Although I wouldn't miss Billy's tobacco spitting, I hoped they made it. I hoped he made it and lived.

Rooke, Matthew, Cade, and I mounted up and continued our trek at an easy pace. I couldn't help but to wonder what the next few days would bring, just the four of us.

"Do you think they'll make it to the ranch before us?" I asked Rooke once we were on the move again.

"Without a doubt. They'll be far ahead of us."

"This doctor . . . will be able to help Billy?"

Rooke smiled. "What Cade did might have saved his life. By squeezing out what venom he could, even though it likely hurt like a . . . " He looked away, sheepishly. "Like a son of a gun, he gave him a fighting chance to get to the doc in time."

That gave me hope. Enough hope to leave it alone.

When my gaze met his, I felt the raw emotion in his eyes. If I wasn't mistaken, a tear glistened in the corner of one of his eyes, but he looked away before I could be certain.

Chapter Twenty Seven

Making camp that evening proved much more difficult than any other night, being only four of us. I made quick work of getting the fire started, thankful that Cade had stayed behind with some matches. We ate a supper of dried meat, hard biscuits and whiskey, passed around in a flask.

I tried not to drink too much of the whiskey, but I couldn't swallow the biscuit without something to help it down. I'd vowed not to drink the stuff again, but here I was. Before long, I weaved back and forth on my way to the woods, followed by laughs from around the campfire.

If it hadn't been so blasted dark out, I'd have shot a glare at Cade and Matthew behind me. Instead, I held out my hands to find my way from tree to tree, every once in a while stumbling on twigs and branches. I shuddered, hoping there were no snakes out here. They liked warmth, but that didn't mean they couldn't be somewhere I'd disturb.

Far enough away, I reached out and felt for a tree to lean against, but all I found was air. A warm, calloused hand curled around my upper arm, preventing me from toppling over.

"Not sure you should wander in the dark alone." Rooke's husky voice washed over me, sending shivers dancing along my skin.

He hadn't released my arm yet, the length of his fingers

branding his touch into my memory. With a slight tug, he pulled me back, sending me in a spin against him except the whiskey had made my balance topsy-turvy and I stumbled chest first into him.

Strong arms wound around me, slipping under my arms with a firm hand pushed against my lower back. I could see the contours of his face in the dark, feel the warmth of his breath laced with whiskey against my cheek.

With a gasp, his other hand slid up to cradle my face while the other dragged me even closer against him. The feel of his muscles against me made my stomach flutter, a warmth spreading inside my loins.

"Georgie."

My name on his tongue, the hoarseness of his voice while he said it, nearly undid me. Then his mouth came down against mine, strong and insistent. A breathless moan from deep in my throat provided him enough opportunity to sweep his tongue against mine. He moved closer until I felt a tree against my back, his mouth plundering mine and catching every gasp that escaped.

When his hand slipped from my jaw down to my ribs, he groaned and pulled my hips against him. His lips moved to my jaw and down to my neck, igniting a fire within my limbs at the feel of his hands and mouth on my body. My fingers slipped through the soft hair at his nape.

I couldn't recall being kissed like this, as though he wanted to have all of me. His hands, steady and practiced, only instigated my body's response.

"We can't do this," he murmured against my mouth, hands lifting me until my legs coiled around his waist.

"Why not?" I closed my eyes, relishing the feel of pulsating waves coursing through my body. Only he could tame them.

"I'm not a good man." His mouth paused against the curve of my jaw, his fingers flexing against the flesh of my hips. "You're mar—"

"Don't say it," I warned. "You don't need to say it. I left. I'm not going back."

Slowly, he released his hold on my hips until my legs dropped, keeping his palms molded against the curves there. "I won't do this to you."

I jerked away, suddenly sobered. "You aren't doing anything *to* me."

Pushing his hands away, I needed to put distance between us. Quickly. What had started a burn inside of me suddenly made me realize I was now a free woman. My decisions up to this point were mine, and mine alone. And he had taken that all away as quickly as it had started.

"Georgie," he warned, trying to snatch me back.

"Don't touch me, Rooke. I'll relieve myself and return to camp after. You need not bother yourself with worrying about me."

I stumbled but righted myself quickly. My face burned hot, hoping he wouldn't linger while I relieved myself. Ever the protector, Rooke likely wouldn't leave me alone in the dark woods.

"You may go," I insisted.

"I'll stay and see you safely back."

"You mean stay and watch me piss?" I winced at my language, the behavior of the men beginning to rub off on me. "I'd prefer you not."

"I'll turn my back," he growled. "Suit yourself."

I continued to stumble on a few more steps before undoing my trousers and yanking them down, seething the entire time and still simmering when we were on our way back to the camp a few moments later. We said nothing else to each other and when we neared the fire, I immediately sought my bedroll and lay down to sleep.

◆

Silence continued between us the following day, not having said more than a few words to each other in the morning while breaking camp. Sleep had not come easily while I'd lain in my bedroll during the night, despite the amount of liquor I had consumed, my emotions in turmoil.

When he wrapped his arms around me, put his mouth on me, it had felt so natural. The molten desire running through my body had been definitely nothing I'd experienced before. Not once. Had he been right to stop what we'd started last night? I wondered, riding next to him late in the day. What would have happened if he hadn't stopped?

Flames shot through me, heating my already inflamed skin. A light rain fell, but it did little to dissipate the heat. If anything, it felt more steamy. His lips, so strong and insistent, had pressed against mine as though he'd done it hundreds of times before. I scoffed. Perhaps he had.

His hands fit against me perfectly, as if made to be there. Sweeping the hat from my head, I fanned my face without a care to my hair getting wet. I needed a reprieve from this heat.

"We're nearing town." Rooke's voice snatched me from my thoughts. "We'll be staying with friends tonight."

My eyebrows kicked up. "Friends of yours?"

He nodded. "I spent time as a boy here. Rory and Sarah would never forgive me if I didn't stop on my way back through." When his eyes met mine, they held sadness. "I'd never forgive myself if I didn't."

"I would be delighted to meet any friends of yours."

A smile lit his eyes. "There you go talking all educated again."

"I am educated. By the very best schoolmarms in northern Britain. We don't call them schoolmarms back home, however.

We call them governesses. My governess had a pinched face and smelled like tonic."

I caught his quiet laugh. "What was her name?"

"Miss Martha."

His outright laugh had me grinning. Oh, how I hated her. She had the meanest personality, strict and unrelenting. And although I suffered through her tormenting lessons, I learned to be educated and poised. I snorted, earning myself a quizzical look. I didn't look like an educated and poised lady anymore.

"I'm sorry," came his whisper.

"About?"

"Last night."

I purposely looked away from him. His apology fell on deaf ears, for I didn't care for it. An apology only meant he'd regretted it, and I didn't want him to regret it.

"I feel like I should explain."

"You shouldn't."

"I may not be a good man," he continued, regardless of my insistence that he didn't need to, "but I'll be damned if I'm going to take you on the ground. You deserve better than that. That you're married had nothing to do with me stopping what might have happened."

My mouth popped open, but I couldn't utter any words that formed in my head. Knowing that what we'd started last night, with only the four of us traveling together, it would undoubtedly happen again unless we kept our distance.

The landscape through town changed to trees heavy in greenery with spacious fields between. Rooke led us toward the left of the road into a line of trees that eventually separated into a round clearing with a log cabin.

A woman sweeping the front porch stopped and leaned on

the broom as we drew closer. She had the fiercest red hair I'd ever seen, and when we stopped and dismounted, I saw the bridge of her nose had a smattering of freckles.

"I's wonderin' when you'd come back, Rooke Preston," she said, propping the broom against the railing and stepping down to us.

Wiping her hands on her striped apron first, she threw her arms around his waist and pulled him into a hug. The embrace reminded me of something siblings would share. Rooke rested his chin on top of her head as a man with dark, scruffy facial hair and a tall cowboy hat rounded the corner of the house. Tearing around his legs came two boys, laughing and darting around him while he walked. They had the same red-colored hair as the woman.

I looped the reins over my horse. I turned back to Rooke, who'd released the woman as the man curled an arm around her waist. Matthew and Cade jumped down from their horses, giving greetings to the couple in front of us.

Rooke looked at me, his head tilted to the side. "This is George." He looked down at me. "Rory, Sarah and I grew up together."

"Nice to meet you," I said, keeping my voice low.

"What brings you down this way? Thought you was in Kansas," Rory said, his arm slipping away from Sarah when she moved toward the boys, who'd taken to rolling around in the dirt.

"It's a long story, but I'm heading back to Rutherford Ranch. George knows Anthony and needed a guide. I . . . volunteered."

"The others?"

"Billy got himself bit by a cottonmouth," Cade said, untying his bedroll and bags without looking at Rory.

"Geezer took Billy. Headed straight to Salado yesterday," Matthew added.

Sarah pulled our attention away, taking our horses and

leading them to the barn out to the right. Another boy, older, appeared in the barn's doorway and she handed off the reins to him. I was too far away to hear them, but he nodded to her before disappearing into the barn with the horses following behind him. I noticed he had the same color hair as she and the other two boys had.

"That Robbie?" Rooke jerked his chin toward the barn.

"Sure is." The grin on Rory's face was pride. "Going to be fifteen this year. Luke and Liam just turned six and seven."

An ache settled in my heart. Jealousy of Sarah and her family. They had what looked to be a thriving home and farm with three boys to help. There was a light in her eyes when she rejoined us. I couldn't miss it. Happiness.

I could feel Sarah's eyes on me, purposely avoiding her gaze. There was something that made me look anywhere but toward her, and I had a feeling it had to do with my farce. Instead, I looked at Rooke.

"You've got room for us, then?" he asked.

"Course we do." Sarah patted his cheek fondly. "By the smell of it, you could use some bathing. I've got leftover stew and biscuits. You'll eat after you've bathed."

Rory caught my eye, the deep-set blue eyes burrowing into mine while Sarah turned to go back up the steps into the house. She barked orders to the two boys to get buckets of water.

"Cade and I will help," Matthew offered, elbowing Cade and earning himself a frown before they followed the boys.

"Look kinda young." Rory studied me. "You sure you're cut out for ranching?"

Rooke snorted. "Wyatt was far younger when he started ranching. George will do fine. He outsmarted Geezer."

This brought out another barking laugh from Rory while they turned to go into the house, his large hand slapping Rooke on the back. I wondered why Rooke didn't tell Rory that Anthony and I were siblings.

"How'd he do that?"

"Come on, George," Rooke called over his shoulder. "You can bathe first."

How kind, I thought. Did he forget I would need help to get back into my bindings? Did he intend to do that, and how would he explain it to his friends? My feet shuffled while I followed behind them into the spacious cabin.

Inside, I found a cozy sitting area with a stone fireplace to the left and an open kitchen area with a table to the right. Instantly comforting, with the warmth and touch of a woman but the strength of a man. Looking at the open stairway at the back of the sitting area, it led to the upper floor where bedrooms were.

"The bath is over here," Sarah called from the kitchen area.

Cautiously, I stepped over to her and followed her to a room behind the kitchen. The small room had a large tub with some racks with towels and a table with soaps and a washbasin. An oval mirror hung on the wall above the washbasin, giving me a shiver of excitement to see what I looked like after a month of traveling.

Before following her into the room, I stopped and looked back at Rooke. He gave me a nod of assurance. It was enough for me, and I went into the bathing room with her.

"Do you have another change of clothes?" She eyed my filthy clothing. I shook my head. "Ain't got a tongue in your head?"

I stood up straighter. "I do."

"You gonna tell me your story? George?"

She knew. It didn't surprise me, but I didn't know if I could admit it yet. Rooke knew, and everyone else had left so there wouldn't be any danger in keeping the charade while we were here unless Rooke thought different. He had introduced me as George, not Georgie.

"Not gonna admit it, huh?" She put her hands on her hips. "And how old are you, anyway?"

My mouth shot open defensively. "Almost twenty-five. I . . .

I've had some issues along the way."

Her gaze softened. "Other than travelin' with a bunch of dirty men and not being able to bathe?" She wrinkled her nose. "Anyone else know?"

"Matthew knows, but the others don't."

Noises behind us had me pressing my lips together. The two boys and Matthew hauled in buckets, emptying them into the tub before turning to leave. Matthew stuck his head back around the frame of the door before leaving us.

"You got a bar of soap? Us men will bathe in the lake."

She nodded, and he hurried to grab a bar of soap from the table before whooping and hollering on his way out of the house. I watched her move toward the door, closing us in before turning back to me.

"Okay, then." My eyebrows raised. "Let me help you get those bindings off."

"How . . . how do you know?"

She scoffed. "Ain't no way you've traveled all this time with those men and hid something so vital to a woman without such a thing. I'll lend you some of my things while I launder your clothes. Nothing worse than puttin' on dirty clothes."

Once I'd peeled off my vest and shirt, she helped relieve me of the tight bindings and I nearly toppled over while my lungs took in full breaths. She mumbled under her breath, waiting for me to recover enough to remove my boots, stockings, and trousers.

"Go on and get clean. We'll be having a talk about continuing this godforsaken disguise." She tsked, gathering up my clothing and leaving me standing naked next to the tub.

I stepped into the shallow water, tepid but enough to get clean enough. When the door opened, I whirled around in horror that someone would see me in my state of undress, but it was only Sarah returning to help with my hair.

"Tell me." At her command, she sat down on the stool to pour water over my hair and wash it for me.

My entire sordid ordeal fell from my lips, finally confiding in someone about everything and feeling immediately better. Even Rooke didn't know the full story of why I'd left my husband. With my back turned to her, I didn't know if she believed that I'd been unfaithful to Charles. She didn't know me well enough to know if I was the type of woman to do such a thing.

"How did you know?" I whispered. "You knew that I'm a woman immediately after seeing me. How?"

She stilled. I swiveled, watching her face soften. She set the cup on the table, folding her hands in her lap. "If you must know, it's the way Rooke looked at you."

I turned away. "I'm married."

Rising, she moved toward the table to tidy it up. More so to keep her hands busy than to clean up what had already been orderly to begin with, I noticed. "Don't matter out here. Maybe in that society, but not here. It's lonely out here." She turned around, leaning against the table while her eyes met mine. "The longer you stay, the more you'll realize it isn't going to matter. Not to him."

"And to me?"

She smiled. "Not to you neither."

Chapter Twenty Eight

After Sarah helped me rebind my chest, she left me to dress in a borrowed pair of her trousers and a plaid shirt. After that, I helped her ladle up bowls of a rich, hearty stew with warm, flaky biscuits and set them out for the men when they came in. My mouth watered at the smell, eager to sit down and eat a soft biscuit. If I never had to have another hard biscuit swallowed down by bitter coffee again, I would be happy.

The stew had flavorful gravy with sizable pieces of beef and potatoes, tender carrots, and bite-sized green beans. I sopped up the gravy left in my bowl with the remaining biscuit, refraining from licking my fingers, and eased back in the chair. Rory, leaning against the counter with his arm slung around loosely over Sarah's shoulders, eyed Rooke.

Rooke kicked back from his chair, settling his hat down on his head. "I'll be back later."

I didn't miss the nod Rory gave him before he disappeared out the door. Watching him go, I wondered where he was going. Matthew stood, collecting the dishes while Cade engaged Rory in a conversation about farming.

While Sarah helped Matthew, it was easy to slip out of the house. I spotted Rooke heading across the field toward the line of trees, the length of his legs eating up the distance. I couldn't run with these blasted bindings, so I waited until he reached the line of trees before I hurried after him.

The woods were thick, but I used the sound of him walking through the woods to guide my way. Darting to the right, I followed the narrow dirt path through the low bushes until it opened to a clearing.

Rooke dropped to his knees on the other side, removed his hat and bowed his head. My brows drew together, wondering what he was doing. He didn't move for several minutes. I grew fatigued waiting until he stood up. I scrambled to get out of the path and hide behind a tree, while he stared down at the place where he'd been kneeling before setting his hat on and turning to come back.

He took the same path he'd come from, and I waited until I felt he could be a safe distance away before I slipped out of my hiding place and hurried over to the place where he'd just been. Nearing it, my heart thumped wildly in my chest.

I covered my mouth, a soft cry escaping when I looked down at the grave marker. There was no elaborately engraved headstone with a name and dates. Only two boards nailed together as a cross with a name carved into it. Jesse Preston. Whoever this person had been to Rooke was special. I had a feeling whoever this person had been was the real reason we stopped to see Rory, Sarah, and their boys.

I looked around, spotting some wildflowers. Quickly, I gathered some into a bouquet and carefully tied them together with the longest blade of grass I could find before setting them in front of the simple marker. I knelt down, clearing away some twigs from in front of the cross.

"My brother."

I nearly fell over at Rooke's husky voice behind me. The beating of my heart was so fast, I thought it would beat right out of my chest. Laying a hand over it, I attempted to slow it.

"He died in the Battle of Antietam." Kneeling beside me, he reached out to touch the flowers I'd placed there. "He was twelve."

I gasped. "How was he allowed to fight so young?"

"He wasn't. When Wyatt and I left, he felt left out." The corner of his lips curled up. "Always curious. Like you. He didn't want to be left behind and escaped from his charge. By the time he found me, and by the time I knew, it was too late."

A deep sorrow quickly replaced the heavy beat of my heart. I felt it might have reflected off him and into me. It hurt him, therefore it hurt me.

"I saw him get hit on the battlefield. Ran for him as fast as I could." He hung his head. "He died in my arms."

I laid my hand on his arm. "I don't know what to say, Rooke, other than I'm so sorry that happened. To him. To you."

"Why'd you follow me?"

He didn't sound angry, but he didn't sound happy that I'd done so. "I . . . was curious about where you were going," I admitted. "And I wanted to talk to you about Sarah."

"Curious like Jesse. Someday, that's going to get you hurt."

"I'm not him, Rooke." I rose quickly to my feet. "What happened to him should have never happened, but that doesn't mean it will repeat itself."

When he stood up, there was a clench in his jaw. "That was the single bloodiest day of the war. Over twenty thousand men were lost, from both sides." He ran his hand over his face. "Rory got injured and brought Jesse home to bury. Any time I come this way, I stop in."

I nodded, turning to leave and stopped by Rooke's hand on my wrist. His hand easily curled around the delicate bones there, holding me hostage and not drawing me any closer.

"Thank you for the flowers." His voice had taken on the huskiness of a man with a broken heart.

"It's the least I can do."

I pulled, but he wouldn't relinquish my wrist. Instead, he tugged until I fell back to him. It took only a second for his mouth to come down on mine. Sarah's words came back at me full force. It didn't matter to him that I was a married woman.

His arm snaked around my waist, pulling me flush against him while his other hand threaded through the growing length of my hair and coming to rest against the nape of my neck. I couldn't help but draw my arms around his waist and meet the thrust of his tongue against mine.

It was like a hunger unleashed, and we could no longer contain it. I couldn't resist melting into his arms, feeling the heat rise in my body from the feelings his mouth drew out. Denying them would be useless.

"Damn, but you smell good," he said against my mouth. "I want you, Georgiana. Holy hell, but I do."

A groan bubbled deep in my throat, staying though I wanted to let go of it. The feeling couldn't be more mutual. I couldn't respond, even when his lips moved to my jaw, pressing there before lowering to my neck.

"I'll not take you here in the grass like some bastard." He lifted his head but kept me locked in his arms. "I told you before. You'll at least have the benefit of a bed and even then . . . "

I frowned. "What is it?"

He shook his head. "It might be too soon since . . . "

Understanding hit me. He had concerns about my full recovery after losing the baby. A slight smile touched my lips. "The baby. I don't think I was far enough along to be worried about hurting me, Rooke."

When he tucked a wayward strand of hair behind my ear, my heart lurched from the simple gesture. His thumb smoothed across my cheekbone before he leaned down, pressing his mouth to mine. I breathed in the scent of him, the cleanliness.

"Won't be long and you'll be home." He pulled away, slipping my hand into his and leading me away from the grave marker.

Home, I mused. Would it be my new home? I allowed him to lead me through the woods, wondering silently about my future in Texas. Or anywhere.

Rooke knew nothing about my circumstances. He'd not asked much about my marriage and I'd not offered much to him. His only knowledge of my life was the very limited things I'd given him. Guilt ate at me for hiding so much from him, but he hadn't offered me much either.

"Rooke?" I asked, noticing he'd shortened his strides for me.

"Hmmm?"

"It might be suspicious, you holding my hand when we arrive back at the house." He stopped, plucked off his hat, and ran his hand through his hair. "Cade doesn't know about me."

"Nor does Rory, although Sarah might have told him by now."

Night closed in on us quickly, and we resumed walking without him holding my hand. Instead, we walked as though amicable friends instead of two people who had only moments ago shared an undeniable passion.

The walk wasn't a long distance, Sarah ushering Luke and Liam into the house while Rory rocked in a chair on the porch. Matthew sat on the edge, swinging his leg while Cade leaned up against the outer wall, playing his harmonica. Rooke bypassed me without touching, prompting me to follow.

With the boys tucked into bed, Sarah rejoined us and we all sat around while Cade regaled us with music. I sat with my knees pulled up to my chest while Sarah smiled knowingly at me every now and again. When Rory pulled her down onto his lap, I resisted the urge to look longingly at Rooke. They looked so happy, I envied them. Instead, I lay my cheek on my knee and drifted into my own daydreams.

Chapter Twenty Nine

We reached Austin the next day, riding at a brisk pace. As we entered the town, I gaped at the liveliness of the activity on Congress Avenue. Although New York was a much larger city, this city with its saloons, schoolhouse, hotel, department stores, courthouse, and many other places of business was bursting with energy.

Today marked Independence Day and the city would be celebrating. Cade graciously checked our horses into the livery while Rooke and I went to get a table at a restaurant. I hadn't eaten in a restaurant for over a month, my mouth watering at the thought of not having to eat with my fingers. Tea, perhaps a serving of fish or duck, braised vegetables.

Matthew trailed behind us, going to check about securing rooms at the hotel next to the restaurant. Although Sarah had allowed me the option of sleeping in the spare bedroom inside the house, reserved for Rooke when he stopped in, I'd declined. Cade would have questioned the need for me to sleep indoors when the rest of them were sleeping outside on the hard ground. And so, I passed another night under the stars.

Strolling by a department store, my gaze lingered on the dresses in the window. These were dresses I knew. Silken fabric with lace petticoats, embroidered stitching with hand-sewn buttons and beaded adornments. I continued to stare until

Rooke had to take my elbow, helping me step onto the boardwalk and into the restaurant.

When Cade and Matthew joined us at the table for four, we laughed about our harrowing tales along the trail while we ate soft biscuits. I longed for a cup of tea, but settled for beer like the others were drinking. The taste, far different from whiskey, would take some getting used to, but I drank it down with joy.

Elated that I would sleep in a bed that night, and reach the ranch in another two days, I fairly danced my way out into the streets following supper.

"I've got a hankering for some poker." Cade's eyebrows waggled up and down.

Matthew whooped. "You're on. Rooke?"

"Not today."

Rooke and I followed the two of them into the closest saloon, walking through the half-doors into a smoke-filled room with a man playing an upright piano at the far wall and several tables occupied by games. No scantily clad ladies with ruby-red lips could be found. Only men playing poker, smoking cigars and drinking beer or whiskey. Mounds of coins lay scattered in the center of some tables, while some players had more coins beside them and some had less.

Matthew and Cade found a vacant table, leaving Rooke and me to seek the barkeep for a drink. Although I was reluctant to drink any whiskey, I consented to another beer and Rooke tossed a few coins on to the bar.

We clinked glasses, grinning, and sipped our beers while we took in the room. "Are you lookin' forward to sleeping in a bed tonight?" he asked, turning toward me.

I nodded. "You?"

He shrugged. "A nice change from sleeping on the hard ground. Can't imagine how you feel."

"I've managed. It's getting out of these bindings that will feel heavenly. More so than the thought of sleeping on a mattress."

I glanced at him sideways.

"I can help you tonight. If you'll allow me." I watched the lump in his throat bob. "Will you?"

I nodded, eager to be out of the bindings more than anything. The way he looked at me caused my breath to hitch, my pulse to race. In a saloon full of men, we shouldn't look at each other this way, but I found myself drawn to his gaze.

"Think I'll take a walk."

I gulped down my beer as quickly as I could and set the empty tin on the bar, hurrying out of the saloon without a backwards glance. What am I doing? I silently berated myself, pushing out of the doors and jumping down off the boardwalk into the street. My heart thudded in my chest, the beer going quickly to my head.

Looking around, couples strolled down the street along with carriages and lone riders. I stayed close to the side of the street, weary of being run down by any of them. Rooke stepped out of the saloon, a worried frown creasing his forehead beneath the shade of his hat.

"Shouldn't be out here alone," he murmured, stepping down to me.

"I also shouldn't be drinking. Brought me nothing but trouble." I smiled. "Looks like there are some festivities down by the city hall. Shall we?"

We headed over to the city hall where a three-man band played while couples danced. Across the way, there appeared to be a roping contest in a makeshift coral with calves.

"Tell me about your life," I said, a touch demanding.

"We moved around when my old man found towns worthy of gaming. When he didn't, we stayed where we were and he traveled around. I know what I know by teaching myself."

"And your mother? She wasn't around much?"

"No. As a prostitute, she was out doing what she needed to do." I pulled a face, thinking of Birdie. "Wyatt and Jesse don't have the same pa."

"Where is your father now?"'

He chuckled. "Last I heard, California still. Rory and Sarah are my family. And Billy. They're family to me and Wyatt."

"Wyatt's at the ranch?"

He nodded. "We took jobs at the ranch at the same time. I moved on. He's been there ever since."

We stopped near a fence, Rooke putting his booted foot on the first rung and leaning his arms over the top. I studied his chiseled profile for a moment, considering the information he shared. Bringing up the war, I knew better than to do. Especially now that I knew his brother had perished in it.

I sucked in a deep breath. "I suppose I ought to tell you the truth about me."

"Would be nice."

"My grandfather is a viscount. When Anthony ran away for his big adventure, and my parents died in a shipwreck, it made me the next in line. Although now that I've run away as Anthony did, I'm uncertain what might happen."

He looked over at me, his eyebrow arched. "Why'd you run away?"

The sordid tale of Benjamin and his lies spilled forth, and how society had shunned me. How Charles had shunned me along with them. The line of his jaw hardened when he cast his gaze away from me, but he said nothing.

"I'm uncertain what I'll do if Anthony doesn't allow me to stay. With no money of my own, if Anthony insists, I suppose I'll need to return to my grandfather."

His eyes clashed with mine, eyes filled with fury. "The hell you will." When I opened my mouth, he continued. "I won't let you go back. You belong here."

"I didn't grow up here, Rooke."

"No, but your brother came here and managed. And you will, too. Because you are . . ."

"Georgie Victoria Rutherford," I offered, purposely using my given name instead of my married name. No one would know me by that name, and they shouldn't.

"Because you're *Georgiana* Victoria Rutherford," he growled.

I couldn't help but to smile at the vehemence of how he said my full name. Not George. Not Georgie. Georgiana. Very few people called me that. The way Rooke said it made it sound so much better than when anyone else said it.

"Are you surprised that I come from wealth?" "Should I be?"

"I suppose not. I've hidden so much. From everyone. I've hated every minute of this, and not being able to tell anyone the truth about me." It felt good to admit it. "I cannot wait until I can shed these clothes for a dress."

I noticed the smile on his mouth, a devilish smile. "I can't imagine you in a dress, but I look forward to it."

When I pictured myself in a dress in front of the men I'd traveled with, it didn't seem right. I had a feeling Cade would be on to me before long. My hair had gotten longer, and as Sarah had pointed out, my facial features were feminine. It was no wonder Rooke had known I was a woman from the start.

As darkness fell and the band continued to play, the dancing grew to more couples. Gunshots being fired in fun had me jumping with each one, Rooke moving closer to me while celebrations for Independence Day continued. While we couldn't dance, as much as I would have loved to, Rooke and I moved away from the band toward the hotel.

When we looked in the saloon window, Cade and Matthew still played cards, serious in the game they were involved with. The evening felt cooler than usual, and I enjoyed the breeze on my face.

Colorful fireworks lit the night sky above us. Surprise had me grabbing Rooke's sleeve, pulling him toward the display at the end of the street. Loud booms overhead followed by red, white, and blue displays of lights raining down had me gaping like a young girl. It had been so many years since I'd seen fireworks.

I removed my hat to see better, gripping it in my hands while I stood in the street next to Rooke with my eyes toward the colorful skies. The show was a spectacular sight. I noticed Rooke staring at me instead of the fireworks. Only when I looked over at him, catching him staring at me with eyes full of something akin to desire.

It stole my breath, his gaze so intense it gripped me and wouldn't let go. The blasts of the fireworks faded away while we stared at each other. Time momentarily stood still, the sounds of cheering around us distant. Words failed me. Instead, I turned and walked toward the hotel.

Rooke caught up to me a moment later before we reached the steps of the hotel. He reached out, turning me by the arm. My eyes burned from the intensity of my own emotions.

"You can't look at me like that," I whispered. "We both know I'm not innocent in these things, and neither are you."

"We both know you aren't leaving."

"But you can't look at me like that when I'm dressed like this. It's bound to raise questions. Questions we don't need to answer. I'd like to retire now. I'm rather looking forward to sleeping in a bed."

He nodded. "My offer stands."

Turning away from him, he didn't see the rise in color to my cheeks. Sleeping without the constraint of my bindings sounded perfect, but I couldn't answer him. Too many things ran rampant through my head.

Chapter Thirty

I stared at myself in the full-length mirror in the corner of my room, not having had the chance to take in my appearance aside from the small mirror after my bath yesterday. Slowly, I took off my hat and tossed it to the bed behind me without looking. I heard it bounce off and fall to the floor.

Tentatively, I reached up and touched the chopped ends of my dark hair. It had grown quite some in the last month. It wouldn't be long before others came to know me for the woman I was. I shrugged out of the vest and flung it to the chair as a knock resounded on my door.

Heat swept from my head to my toes, knowing it would be Rooke. When I pulled it open a moment later, he filled the doorway with his hands braced on each side of the door, head bowed. When his head lifted, revealing his eyes, I gasped at the intensity in his gaze. Pure desire stared back at me.

Pushing back, he straightened. "I don't know that I've ever wanted a woman, craved a woman, as much as I do you. A good man wouldn't be having these thoughts."

I opened the door fully. He stepped in, kicking the door closed with the heel of his boot before stalking into the room. I watched him bend to retrieve my hat from the floor, dusting it off on his pants before setting it on the dresser.

"Are you certain?" I whispered.

The slow nod of his head, combined with the heady look in his eyes only heightened my awareness that this would be our first time utterly and completely alone with each other. No one would stumble through the woods upon us. Certain that Cade and Matthew would be playing cards for a while, no one would come knocking at the closed door.

Warmth consumed me while I unbuttoned my shirt, dragging it up my torso and letting it fall heedlessly to the floor. When his hands curled around my bare shoulders, I heard the sharp intake of his breath.

"Turn around."

The air crackled around us like lightning bolts in a thunderstorm. I turned, trembling, when his fingers found the end of my bindings and slowly unwound them. In the mirror's reflection, I caught his hooded gaze while he peeled them away and away until I stood before him. This time, I didn't shield myself. After all, he'd seen me before on more than one occasion.

"Holy hell . . . " his fingers curled around my shoulders, turning me toward him.

I sucked in my breath, my heart hammering an erratic thump in my chest while his eyes devoured me. Being looked at like this by a man, it unnerved me and excited me at the same time. It's like he studied every curve, every angle. His hands raised, fingertips tracing the angry red lines where the bindings had clung to me.

He raised his eyes to mine, silently asking for permission. Finally, I took his hands and brought them to my body for him. My eyes closed at his rough hands molding to flesh that had ached to be exposed for weeks, a heavenly sigh escaping from my parted lips when his fingers splayed around the curves and his thumbs brushed against sensitive peaks.

Heat engulfed me, settling low in the center of my body, my limbs turning liquid at his touch. When he leaned down, capturing my mouth in a searing kiss that left me wanting more, my arms twined around his neck. I plucked his hat off, tossing it to the bed while plowing my fingers into his hair with my other hand. He deepened the kiss with a low growl that hit me with its fierceness. Have two people ever fit so well together? I thought, meeting the demands on his mouth while his hands changed course to my hips.

The wall met my back, his mouth giving no mercy while I felt his hand working the buttons of my trousers. He caught my gasp as his hand slid in.

I cried out when his fingers brushed against me, expertly teasing until my legs trembled and I writhed against him like a wanton woman.

"More," I murmured against his lips. I wanted more. And he gave it to me until I melted beneath his touch, seeking release. A catastrophe of swirling engulfed my body, building and begging for me to burst from the sensation he wreaked.

"Let go," he rasped.

"Rooke." My head hit the wall with a light thud. "What . . . is happening . . . "

My question died away, my breath caught when the sensation of his thumb combined with the slide of his fingers hit a nerve, blasting a wave of heat from my head to toes. He caught my cry with his open mouth. But he hadn't finished with me yet.

"That, darlin'," he murmured, mouth moving down to my neck, hand down my trousers and other hand holding me up, "is how it's supposed to feel."

And I would, again and again, under the expertise of what his hand did to me. This was unlike anything I'd ever experienced before, stars swimming before my vision until I thought I would die from the thrum of my body. An explosion from within had my body sagging against his, the flames completely engulfing my pulsating body.

"That's better," he said against my neck, hitching my legs up around his waist to carry me to the bed.

I buried my face in the crook of his neck, the feel of the stubble against my cheek doing very little to cool my still rising ardor. When my bare back met the mattress, I resisted the urge to stretch like a cat at the feel of such comfort but watched him stand back and strip off his shirt.

I'd never tire of seeing him without his shirt. His bronze skin dancing in the dim light of the room. He removed my boots and stockings first before slowly divesting me of my trousers. The cool air whispered against my skin.

Completely bare to him, he studied my every curve again, his gaze sweeping over me. He kicked out of his boots, looking back at me with an arch to his brow while his hands moved to the button of his trousers. I'd never fully looked upon Charles, not having the desire to. I didn't think I could get enough of looking at Rooke, the way his virile body fairly glowed in the light of the room. I sucked in a sharp breath at the sight of him.

Once gloriously naked before me, he picked up my foot and smoothed his hand up my leg. I shivered, propping myself up on an elbow while he placed a kiss on my inner knee. The bed sagged beneath his weight, but I sat up to meet him halfway.

Boldly, I reached for him. A groan escaped from deep in his throat when my hand wrapped around him, sliding down the impressive length and back up again. I didn't know what had come over me. I'd never been this wanton before.

"Holy hell woman," he whispered. "You need to stop that before this is over too soon. It's been a long while since . . ."

I grinned, releasing him and smoothing my hand up his rigid abs. My legs wrapped around his waist when he came down over me and gathered me in his arms.

"You might be the death of me yet."

"Me?" I asked, feigning innocence while I moved sensually beneath him. I didn't know who I was in the moment. This was a side of me I hadn't known existed.

Grasping my leg with one arm, he looked deep into my eyes while guiding himself into me with the other, his mouth coming down on mine as he eased slowly in. I knew he went cautiously on purpose to not hurt me. But that wouldn't do.

My hips moved with a confidence I didn't know I possessed, and he sat up, hands on my legs that were still around his waist while his face marked concentration. I pushed closer, his hand pressed against my stomach.

"Stop," he uttered, closing his eyes. "Give yourself time."

Still worried about me, I thought. An unladylike snort escaped, and I pushed up on my elbows, biting my lower lip.

"No." My hand wound around his neck, pulling him back down to me until he could take no more, and plunged into me with a growl.

A cry of pure ecstasy tore from my throat, hips meeting his every thrust. My body sang in response, reacting to his movements in ways that brought out a deep passion that surprised me. Vibrations deep in my core lifted me until I couldn't stop it and I cried out release after release.

"Georgiana," he murmured, continuing his concentrated plunges so deep I thought he couldn't fill me any further, and then he would and I would cry out as another wave crashed through me, leaving me breathless.

Deliberately, he slowed until only the sound of our heavy breathing permeated the room. When his eyes met mine, the light behind his gaze caught my breath. He caught my hand in his, placing a kiss to my palm before pulling me up until I straddled him.

Mouths clashed, tongues warred and teeth clinked together while my hands fisted in his hair and his hands smoothed across my curves. Rooke possessed me. All of me. Nothing in the world could part us from what we'd started now. His lips burned a path down, a shocking cry bursting from my lips when his mouth closed around my breast. My hips moved of their own accord, seeking to find a cure to this maddening frenzy building within me.

While he feasted on my flesh, teeth creating a sensual pain quickly doused by his tongue, I thought my eyes would roll into the back of my head. "Rooke," I moaned. "I'm . . . oh . . ."

"Yes." His mouth tore from me, jaw tense while he took over control and plunged into me so deeply that I felt it in my toes. "Come with me, darlin'."

Shaking from the fierceness of our two bodies coming together, the waves crashed into me until I swore I saw stars behind my eyes. I clung to him, hands banded around his powerful arms slicked with sweat.

His body shook, grasping my legs and pulling me closer with a growl, a deep thrust and a stillness that stole my breath away. Neither of us moved, only our breathing filled the quiet of the room.

After a moment, he looked down at me with glazed eyes. "Holy hell, darlin'."

A smile slipped out.

"Pleased, are you?" His teasing growl was endearing. Even more so when he released me but fell to my side and pulled me toward him.

Sprawled over his bare chest, my legs tangling with his, I breathed in his manly scent and let it fill my senses. I was fairly certain I wouldn't get enough of him. As though he had shown me the light, and the light was a new life.

Chapter Thirty One

A feeling swept over me, an unexpected warmth unlike the sweltering heat I'd experienced both day and night for the last several days. It comforted me, beckoning with promises of protection. Something moved, rousing me from my state of euphoria. Hair against my legs tickled, the rise and fall of a chest moving beneath me. My eyes fluttered open to a pair of deep hazel-blue eyes lazily drinking me in.

"Darlin'."

The beat of my heart skittered at the huskiness in his voice. How could one man make me so deliriously weak? The way his eyes roved over me, the skate of his fingertips while they danced along the bare skin of my arm to my shoulder. A moan slipped out, caught by his lips while he pressed me against the mattress.

Despite how much I'd been looking forward to the comfort of a bed, we hardly slept. I would never complain about it, I mused, wrapping my arms around his neck.

"I daresay." I sucked in a breath when his mouth coasted over sensitive skin where bindings had once been, teeth grazing. All thoughts in my head fled.

"Daresay what?" came his muffled reply, his hand traveling up my thigh.

My heart dipped when he looked up at me, lips parted and eyes soft. My palm cradled his rough cheek, wishing things had been different. I wouldn't think about it now. Even when his lips pressed against the center of my hand, his body slid up mine until I cradled him between my legs.

When his finger traced down the side of my face, I closed my eyes and gave into all the feelings he gifted to me. Everything he gave, I took until we were both depleted of energy.

Several minutes passed us by, our uneven breathing the only sounds of the room until a crude knock ripped open our temporary haven.

"George?" Matthew rapped again. "Cade's waiting outside with the horses. Not sure where Rooke is, but we've got to get on."

My front teeth sank into my bottom lip, refusing to look at Rooke even though I knew the devil had a grin on his face from ear to ear. With both hands on his bare chest, I gave him a push, but to no avail. He wouldn't budge.

"I'll be down as soon as I can."

Playfully, he wound his arms around me again until I laughed. Not the laugh that would come from someone pretending to be a boy, but the full laugh of a woman.

"Rooke in there with you?"

Bugger it! My eyes grew wide. While Matthew had known my secret, that didn't mean he needed to know about this. I scrambled out from under Rooke, throwing my legs over the side of the bed and hurrying to find my trousers. When I looked back at Rooke, he lay on his side with his head cradled in his hand while he watched me picking up scattered clothing.

His shirt smacked him in the face when I threw it at him. "Get dressed."

"George?"

"Matthew, I'll be down. Give me a moment. Please."

Grudgingly, Rooke slid from the bed and dressed. As hard as it was not to watch his powerful muscles ripple with each movement, I got what clothing I could on before he had to help me into the bindings.

He caught my wrist before I reached the door, spinning me into his arms and pinning me with a searing kiss that would have left me stuttering had I needed to speak. Instead, we left the room with my cheeks tinged with red but my hat low over my eyes.

As Matthew had said, Cade waited with the horses outside the hotel. He leaned against the hitching post, ankles crossed and arms folded, when we finally emerged. Saying nothing, his eyebrow raised at us.

"Have a good night, did you?"

Rooke whipped his arm out in front of me before I could take a single step toward Cade. "Cade." And that was all he needed to say.

Straightening, Cade took a step forward, but his eyes remained on me. "Should have known you were a woman." He shook his head. "Walls are pretty thin in this hotel."

Oh God, I swayed. The last thing I wanted to happen was to have someone angry with my deception. Cade had been one of those I'd been closest to, and yet I'd not been honest with him.

"Cade. I'm sorry."

He nodded. "You had your reasons. Now, let's get on. I'm hankering to be back at the ranch like everyone else."

Matthew handed me the reins to my horse. "Shoulda bought a dress while we were here," he teased, watching me swing up into the saddle.

I snorted. "I can't wear a dress riding like we have been."

"Let's go," Rooke snapped.

The four of us lurched into motion, trotting down the street at an easy pace. When we were clear of the town we broke into gallops that brought us racing into the west. I didn't know what awaited us in the next two days, but my anticipation mixed with dread.

◆

Cade didn't seem to mind the fact that a woman traveled among them now. Rooke kept me close when we stopped at camp that night, but we would never disrespect either of the two men by engaging in any inappropriate behavior. Having been heard last night embarrassed me enough.

We packed up camp the next morning and rode the remaining miles until we arrived at the ranch rangeland. It would be another twenty miles to get to the ranch itself, and while Rooke was in no hurry to push the horses in the sweltering heat, Matthew and Cade wanted nothing more than to be back in their beds that evening.

Rooke looked to me for the decision on whether we pressed on or stayed another night without the comfort of a warm bed. I shrugged, having no warm bed to speak of yet. Anthony would be surprised to see me, but as my family he wouldn't deny me a place to sleep. For how long, I didn't know.

"I don't mind staying another night."

Cade and Matthew grinning, kicked their horses into motion and sped across the flat lands on the rangeland, leaving us alone for the rest of the journey. Knowing it would only be Rooke and I that night, anticipation tingled in places I had never realized existed.

"There's a lake ahead," Rooke said. "Be a good place to camp for the night."

"You know better than I."

The ride to the area took less than a half hour, the

shimmering lake with several trees to one side and a rocky crag bordering on the other side a welcome sight. While Rooke unpacked our bags and set the horses to graze, I gathered wood and arranged a fire.

Cade had the matches, I realized when I sat on my heels to look at my perfect arrangement of wood and kindling in a small circle not too far from the trees. Not too close either, for I knew too close could catch them on fire. Rooke tossed a book of matches down to me.

"You've had these the entire time?"

His laugh felt like a gentle caress over my shoulders. "Yes, darlin'."

I had the fire sparking and flickering within a few minutes, handing his matches back to him. When his fingers brushed mine, a jolt of electricity flowed through me and I looked away. After our night together, I knew what it would lead to. I not only wanted it, I craved it.

"If you want to bathe in the lake, I've got soap in my saddlebag."

Moments later, the cool water against my feet felt like silk, lapping gently against my skin as my movements stirred the surface. Rooke stayed back to heat dinner while I cleaned up.

Memories of sitting by the river near my childhood home had me smiling while I floated in the lake close to the shore, relishing the feel of the water against me. The sun had begun its descent, but I didn't want to get out of the water. It felt too good against the heat of the day.

So many days, not being able to be washed, this felt like something not to be rushed through. I paused my relaxing moves long enough to wash my body and hair, rinsing as I dipped beneath the water. As long as my feet touched the bottom, I knew I'd be safe. Rooke wouldn't have to rescue me from drowning again.

When I rose, water running down me while I smoothed back

my hair and wrung out the longer strands, I sensed someone behind me. Elation speared through me, but I stayed where I was instead of turning.

"Should you have left supper unattended?" came my whisper.

"You shouldn't be taking so long."

His hands touched my arms, below my shoulders, sliding up. Wet skin against wet skin, only the sound of droplets of water and nature around us. I inhaled when he dropped one arm, hooking it around my waist, and pulled me back against him. His mouth connected to my neck, the other arm coming around to cup one breast.

"What are you doing to me?"

"Cherishing you, darlin'."

On unstable feet, I turned in his arms. "Why?"

When he crushed me against him, continuing the assault of his mouth in places I didn't think anyone had ever touched, words couldn't form. He hauled my legs up around his waist, wading deeper into the water while it swirled around us.

"Cause you deserve it."

My eyes fluttered, hand cupping his jaw, and my thumb caressing his lower lip. He nipped at it. "Charmer," I murmured, but the deeper he brought me into the water, the more my panic rose. "Rooke, I can't swim."

"I've got you, darlin'. I'm not letting go."

We swirled around in the water. The more my body temperature rose, the more fevered his kisses got and the more insistent his touches became. His handling of my body was practiced and perfect, even as he drew me toward shore, bringing me to the brink of desire.

Later, Rooke carried me back to the fire I'd built earlier, going to retrieve my clothes and reappearing a few minutes later. He'd made a pan of beans mixed with salted pork, but I had little appetite. Still, we ate in the quiet as night fell around us. With

Cade and Matthew having left us, the silence seemed deafening.

After we'd rinsed and put away our dishes, I slipped my shirt back on to ward off the swarming bugs despite the heat. We set the bedrolls close to the fire and sat with our backs against a log.

"I can't understand," he gently kissed the inside of my wrist, "how someone could have let you slip away so easily?"

"I'm adept at sneaking around."

When he chuckled, his voice deep, I realized he did not know how difficult my marriage to Charles had been. How isolating, demeaning and frightening at times.

"He's a fool."

"Perhaps I'm the fool. Leaving my life behind, safe and wanting for nothing."

"Wanting a marriage with a man who has no trust in you? A man who doesn't treat you as you ought to be treated?" He snorted. "Listen to yourself."

Bugger it. Was Rooke right? Did I make excuses for a marriage that was completely wrong? And why?

"You know I'm right."

"What do I do now?"

Rooke picked up my hand, threading his fingers through mine. "You stay at the ranch."

I didn't have a choice but to stay at the ranch, but what wasn't he telling me? I could sense there was something else. Something he wanted to say.

"And what about Anthony?"

He huffed out a sigh. "He isn't the same man you once knew, darlin'. Trust me."

The way he said it made me think there was more to it.

His fingers curled around mine, clutching my hand. "He hasn't been the same man since before the war."

"Why? What happened to him?"

"Promise me something. Promise me you will not reveal

yourself to him yet."

He'd wound his way around my question, purposely not answering me. How could I promise him something when I didn't know what I would ride up to tomorrow?

"Tell me why."

When he looked up with a heavy sigh, I knew that telling me the truth about my brother could hurt me and it was the last thing he might want to do, but I had to know.

"He was injured in the war." His gaze found mine. "Badly. He's not the same man."

"Is that why you left? Is that why Helene left?"

"Yes. I helped her get away from him, and I paid for it with my friendship. The war changed a lot of men, Georgie. Some never recovered from it."

I tried to digest his words. My thoughts scrambled inside my mind at what kind of injury could have caused him to be so different. From the stories the others had been reluctant to share, I knew enough to know the war had been horrid. I wrestled my hand away from his, pressing it to my forehead while I thought of Rooke's young brother's life lost in the war.

The brother I knew wouldn't stay inside the house. Anthony loved the outdoors and everything about it. He'd ride for hours, hunt with my grandfather and the hounds, travel back and forth to London. Being inside, he was like an animal caged.

"Georg—"

"I need to think about this, Rooke. I don't understand it yet. Perhaps I will, but I don't at this moment."

"I'm sorry I didn't tell you sooner, but I can't regret it. You may not save him, and I need you to know that returning to New York is not an option for you, either."

My eyes widened. "You don't know that. If Anthony truly is not the same man he once was, I may have no other choice. I would never willingly return to my marriage. But we cannot be certain what lies ahead, Rooke."

He rose to his knees. "I would take you away from there before I allow him to send you back to the monster you married."

At his outstretched hand, I hesitated for a moment before sliding my hand into his and allowing him to pull me back down. He enclosed me in his arms, stroking my back for comfort before we settled back.

"Do you think Matthew or Cade told him about me?"

"No." His reply came quickly. Too quickly. "Matthew would never betray you. He adores you. And Cade, he and Anthony don't see eye-to-eye."

"But would they tell anyone else at the ranch?"

His shoulders bounced. "Can't say, but I'm thinking no. After weeks away, there's much work to be done. Wyatt and only half a crew can only do so much while the others were away. I suspect the ranch is in full swing, under Geezer's orders, of course."

I brightened. "Do you think Billy's back?"

"He'd better be or I'll be dragging him back."

His hand crept up my leg. I batted it half-heartedly away.

"I need to be out of these bindings." He nodded. "The sooner, the better."

"No one knows better than I, darlin'."

This man, I thought as I leaned into him. I'd been angry with him for not telling me about the truth about Anthony, but he had his reasons. I would determine whether those reasons were valid when I faced Anthony after ten years of not hearing from him, but his way of smoothing me over with his charm, I couldn't be angry with.

Chapter Thirty Two

"You ready?"

Settled into the saddle, reins looped within my hands, I considered Rooke's words carefully. Was I? After his confession last night, I had to question my readiness to face my brother after so many years especially after Rooke had warned he wasn't the same man he once had been after he'd been injured in the war.

Whatever had happened between Anthony and Rooke, the pain in Rooke was still fresh. It would have ripped open wounds he tried hard to bury.

At my grim nod, he clucked his horse into motion, with mine following behind. We trotted the sloping hills and flat landscapes before picking up speed. It would take most of the day to reach the ranch where Anthony's house and the other buildings were located.

Riding across land that belonged to Anthony felt different. Pride swelled in me as he'd succeeded in what he had set out to do. Even if Father had sent him money, Anthony had done this. Being on land that belonged to him made it real. It didn't matter if he was different now than he was then. He was still my brother. The one who protected me, fixed my hurts, and stood up for me. He knew what was best for me, always, and he would know what I should do now.

At the clip in which we moved, with a few rests every so

often, we made it to the ranch by early evening. As we got closer, the smell of the cattle intensified. Rooke only chuckled, telling me that I'd get used to it. Coming up over a rise, I saw the ranch buildings in the distance. Rooke slowed to a stop and waited for me to catch up, allowing me to take time looking at it. The large barn where they kept the horses, another enormous building behind it sat further to the left near a grouping of thick trees. The bunkhouse, Rooke explained, was a place I should not enter regardless of how well I knew the men I'd been traveling with.

My eyes scanned the area from the several paddocks next to the barn to the house across from them. A larger house by some standards of what I'd seen along our travels with a porch that wrapped from the front to around the side. Another grouping of trees behind the house stretched out for at least a mile.

I drew in a sharp breath. "It's now or never."

We lurched into motion and raced across the plains toward familiar faces. As excited as I was to see the boys again, they weren't the ones I wanted to see the most. It was Anthony. It had always been Anthony.

It took less time than I thought to reach the furthest paddock. A few horses grazed within the confining wooden fences, picking up their heads while we passed through. Finding no interest in us, they returned to grazing as quickly as they'd paused.

A man strolled out from the barn, his cowboy hat shading his eyes and a pair of those new popular denim jeans, and a plaid shirt rolled up to his elbows. I didn't wait for Rooke, swinging down from my horse into a slight bounce.

"I'll be right damned. When they said Rooke Preston was heading here, I thought someone was pulling my rope. I thought to myself: that couldn't be right the way you left out of here."

When the man removed his hat, his warm blue eyes caught mine with a smile. Hair, a dark blond, nearly reached his shoulders. "They said you were bringing with you a new ranch hand. Relation to Anthony?" He stuck out his hand. "Levi."

"George."

"Right nice to meet you, George. Them boys got it right? You relation to Anthony?"

"Levi." Rooke handed him the reins of his horse. "Did anyone tell Anthony I was coming? Or bringing with me someone who knows him?"

"No one's seen Anthony for days," came his reply, sending prickles of fear down my back. "We hear things coming out of the house so we know he's in there. But he hasn't come out."

"Where are the others? Did Billy make it back?"

"Geezer and Billy made it back a few days ago. Cade and Matthew did late last night. They're all eatin' and be right glad to know you're back." He grinned. "Why are you back?"

"Figured it might be time for a change."

"It's about damn time," came a deep voice behind us, laced with a British accent that had faded but remained.

The sound of Anthony's voice, rough and slurred with drink, widened my eyes before I turned to look at him. Frightened of what I might find, I kept my eyes shaded by my hat on purpose when I slowly looked up.

Levi gave Rooke a look that shouted 'good luck' before he led our horses away. Both Rooke and I faced the house where Anthony stood on the porch. I nearly cried out at the sight before my eyes, tears burning as they threatened to spill.

The same dark hair, albeit longer, sprouted on top of his head and the same warm brown eyes, except rimmed with red. His face looked haggard and drawn. The white shirt he wore looked about as dirty as mine had been at one time along the trail. Unbuttoned partially, and untucked from one side of his trousers, his suspenders hung down instead of over his shoulders.

He leaned heavily on a crutch, one leg of his trousers tied at the knee where his leg had once been. In his hand, he had a bottle he brought to his lips and gulped from. This couldn't be Anthony. He looked like Anthony, but different. My brother would not have let a war wound dictate his life.

I took a step toward him, Rooke's hand shooting out to grab hold of my arm before I did or said something ridiculous. Anthony's eyes narrowed at me.

"The hell do you think you're doing, you insolent swine?" he snapped, hobbling toward the stairs as though he'd come down to me. "I ought to have you horsewhipped."

"He didn't mean it, Anthony," Rooke said, keeping his hand on my arm. "He likes to help people is all."

Anthony kept his eyes trained on me. Did he see me? His sister? "Are you sure about that? Seems like he had a different idea."

"I'm sure."

Why wasn't he telling him I was his sister? Rooke had known from the beginning this was why I was here, and now we were. Why wouldn't he confess to Anthony who I was?

"What are you doing here? Thought you wouldn't be back. Especially since you left here with my wife."

Rooke stiffened. "I'm not sure what you're implying, Anthony, but I couldn't let her leave here alone. I saw her safely back to her family before settling in Abilene."

Anthony waved his hand flippantly. "Suppose you're looking for a job."

"You offering?"

Anthony shook his head, laughing coldly when he looked down at the floorboards beneath him. He swayed but caught himself before he fell over. When he looked back up, I held my breath in anticipation of what he might say to Rooke.

Rooke had been right. This wasn't my brother. I would have taken the bottle straight away, for it wasn't doing him any good. In fact, it appeared to be thoroughly wrecking him. Anthony wobbled, and I thought he would fall over.

"We'll talk." Anthony's eyes found me again. "Keep him away from me, Rooke."

We watched him hobble back into the house, disappearing through the front door with a slam of the screen behind. I released the breath I didn't realize I'd been holding. How did this happen? I thought wildly. How could he have not sent a single letter? I would have come to America sooner to help him. Didn't Helene try to help him?

Confusion swept through me, and I wanted to speak with Anthony. I needed to understand this. Only then would I be able to help him. And he needed help. I turned to Rooke, his hand dropping away.

"You need to wait until he's sober before confronting him. And even then, I'm not sure it's a good idea."

"What do you mean? I can't live like this forever, Rooke. I need his help, and clearly he needs mine."

After a quick look around to see who our audience might be and seeing none, Rooke took me by the arm again and steered me past the house and walked into the woods.

"Where are we going?"

"When I left here, I left my land and house. I still own it," he said with a grunt. "It's the only place no one will be listening to us, and the only place you can get out of those insufferable bindings. We can figure out what to do after we've had supper and rested."

I couldn't resist a glance behind us to make sure no one had seen us leave together. As far as we knew, there were only two people who knew my secret. Everyone else would expect me to bunk with the rest of the men.

"You have a house in the woods?" I asked, following Rooke along a trail through the woods.

"Wyatt said he's been trying to upkeep it for me on the off chance I'd come back. It's not too much further."

"You lived alone?"

"It's not big enough for anyone other than me."

The woods were brimming with wildlife. Birds flittered between branches while we walked, red squirrels scampered out of our way while I could have sworn I spotted a doe dining on leaves. We arrived at his house a few minutes later.

A smaller version of Anthony's house, it had a front porch and a few window panes in the front. By the looks of it, it looked big enough for more than him. If he hadn't been here in years, the house looked surprisingly sturdy.

When I followed him up the steps, he opened the door to a dimly lit interior that, after he lit the gas lamp, illuminated a cozy three-room cabin. The kitchen and dining area on the left I found surprisingly tidy. It looked like someone was already living here. The other side had a stone fireplace at the back wall and two doors, both open. I frowned.

"This looks big enough for more than one person. There are two doors," I pointed out.

"One is the bathing room. The other room is the bedroom." He hung his hat on a tall rack next to the door, swinging his arm to motion me in.

Mirroring him, I hung up my hat and stepped in. "This is nice."

Without looking at him, I wandered. The kitchen had a simple wood-burning stove and a basin for washing; the table was made of sturdy wood but was heavily scarred. There were only three chairs around it.

In the living room, two chairs near the fireplace looked worn but comfortable. His floors had well-worn rugs covering the hardwood, but where the rugs didn't cover looked free of dirt and debris. The temptation to run over and look in his bedroom pulled at me, but I walked with purpose instead. I turned around in the living room, catching him watching me with a smile threatening his mouth.

First, I looked at the room similar to the bathing room at

Rory's farmhouse with a large wooden tub in the far corner and it looked like a pump attached coming through the wall. Instead of a table, the fourth kitchen chair sat next to the tub with soap, a straight-razor, mirror and cloth.

Charming, I thought, sauntering over to the next door as Rooke ate up the distance between us. A simple mattress on an iron bed frame took up most of the space in the small room, a dark brown trunk tucked against the far wall below the window that faced the front of the house. In front of the bed, a tall oak dresser, likely filled with his clothing, stood.

I leaned against the frame of the door, leg kicked up behind me with my boot on the frame. Rooke leaned his arm over my head, his hand toying with the button on my shirt.

"Is this why you brought me here?"

The lilt of my voice drifted between us, causing the corner of his mouth to curl up. When he had his cowboy hat on, he looked magnificently handsome. Without it, when I could see the twinkle in his eyes, he took my breath away.

"No."

My heart pitched, but I knew why. I needed answers. Answers that Rooke had. Still, I pouted. "I have nowhere else to go."

"Darlin', you won't be leaving here soon." His fingers lifted from my buttons to my hair, threading through the ends until my eyes closed of their own will.

His mouth fell against mine a second later, coaxing my lips open with his tongue, and had my heart racing. If this continued, I'd not have my answers soon. And I didn't give a damn. I offered him a sigh, sliding my hands along his ribs.

"Maybe we should sit down," he said against my open mouth. "You need to know some things that I haven't told you."

I blanched, then sighed. "I need to know everything."

"He lost his leg, and he became an alcoholic. Not only that, but he has horrible nightmares." I followed him to the chairs, sinking into one and biting my tongue, waiting for him to start before I peppered him with questions.

Even in the shade of the woods, the inside of the house was stifling. Rooke opened the window between the fireplace and the kitchen to let air in before sitting next to me.

When he leaned forward, he stretched out his hand toward me and I tangled my fingers with his. "I brought you here because I knew your odds with getting through to him are slim. I have a very small hope that you can bring my old friend, the man we both know is in there, out of that monster." I nodded. "For now, you are not to go anywhere near that house until I can make sure it's safe."

"But—"

Rooke pulled me up from the chair and directly onto his lap, silencing me with a kiss that left me stunned. The strength of his hands molded to my body, even rising with me within his arms to bring me into the bedroom amazed me.

"Enough talking."

The door shut with a bang behind us and we didn't emerge until morning, having forgotten completely about supper.

Chapter Thirty Three

Light filtered in through the window, particles of dust catching my attention while I lay haphazardly wrapped in blankets on Rooke's bed. I would lie in bed all day if I could, but he'd risen long ago and gone to check on things around the ranch. Although I hadn't wanted him to leave, I knew he had things to do. Se- cretly, I'd hoped he spoke with Anthony and told him about me, although in my present position, that might not be wise.

He brought me a soft biscuit and a cup of coffee in bed before leaving with a tender kiss and a light slap to my backside. I couldn't eat the biscuit fast enough, ravenous after not having eaten for so long.

After a long stretch, having thoroughly enjoyed sleeping in a bed after so many nights on the uncomfortable ground, I vacated the bed with a blanket still wrapped around me while I went to the kitchen to pour out the cold coffee and see if there might be another biscuit.

I'd expected Rooke would be back soon, but I also knew that after so long being away, he likely had several things to get to. If he wanted to stay, he'd need to secure a job.

I glanced out the window on my way to the kitchen, eager to see Billy after his ordeal and Matthew and Cade. But more than anything, I wanted to see them as a woman, not a boy. It had been incredibly freeing to be without the bindings, and I wasn't sure if I'd put them back on. Rooke certainly didn't seem to want me to put them back on.

I opened the back window, emptying the coffee into the bushes before setting the cup on the counter in the kitchen as the door swung open.

"I hope you have more delicious biscuits," I said, opening a cupboard only to find dishes.

When I turned around, thankfully clutching the quilt to my chest, I gasped and stumbled back at the man staring at me with wide eyes. He had short dark blond hair and eyes that were the same color as Rooke's. When a grin spread across his face, dimples appeared on each side.

While he took in my appearance, I took in his. He wore a white shirt, trousers and suspenders and, unlike Anthony yesterday, he actually had his suspenders on. I pulled the quilt up higher. With my shortened hair, I wondered if he knew I was a woman.

He looked around. "I'm looking for Rooke."

"Rooke isn't here."

His gaze found mine again. "I can see that. I'm Wyatt. And you must be the new ranch hand?"

Oh no, I thought. Everyone expected Rooke to be returning with me, and I'd not appeared yet. "I'm, well, yes. And no." I sank into a kitchen chair, the wood creaking beneath my weight. "It's complicated."

As though remembering the door was open, he closed it with a quiet click but remained where he was. "You're not George?"

"I prefer Georgie, but those we traveled with only know me as George."

"You aren't a man."

My smile slipped. "No."

"Holy hell," he uttered, grabbing a kitchen chair and plopping down across from me. "What in the hell is wrong with my brother? Has he lost his mind bringing you here?"

"As opposed to where?"

When he looked back at me, his eyes narrowed. "You talk like Anthony."

"My brother. No one can know that yet. I've been searching for him. But I didn't know what happened during the war, and Rooke isn't sure what we should do yet."

"He can't keep you here!" He jumped up and paced. "What's he gonna do? Keep you hidden away, naked?"

Heat rose to my face, and I pressed a cool palm to one cheek. "I have clothing, I can assure you. I was . . . um."

He pinned me with a condemning look. "I know he's only got one bed. I *know* what you were doing." He shook his head, continuing to pace. "In all my years, I've never known him to do something so foolish."

The chair precariously teetered when I stood quickly. "Please don't tell. Please. Until we can figure this out. I will need to speak with Anthony, and I'm not sure how."

When he stopped pacing and we stared at each other, I felt self-conscious not being clothed speaking with a complete stranger. And asking him to not tell anyone about the situation, even with him being Rooke's brother.

He folded his arms in front of himself. "I'm sure as hell not going to tell Anthony. The man may be a cripple—"

"He is no such thing!"

He blinked a few times, likely surprised at being snapped at, and started again. "The man may have a hard time getting around, but he won't hesitate to have someone beat me senseless. I'm not telling him about you."

"Or anyone else," I prompted. "No one else can know."

"Sheeet. They said a new ranch hand was coming." I took a step toward him, not sure what I would do in only a blanket and nothing else. He held up his hands in surrender. "I won't say nothing to anyone else."

"Swear it."

He chuckled. "I swear. Damn, woman." I watched him hurry toward the door, yanking it open. "If you see Rooke, tell him I'm looking for him."

At the sound of someone approaching, Wyatt shot me one last look. "Never mind, I hear him coming."

As Wyatt was about to step out the door and close it behind him, I grabbed the door to go with him. Except we were both surprised that we were mistaken at who came down the path. I watched Anthony hobble over, stopping short at the sight of me.

My breath caught in my throat while he stared at me, his mouth popping open.

"Excuse me," he said. "Didn't know Rooke had company."

He didn't recognize me! I couldn't believe he didn't recognize his own sister, even with shortened hair. Not that now would be a good time for him to know I'd arrived on his doorstep after having traveled with his men to get here.

"He isn't here," Wyatt said, stepping in front of me. "Did you walk down here all by yourself, Anthony?"

"I need to see Rooke. He's been gone for years. Need to speak with him."

"I'll help you find him." Wyatt stepped off the porch, leaving me in the frame of the front door.

While Wyatt helped Anthony get turned back around, I couldn't help but see the look that Anthony cast over his shoulder at me. Caught off-guard that Rooke had a woman here, as Wyatt had been, but there was something else in his red-rimmed eyes. Was it recognition? I couldn't be sure until I spoke with him. Looking down at the quilt still fisted in my hand, I dragged it up further and retreated into the house.

Chapter Thirty Four

"You can't go wandering up to his house, demanding to speak with him."

I rose onto one elbow, looking at Rooke lying beside me. "And why not?"

"He's unstable, for one reason. And he's likely deep in his cups, is another. You need to wait until he sleeps it off, or until he's in a better mood." He reached out, toying with the end of my hair. "Trust me in this, darlin'."

"I am his sister. He will listen to me no matter what mood he's in." I flopped back, staring up at the beams of the ceiling. "He stared right at me and didn't recognize me."

"And a damn good thing he didn't."

His growl sounded charming.

"You know that he'd likely kill me for having you naked in my bed, don't you? This is not something I would like widely known."

I grinned. "You can't keep me here forever, Rooke Preston."

"Maybe I will."

In the haven of his house, cozy in his bed, I would consider it. But without being able to leave, and especially without the benefit of an excellent tea, I could never stay hidden away forever.

Even when darkness came as we lay entwined, Rooke sleeping in exhaustion beside me, I stared at the ceiling while wondering about my predicament. There had to be a way out of this. And the only way I could think of would be to go to Anthony and show myself. The hour grew late, and the longer I waited, the deeper he'd be in his drinking.

Carefully, I slipped out from under Rooke's arms and untangled my legs from his. Thankfully, his cabin was sturdy and had very few creaks in the floor. Able to dress myself quickly and slip out the door without a sound, I bounded across the forest floor toward the ranch. It was easy to find my way back, following the line of trees and delighted to find Anthony's house well-lit.

The closer I came to the house, the more anxious I became. While I didn't know what to expect, I knew that deep down, my brother was in there. Whatever may have happened between Anthony and Helene, my determination to help him overcome his internal battles had become more important than anything in my life. My own issues would wait.

As quietly as I tried to be, my boots still made scratching noises that made me cringe with every step. Other than an occasional hoot of an owl and the yaps of coyotes in the distance, the night seemed rather quiet.

When I reached the side of his house, I slowed my pace. Obnoxiously loud laughter from the bunkhouse carried across the lane, nearly drowning out the voices coming from Anthony's house. I walked carefully toward the front, until I stood at his open front door. The hallway directly in front of the door didn't allow me to see into the parlor or the room adjacent, but from the plume of smoke drifting out of the door on the left, I could deduce Anthony and his company were in there.

The inner door was open, with my only barrier being the screen door. Grasping the handle and dragging it toward me, I winced when it screeched in protest. The voices within continued, oblivious to the intruder sneaking in.

Once I stood in the hallway, I smoothed down my freshly

laundered white shirt. I'd purposely left off the vest and kept the two buttons at the neckline undone because of the heat. With any luck, Anthony would know exactly who had traveled thousands of miles to find him tonight. I'd also left off my hat, hoping he'd be able to see clearly this time.

"You've got plenty of land here, Anthony," I heard a man's scratchy voice. "Let me take some of it off your hands."

"Owen, you've got plenty of your own. Stay off mine."

"Helene left you. Who're you going to leave it to when you're gone? That no good friend of yours?" The man scoffed. "Run it to the ground, he will."

My heart thundered, and I became immediately irritated at whoever had spoken ill of Rooke. Taking in the deepest breath I could, I rounded the corner until I stood in the doorway and stopped when I saw not two of them, but four. All eyes immediately landed on me.

"Excuse me," I said, but my voice caught at the sight of Anthony in the chair with a glass half full of amber liquor.

"What the bloody hell?" he growled, struggling to rise and motioning to the two taller men.

I found my arms seized immediately, pulled into the room roughly. One of them had the blackest hair and eyes I'd ever seen, the other the opposite with light hair and pale blue eyes. The only other occupant stood back, amused at the unfolding drama.

I tugged, first one way then the other. All I succeeded in doing was being held more firmly. "It's me, Georgie."

Taking up his crutch, he tossed his head back in laughter. "How do you know that name? This has to be a jest. She wouldn't have come all this way. Not alone."

"I wasn't alone." I tugged against the two men, only to have them each firm their hold on me. They didn't know I was a woman. It only made me struggle more. "Unhand me. I am your sister, Anthony. I've come for your help."

He stepped toward me, eyes bloodshot. I watched him toss back another gulp of his drink. "Prove it."

"When Nigel Chrisley kissed me in the woods, you forbade me from telling anyone about it." I took in a few deep breaths. "Then you went over to his house and punched him in the mouth for daring to kiss your sister."

The lighter haired fellow kept his eyes trained on me while the darker-haired one looked at Anthony. "This true, Anthony?"

Anthony seemed to hesitate for a moment before sitting back down. "She could have told someone about that."

My mouth shot open. "Why ever would I tell anyone about that incident?"

At that moment, the screen door slammed open with a bang and a moment later, Rooke rushed in. Missing his hat and his shirt hanging open, his eyes found me immediately before turning on Anthony.

"Tell them to release your sister, Anthony."

I'd heard Rooke angry before. I'd heard him stand up for me before. But I'd never heard such a sinister growl come from him. Shocked that he'd spoken that way to the man who held his livelihood in his hands, I could only stare at him. As did the rest of those in the room.

Part Three

The question isn't who is going to let me.

It's who's going to stop me?

Chapter Thirty Five

Time held still, as though frozen, until someone made a move or said something to break the silence. Everyone looked at Rooke. Rooke looked at Anthony.

"Cash. Owen. Release her," Anthony finally said.

Abruptly, my arms were free. Rooke made no move to get closer to me. Even when the blond-haired man patted down my sleeve as though getting wrinkles out of the fabric. I yanked my arm away from him with a glare, stepping toward Anthony.

He wouldn't look at me. I cast my gaze over my shoulder until the darker-haired man walked forward. Although the darkness of his hair and eyes gave him an ominous look, when he smiled, it reached his eyes.

"Cash Tucker." He took my hand without my say-so, placing a kiss on my knuckles. "Town sheriff and your servant, ma'am. My apologies for my rough handling of you."

"Georgie. My name is Georgie."

"Yes, Cash." Rooke moved fully into the room, his presence a formidable force against the other men. He commanded without trying to. "We know you're everyone's servant. I'd like to know what Owen and Robert are doing here."

"Just leaving," Anthony said, remaining seated while draining the rest of his drink.

The man who'd been holding my other arm sidled closer

to me, his grin so wide I could see his crooked front tooth. "Owen Appleton, Anthony's neighbor." He tried to grab my hand, no doubt to kiss my knuckles as Cash had, but I clasped my hands behind my back. "I hope we see one another soon, Miss Georgie."

I'd rather not, I said silently to myself while he stepped toward the door and came face-to-face with Rooke. The men had no love lost between them, not bothering to hide their loathing for one another. The other man passed by me, casting his eyes down as he went.

Owen jabbed him with his elbow. "Address the lady, Robert."

His eyes met mine, a light brown that gave me a sense of wayward kindness. "Robert Appleton, at your service."

"You needn't be at my service," I said.

Owen and Robert slipped out while Cash lingered by the door, his black cowboy hat turning over in his hands. He gave me a crooked smile before settling it on his head and looking at Anthony. It seemed he waited for the two brothers to leave.

The door slammed shut after Owen and Robert and minutes later, the sounds of horses leaving echoed throughout the room.

"Anthony, please don't tell me you're thinking about it," Cash said.

"About what?" Rooke asked.

"Nothing for *you* to worry about." Anthony struggled to his feet, going immediately to the side table to pour another half glass of liquor. "I appreciate you stopping by, Cash."

Cash departed without another word, leaving Rooke and Anthony in awkward silence. I looked between them, prepared for an argument. Watching Anthony drink more alcohol grated my nerves, but I pressed my tongue between my teeth to keep from saying anything. He'd had the shock of the night with me barging in. I didn't want to upset him by lecturing him about his lifestyle of choice.

"Rooke," he said, settling back into his chair. "We'll have words tomorrow. You may leave."

It didn't look like Rooke wanted to leave me with Anthony, but I nodded to him. If I knew Anthony, he wasn't too happy that he'd found me at Rooke's house earlier that day wearing only a quilt around me. I'd need to explain my way out of that or Rooke would suffer his wrath. That was the price I paid for sneaking out the way I had.

"Georgie . . . " Rooke said.

"Her name is Georgiana." Anthony's slurred words contained a bitterness I'd never heard from him before.

Rooke didn't look bothered by it.

"I'll be fine."

"Rooke," Anthony said, his voice agitated. "You'll leave here now before I get angrier. We'll talk tomorrow. *Georgiana* will be fine in my care now."

With a tight jaw, Rooke turned and left. Before I strolled further into the room, I noticed that while Rooke had left the room he hadn't gone far and stood just outside the door. Anthony couldn't see him, but I could see part of his shirt. Ignoring the fact that he stayed to listen to our conversation, I continued looking at my surroundings. I noticed the fabric of the armchair Anthony sat in and how worn it looked. He must not be able to stand for long, I thought to myself. The rugs I walked upon were filthy. As I wandered toward the front windows, I noticed that there were layers of dust, as though no one had cleaned for years.

"That was you at Rooke's house earlier today."

I braced myself.

"What do you think you're doing?"

I rounded the room behind the chair next to his, glad there hadn't been a fire in the fireplace. Likely, it would have started a bigger fire as filled with old ashes as it was. The walls looked in decent enough shape with a dark blue floral wallpaper.

"Wondering how long it's been since anyone has cleaned this house. I'm assuming you have no regular housekeeper?" I said, sinking down into the chair next to him and swiping my finger on the circular table between us. It left a mark on the layer of dust.

"That is not what I asked." His voice remained the same, accent and tone, except for the slur in his words. "What do you think you're doing *here*?"

"I've been traveling for over a month to get here." I pursed my lips. "You never wrote. You promised."

He snorted. "You've known where I've been. I wrote to you as soon as we settled here. You never wrote back."

"I've never received a single letter from you. What I know, I only know from listening at doors when you wrote to Father and Mother."

When he looked at me, his eyes were half-closed. This could be the worst time for this conversation. What had happened that I hadn't gotten his letters?

"Mother," he growled. "She likely intercepted my letters, not wanting you to go running after me. She always feared you would."

"I'm in trouble, Anthony," I whispered.

Another snort. "I can understand that. It *was* you who I saw earlier. At Rooke's. Wearing nothing more than a bloody quilt."

"That's not the trouble I'm in."

"The hell you say!"

I couldn't stay seated while he berated me for my actions of late. This had nothing to do with Rooke. While I paced, he sipped his drink. "I left my husband in New York."

"You married?"

"Seven months ago. I wouldn't have, had I known it was Mother trapping me. He's as bad as she was. Controlling everything about my life. And then they left me there." I frowned.

"At least you're rid of her."

"They died, you know." I couldn't help the sadness sink in for losing my father. I'd always thought I would see him again. "In a shipwreck, after seeing me wed."

He frowned, then shook his head like he was trying to clear it. "Seven months ago, you say?"

"Mother pushed me to accept his proposal."

"But I received a letter from Father only a few months ago."

That couldn't be. Charles told me they'd died. I'd received no letters from them, only Grandfather. And he'd read them to me. I looked back at Anthony, wondering if now was the right time to be speaking of such things. Perhaps he was confusing a letter from Father from long ago. He had to be.

"And you ran away because?"

Everything that had happened since spilled out, even though by the time I'd finished he looked half asleep. I had no way of knowing how much he'd had to drink, or if he'd remember anything I'd told him.

"Perhaps we should continue this in the morning, Anthony. You look as though you're ready to be abed, and I should be—"

He looked at me sharply. "Don't even suggest it. You'll not be returning to Rooke's house. The spare bedroom is where you'll sleep. And you can use the clothes Helene left behind."

Anthony used his crutch to stand, swaying. Instinctively, I reached out. "Allow me to help you to your bed."

He swatted away my hand. "I don't need your bloody help. We'll discuss what you'll do tomorrow. I'll show you to your room."

It took him a painfully long time to get up the steps to the second level, but once we reached the top, he brought me to the door on the right and opened it to a room with a simple bed and dresser. Unwelcoming, I thought. Still better than sleeping on the ground. Looking at the bed, I realized I missed Rooke already. How I'd grown used to having him beside me at night, regardless of where it had been.

"The bath is downstairs behind the kitchen. Rooke figured out how to fill and drain the tub from the outside."

I chuckled. "I've seen."

That earned me another sharp look. "There is a trunk of clothing in here. Make use of what you can. I'll have the seamstress in town make you a suitable wardrobe ."

Once alone in the room, I sat on the bed, which felt surprisingly comfortable and clean, but dusty. Exhaustion claimed me, and I realized I had slept little the last few nights. I quickly shed my boots, stocking and trousers, wandering over to the window that faced the trail of trees, disappointed that I couldn't see Rooke's house. Elated that I finally had my brother back in my life had lifted me up, only to feel desolate without Rooke. He'd been my stability, my only stability, these last weeks. His absence affected me more than I expected it would.

I didn't bother with the trunk that night, simply lay down in my shirt and allowed the bed to swallow me up. When sleep claimed me, it claimed me quickly, and I sunk in so deeply that I didn't dream.

Chapter Thirty Six

I'd never felt so alone as I did upon waking the next morning, but I was so well rested I nearly bounced out of the bed. Sunlight streamed through the panes of the window, highlighting the dust in the room that I'd missed last night.

When I opened the trunk, it creaked and hissed like it'd been several years since opened. Inside were very few things. A couple of dresses, a petticoat, a corset and a pair of trousers that looked far worse than what I'd been wearing.

I put on the corset, but I didn't lace it as tight as it would have been with a ladies' maid to assist. However, it was enough. The fabric petticoat felt heavenly soft against my bare legs, but when I slipped into the light blue dress, I found it big on me. I fixed it enough so nothing indecent would show and went downstairs in my bare feet.

I hoped to find tea. Anthony, being an Englishman at heart, should have tea. The kitchen didn't differ from Rooke's except being enclosed with a longer tabletop and several cupboards. In the cupboards, all I found were some mismatched dishes with most of them chipped or broken and some biscuits that appeared old.

I shrugged, having eaten hard biscuits for many weeks. There was no tea, not even any intolerable coffee to wash down the biscuit that tasted like sand. Wandering into the dining room, it didn't take an educated guess to know Anthony rarely used this room with dust on the tabletop and eight chairs. The sideboard with a candelabra had as much dust.

I'd wandered back into the kitchen when Anthony came in, looking twenty years older than his true age. I wrinkled my nose. He needed a bath, a shave, and his clothing needed severe washing.

"That dress suits you," he said gruffly.

"It'll have to be taken in. I couldn't find any tea. If I'm going to be staying here, we'll need decent food and—"

"I never said you'd be staying here, Georgiana."

I leaned against the counter, folding my arms across myself with what I had left of the biscuit clutched in my hand. He hadn't called me Georgiana . . . ever. Anthony always called me Georgie. How much did he recall of our conversation last night?

"You would send me back to a man who would put me in a place I would likely die in?" I asked, appalled he would do such a thing. "Why would that be better than staying here with Rooke?"

A mottled color came over his face at the mention of Rooke. "You will not carry on with him. I forbid it. And you will go nowhere near the bunkhouse, either."

"I am a grown woman." I drew up my spine, standing rigid. "I've crossed half the country to be here, ridden with cowboys, been chased by outlaws. You may think you left behind a silly helpless girl, but I'm not her now, Anthony. I can make my own decisions, and I did so when I took my life in my own hands and left rather than be sent to a place to be experimented on, living in unhealthy conditions, and be forgotten. If I should decide to stay here . . . I shall do so."

He stepped toward me, unstable but menacing. "I never said you were not able to make your own decisions, but showing up on my doorstep unannounced doesn't make me liable for you. It doesn't force me to provide you food and shelter." I gasped. "I'm asking you to stop taking up with Rooke until this is settled."

We stared at each other. Moments ticked by.

"What happened to you?" I whispered.

There was a chill in his gaze. "I lost my leg in the war."

"But you're still alive, Anthony!"

"No." He shook his head. "I should have died that day in battle. Even my wife left me. I've lost everything but this ranch."

"Hmph, and you haven't lost it. Why? Because you have good people working for you. Wake up! Just because you lost part of your leg does not mean your life is over!"

When he took more steps toward me until we were nearly nose-to-nose, I witnessed the anger deep in his red-rimmed eyes. It took every bit of courage for me not to back down. This Anthony frightened me.

"You've come here to seek to tell me what I have?" The laugh that followed filled the kitchen with bitterness. "You know nothing. Nothing!"

"I know that I'll not return to a man who controlled me every bit as Mother did. And I'm not crazy. I'll not be sent to an institution. I'd sooner live the days as . . . as . . . "

"A man's whore?" He swayed back, using his crutch to steady himself. "That is what they'll know you as here. And that is all they'll know you as."

Warmth flooded my cheeks, and I pressed my palms to them as if to cool them. It did no good. I'd be as shunned here as I'd been in New York.

"What can I do, Anthony? Please. Tell me. And don't tell me to return to Charles. I did not cuckold him. I would never do such a thing. You know I would not."

The look he gave me didn't reassure me. "Ah, but you have. Have you not been carrying on with Rooke?"

A frustrated cry escaped from deep down. "You aren't listening to me! I only took up with Rooke *after* I left Charles. We're as good as divorced."

"I will deal with Rooke later. You will have decent clothing while you are here, and I will think about what I can do to better your situation."

"I'd just as soon write to Grandfather than return to my husband." I wanted to squeeze my eyes shut. "You said last night that Father had written to you recently."

"Three months ago." His eyes burned into mine. "Grandfather has died. I'm assuming by your suggestion to write to him that the information did not get passed along to you?"

I felt dizzy, clutching the counter for support. No . . . I whispered to myself. Not my grandfather. Not my sweet grandfather. And Charles had said nothing to me! That bastard!

"If there is anything to do about it, I may write to your husband to get a clearer understanding. This is not the place for you."

"You can't know that! Do you even know me anymore? You don't know yourself!"

Anthony turned to leave the kitchen. "You'll need to have someone bring you to town for supplies." He looked back at me over his shoulder, looking as though he swallowed a maggot. "Find Rooke and tell him to send someone with you to town."

"But, I thought you said—"

"I know what I said," he snapped, rubbing his hand over his forehead and squinting his eyes. "Find him and have someone *else* go with you. And that is all you'll do."

As I watched him leave, I noted his grimace. If he lost his leg three years ago, and it still gave him pain, it was no wonder he had fallen so deep into his drink. I shook my head, determined to stay and help him. If my mother hadn't interfered, I could have helped him years sooner. I wouldn't lay blame on her, but I would help him. And now I found out that everything I'd been told had been a lie. My parents were alive. Grandfather was not. Determination that I helped Anthony in exchange for not being sent away shot through me like lightning. I vowed to do everything I could to help him.

◆

"Excuse me."

I felt different wearing a dress after wearing trousers for so many weeks, the swish of soft petticoats against my legs instead of rough fabric a pleasant turn. While I'd been fearful about how much longer I'd need to continue the farce, it had been shockingly short-lived. Now, I approached Wyatt and Levi while they stood next to the paddocks closest to the barn as a woman.

I'd never been self-conscious, but the moment their eyes fell on me, I stopped. One shoulder of the dress continued to slip, forcing me to push it back. They stared at me with renewed interest.

Levi swallowed thickly. "Where did you come from?"

Sensing Wyatt would spill my secrets, I rushed forward. "I'm George. Georgie. I arrived with Rooke." Confusion flooded his eyes. Pink touched my face. "We met two days ago."

"Georgie." Wyatt smiled, smoothing his short hair back with his palm. Of all the men I'd met, he was the only one I hadn't seen in a hat. "You're looking fine this morning. What can we do for you?"

"I need someone to bring me to town for supplies. Anthony has next to nothing in the house, and I'll need to see a seamstress about some clothes." Wyatt's eyebrow raised a fraction, amused. "Anthony told me to find Rooke."

As if hearing his name as soon as it left my lips, Rooke strolled out of the barn and caught sight of us. It took him less than a moment to stride toward us, his eyes lighting when he saw me, quickly replaced by a frown marring his handsome face.

"Georgie," he breathed. "Everything all right?"

"As much as it will be, considering."

His gaze swept over me, from top to bottom and back again, a slow smile appearing on his lips. "You look . . . well rested."

That was most assuredly not what he would have said if Wyatt and Levi hadn't been our audience, but I kept quiet about it. "There wasn't much to say last night. Anthony was quite drunk."

"He's always like that," Wyatt quipped, earning a glare from Rooke.

"It won't be easy, getting him to open up." I nodded, remembering his warning. "I don't doubt you'll keep hounding him."

"Unless he sends me back."

"He wouldn't," Rooke said.

"He would. However, I might have bought myself time. He may be sympathetic to my plight, but that . . ." I looked at Wyatt, then Levi, before looking back at Rooke. "He isn't happy with my actions."

That knowledge soured Rooke's mood instantly, much to my dismay. We were both to blame for those actions, even though I wouldn't regret them. Anthony had been right that I'd been unfaithful to Charles, yet it wasn't the same as what had driven me away from New York. Anthony would never see what was between Rooke and I was different. It hadn't been me who had broken my vows. Charles had done so. Regardless if he accepted that our marriage had ended, it was to me.

I badly wanted to tell him what I'd learned in such a short time, but I didn't want anyone to know that I had a husband. Even estranged, those around would judge.

"I need someone to bring me to town for supplies. Anthony told me to find you and tell you."

"I can do it." Wyatt wasted no time volunteering.

Rooke scowled. "Don't you have things to do, Wyatt?"

A smile played on my lips at Wyatt's lazy shrug.

"I will take you to town," Rooke said.

"Wagon or horses?" Levi asked.

"Wagon. If we need things from town, we'll need something more than saddlebags. Knowing Anthony, he's unprepared to host his sister, even for a short time."

Levi graciously tipped his hat and wandered away to prepare a wagon. As much as I wanted to ride, a wagon ride would prove pleasant having not had one in such a long time.

"I don't believe Anthony had any interest in you taking me to town," I said. "In fact, it may make him angrier."

"I don't give a damn."

"Brother, you know how irate Anthony can get." Rooke only scoffed at Wyatt's point. He stepped closer, attempting to whisper. "Do you know what you're doing, Rooke? I mean, this is his *sister*."

"His *sister* can still hear you," I snapped. "I'm fairly certain I'll be safe enough going to town with Wyatt. You needn't suffer Anthony's wrath anymore, and you already will, given the circumstances."

Rooke wouldn't have it.

"You will go nowhere with anyone else but me."

There wouldn't be any changing his mind. Levi had the wagon hitched with a team of horses within the hour and I sat on the bench waiting for Rooke to finish what he'd been doing. Without a job here, I did not know what he could be doing.

While I sat there, I caught the eyes of several men coming and going from the bunkhouse. There were no hats or bonnets within the trunk to cover my short hair and continuing to wear the cowboy hat, even though it would have shielded the sun, didn't seem a good idea.

I saw Cade and Billy stride out of the barn and stop short, staring up at me with open mouths. The gesture brought out my smile, and I gave them a wave, despite my refined upbringing. It felt good not to need to be formal, even now when the farce had faded. Seeing Billy looking so much better than when I last saw him made me feel good.

Matthew, coming out of the horse barn and talking behind his shoulder, bumped directly into Cade. Cade spun around with a nasty glare and a few vulgar words that would have made my ears burn had it not been for the weeks I'd spent around these men. By now, I was well used to their ways.

"George?" Matthew grinned, bypassing Cade to approach the wagon.

"It's nice to see you, Matthew. Glad you made it back."

Matthew draped his arms over the side of the wagon while Cade and Billy strolled up beside him. Cade shook his head, squinting up at me despite the shade of his cowboy hat. Billy spit before looking up at me.

"I'll be goddamned," Billy murmured. "Now, I understand why you never jumped in the river with us. All of us . . . fools."

"Rooke wasn't." Matthew's sly admittance brought a fierce blush to my face. "He knew from the start. Can't fool him."

At the sight of Rooke striding from the bunkhouse, followed by a grim-looking Geezer, I couldn't help the flutter of my heart. I berated myself, knowing this needed to stop before I landed in a bigger heap of trouble. Already on shaky ground with Anthony, showing my feelings any time Rooke came around would only make it worse.

Saying nothing, Rooke climbed swiftly into the wagon and settled next to me while Geezer folded his arms across his chest, standing behind Matthew, Billy and Cade. His eyes narrowed, staring at me hard. I met his eyes, unwavering and refusing to be bullied. If anything, he wouldn't be able to do so now. Anthony wouldn't allow it, would he?

"Is there something you'd like to say to me, Geezer?"

"Leave it alone, darlin'," Rooke said, taking up the reins.

Matthew, Cade, and Billy touched their hands to hats in farewell as the wagon lurched forward. I presented him with my brightest smile while we pulled away. Geezer remained rigid, eyes never leaving me while we left.

"Can't let him get under your skin like that."

I huffed. "What makes him dislike me so much?"

"That's just how he is, and always will be. You need to leave it, and him, be. You may make a dent in Anthony, but you'll never be able to change Geezer. He's a hard old man, set in his ways. With Anthony, there's hope."

If Rooke thought so, then it must be true. Optimism swelled. I'd need a plan of action on how to approach him. Nothing I'd said or done last night had stuck, and this morning it had been worse. I could be short on my time here unless I convinced him otherwise.

"How much did you hear last night?" I asked, starting slowly.

"Enough."

"Anthony has asked me to stop taking up with you. Until this has been settled." I swallowed, watching him for a reaction. He stared straight ahead. "I thought you would want to know."

"He's right."

Inwardly, my heart sank to my toes. "I am a grown woman."

"And married."

"I left him, Rooke. Charles could have set the marriage aside by now." I doubted he would have. Charles had too much pride to have divorce taint his good name. And he'd lied to me about my family. What cause would he have to do such a thing?

Rooke looked at me then. "Do you think he's done that?"

Shoulders slumped, the dress slipped again, and I yanked it back up. "No."

"Anthony is right. I should have never taken advantage of you that way. I told you I wasn't a good man, and I meant it."

That straightened my spine. "You didn't take advantage. Did I give you any indication that I wasn't interested in participating in the hotel or in your cabin? What if I return to New York and Charles locks me in my room, starves me to death? Being sent to an institution for insane women is quite possibly the worse. Living with Charles, under his control, was terrible. I needed his permission to leave. He managed what I ate, how much I ate." I scoffed, recalling the night Benjamin asked me to be his mistress. "From time to time, he would advise me on what to wear."

His jaw clenched. "I won't let Anthony send you away."

Rooke saying it made me feel better. I'd trusted him from the beginning, and I still did.

I looked around at the passing scenery, groups of green trees dotting the landscape surrounding us with the rolling hills between. The dirt ahead of us was wide enough for two wagons to pass by one another, dry as the desert. Looking behind us, a whorl of dust followed.

We passed a wooden signpost that showed the way to Appleton Ranch. It had a similar look as Rutherford Ranch, a lane leading to the house and a ranch with hills, prairie and trees surrounding.

"Those boys last night . . . this is their ranch?"

Rooke shot a glance toward the lane leading to the Appletons. "Only after their old man, Wilbur, dies. Not sure that old goat will ever leave this earth. Not without a fight, anyway."

"Doesn't seem to like you much, that Owen."

"The feeling's mutual. He's nothing but a greedy bastard. Been after Anthony's land for years, but even on his worst day, Anthony will always refuse. There's no reason for Owen to have a need for more land. He's got plenty."

I let his words sink in. Having overheard part of their conversation last evening, it sounded like the sheriff had been there at the right time as well. Owen had been pressing Anthony for some of his land again. I gnashed my teeth together. All the more reason for me to stay.

"You'll need to see Delilah Burns when we're in town."

"Who is she?"

"She is the wife of the owner of the general store. Thaddeus makes sure the good people of Lone Point River have everything needed for supplies while Delilah makes sure everyone is clothed. She'll make you some decent dresses to wear." He smiled at me then, making my stomach flutter. "Not that you don't look fetching with it slipping off like that."

I took a swipe at his arm. Teasing me would not help matters if we were to stay away from each other. One misstep and we'd be right back in each other's arms. I was filled with anticipation, longing for that moment to happen again, and my heart leapt. This wasn't the time or the place. To make sure, I folded my hands in my lap and stared ahead to enjoy the rest of the ride into town.

Chapter Thirty Seven

The jingle of a bell overhead announced our arrival into the general store. Lone Point River had only the jail, general store, church, saloon, and livery. Being so small, the church served as the school, and the livery also had the blacksmith shop. For any other needs, someone would have to travel to Austin.

An older man with thick gray sideburns strolled out from a curtained doorway, beaming with excitement at the prospect of customers.

"Rooke Preston, I haven't seen you in years!" His voice carried loudly across the store.

"Good to see you, too, Thaddeus. I'm back now and not likely to leave soon." Rooke ushered me in by my elbow. "This here is Georgiana—"

"Georgie," I interrupted.

Rooke cleared his throat. "Anthony's sister. As you can see, she needs the help of your lovely wife and if you know Anthony as I do, she desperately needs supplies."

"Ah, my dear! Come in, come in. It's lovely to meet you."

"I leave you in capable hands," Rooke whispered into my ear. "I'll be at the saloon."

"Rooke!" I heard a whimsical voice, watching a much younger woman sweep through the same curtained doorway Thaddeus had. "Who's this?"

The woman, at least ten years younger than the man, had beautiful coppery-colored hair that wound and coiled around her head. Her eyes were bright with happiness.

"Georgie Rutherford," I said, hurrying over to take her hand. "In need of several supplies and a new wardrobe." I turned toward Rooke. "Are you still here?"

Rooke grinned, settling his hat back on and strolling out of the store. Thaddeus and Delilah seemed a delightful couple of people as they ushered me over to the counter.

"Do you have a list, dear?" Delilah asked.

"No. I'm not..." Oh dear, how would I say this gently without them taking offense? "I don't know much about keeping a home and what we would need to stock." I wrinkled my nose. "Anthony is not one for cooking or cleaning."

Delilah patted my arm. "Thaddeus will know what you need. He'll put it on Anthony's account. In the meantime, let's you and I talk about garments."

"I'll leave you ladies to it."

It warmed my heart to see Delilah glance after him while he sauntered away, looking up and down shelves and beginning to pluck things to set on the counter. She leaned over the counter with a piece of paper and quill.

My eyes widened, and I turned. "Might you have any tea?"

"A good English tea?" His eyebrow curved, and I nodded eagerly. "I do. I'll add it, and I will also make sure we keep it in stock for you."

With a sigh of relief, I turned back to Delilah. "My apologies. It's been so terribly long since I've had a good cup of tea. I can't go much longer with coffee."

"I'm not much for tea, but coffee with a nip of whiskey does wonders for me." I laughed softly. "Now, tell me what you have for garments and we'll narrow it down to what you need me to sew for you."

"It isn't much, I'm afraid. I arrived in trousers and a shirt. All that I found in the trunk Helene left is this dress, another poor excuse for a dress, a corset and petticoats. I'll need everything else."

She stood up straight. "Oh, dear. You really do need everything." I nodded. "Let's take your measurements and you can pick out fabrics, and I'll get started. I'm afraid I only have a dress or two that might suit you in the meantime. Follow me."

We walked back through the doorway into a parlor set with racks of clothing and bolts of fabric strewn over several surrounding tables. Another doorway led to a kitchen of sorts, and I assumed they lived upstairs.

Delilah showed me the fabrics that she had, and I picked out which types I would like dresses made from. I wouldn't need many things, a few day dresses and perhaps a pair of trousers and shirt tailored for me when I'd want to do more heavy work around the ranch or go riding.

"We come from Pennsylvania," she said, once she started taking measurements. "The winters became too cold for Thaddeus. We came down here to open a store."

"You have no children?"

Measuring the size of my waist, she shook her head. "We were never fortunate enough in that area. We are content with each other. What about you, Miss Georgie?"

"My marriage, in New York, has ended badly." I bit the inside of my cheek at my gentle lie. "I suppose it is a blessing not to have had that fortune."

"And Anthony?" she asked, switching to measure my inseam. "How is he faring these days?"

"Not good, but I aim to fix that."

When she stood up, eyes sparkling, I smiled. I liked her. I liked Thaddeus as well. Having a general store suited them well, for they were amicable people. I knew I'd be back getting more supplies before long.

"I wish you luck, but I'm not sure you'll need it. Seems like you have a good head on your shoulders, and a good heart as well."

"How long will it take you for the garments?"

"It will take me some time, but I will start immediately and send word when I have some of it done for you. In the meantime, let's see what might fit you over here." I followed her to a rack, and she pulled out a pale pink dress trimmed with white with belled sleeves at the elbow.

I nodded in agreement, and she pulled out an ivory colored dress with tiny green flowers. Again, I nodded. She ushered me into a small alcove with another curtain to try them on.

Delighted that at least one of them fit, I called her and handed the pale pink one back with good news that the ivory dress had fit perfectly. "You keep that one on then," she said. "If you want this blue one, I can take it in for you. No charge."

"I must insist on paying you for all your labors, Miss Delilah!"

"Please, call me Delilah. And I insist. Think of it as a welcome to town gift. I do hope we'll be seeing more of you."

I emerged from the alcove, unable to resist a twirl. It felt liberating to be in a fitting dress again. Thaddeus chose that moment to duck his head in with news that he'd brought the supplies out to the wagon already, including tea.

"You've been angels sent from heaven," I said while we walked back to the front of the store. "I am so glad Rooke brought me to you. There is no doubt I'll be back."

Delilah clasped my hands. "You'll need to be! I'll send word when I have your clothes done. Shan't be long."

At the door, I turned to give them a friendly wave. Two of the best people I'd possibly ever met in my life, they'd made me feel welcome and wanted in this town. And Thaddeus had tea! That itself delighted me so much I had a spring in my step, crossing the street toward the saloon where Rooke said he'd be.

Sheriff Cash Tucker sat outside the town jail in a rocking chair and tipped his hat toward me when I passed by. I gave him a nod on my way, unsure if I should stop and talk with him yet. Having the town sheriff as a friend wouldn't be a bad thing.

"Georgiana Rutherford?" he called, rocking up to his feet. "A word?"

Bugger it, I thought and stopped in the middle of the street. Changing my course of direction, I moved toward the lawman and hoped it would be a brief conversation. I didn't want any trouble.

"Good afternoon, sheriff."

"Afternoon, ma'am. I'd like to apologize for being rough with you last night." His mustache twitched. "I didn't realize you were Anthony's sister."

"No apologies are necessary. You couldn't have known."

"Anthony is well today?"

"As well as can be, I suppose."

"All the same, I thought it would be fair to give a warning about Anthony."

Chapter Thirty Eight

My ears perked up. A warning? What could he possibly have to warn me about my own brother?

Cash tucked his thumbs into his pockets, rocking back on his heels. "You ain't going to change him, you know."

His words had anger simmering the moment they were out of his mouth. My eyes narrowed. Sheriff or not, he didn't know what I might be capable of. As he hadn't known Anthony as long as I had.

"With all due respect, I'll not be leaving here until I try."

He untucked his thumbs, standing up straighter. "Don't get me wrong, ma'am, I'd like to see him back to his old self."

"As would I. And you may call me Georgie."

The smile beneath his mustache brought out a kindness in his eyes I didn't think I'd see in the sheriff.

"You'll call on me should you need me?" I gave him a quick nod. "Good day to you, Georgie."

I watched him stroll back to his chair and continued to rock. The man had a thing with rocking either in his chair, or on his heels. Despite that, I stepped up onto the boardwalk across the street, pushing open the double doors under the eaves of the saloon.

There were few inhabitants within the hazy interior, some men playing cards at a table while others leaned up against the bar at the back. Rooke had his back to me and when my eyes swept the rest of the room, I saw Owen Appleton at the other end of the bar with his eyes on me. Disgust crept over me.

"Good afternoon."

A woman with dark hair, swept into a bun and wearing a stark white apron, walked smoothly between the tables, a dirty rag clutched in her hand. While her face seemed severe, her dark eyes were warm in greeting.

"I'm here to collect Mr. Preston."

"Rooke said you'd be by. I'm Stella. That's my brother behind the bar." I darted a look around to see a man with much lighter hair than she, sweeping a rag over the top of the bar while speaking with Rooke. "You're Georgie?"

I nodded. "Anthony's sister."

"Anthony didn't join you?" I shook my head, noting the fall of disappointment in her eyes. "How is your brother these days?"

"As well as he can be." I'm an eavesdropper, not a matchmaker. But I could see something in her eyes. The tiniest spark of interest."Do you know my brother well?"

Her eyes dropped. "I haven't seen him for the longest time. Before, when he used to come in from time to time, he was so kind to me. Always laughing and teasing."

There it was. But Anthony had been married then. He was free to remarry, even if he didn't know it yet. "I'm here to bring him back to the way he used to be."

"Oh, I do hope so. The last time he was in here, he threw a fit when Tanner wouldn't allow him any more whiskey." She waved her hands. "Please come in. Can I get you some cider? A beer? Maybe whiskey?"

"You don't have any tea, do you?"

She laughed, darting out of the tables to the open aisle and leading the way toward the back. I could feel Owen watching me while I followed her but kept my eyes anywhere but on him.

"Afraid not."

"Cider will do fine." I stepped up next to Rooke, who looked over at me lazily with a wink.

I couldn't help but notice his eyes sweep over my change of dress with an appreciation in his hazel-blue eyes, warmth blooming in my chest at his daring perusal. "Everything taken care of?"

"Thaddeus loaded the supplies in the wagon. He'll need to order some things, and Delilah will send word when she has some of the clothing done up for me." Stella set a cup of cider in front of me. "They're wonderful people."

"Aren't they just that?" Stella's brother said. "Tanner Strahan, at your service."

"This is Georgie." Stella elbowed him lightly in the ribs. "Maybe her being here will do Anthony some good."

"Now, wouldn't you like that, little sister?"

I watched Tanner sidle away, a devilish gleam in his eyes that made me wonder what the sibling bantering was about. Either way, those I'd met in town seemed friendly enough.

"Nice to see you today, Miss Georgie." I wanted to ignore Owen's voice from the end of the bar. "My apologies for the misunderstanding yesterday evening."

Rooke straightened, the line of his jaw hardening.

"The next time we have a chance meeting, I'll behave myself." When I caught his eyes, it was filled with a promise that chilled me into believing I would be better off not having another meeting with him.

"We should go." Rooke gulped down the rest of his whiskey.

I looked down at my cider, picking it up and drinking down as much as I could before Rooke had me by the arm, pulling me away. Stella's eyes widened, but she darted quickly around the bar and followed.

"Might I call on you, Georgie?"

"I'd like that. Very much so." I called behind my shoulder. "Thank you for the cider."

Once outside, I yanked my arm away and gave Rooke one of my nastiest glares before striding toward the wagon. I only knew he'd followed me by the sound of his boots crunching on the dirt.

Despite my skirt, I scrambled into the wagon, feeling his firm hands at my waist. I quickly pushed them away, pinning him with another glare when I turned toward him. "That was uncalled for."

When he sat down beside me and picked up the reins, he merely smiled. I swatted his arm, huffing when it went unaffected and flounced back down with my arms folded over my chest.

"If we'd have stayed, there'd have been a fistfight."

"You?"

"I'd have knocked his teeth down his throat. And I'll be damned if I'll let you have another *chance* meeting with him." His eyes found mine. "There shouldn't have been one last night."

I'd been wondering when he would bring it up. "I'm sorry for sneaking out last night, but I had to. You wouldn't have let me go otherwise."

"For good reason. Talking to Anthony when he's drunk won't do any good. He won't listen. Sneaking out last night to approach him was stupid."

I pulled a face at the insult. "Stupid? Stupid, am I?"

"That's not what I said."

I huffed again. "What would you have me do? He'd already been there earlier, and after everyone said he rarely left his house. And he didn't even recognize me! His own sister. Were you going to keep me naked in your house forever?"

That smile teased his lips. The one that had my heart thumping in my chest. Damn him, I thought. Why did he have to be handsome? I looked away before doing something stupid again.

"As much as I like the thought, it wouldn't do either of us any good. You'd be trapped, and I'd . . . not be worth a damn knowing you were naked in my house."

We'd need to get back to the ranch before I got into serious trouble. I needed to stay here and help Anthony, but with Rooke here made me doubt my self-control. I didn't know anyone like him. Had I met him in New York, had he been the one to approach me on becoming his mistress, I might have taken his offer.

"What are you going to do?"

I straightened my spine. "I'm going to learn everything I can about ranching." When I looked at him, I thought he was choking until I realized he was only shocked. "And somehow, you're going to be the one to teach me."

◆

Rooke didn't know what to say to me after that. If he agreed, he'd be giving me reason to believe he would, and that would be as good as his word. If he didn't agree, he knew I'd be upset.

"There's a lot more to learning to ranch than you think. And I'm certain Anthony won't let you anywhere near me for the time being."

"I won't give him a choice."

"You're playing with fire."

"I'm playing with my life. Mine. Anthony has no say, and he hasn't for many years." Not that it had been his fault my mother had interfered. "But I am determined to help him overcome whatever has him in a bind. Maybe then he'll see reason."

Rooke slapped the reins, the horses picking up speed as we moved further away from town. He was likely eager to get back to any kind of work this late in the afternoon. "Do you think he'll try to send you back to New York?"

"It is a possibility. But I'll put up a fight. If he knows me at all, he'll see it coming."

Rooke leaned back against the seat and laughed deeply. "I can't wait."

When we arrived at the ranch, there were more ranch hands standing outside, gaping at us. Thankfully, Anthony was not present. Rooke stopped the wagon outside the horse barn and jumped down, his hands firmly on my waist until my feet touched the ground.

"Let's get you home," he said, putting his hand to my back and pushing me gently toward the house.

At Anthony's doorstep, I wanted him to kiss me but knew it would be impossible now. Even with the house silent behind me, there were too many ranch hands around. Too many eyes and ears. I couldn't risk it. Rooke wouldn't risk it.

"You know where I'll be should you need me."

Rooke strolled away, leaving me on the front porch. The house seemed oddly quiet, but I'd not been here long enough to know Anthony's habits. I went inside, slowly stepping down the hallway. Sprawled in the same chair he'd been in last night, he had a decanter in his hand instead of a cup.

"Damn you, little sister," he slurred. "Couldn't have stayed away. Had to come here to dredge up the past."

"Oh, Anthony. Really." I marched over to him, grabbing the decanter out of his grasp.

"Give that back."

"I absolutely will not. You'll be going to bed, and you'll be staying there until you sleep, whatever this is, away. Then you and I are going to talk. When you are sober. And you won't be taking up another drink until I say so."

I helped him up from the chair, but he staggered and nearly toppled us both over. After I grabbed his crutch and leaned him on it, he seemed to stabilize but getting him up the stairs had its own challenges.

"Why did this happen to me?" he wailed when we reached the top, me pushing against his back so we didn't both fall backwards down the stairs. "Why? I've lost everything. Everything!"

"Not everything, you fool. You have a lot to live for. Stop wallowing."

I helped him into his room, which smelled so foul I had to be quick to get him to lie down. This house needed a good cleaning, and I didn't know the first thing about cleaning a house.

Anthony lay on the bed, moaning, and I rolled him to his side to make sure he didn't vomit and choke on it before I propped his crutch near the side table. The curtains remained shut. I pulled his boot off the one leg he had, pulling the blankets up over him.

When he had quieted, I went to the door and looked back at him. My heart ached for my brother, for whatever he had suffered through had to be tormenting him. Nothing I could do would take those horrors away, but I would stop at nothing to improve his life again. I would do anything.

Chapter Thirty Nine

To my delight, Stella came by the very next day, helping me hour after tireless hour to get the house clean enough to live in. Not only did my newfound friend help me clean, she showed me some things in the garden that I could easily do, as well as some simple recipes to prepare.

Since then, I ferociously continued to clean the house. After having servants my entire life, it surprised me to no end how many things within a house needed to be cleaned. I would never take help for granted again. There was nothing to be done about the sad shape of the dishes in the kitchen, but it didn't stop me from cleaning out the cupboard.

I didn't know the first thing about cleaning out a fireplace, but with a bucket and a shovel, I figured it out on my own. Cooking took on a whole new meaning, starting out with a few simple things. Although edible, I admitted to needing a lot more practice. I'd not had the chance to meet the bunkhouse cook, Mack, after being forbidden from going to the bunkhouse, but I knew the men had one. He might be a dual-purpose employee, but he made sure the men ate.

Anthony hadn't been happy when I announced there would be no liquor in the house, throwing his crutch at me. It had promptly hit the wall, his aim awful. He stayed in his room sulking throughout most of the days I'd been cleaning.

Finally, days later, I'd done enough chores to deserve a day off.

I leaned against the house in the shadows of the porch, wearing the same ivory dress Delilah had given me when Rooke and I had gone to town, but I'd left the petticoats off because of the heat and my feet were bare.

No one knew I was there on the porch, watching.

Rooke and Cade were in the paddock directly across from the house, working with a horse that didn't appear to like what they were attempting to do. It continued to buck and skitter away from them, even Cade. Billy, Wyatt and Levi sat on the top rung of the wooden fence next to the barn, watching.

Pushing away from the house, I moved toward the steps until I could feel the sun on my face and leaned against the post. My hair was a bit longer now, although still short enough to still pass as a boy to some. I could feel the tickle of the strands against my neck beneath my ears. I'd be the first to admit how much I wanted my hair back. The entire length of it. That would take years.

Levi saw me first, catching my gaze and grinning at me from beneath the rim of his hat. Wyatt's eyes followed, settling on me with his hawk-like eyes. I sank down, sitting with my back against the post and my legs stretched out along the top step. With my bare ankles crossed, I sighed in content while watching the men in the paddock from my perch.

"He'll never love you like that."

The sound of Anthony's voice, not slurring and not rough, would have been welcome to my ears had he not said such a rude thing. I hadn't heard him come out of the door, having fixed the screech of the screen door while I'd been ferociously cleaning.

I didn't look at him, even though I wanted to know what he looked like after so many days of being shut up in his room. Instead, I kept my eyes on the man within the paddocks.

"I don't need him to. I'm married." Even as I said it, Sarah's words haunted me that it didn't matter to Rooke, and it wouldn't matter to me. I knew that it didn't matter to me, but I'd be damned if I admitted that to Anthony.

"Doesn't matter if you're married. Are you going back to your husband?"

"No," I whispered. "The minute I left, I knew I'd never return."

"You'll stay away from Rooke."

I whirled to stare at him, fire in my eyes. "I won't."

Anthony limped toward me, looking haggard but well-rested. "You'll stay away from him and every other damn man on this ranch. Or I'll start picking them off one by one."

I gasped, unsure if he meant he would kill those who worked for him or leave them without a job. But it mattered to me. I wouldn't see anyone hurt because of me. Especially Rooke, who had done so much for him. He'd have lost this ranch had it not been for Rooke stepping up.

"I mean it, Georgiana."

"Georgiana, Georgiana," I mimicked. "You never used to call me by my given name. I've always been Georgie to you. I am a grown woman now and deserve to be treated with some civility."

When he came closer, I clamored to my feet in case I needed to catch him from falling. We stood on the porch, nearly nose-to-nose. Eyes still bloodshot, he sorely needed a bath and a shave.

"I'll be damned if anyone lays one finger on you. And that includes Rooke."

I moved past him, unable to stand hearing his threats any longer. Hand on the handle of the door, his next words crashed into me so hard I had to grip it or fall into the door.

"Besides, he's married, too."

Chapter Forty

"Where is his wife?" I forced myself to speak calmly, hand still on the door handle. I turned away from Anthony.

"Gone. She left him, just as Helene left me."

"After the war?"

He chuckled. The first time I'd heard such a sound come from him since I'd arrived. It wasn't a joyous laugh. More like a menacing one. I counted it as a laugh, all the same.

"Not long after they were married."

I spun around to face him, laughing so loudly that the eyes in the paddock turned toward us, curious. "How do you know he's still married, Anthony? How do we know *I'm* still married, for that matter? Charles could have set the marriage aside as soon as I left. He never could stand for embarrassment and a wife accused of being unfaithful, then leaving in the middle of the night. That might have been too much for him."

He shrugged.

"That's all you've got?" I snapped. "Anthony Edward Rutherford, I've spent the last two days cleaning your house, scouring surfaces, beating out rugs, digging out the fireplace and trying to figure out how to cook. You will not send me back to New York." I poked a finger into his chest. "Unless it's in a black box. Dead is the only way I'll return to my husband."

His eyes lit in surprise at my audacity, but he didn't back

down. Nor did I.

"You'll go down to the creek to bathe because you stink to high heaven while I scour your bedchambers, then you'll have some of that bread and jam Stella was kind enough to bring us. And then, only then, will you and I sit down to talk."

He opened his mouth, but I pointed to the creek.

"Go!"

I couldn't be sure I'd ever been so angry at him, or that Rooke had a wife he'd never mentioned, but while Anthony took himself off to the creek for washing, I busied myself with getting his bedroom cleansed and aired out. Several times I'd had to bite back vomit while I cleaned, but by the time I heard him return, I'd had it clean enough. The window would need to remain open for a long while, if not all night.

When I met him in the kitchen, he made good on my order to eat and with his wet hair; he looked as though he'd needed a haircut months ago. I knew nothing about cutting hair and shaving. I'd need Stella's help again, help I would assuredly get with no issue.

I slid into the chair beside him, noting he still looked tired.

"Anthony, things will get better." I reached out for his hand, only to have him yank it away from me. "I promise you, they will."

"You haven't any idea what I've been through." His voice held such vehemence. I flinched. "You need to leave me alone. And best to do that by going back to New York."

"You would send me back to the lion's den?"

"If I have to, yes."

"And if he does send me to an institution for crazy women because of a misunderstanding? You're fine with his decision?" That forced his eyes to meet mine. "Are you?"

He slammed up from the table, walking faster than I thought he would be able to with only part of his leg. Calmly, I gritted my teeth at the table while he left the room to give him a few moments before I went after him.

I found him in the parlor, sitting in his chair. Without a drink in his hand but looking as though he needed one badly. I drifted in. He'd need to go through me first to get one, and I wouldn't buckle so easily.

"You're rotten," he said, red creeping up his neck. "You're a rotten sister, Georgiana. Give me my bottle back."

"No."

"Give it back!"

Yelling certainly wouldn't get it back, I thought. "You'll not have another drink, Anthony. It is making you worse every day. You don't need it. It won't make any of your problems disappear."

"It will, damn you!"

At the sight of him nearly in tears, my heart cracked wide open. I needed to remain firm. He would drink himself to death. It surprised me he hadn't already. When he stood back up and reached for me, I shrieked and moved away quickly before he could grab me.

"You will not have it, Anthony. I swear, you'll not touch another drop of it."

He turned angrily. "You will not order me around like our bitch of a mother. If I want a drink, I shall have one and no one is going to stop me. Not you. Not Helene. Not anyone."

I whirled, unable to take his shouting any longer. He could tear the house down looking for a bottle, but he would never find one. They were gone. I ran out into the sunlight, teetering on the top step at the five men rushing at the house.

One by one, except for Wyatt, they removed their cowboy hats while looking up at me. I braced myself against the posts, catching my breath. Did they think to rescue me from Anthony's wrath? If so, we'd only begun.

Rooke stepped forward. "We heard shouting."

I looked past him at the horse dancing around in the paddock, in celebration that the men had left him alone. Leaning against the post, I tilted my head up.

"It's not the last you'll hear."

"If you're in danger . . ." Rooke took another step forward.

"I'm not in any danger. Anthony is my brother. I can handle him." Doubt shone in his eyes. "I will handle him."

"Pardon me." Cade stepped closer. "If you don't mind me saying, Miss Georgie, but Anthony isn't the same."

"Yes, yes." I waved my hand. "I know. We'll get through this. We will."

"And if you don't?" Rooke asked, concern set deep in his eyes.

I shrugged. For I truly didn't know.

Chapter Forty One

Shouting roused me from sleep the next morning. I wondered briefly if I'd been dreaming about it until I heard it again. I scrambled out of my bedchambers, running down the stairs to see Anthony on the porch through the screen door.

The door slammed into the house when I ran outside. Rooke and Anthony stood on the porch. My brother had his fist wrapped in Rooke's shirt as though he would strike him.

I did the only thing I could think of. I grabbed Anthony's arm until he released Rooke. A crowd had gathered outside of the house, some men I recognized and others I'd never met before.

"Stop this right now." I released Anthony. "What in God's name are the both of you doing out here arguing at this time of the morning?"

Both of them turned to me with wide eyes. I staggered back at the anger brimming in Rooke, then in Anthony. What was wrong with them?

"Get back in the house!" Rooke yelled.

"What the hell do you think you're doing?" Anthony yelled at the same time.

Looking between the two of them, I wondered why they were turning their anger on me when I realized I'd run out of bed in nothing but my shift. I covered myself with my arms and backed up toward the house.

"I heard shouting," was all I could utter before fleeing back inside.

When I ran back up to my bedchambers, I didn't hear any further arguments outside and hoped I'd at least put an end to anything between them. My back hit the door as soon as it closed, face reddened. I pressed my palms to my cheeks, feeling the warmth in utter dismay.

It would be a miracle if Anthony didn't give me a set down. After that display, he had every right to send me packing. My first misstep, and it had been a big one.

"Georgiana, get down here."

I bristled at Anthony's distant voice, as though he were standing at the bottom of the stairs. With his struggles to get up the steps, I didn't doubt he hadn't come up. Bracing myself, I shoved away from the door.

Several minutes passed before I had the courage to leave my bedroom to face him. I found him glaring at the unlit fireplace, hands braced on his crutch and his remaining leg stretched out. I knew I'd behaved badly. He didn't need to remind me of it. But undoubtedly, I knew he would. Not only had I shamed myself in front of half the ranch hands, I'd brought shame upon him. But I did so under duress.

When I wandered into the parlor, fully dressed, I deliberately slowed when I walked around to face him. Lips set in a thin line, his eyes stared into nothing, and his jaw was tense.

"Anthony, I thought someone was getting hurt."

The words tumbled from my lips quickly. When his eyes snapped up to meet mine, it was impossible to mistake how upset he was. Animosity danced in his blue orbs. There were no words I could give him to right the wrong that I'd done.

"If you are to stay here, even for a short amount of time, you will behave as a young lady should." He pushed to his feet, using his crutch and moved to the fireplace.

When he looked my way, my excitement leapt. The words

I heard were that I would stay. Yes, of course I will behave! I wanted to shout, but I clasped my hands before me and stayed quiet. Knowing Anthony, he had more to say.

"There are reasons I told you not to go into the bunkhouse." I opened my mouth to argue, snapping it shut at his glower. "These men out here, they don't see women prancing around, especially in a state of undress. Women are so few out here that men order brides from the east. Things are different. I risk trouble among those men were you to get involved with any of them. Stay away from them."

I nearly trembled in anger, but my excitement won over. Biting my lip, I hoped he wouldn't see through me, for I had no intention of staying away from everyone, but I didn't plan to go into the bunkhouse, stepping outside like I had, or entertaining any man on this ranch alone. Aside from Rooke, there were no other men I would take an interest in. And I'd only found out he was married, too.

"I meant what I said, Georgie." His voice softened a fraction. "Including Rooke."

"I haven't—"

"You don't think I know he was the one who accompanied you to town?" His eyebrow arched. "I may not leave this house often, but I know what happens around this ranch. I won't have your name sullied more than it already is. I can't."

"He brought me to town for supplies, and that is all. I promise. Haven't you seen everything I have done here for you? Everything I am trying to do for you?"

"You mean to stay, then?"

I nodded, my eagerness betraying me.

"I need my whiskey, Georgie. But I will delay any messages and not send you away. For now."

"You cannot have your whiskey. It's killing you. I won't let you die, Anthony. I won't, even if you try to send me away." Stepping over to him, I grabbed his hand. His face turned sour. "I will help you."

He tried to shake me away. "You can't help me."

"I will. You only need to give me a chance. We will do this to-gether, you and I."

My expectations that he'd trust me were not high, but I hoped it would give him a small bit of acceptance. And he'd called me Georgie. That little hope was all I needed.

A knock resounded on the front door. I heard Stella calling through the screen door. Anthony scowled at the intrusion, but a grin split my face and I hurried away from him.

"Stella, come in! Come in!"

Arms laden with garments, I pulled her in. "Delilah caught word I'd made plans to come back to help you today and asked that I bring you these."

While she transferred the load into my awaiting arms, her eyes caught Anthony coming to the door of the parlor and leaned against the frame. I watched her mouth fall open at the sight of him, and I suspected it had been a while since she'd seen him.

"Stella, do you know how to cut hair and shave? Anthony sorely needs both."

I left a flustered Anthony to Stella while I brought the gar-ments to my bedchambers. There wouldn't be enough time to sift through them, so I laid them out on the bed and marveled at the work Delilah had done in such a short amount of time.

By the time I returned, Anthony was ticking off all the reasons he didn't need a haircut and a shave, or any help, for that matter. I scoffed, and by the look on her face, she didn't believe him.

"Anthony, you'll feel better if you have a cut and a shave. Please."

"You will," she prompted. "I do it for Tanner. You can trust me."

Anthony rolled his eyes. "If it stops the two of you from con-tinuing to badger me, I'll do it. Helene left toiletries in that room back there." He pointed to the room opposite the kitchen.

While Stella settled Anthony in the kitchen, I ventured into the room with a neglected, oversized bathtub. I found a comb and scissors, returning to Stella. After filling a bucket with water, I collected a handful of towels and returned to the kitchen. "I'm sorry for putting you to work. Again," I said, setting the bucket and towels down on the table next to her. "It seems that's all you do when you're here."

"I don't mind." The look she gave Anthony couldn't be missed.

"One day, I will have you over for tea and we shall not do any work."

"I would like that very much." Her timid smile gave me some relief, and I had a feeling she had found joy in being in Anthony's company, though he rudely said nothing.

I busied myself getting Anthony a biscuit with jam while Stella set to cutting his hair. I heated some water in the kettle over the stove and after a short time, handed him a cup of tea.

He looked at it as though he'd never seen such a thing before. "It's tea," I said.

"Why are you giving me tea?"

"That's what we drink." He pinched his lips together but sipped it to appease me and said nothing else.

It didn't take long before he handed the empty cup back to me. Victory! I wanted to shout. A small one, but a victory all the same. We would take this one day at a time. I knew it wouldn't be easy, for he'd changed from a happy, jovial young man to a bitter old man instead of nearly thirty over the course of ten years. Even a miracle wouldn't change him back overnight.

"What was it you and Rooke were shouting about this morning?" I asked, making myself busy with kneading dough for more biscuits.

"You," he growled.

"Me?" I whirled around, heedless of the flour on my palms.

"Why ever for?"

"He wants you to learn things around the ranch. I told him you have enough to do around the house, and don't need to learn anything about ranching. That's for him and the boys to handle."

"Does that mean you're hiring him back?"

"That's between us, not you."

I glowered. "And what about defending myself?"

Snip, snip, snip. I tried not to pay attention to his dark locks falling to the floor, hard to forget my hair getting cut. Stella had done wonders on his hair already, making him look cleaned up before having given him a shave.

"You'll never need to do that so long as there are men around here."

"I'd like to defend myself."

"This is not up for discussion."

With a huff, I turned around and continued my assault on the dough. Poor Stella had to listen to this. I was sure she'd heard enough when she'd arrived. Perhaps she'd have some advice on how to navigate this situation. She and Tanner took over ownership of the saloon after their parents had passed on. Surely she knew about men who drank whiskey and couldn't stop.

I finished my biscuits while Stella shaved Anthony's face clean. He looked ten years younger by the time she'd finished. I had to bite back my grin before he shuffled off to the porch to glower.

Stella assisted me in the garden, praised my efforts in tidying up the house, and taught me some things about the chicken coop. After she assured me of her return in a few days, I waved goodbye and continued with my chores.

I'd promised Anthony I wouldn't go into the bunkhouse, and I didn't. After supper, which he'd had the good manners to eat even though I'd burned the chicken, he'd gone up to bed. It would take time for him to get better and I let him go. It hurt me to watch him struggle up the stairs and not try to help him.

I'd also given him my word I wouldn't leave the house half-dressed, and I wasn't.

My promise to not entertain any men alone grated on my nerves while I wandered across from the house toward the paddocks. A few horses were grazing, but I didn't see anyone. The evening grew later, but the sun shone through a few wispy clouds. The dust kicking up from my footsteps attested to the rain that the land needed badly.

Stella had told me that most women in this area saved their boots for church on Sunday or going into town when warranted and went barefoot much of the time. While I walked, the dirt irritated the soft soles of my feet. It would take some getting used to. I knew there were snakes and other things that could bite, so I had to step carefully.

A welcoming light illuminated from the open doors of the barn, soft and glowing. I ducked my head around the corner but saw no one about, though I could hear voices. Horses in their stalls whinnied their approval of my arrival while I walked down the wide aisle. The horse I'd ridden for most of the way from Abilene hung his head outside the stall, and I couldn't resist paying him some attention first.

His wet muzzle found my neck while I rubbed his face and forehead, causing me to laugh abruptly. "Dusty, that tickles," I said, trying to sound stern. "But I share your love."

"Georgie."

Levi's voice made me jump a foot away from the horse. "I'm sorry for intruding."

"Is there something we can help you with?" Rooke appeared behind Levi.

The sight of Rooke with his shirtsleeves rolled up to his elbows with bridles slung over his shoulder nearly undid me. He didn't wear his hat, and it looked like he'd recently bathed. My fingers itched to thread through his hair, stretch onto my toes and press my lips to his throat, then his jaw and finally his mouth.

"Georgie?" I looked at Rooke, my eyes widened as he caught me daydreaming about things I shouldn't be. "Is everything good at the house?"

Licking my lips, I nodded. Now? After all this time I couldn't find my voice now? What in the world is wrong with me? I mentally shook myself awake.

"I'm . . ." What am I doing?

"Levi, leave us."

Levi said nothing, spinning and leaving as Rooke ordered. That was very rude, I thought, sliding my hands to my hips to prepare for giving him a piece of my mind.

"Don't look at me like that," came his growl. "Neither of us will like the consequences. Not after this morning."

"Speaking of this morning, it's what I came to talk with you about. Anthony said you argued about me wanting to learn about the ranch."

A crease appeared between his eyebrows. I wanted to smooth it away. "He doesn't see it the same way I see it. He'd sooner see you on a train back to New York. I'm not about to let that happen."

"Why didn't you tell me you were married?"

I hadn't meant for it to slip out at that moment, hoping to mention it when a better time had come around. Would there ever be a better time? I wondered. By his look of guilt, I knew instantly that Anthony had told me the truth.

"That was long ago."

"And you never heard from her again?"

"No." He turned, hanging the bridles on a peg near the interior door. I stepped toward him, noticing the door Levi had gone into led to living quarters much the same as when I'd first met Rooke in Abilene. This one had a small hallway leading presumably to more rooms.

"I deserve to know."

"She left within a week of us getting married. I knew she had her sights set on bigger things in life. Life with me would have been simple. Leanora wanted the life that you had."

"How old were you?"

I saw his shoulders rise and fall like he'd laughed, but I didn't hear a sound. "Eighteen." He turned to me. "And that was the last I heard from her. Not the same situation as you, I'm afraid. My marriage was done over ten years ago."

I searched his intense gaze. "You and I both know I won't return to New York. I know he doesn't see it now, but he will. He's agreed not to do anything rash, but he is putting up a fight about the liquor."

"I'm sure he has. It's been his constant companion these past few years."

"I'm aiming to change that. I need to know if you're intent on helping me learn to ranch, despite what he might think."

"He thinks otherwise."

"I need and want to defend myself."

The night air brushed against my bare shoulders when I followed him toward the barn doors. Finally, not rain but the slightest cooling in the air for a brief reprieve against the onslaught of heat.

"I want you to defend yourself. If I'm too far away and something happens, you need to learn how to fire that pistol I gave you. You still have it?" I nodded. "I'll keep working on him. You need to keep working on him, though. He's still your brother, and I still need to abide by some of his wishes."

"I understand."

Chapter Forty Two

A few nights later, I awoke to horrible shouting and screaming. Thinking someone had gotten into another fight, I ran from my bedchambers. Even half asleep, I knew I couldn't go outside of the house dressed as I was, but no sooner had I stepped outside my room when I heard it coming from Anthony's room.

I crept down the hallway to find his door ajar. Only a small bit of light came from within, but I pushed the door open to find Anthony standing by his bed, shouting. I couldn't see anyone else in the room. Who could he be yelling at?

"Anthony?" I whispered.

When he turned toward me, his eyes had taken on the red tinge again and although he looked better since his shave and haircut, he had taken on a look of pure rage. I gasped at the bottle clutched in his hand.

"Where did you get that?" I snapped, rushing toward him to snatch it.

As garbled as it sounded, Anthony shrieked at me and yanked the bottle away. Only it slipped from his grip and flew across the room. When it struck the wall, it shattered and left a stain.

I'd never seen a person in such a fury before, especially my brother. He came at me with such force that I didn't have time to block him before he had me pushed up against the wall and his hands at my throat. Tearing at his hands with my fingernails didn't deter him from releasing me, my breathing slowly dying away from the pressure. I lifted my knee and kicked him, giving myself enough leeway to scream as loud as I could and as long as I could.

I couldn't get him to stop coming at me, despite having kicked him. When I tried to get through the door, he grabbed my hair and yanked me back until we crashed to the floor. Who did he think I was? I thought frantically. Did he mean to do me harm? Kill me?

"Get off, you bastard! Wake up! You're drunk!" I screamed.

He threw his arm around my neck, abruptly cutting off my screams. Writhing, I kicked my legs and grabbed at his arms, screaming until my throat grew sore from it.

"Damn you," he said, repeatedly. "Damn you to hell."

Footsteps coming up the stairs sounded like fists beating against the floor. When I looked up, Rooke appeared in the doorway without a shirt and only his trousers on. He grasped Anthony by the armpits and hauled him up, even when Anthony continued to fight. Crawling backwards until my back hit the wall, I watched with wide eyes while Rooke dodged every swing.

Anthony's feeble attempts at punishing whoever he could were weak at best. Wherever he'd gotten the liquor, it had done its job. When Rooke's fist caught Anthony in the jaw, he fell back onto the bed without another sound. Silence surrounded us, only the sound of my heavy breathing filling the room.

Bugger it, I thought. I'm not supposed to entertain any men. I crawled, not having enough strength after nearly being strangled, into the hallway. A minute later, I felt Rooke's hands helping me to stand.

"Did he hurt you?" His voice was rough, angry.

My throat burned. I could only shake my head.

"Tell me the truth."

"He hurt my neck," I whispered. "That's all."

Rooke got me back to my room, sitting me down on the bed and, much to my surprise, sat down next to me and pulled me into his arms. With my head on his chest, I breathed him in and let my tears go.

Just as I thought we'd been making strides, Anthony and I, it had all been for nothing. And now it was worse. Every fear, every challenge, every single thing I'd been through to get here came out in sobs that shook my body against Rooke's while he held me and didn't let go. My tears soaked his chest and still he held me tightly, his strength holding me together.

"I'll stay tonight."

When I tried to lift my head, he kept it against his chest with the barest pressure of his palm. "Rooke, no. He'll kill you if he finds you here in the morning. I won't have that."

"I'll leave before morning. Besides, it's to make sure nothing else happens tonight. I doubt Anthony would disagree that your safety is the most important, especially to protect you from him." This time, he let me move enough to look at him through watery eyes. "I promise you I won't do anything untoward."

I smiled weakly, silencing my thoughts that I might want him to do something untoward. I would do anything for Rooke, but risking Anthony finding us in an uncompromising position under his roof was not something I would take a chance on. The only thing I could do was agree.

Already in my shift, Rooke tucked me back into bed. He removed his boots and slid in next to me, pulled me into the safety of his arms once again, and the curve of his muscles lulled me into the security I knew I had with him.

"Thank you," I whispered.

His arms contracted around me. "Georgiana . . ."

As tight as he held me, I couldn't see his face to know if he intended to finish his thought. From the sounds of it, he wanted to say something else, and I waited. My full given name being said was rare, even for Rooke.

"I want you to know . . . I . . . " His chest rose and fell deeply, taking me with it. "I'll protect you with my life."

I released the breath that had caught in my throat. Had I thought he would profess love for me, after only knowing me for little more than a month? I chastised myself. Yet that little voice inside my head still yearned for it.

Chapter Forty Three

I woke to an empty bed the next morning. As promised, Rooke had left before dawn. After dressing carefully, I checked on Anthony to make sure he still breathed. Still in the same position as Rooke had left him, his chest rising and falling steadily with each breath, satisfied me enough to leave him to rest further.

The sun had barely made itself known in the morning when I set out. The world remained quiet. Even wildlife was not fully awake at this hour. It wasn't a long walk to get to Rooke's little house in the woods, and I hoped he was there instead of working already. Waking to find him gone had deflated me.

If it hadn't been for him last night, Anthony might have succeeded in hurting me more than he had. There wasn't a doubt in my mind that it would happen again, and I couldn't think of a way to help him that wouldn't endanger me in the process.

Silence greeted me when I cracked open the cabin door and tiptoed in, my boots in my hand. Setting them quietly down next to his under the coat rack, I moved with the same stealth I had while sneaking around as a young girl. It took me less than a minute to shed the dress I'd hastily put on, but I took a minute to lean against the frame of the door to gaze upon Rooke.

My heart swelled in my chest while I took in his sleeping form. Disheveled hair, the line of his upturned jaw and the rise and fall of his chest. The heat had the blanket down around his waist, but I didn't have the decency to blush.

His eyes opened to find me standing there, lips curving into a sleepy smile before he realized I stood in his house half-dressed. Eyes opened fully when he propped himself up.

"Did something happen?"

I shook my head, walking to the bed and joining him. "I can't live with him anymore, Rooke. Will you let me live with you?"

With a groan, he pulled me to him and we lay back. "Darlin', you can stay here. What did I tell you last night?"

"My safety is most important, even against him."

I heard his deep sigh. "Yes, that. And I'll protect you with my life."

"He won't listen to me, and he'll only get worse."

"You are the only one who can help him. And you will."

Looking at Rooke, I saw faith. Faith in my ability. Faith in his friend. Resigned, I knew what I needed to do. But until then, I wouldn't be sleeping in that house. And that battle would be the hardest one yet.

"I don't know where he got that bottle last night, but no one can sneak him another bottle. He might have hurt me worse than he did last night."

Rooke tugged me closer, his mouth finding the sensitive spot on my neck that had me a sliding into a sea of ecstasy. "I'd have killed him."

A smile teased the side of my mouth, even though I knew he would do no such thing. "I appreciate your rescue tactics last night, though you may be tested when he wakes and finds me gone. It's a shame that we're both legally married. If that were an option, he'd had no reason for his anger."

"He'd find a way to be angry," came his muffled reply, his hands busily shifting clothing around. "I don't want to talk about any other men while you're in my bed."

"Why did Leanora run off? Where did she go?"

"She ran off with another man."

"Why would she-" Thoughts fled at the graze of his teeth where he'd pulled my shift down, warm breath heating my already enflamed body.

"Stop talking, darlin'."

When the scorching heat of his hand touched my inner thigh, brazen fingers seeking to ease any burdens I carried, I clamped my mouth shut until nothing but gasps and moans slipped out. I understood now. This was not the time to speak, or even think, of other people.

◆

Shut up in his room when I returned, Anthony was apparently in no mood to be disturbed. No doubt curing his aching head from drinking so much, I thought. I tended to the bread I'd planned on baking, then went to work in the garden. Using the bandana Rooke had bought me in Abilene, I tied it around my head to catch the perspiration from getting into my eyes while I weeded and watered.

By the time the later afternoon sun beat down, I had dirt smudged on my hands, face and apron. I took a bath, soaking in the lukewarm water to cool me down before I went out to the paddocks.

Rooke worked with Levi in the paddock while Billy, Cade, Wyatt and Matthew stood near me. When the screen door of the house slammed, Anthony would find me here. I had no intention of moving this argument anywhere else. The thump of his crutch while he walked to us came slowly, but when I heard it grow nearer, I turned around. He looked terrible.

Rooke and Levi left their task, coming closer while the boys stayed close. None of them would allow harm to come to me, no matter who signed their paychecks.

"Thought you'd never come out of your room," I said, having to look up Anthony.

"I owe you an apology." He glanced at the men. "Better said in privacy. This is family business."

"Yes, you do owe me an apology. But I'll not go anywhere with you yet."

He scowled. "You needn't make it harder than it is."

"Then don't make it harder on me." The bite in my voice didn't intimidate him. "I am not here to see you die, and I will not stay here to see you die. I'd sooner leave than that, Anthony."

"I'll not have you telling me what I can do and can't do. This is my house."

"You can always build me my own."

Despite the heat of the sun and already being overheated, I grew even hotter. My chest rapidly rose and fell as my breathing spiked, waiting for what he'd say. I hadn't told him that I'd gone to ask Rooke if I could stay with him. Yet.

"Rooke stayed with you last night. I told you not to entertain—"

"I know what you told me. That was not what he was doing. He was there to protect me in case you attacked me again. Nothing more."

He reared back as though I'd slapped him in his face. Had he not remembered that he'd attacked me? Tried to kill me? Did he only remember getting drunk again? The sun beating down relentlessly combined with my rising anger, threatened to explode.

"I . . . Maybe you shouldn't stay here," he muttered, turning to leave.

I grabbed his arm, stopping him. "Or you could stop drinking so you don't hurt me or anyone else."

"It eases my pain."

My hand fell away. As I thought, he'd been numbing his pain from his leg. Surely, there could be something else to do other than drink to ease his pain. There were other men who'd had much worse injuries during the war.

"There are other things you can do to ease the pain other than drink. And we're going to find out what those things are. Will you consider it?" He stared at me, unblinking as though I'd gone around the bend. "Please?"

It took only the nod of his head. I launched myself at him, holding him as I hadn't done for so many years. He didn't move for a moment, letting me hold him like the embrace was keeping me together. When I felt his arm slide around my waist, I smiled.

Chapter Forty Four

Despite Anthony having agreed to consider other treatments for his pain, I didn't have answers yet that day. As soon as I could the next morning, I went to the paddocks to ask questions.

The doctor in Salado who'd treated Billy's rattlesnake bite would be the best option for Anthony to see for help. If I could get Anthony to agree to travel to see him, with someone trustworthy to travel with, that might be the answer we would look for. And that wasn't all I had up my sleeve.

Geezer and Anthony did not get along, neither did he and Cade. Wyatt and Matthew, the only two I knew with calm enough temperaments to handle Anthony, agreed to go. Between the two of them, they could keep Anthony in line.

Elated, I spent the rest of the day learning about the ranch. Following Billy around to learn about the management of the equipment, then watching Levi with the cattle. It would take me a while to learn about everything, but I was determined to do so.

I returned to the house to wash up and fix supper for Anthony before evening set in. When I opened the screen door, I heard pots and pans banging inside the kitchen and hurried to see who'd slipped in unseen.

"Mack?"

The man in my kitchen whirled from the stove, pan clutched in his hand. The surprise on his face twisted to a beaming smile, twin dimples appeared and his eyes glowed. He had curly, dark hair that looked untamed.

"Miss Georgie, it's dang good to meet you."

I glided into the kitchen, lifting my nose to smell freshly baked biscuits as I wondered what had brought Mack into the main house. It couldn't be more obvious that he'd set himself to cooking. But I wondered why.

"I apologize for not seeking you out to meet you sooner." I lifted the linen from the basket, revealing plump biscuits the size of my fist. Much bigger than I had successfully made yet.

"You've no need to apologize. Rooke told me it was only to keep you safe."

I scoffed. "I've been forbidden from the bunkhouse, as though there are dangers lurking there. I know most of the men."

When he laughed, I noticed his belly dance. Setting the pan on top of the stove, he added a healthy scoop of lard that promptly melted before he laid each piece of butchered chicken carefully in until it fit like a puzzle.

He cooked with such ease. It amazed me. I settled into a chair to watch him slice potatoes next, laying each in another pan until they sizzled along with the chicken. He deftly turned each piece of chicken. He cooked with such care, I wasn't surprised my cooking was lacking. I needed to slow down and take my time. Watching him cook would allow me to learn so much.

"I can't wait to taste your supper, Mack."

His grin was answer enough, bashful yet proud. "You go on and wash up, Miss Georgie. Master Anthony will be in soon as he's done with his business."

"What business?" I asked, standing up quickly.

"He's talking business with Rooke, and he'll be in shortly."

"Where is he? What are they talking about?"

Mack turned to look at me, admonishment in his eyes. I tried to tell myself that what went on was my business so long as I lived here, but in truth, it *wasn't* any of my business. I'd need to settle on the hope that Anthony, or Rooke, would provide me with any details of their business.

"I'm only the cook here. I don't know nothing about no one's business."

Sidling to the doorway, I turned into the doorframe to look at Mack with one of my most beguiling smiles. The effort would be pointless, of course. He only told me the truth. Mack cooked for the ranch hands and wouldn't know anything about the business dealings between Anthony and Rooke.

"Won't work, Miss Georgie," he murmured, turning back to his cooking before it burned.

Dancing away, I couldn't help but to laugh. "Can't blame me for trying," I called out behind me before hurrying up to my bedchambers to wash up.

After utilizing the washbowl and a cloth to wipe away the dirt, grime and sweat from the day, I changed into a fresh dress and checked my reflection in the mirror in case Rooke joined us for dinner. Good enough, I thought.

The aroma greeting me the moment I opened the door instantly caused my mouth to water, the eagerness to eat a good meal quickening my footsteps down the stairs and toward the dining room. When I entered, Anthony sat at the head of the long table. The table had been set lavishly with lit tapers, crystal goblets, shining silverware, and those damned chipped dishes.

Glad I'd changed into a fresh dress, Anthony appeared to have taken care of his appearance with his hair freshly combed and face recently shaven. He dressed in wrinkle-free clothing, the way a gentleman of aristocracy would.

"Georgie," he said, waving his hand at the chair beside him.

"Anthony, you look well." I swept into the room, sitting down as Mack appeared behind me to push my chair in closer. "It smells wonderful, Mack."

"I couldn't agree more. You've outdone yourself." Anthony snapped his napkin open and set it on his lap.

"Are we celebrating?"

Anthony's eyes, nearly the same color as mine, sparkled. "Thought I'd allow you a break from trying to cook. I realize how hard it must be for you, managing this household, cooking, gardening."

I couldn't be sure he told me the truth, although I'd never known him to lie to me. These past several days, I wasn't sure he'd noticed me trying, although the cooking had been quite challenging.

Mack briefly left, returning with two plates laden with golden fried chicken and crispy potatoes with freshly baked biscuits. My eyes widened at the display of culinary goodness. I had to force myself to wait a few moments before picking up my fork. I didn't want to look like a barbarian.

"Is that all?" I asked. "Or is there something else you wish to tell me?"

Anthony picked up his fork, giving me all I needed to dig into my food with gusto. I had to remind myself after a few bites that although I'd been living in the wilderness for more than a month, I was still a lady. Immediately, I slowed.

"What else could there be? I behaved badly after all you've done to improve my life here, and I wanted to repay your kindness." I snorted, nearly choking on a biscuit. "You think I have some other reason for treating you as you are accustomed to?"

Speaking as he did, his British accent came through thickly. I smiled, remembering the old Anthony and how terribly I'd missed him. The man who sat beside me, the one looking at me with kind eyes, was my brother. Not the man last night who was in a rage because of poison running through his body, left damaged from the war.

Before I realized what I was doing, I reached across and curled my fingers around his hand. And he allowed me to do so. I squeezed.

"I've missed you so much," I whispered.

When he squeezed back, I nearly burst into tears.

"We shall get through this, Georgie. No promises that it will be easy, but we will get through this." I released his hand. "I spoke with Rooke. He told me of your idea of seeing a doctor in Salado."

Hope swelled. "And?"

"I've agreed." I thought I would burst from happiness. "Wyatt, Matthew, and I will leave at first light."

I leapt from my chair to throw my arms around him, tipping his chair backwards until he grabbed the table to steady himself. Although barely there, I heard his chuckle. I could not give him my thanks enough, even when I sat back down.

"In the meantime, you will abide by my wishes and stay away from the ranch hands while I'm away." He looked at me hard. "I mean it. These men would, and could, do you more harm than good."

"And half of them, including Rooke, I traveled with for more than a month." I shot back, my tone soft. "Most of them thought they traveled with a boy, but now they know differently. And Rooke would allow none of them to harm me."

I didn't like the look in his eyes. "You are my sister, and he trifled with you. He knew you were my sister when he did. I cannot forgive him for that."

"You can't forgive him? Or you won't?"

"I told you before. He is married."

"As am I. But we are both adults, and both have estranged marriages. Marriages that are over and done with, as far as both of us are concerned." I sighed. "We can continue to argue this, Anthony, but Rooke will teach me what I need to know about this ranch without compromising my safety. He'll teach me to protect myself."

With finality, Anthony set down his fork and leaned back as he drew his arms across his chest. Here it comes, I thought.

We can't have a simple conversation without it turning into a wicked argument. When we were young, we would agree on everything and now, we agreed on nothing.

I would have reached for his hand again, but I knew he would have snatched it away. "You remember when we were younger? You would have protected me against anything and anyone?"

"And I am still doing so, yet you seem to challenge me at every turn!"

"I'm actually not. I'm helping *you* to protect me, as is Rooke. You are only seeing him as a threat when he would lay down his life for me. Has he not told you that?"

While he stayed silent, I could see him thinking about it. I knew it would be a very large margin that he would understand what I tried to tell him, but there were only so many things Anthony could do to protect me. And Rooke being further away from the ranch, I needed to protect myself.

"Let Rooke teach me what I need to know, Anthony."

His jaw clenched, followed by a long, drawn-out sigh. "Very well. But I still won't forgive him."

If that was all I had to live with, I could do that. I'd take the victory I'd won. Every day I had a victory. I'd celebrate if I had to. I knew there could be setbacks, and I would need to deal with them as they came.

"Now, let's speak about your estranged marriage." He resumed eating.

I tipped up my chin.

"You believe your husband let you go? You don't think he followed you?"

"I'm not sure how he could have. I left no trace."

"If I'd been in my right mind, I might've gone after Helene."

His words were like a punch to my stomach, knowing what I did about Helene and the child. I didn't know if he knew that she'd died along with their child, but I didn't want to tell him in fear that he'd reach for his drink again. I knew it was selfish of me to decide to do it. And I did it anyway.

"You would have?"

"I might have, but I was so far gone with drink that I didn't. She was quite mean before she left here, though. Said awful things to me. Things I would have never said to anyone, even as angry as I am now." He looked away, pain laced through his tone.

"You would have brought her back?"

"If she's changed, I may consider taking her back, even now."

It tore me up inside, gutted me. Anthony didn't know. "Anthony," I whispered. "I have something to tell you."

When he looked at me, I thought he'd be able to tell by the tears gathered in my eyes that I was about to deliver him the worst news. I hoped there was no drink to be found on this ranch, though I knew the ranch hands likely had some in their quarters. It had to have been where he got it yesterday.

"When I was trying to find you, I went to North Carolina to see if I could find Helene first." He sat up straighter. "She died, Anthony."

Expecting him to be angry or cry, something to show emotion about how he might feel, I waited. But he remained stoic. Nothing. He continued to eat as though I hadn't told him he was a widower.

"How?" he asked after another moment.

Oh, God, I thought. He had to ask me that. "Childbirth."

His head snapped up. There it was, the emotion that I waited for glittering in his eyes. While I thought he would stand up, anger and sorrow bursting open, I saw the hardness return to his eyes into a full anger that had redness creeping up his neck.

"Wh . . . Anthony? Are you unwell?"

His palm slapped down on the table, causing me to jump up and my fork clatter against my plate. "Then she truly got what she deserved."

Chapter Forty Five

At first, I thought I hadn't heard him correctly. Never had I thought I would ever hear him say someone deserves to die. Anything but that.

"I've been a bastard since coming home from the war." His admission was not news to me. I knew. I'd seen it. "But Helene was not the same as when I left. She'd not been faithful while I was away, you know."

"You accused Rooke of being with her."

He sighed. "I'd convinced myself of it. Especially when they left together, and he never returned. Helene was quite a woman. I never understood her power until she was gone. She had power over nearly every man here. Except for one man."

I frowned, unsure what he was talking about.

"Rooke. When Helene let Jesse slip away, he never forgave her for it. I'd been a fool to think that they had an affair. She had an affair with everyone else, including Owen Appleton." He looked uncomfortable. "That child could not have been mine, Georgie. We hadn't been intimate since before the war."

I'd let out an awful gasp. But her mother and sisters didn't seem to know anything about Anthony, and they did not know that the child she'd born had not been Anthony's. Everything I thought I knew, I'd been wrong about.

"If that's true, why are you giving me such a hard time about carrying on with Rooke? Helene did the same thing to you and left. You could have found another woman, moved on and had a better life. Why didn't you?"

He stared at me. "What woman? Do you see me, Georgie?" I saw him. I wasn't sure he saw himself.

"I've lost my leg. I'm an alcoholic with fits of rage at night. What woman would want me?"

My thoughts drifted to Stella, although I had yet to find out what attracted her to my angry, bitter brother. Instead, I reached out to grab his hand. "Anthony, you will get better. You are young. There is still so much life in you. Please, have faith."

The nod he managed was enough for me.

◆

Anthony, Wyatt, and Matthew were gone before the sun rose the next morning. I woke shortly after dawn, dressed and took my tea on the porch to watch the sunrise while I thought about what Anthony had said at dinner.

Now, I rocked in the chair while I sipped my tea and thought about the hardships Anthony had faced. First, the horrors he'd seen in war. He'd lost part of his leg and suffered not only a great deal of pain, but the worst conditions of some hospitals, disease, and shortage of medical supplies. And when he thought things couldn't have gotten worse, they sent him home to find that his wife, whom he loved with his whole heart, had been involved with other men while he was away fighting in a war he hadn't wanted to fight in. It was no wonder he'd turned to drink.

"Well, hello there, darlin'."

Arching my bare foot, I stopped the rock of the chair as Rooke strolled around the corner with his cowboy hat pulled low against the attack of the bright morning sun. His blue denim shirt, rolled up to his elbows had been left unbuttoned at the neck and covered by his bandana.

Lips curling, I hid my smile by taking another sip of my tea before standing. With a purposeful sway to my hips, I set my cup on the plank of the porch and peered down at him. The way his hip cocked out, the gun slung in its holster and his hand resting on his other hip. The way his eyes glided over me despite the porch being in the way. He made my heart pound.

I swung around the post, giving him a clear view of me. His head tipped up, his eyes sparkling with appreciation. Warmth spread through me. With Anthony gone, he shouldn't look at me that way or I wouldn't be able to keep any promises.

"You're mighty cheerful this morning," I said. "Any reason?"

"Should you be wearing that? Surely Anthony told you before he left."

My brows furrowed. "What should he have told me?"

"I'm going to teach you how to shoot. To protect yourself." He took several steps towards me until he had to angle his head to look up at me. "Might want to change into trousers. It's going to be at least a half-day ride."

"You can't show me around here?"

"I'm not taking the risk of scaring the horses or the cows. Now, let's get to it. Cade's already preparing our horses."

Tea forgotten, I whirled and disappeared into the house before someone could change their mind. How could Anthony have kept something so important to me last night? As adamant that he'd been to make sure I stayed away from anyone who'd protect me, or teach me how to protect myself, and he'd been keeping it a secret that he'd commissioned Rooke to do it after all.

Nearly dancing around my room in eager anticipation to learn something of use, I tripped twice trying to pull on my trousers. I grabbed my hat from the rack and hurried out, slamming the door when I left the house.

Rooke stood where I left him, except he had two horses saddled and waiting. So excited, I nearly jumped into the saddle. The horse, a beautiful black stallion similar to Rooke's horse, skittered away from me and I knew I needed to calm myself or I'd be scaring him.

"Easy now," Rooke said. "Hasn't been that long since you've ridden. While we're out, there's some fences that need checking."

A few pets to his forehead and the horse calmed. Minutes later, Rooke and I rode away from the sunrise toward nothing but land. First, we rode along the fences at the southernmost border to ensure we didn't need to repair them before turning back north. I focused on the lush green trees dotting the horizon, bountiful against the swath of blue sky behind them. The gentle swells of the hills before us appeared like something out of a picture book.

Soon, we raced toward that horizon and I wondered again why we needed to ride so far to practice shooting. Surely, we wouldn't need to be so far from the animals.

We stopped in the late afternoon near a stream that glittered in the sun as though the light kissed the ripples of water. Rooke took care of the horses while I made a place for our saddles and the food Rooke had brought from Mack. I couldn't resist peeking into the bundle, surprised at how much food he'd packed us.

I sat on a fallen tree, pulling out some jerky to munch on when Rooke found me. He'd let the horses loose to graze. The purpose of his stroll, the intensity deep in his eyes, spread a warmth down my spine that had me on my feet with nervous anxiety.

When he took a long step toward me, a jolt shot through me. Another step. What I had left of my jerky fell heedlessly from my fingers, his arm slinging around my waist and pulling me flush against him in a single movement that brought my mouth to his at the same time. My hat fell off, making way for his other hand to tangle within my hair, the length having swept down the back of my neck with a slight wave to it. I felt a tug, and my face angled up, giving him better access to plunder my lips until I was sure they bruised.

Of their own free will, my hands slid up his chest and traveled the chiseled slopes. Fingertips tingling, itching to touch his bare skin, I released a breathy sigh, only to have it caught by his growl.

When his hand left my hair, sliding down my body to my hip and joining the other to cup my backside, I trembled when he lifted me and my legs wound around his waist. I could never grow tired of him kissing me, touching me.

"Still wondering why someone would let you get away," he murmured.

"Is this why you brought me out here?"

He pulled back. "No, darlin', but it's a damn good idea. Would you rather stop?"

With both hands along his carved jaw, I pulled his mouth back to mine and sucked his lower lip into my mouth until he chuckled. Now he knew my answer. As unladylike as I'd been acting lately, at least we were alone here. No one could stop this. No one could interrupt. It was only us.

Lying in his arms in the aftermath of what still felt like the first time he'd made love to me, the sun fading away with the day, I couldn't be angry. He'd had the foresight to bring a blanket which was a dead giveaway that I knew he'd planned to ravish me all along.

"Does it bother you?" His nose nuzzled my temple, arm tightening around my midsection while I lay sprawled against him.

"Does what bother me?"

"That we can have only this?" He picked up my hand,

studying my fingers while he threaded his fingers into mine. "That we can never be married?"

"Is this your way of proposing to me when you can't?" I teased.

"In a way, I suppose. But does it bother you?"

I pulled away a fraction to look into his eyes. "If this is how we're meant to be, this is how we'll be. Does it bother you?"

"It doesn't bother me so long as no one mistreats you because of it. But I know it bothers Anthony, which is why I waited until he left before stealing you away."

"Anthony didn't tell you to teach me how to shoot before he left, did he?"

The devilish grin slowly curving his mouth answered me, and damn it, but I couldn't be angry with him when his arms drew me closer and that grin lowered down to me until his lips connected with me in a searing kiss.

A breathy sigh slipped from deep in my throat, his hand slithering down around the curve of my hip, continuing its descent until he gave me a tug that slid me on top of him. A husky chuckled followed.

The sound of a rider in the distance had my head snapping up a second later. I rolled away from him, grabbing my shirt and shrugging into it quickly. Getting caught in his house had been one thing, but out here would be something entirely different. And not something I wanted to happen.

Rooke cursed colorfully, leaping to his feet and stepping into his trousers. The sight of him in only his trousers, no shirt and feet bare, had my mouth dry. I swallowed the thickness in my throat, looking away to slip on my own trousers.

With only a moment to spare, Geezer rode swiftly across the hilly embankment that partially shielded us. Rooke finished rolling up the blanket, attaching it to the saddle before turning to face him.

Hard eyes on me, Geezer looked down. I resisted the urge to

make sure my clothes were straight, sure he knew what we'd been doing out here. Looking back at him with narrowed eyes, I put my hands on my hips.

"Is there something we can help you with?"

I saw the edge of Geezer's mustache quiver. "Was told you headed this way."

"And?" Rooke came to stand next to me.

"Did you check the southern fences on your way out? Billy said he thought a tree might have fallen on it." Geezer looked at Rooke, giving me some relief from his chilling stare.

"I checked. That why you came all the way out here, Geezer? Or something else brings you out here?" When Geezer remained silent, Rooke continued. "You worried about Georgie?"

"No," came his quick reply.

Too quick.

"I will assure you we are out here for a reason. Georgie is going to learn how to shoot, so she might defend herself if there's a need. There may not always be someone around, and out here in the wilds of Texas she'll need to know how to shoot to kill if need be."

Geezer's gaze found me again. He leaned forward in his saddle, arms crossing each other. "Is that true?"

I couldn't believe it. There had been no other time he had spoken to me decently, and here he was, asking me if Rooke told the truth. "It's true. There's no need to worry about me. Rooke's been teaching me how to shoot straight."

With a nod to me, Geezer wheeled his horse around. Soon, the sound of the hooves faded into the distance. Rooke and I exchanged confused looks.

"Suppose I should do what we came here to do." I snuck in a smile. "Teach you to shoot, Georgie." My grin widened. "Teach you to shoot."

With our gun belts slung around our waists, Rooke and I walked out toward a bank of trees. One tree had a large knot in it, perfect for aiming. Rooke took his stance behind me, the same way he had many weeks ago when I didn't know he knew I was a woman.

This time I had the same issue with concentrating. No. It was worse than last time, because every feeling had come to life with him pressed against my back and his warm breath brushing against my neck. His hands were against mine, the strength of him to me was more than I could contain.

"You're going to pull the trigger this time," his husky voice said in my ear.

A shiver snaked down my spine. My finger curled and when I pulled back against the trigger, it knocked me back into him. He held me steady, making sure we didn't both topple backwards.

"Again."

The bullet had gone nowhere close to my target. But I did it again. And again. Each time I shot the pistol, I got closer to the target and I no longer rocked back into Rooke. Eventually, he didn't stand behind me and my stance became much stronger.

Victory came soon after, but instead of jumping up and down in excitement, I sheathed the pistol in the holster and turned to Rooke with a grin. That girl that danced at balls and never raised her voice to anyone had shot at a tree and won.

Rooke said nothing, giving me a nod of his head. He didn't need to say anything. I could see the pride in his eyes. And that pride only gave me more urge to press on.

Chapter Forty Six

Over a week later and there still hadn't been a word from Anthony, Wyatt, and Matthew. I knew they'd be returning soon. Delilah sent word that the rest of my clothing order was complete and ready for pickup, and there were other things that needed attention. Rooke and I had spent evenings before the sun went down riding out as far as the sun would allow to practice and I'd gotten rather good at hitting the target.

Confident in my abilities, I had Levi hitch a team of horses to the wagon for a trip to town. I knew Rooke would disagree with going to town alone, but I didn't want to bother him. It seemed he always had things to do around the ranch. Numerous men had abandoned the ranch to find employment under more favorable leadership since Rooke had been gone. Rooke was not yet officially part of the staff, but Anthony still entrusted him with responsibilities. I brought my pistol, even though strapping a gun belt around a dress seemed strange.

No sooner than halfway to town, I heard a rider behind me. With a sigh, I prepared myself for an argument with Rooke. He didn't need to coddle me along with everything else. I'd never learn to fend for myself with him hovering.

"Good afternoon, Miss Georgie."

Trepidation skittered across my skin at the cocksure voice. I'd barely turned when Owen Appleton came into view beside the wagon. Robert trotted up beside him, tipping his hat to me.

"Mighty fine day," Owen continued. "Looks like you could use an escort to town. Assuming that's where you're headed."

"I've no need of an escort. I know my way."

He scoffed. "Now what kind of gentleman would I be if I let a woman travel alone on these roads? No, no. I'll see you safely in town and I'll not hear another word about it."

I could only thank the stars we were nearly to town. His company wouldn't need to be tolerated for too much longer. Craning my neck to look at Robert, he said nothing while they rode. Quiet one, I thought. He let his brother overshadow him.

"How've you been getting along with your brother?"

"I've been getting along with Anthony fine. Why do you ask?"

Owen studied my profile, giving me a feeling of unease. "Anthony's not a simple man to get along with. A woman alone, I'd think it would be poor company to have. Brother or not."

"It's disrespectful to speak to a woman of her brother that way," I said tightly. "Where I come from, we don't do that."

"Now." He drew out the word as though he were chastising me. "I didn't mean no disrespect. To you, or Anthony. I'm trying to be a good neighbor."

I whipped around, looking at Robert. "Robert? Is that true?"

Robert visibly gulped. "Yes, ma'am."

I wouldn't get a straight answer out of him if he writhed on the ground with a gunshot wound. The feeling that Robert only went by what his older brother said overcame me. I gave the reins an extra snap and the horses picked up speed. The sooner I reached town, the better.

"What is it you want with Anthony?"

"I'd like permission to court you."

My breath nearly choked me. "Excuse me? Why ever would you want to do such a thing?"

He stared at me, and I swallowed the rest of my words. I needed to tread carefully. A woman alone on the road with two men. Armed, yes, but easily overpowered by two, more than likely. Looking at Robert, I doubted he would touch me at all.

"Come now, Miss Rutherford. You're a pretty lady. What man wouldn't want to court a pretty woman?"

Ah. Owen Appleton thought, because I'd arrived, I was available to court. He didn't know I was a married woman. And I wouldn't tell him, either, even though I had no intention of allowing him to court me. Anthony would never consent to it.

"I'd rather not court anyone yet."

I heard him sigh. "You'll change your mind soon enough."

I'd sooner get bitten by a rattlesnake, I thought. Even after seeing how much Billy had suffered after such a thing. The uncomfortable company soon ended as we trotted our way into town. Owen and Robert hitched their mounts at the post in front of the saloon before helping me down from the wagon.

"We'll leave you to do your errands then," Owen said, eyes twinkling with mischief.

"I'm stopping to say hello to Stella first."

Owen swept out his arm, nearly ramming it into Robert. I'd had enough of these two dunderheads and moved quickly past, pushing open the saloon doors. The murmur of patrons greeted me, the pungent smell of cigar smoke permeating the air.

Tanner poured glasses of whiskey behind the bar, nodding to me when he noticed me coming in. Stella stood at the bar and with her back to me was another woman, light of hair. When Stella saw me, her eyes grew wide.

"Georgie, I didn't expect you today."

"Delilah sent word that the rest of my order is complete." I stepped up to the bar beside her. "Good afternoon, Tanner."

"Afternoon, Miss Georgie."

Tanner eyed Stella suspiciously, and I turned to her, looking around her at the woman. "Who is your friend, Stella?"

"Um . . . Georgie, this is Nora." The woman passed me her hand. "Nora, this is Georgie."

I shook her hand, noticing the color blue of her eyes. "Very nice to meet you. What brings you to Lone Point River?"

"Nora is Rooke's wife."

I dropped her hand, stunned. "And . . . you're looking for him?"

"My brother told me I could find him this way. Rory never was one to give complete details for anything." I could barely catch my breath.

Rory? As in the man Rooke had grown up with? The world seemed like it had tipped on its axis, bringing me with it. I put my hand on the bar to steady myself.

"Can I get you something, Georgie?" Tanner asked.

I waved him away but thought better of it. "I'll take a whiskey."

Stella's eyebrows shot up nearly to her hairline. "No tea today, Georgie?"

"Today calls for whiskey, don't you think? Rooke's wife has come back after . . . how many years has it been?"

Nora gave me a demure smile.

"Well, I'm certain the reunion will bring him great joy."

Stella didn't look certain about it while Tanner set a glass in front of me and poured the dark-colored liquor. As much as I'd come down on Anthony for this, I grabbed the glass no sooner than it had two fingers full and downed it. Tanner chuckled, but Stella's eyes widened.

"You'll bring Nora back to the ranch with you?" she asked.

I'd as soon leave her here and fetch Rooke, but since Stella had asked it left me little choice. As much as she had done for me, I owed it to her to take the woman off her hands.

"Of course. I'll need to collect my order from the general store, but I can return for Nora before I leave." I doubted my ability to keep my judgments to myself, but I would try.

Nora had a beauty most women would be envious of. Light hair, green-flecked eyes, and flawless porcelain skin. The dress she wore was made of expensive fabric that I used to wear. I looked down at my ivory dress. Having been wearing it for so long, it was well worn now. Thank heavens, I'd had the good sense not to dress in trousers today.

"Another one?" Tanner asked.

I shook my head. "I shall collect my things and we can get to the ranch straightaway. I'm sure Nora is excited about her reunion with Rooke."

Nora managed a tight smile but said nothing.

"I'll be back," I said to Stella and Nora without looking at either of them.

I pushed away from the bar and whirled without another word, my feet taking me quickly away until I felt the hot air outside against my face.

No matter. I'd return for Nora after my errand. And that would be too soon. Dizziness swept through me while I crossed the street, but I managed my composure when I stepped into the shade of the general store to the beaming smile of Thaddeus. I knew my friends in this town, and I had them. I could count on them.

A half hour later, Thaddeus loaded the wagon with my things while I returned to the saloon to collect a surprise that would be sure to knock Rooke back. He had said he hadn't seen her since they got married. By the looks of her, she'd found what she'd been looking for. I wanted badly to ask what had brought her back, but it would be rude and not my business.

I ignored Owen's goodbye when Nora and I left the saloon, getting into the wagon. Thaddeus had packed everything into crates neatly in the back to not roll around. Picking up the reins, I started home.

She asked, idly toying with the satchel around her wrist, "Do you think he'll be surprised to see me?"

"One might say he will be, but I don't know your relationship history well enough to know how he might react. Nor have I been on the ranch long enough." I saw her nod, looking into the distance. "How far did you travel to get here?"

"From Boston."

"Were you there long?"

"Yes, many years."

I itched to ask, gripping the reins instead. "This must be very different for you, being out on the frontier. All this dust, and the sun."

"It is different, yes. You said you haven't been here long. Where did you travel from? I noticed you have an accent."

"I'm from Britain, originally. But I've recently come from New York City."

She smiled. "That isn't far from Boston."

I couldn't do this, I thought. I can't sit here and idly chat with a woman who'd likely broken Rooke's heart all those years ago. Although Rooke had said it had been over ten years since she'd left, he didn't appear to be heartbroken.

"I suppose you're wondering why I've come back."

"It isn't my business," I said, my voice tight. "This is between you and Rooke. I'd rather you speak with him about it. Not me."

We lapsed into silence again, not a comfortable companion silence, but awkward and lengthy. If I thought I wanted to get into town quickly to escape from Owen's company, this was worse. But hurrying the horses with a wagon behind wouldn't do any good, so I forced myself to be calm.

"How long are you planning on staying?"

"I suppose that will depend on Rooke."

My heart hammered in my chest. Did she plan on reconciling with him? And would he be open to the possibility? I scolded myself for even thinking about it. And yet, the thought crushed me.

When the ranch came into view, I breathed in a sigh of relief. Rolling the wagon to a stop in front of the barn, Cade strolled out to greet me with eyes immediately on the pretty woman next to me. He reached a hand up to her, helping her down.

"Name's Cade."

I rolled my eyes, clamoring down from the wagon with no one helping me. I wanted to tell him that she preferred men that had money. Ranch hands likely didn't hold a candle to the life she'd been living in Boston judging by the dress she wore. Brushing the dust from the road off the front of my dress, I came around the wagon.

"Cade, this is Nora."

"It is a fine pleasure to meet you."

Would he have greeted me this way, had he known I wasn't a boy when we'd met so many weeks ago? I thought. It irritated me, regardless of what the answer could be.

"Do you know where we might find Rooke?" I asked.

After a long, drawn out whistle from Cade, Rooke came strolling around the corner of the barn. I'd never seen Rooke stop so abruptly, his jaw hardening and eyes narrowing at the sight of my companion. When she fluttered her eyelashes, her mouth turning into a beguiling smile, I felt my insides churn like butter.

After a moment, he strode closer to us with his eyes flashing in anger. "You wanna tell me what the damn hell you are doing here, *Leanora*?"

Chapter Forty Seven

"Nice to see you, too, husband," she cooed. "I go by just Nora now."

Gone was the demure woman who'd sat beside me in the wagon on the way from town, acting as though she didn't know how he'd react. In her place seemed like a woman who knew full-well what game she played. A woman who knew how to wrap a man around her little finger with the batting of her pretty eyes and the pout of her lush lips. It enraged me. Made me want to pull Rooke aside and tell him not to believe her for one minute.

"Cade, would you and Levi be so kind as to help me bring my packages inside?" I asked, eager to be away from the pair of them.

Levi quickly moved into action, but Cade seemed to want to linger until I pinned him with a glare. He mumbled but moved. Grabbing crates, they followed me into the house. Before I disappeared into the house, I looked back across the lane to Rooke and Nora. He didn't look happy, and she looked like she wouldn't be getting her way.

I smiled, going into the house behind Cade and Levi. They set my packages in the kitchen and I shooed them away, but not before I gave them strict instructions to leave the two outside the barn alone with their discussion.

"Aren't you at least curious?" Levi asked, staying behind after Cade left.

I leaned against the door frame, thinking how easily I could eavesdrop just as Rooke had done the night I snuck into Anthony's house. Except I didn't want to. I knew Rooke would tell me. My heart swelled with love for this man.

"I am, but Rooke will tell me what he feels I need to know."

"How'd you get so smart, Georgie?"

I wrinkled my nose. I wanted to tell him it had nothing to do with knowledge but growth. I think I'd outgrown listening at doors. And being with the right person. I knew Rooke was the right person for me. "Blame it on my brother."

He laughed. And laughed and laughed as he walked out of the house. I could still hear his laughter even while he walked away from the house. I busied myself with putting the kitchen goods away before trekking the clothing upstairs and folding each of them away into the trunk.

I admired the clothes that Delilah had so carefully sewn, her craftsmanship to be respected. Even the shirt and trousers were of impeccable quality. There was a fine pale yellow gown the color of the sunrise on a hazy day for a special occasion, and two day dresses. None of them were like those I'd worn in high society, but modest, with scooped necklines and quarter sleeves. These dresses were of more durable fabrics. Calico, she'd called the fabric. She included a shawl for the cooler evenings, fresh new stockings and a new petticoat. I felt like a brand new woman.

The house seemed empty without Anthony grumbling about, and I hoped that the doctor had given him some help. For hundreds of years, men had lost part of their legs. There were solutions that could help him. I knew it had to be true.

I wandered back downstairs, my mind drawn to the couple by the barn. When I looked out, they were no longer there. Not able to stand by idly without thinking about what might be transpiring, I went out back to the garden and busied myself with watering and weeding.

I worked until I couldn't be sure how much time had passed. Brushing the dirt from my palms, I stood back to survey my pretty garden with its plump tomatoes, sprouting carrot tops, green beans, and rows of turnips. Stella had taught what I had been sure I couldn't learn.

"Georgie."

Rooke, hat in his hand, strolled with uncertainty toward me. A frown creased his brows, giving me no sign of what I might expect from him.

"I knocked at the front door but got no answer. Thought you might be back here."

I swallowed the lump in my throat. "I couldn't sit idle."

"I don't blame you none, darlin'." He threaded his fingers through his hair, the strands sifting through softly and landing right back where they'd been.

Damn him, I thought. How could he stand there looking so sinful while I'm in turmoil? I wanted to scream, shout, rage at the heavens at how unfair this was. I yearned to run into his arms and beg him to make this right.

"What does she want?" came my soft question. "Does she want you to repair your marriage?"

He chuckled quietly. "No. Well, yes. And no."

"What does that mean?"

I walked straight up to him, keeping my fists clenched at my sides. Would he take her back? Why, after all these years, would she want him back?

"Did she tell me the truth? Is she Rory's sister?"

He blew out an aggravated breath. "Nora is Rory's sister, yes. I told you the truth when I said we'd married young. And also that she'd run away as soon as she had the chance of someone with more money. I should have told you Rory is her brother."

With pent up energy, I paced. "I don't understand, Rooke. If she ran away to be with a man with more money, why is she here now?"

I felt his hands curve over my shoulders, stopping me from taking another step. "Georgie," he breathed out. "Let me finish. Please. She wants money."

Spinning around, I would have cried out, but he pulled me into his arms and held me there. Like iron bands clamped around me, it immobilized me. Enraged, I would have gone straight for her. How dare she?

"Shh. She wants money, and she'll go quietly away."

"How does she know you have money?" My temper simmered, ready to explode into unleashed fury. "Do you?"

He shrugged. "I have some. She didn't remarry when she left, and the man she ran off with has found another. Someone younger. He left her destitute, barely enough money to get here. She needs money to start anew."

"What are we going to do?"

When he loosened his hold, he smoothed my hair back with his palm. "Darlin', this isn't a two-person problem. This is my problem, and I will handle it."

"How?" I tried to shake him loose, but he wouldn't budge.

"Cade and I will bring Nora back to Austin tomorrow. We'll petition a judge for a divorce. I'll give her what money I have, and she'll leave. I'll be back here before you know it."

"You make it sound very easy, Rooke. But you are forgetting one simple thing. Divorces aren't just granted. What makes you think a judge is going to agree to give you one after so many years? And why would you give her all of your money?"

"All I can do is try. And the money isn't worth a damn to me."

The hope in his eyes was enough for me. Resigned, I laid my head on his chest. For his sake, I hoped he'd get his divorce. But at the cost of all he had? How much money would it cost him to be rid of a wife? The answer scared me too much to ask.

In the garden's quietness, nothing but nature around with

birds flying from tree to tree and insects buzzing around, we basked in the moment. God only knew we'd had enough setbacks.

"I've one more thing to ask of you." His lips against my hair sent a shiver down my spine. "I would not ask it if there were any other way."

"Hmmm?"

"Can Nora stay at the house with you since Anthony is not home?"

Inwardly, I groaned. There wasn't another alternative. I would not have her staying with Rooke, and she couldn't stay in the bunkhouse. We could send her back to town and stay in the hotel, but it would be best to watch her.

"She can stay here. I'll sleep in Anthony's room, and she can sleep in mine."

When he pulled away, he cupped my face in his large hands and looked deep into my eyes. As though he gazed right into my soul, searching for the most intimate part of me. He had to know. He had to know that there wasn't anything he could ask that I would deny him. Married or not, this man had my heart.

"You're an angel of mercy."

I raised an eyebrow. "Perhaps you should hold that statement until you come to collect her tomorrow." He chuckled. "Where is she now?"

"In the front of the house with Cade."

"I'll give her supper, and she'll be ready to go in the morning."

Rooke and I walked around to the front of the house, keeping apart as we neared the porch. I didn't look at Nora or Cade. All I wanted to do was get this evening over and say farewell to her in the morning. I stepped onto the porch, turning to look down at Rooke.

"Thank you again, Georgie," he said, standing at the bottom of the porch. "You don't have to do this, and yet you are."

Nora stepped up onto the porch, averting her eyes from me.

I wouldn't lie to him and tell him it was a pleasure, when it most certainly wasn't. "You're welcome. Come in, Nora. I've got biscuits and honey."

She followed me to the door, turning back at the last moment. "Goodnight, Rooke."

He grumbled something inaudible and walked away, putting his hat on as he went with Cade. The way she'd said it sent a shot of anger right through me. Taming it down, I led her inside and toward the kitchen.

"You'll take my room, and I'll sleep in my brother's room since he's not here." She only nodded as she sat on a kitchen chair. "Are you going to speak with me whilst you're here, or no?"

"I'm not certain you'd like me to," she said with a sniffle. "I'm sure Rooke told you what I've told him I want."

"I think it's awful what you are asking of him, yes. But he did not tell me the details. He only asked me to take you in tonight, and that you are leaving tomorrow."

"I need the money to start over." The tone of her voice put my defenses up. I didn't trust her. "I barely had enough to get here. I wouldn't do this if I wasn't desperate."

"Why didn't you go to Rory and Sarah? Surely, they would have taken you in."

She wrinkled her nose. "I'm not meant for a farming life. Sarah would've put me to work the minute I stepped foot in the house. She never did like me, even when we were children."

When she caught my gaze, she looked as though she had when I'd met her in town. Innocent. Lost, even. What game was this? I thought. No, I wouldn't believe her so innocent if she threatened Rooke for money. His only way to be rid of her would be to give her money. How destitute it would leave him, I didn't know.

I set the basket of biscuits with the jar of honey down on the table. While I gathered plates, careful to select ones that weren't chipped, and flatware, I didn't look at her. My anger simmered again, and I'd need to calm down before facing her.

With a slight clunk, I put the plates down before sitting down across from her. Silence greeted us momentarily while we ate. I made myself a cup of tea, but she declined.

"I'm not a monster, you know." She brushed the crumbs from her hands over her plate. "Rooke may make it sound like I am, but I need the money to reach Maryland."

"Not Boston?"

She shook her head. "I have friends in Maryland."

The way she made it sound, she hadn't demanded a large sum from Rooke. But any money at all from him would be too much, in my opinion. I didn't trust her. "I wish you luck, but I don't agree with extorting money from Rooke."

"Rooke won't need to worry about me coming around again. He can move on with his life, once and for all." She kept looking at me, watching for any sign. "You seem to be sweet on him."

I laughed, but it came out nervously. "Rooke is a good man, but I'm married." As soon as I said it, I regretted it. "I escaped from a terrible marriage, coming here for my brother's help. Rooke has been nothing but kind to me."

"I think I shall seek my bed now. Or rather, your bed."

Once I had the kitchen tidied up, I led Nora upstairs to my bedchambers. She looked around but said nothing. I could imagine she thought it was plain. I cared little for what she might think of it, or for me, for that matter.

"I'm down the hall should you need anything."

Anthony had tidied his room before he'd left. The glass had been cleared, and the wall washed. Clothes once scattered on his floor were now folded and put away. I smiled at the perfectly made bed. Proud that Anthony had been trying as hard as it had been for him to do so. A long way to go, but it was a start.

The bed had a slight bounce to it when I sat down, pulling off each boot and sock and setting them aside. I stood up, removing my dress and folding it neatly over the trunk beneath the window. The room had a bigger space than mine did and overlooked the lane coming from the road and part of the bunkhouse. I swept away the curtain but could see nothing of interest below.

This time when I sat down on the bed, I lay back and thought of nothing except Rooke. I wondered if he thought of me. For his sake, I hoped this helped him, for I couldn't stand the thought of this woman holding anything over his head. Sleep eluded me for a short while, but once it grabbed me, it took hold and refused to let go.

Chapter Forty Eight

Sunlight streamed through the window despite the curtains, creating beams of dancing light across the floor and bed. The day had dawned bright and new, bringing hope with it. I pushed the blankets away, hurrying to dress to meet Rooke and Cade downstairs timely.

After splashing water on my face to chase away the dark smudges of worry, I went to see if Nora had awoken only to find my bedchambers vacant and bed already neatly made. Voices drifted upstairs from below.

I found Nora along with Rooke and Cade on the porch, ready to go. Horses saddled, bags packed, and Nora looked refreshed, as though she'd slept every wink she could. I grumbled with each step until I reached the door, strolling out with a smile plastered on my face. Only Rooke would know it was less than genuine.

"Mornin', Miss Georgie." Cade tipped his hat.

"Good morning. Nora, I trust you slept well."

"I did, thank you. Your bed is quite comfortable."

This time, my smile reached my eyes. "Good morning, Rooke. Are you ready? Do you have everything you need?"

He nodded. "We're ready to get on our way so we can get back." His eyes remained on me, silently assuring me. "With Anthony away, I'll need to get back soon to resume my tasks."

Nora didn't like that Rooke's attention stayed on me. She huffed, walking down the steps to the horses. Cade merely smiled, as though her frustration amused him. I walked to Rooke, placing my hand on his arm.

"Be safe," I whispered, for his ears only.

His eyes burned into mine. "Five days, at most. And we'll be back. You've got your pistol?" I nodded. "You use it if you need to. Never hesitate."

I watched Rooke jog down the steps to join Cade and Nora, trying to keep the anguish of his leaving away. Even a reminder that he wasn't mine, could never be mine, didn't stop the thoughts that Nora would try something while in his company.

They mounted the waiting horses and left within minutes. The cloud of dust that followed in their wake slowly died away while I stood on the porch watching them get further away. I couldn't help the feelings of anxiety that crept in.

Rooke would be with Nora nearly two full days before reaching Austin. It didn't matter that Cade had gone along. Anything could happen. Given the rapid transformation from innocent to bold in her reaction to seeing Rooke for the first time, it wouldn't be surprising if she attempted to win Rooke back. Most fervently, I hoped I read the situation wrong, but it stuck in the back of my mind and refused to leave.

I busied myself with sweeping the porch, cleaning the house from top to bottom, paying special attention to my room. I'd even taken out the bedding and scrubbed it clean in the wash basin out back. Chicken eggs collected, garden watered, and kitchen scrubbed down. I kept busy.

Beginning to run out of things to do in the late afternoon, I hauled the rugs out to the hitching post around the back of the house and beat them with a large stick. Dust puffed out with each whack of the stick, and at each strike I felt better and better as though my frustration released.

"Thought I'd find you out here." A gruff voice came from

behind me.

I ceased swinging mid-swing while Geezer strolled toward me, the familiar pair of leather chaps slapping against his legs while he walked. For once, the hardness in his crystal blue eyes wasn't there. No clench in his jaw, no pinch in his lips beneath his bushy mustache.

"You were looking for me?" That couldn't be right.

"Think it's time to clear the air between us."

I set down my stick and wiped my hands on my apron. "That's a good idea. Let's start with why you dislike me so much."

His laugh rumbled deep. "Who says I don't like you?"

"You were so hard on me along the trail. Always glowering at me, barking orders."

"Think you would've survived if I didn't?"

Rooke had said as much at one time. There had been so much I had learned along the way, regardless of who I'd been pretending to be. Forcing me to learn did help. Being tough on me could have been the reason I took to it so quickly, but I couldn't be sure.

"But it still seems you don't like me much."

He heaved a long sigh. "You're similar in age to the son I lost. Same stature, even. Guess I took that against you, though I didn't mean to. I've nothing against you, Georgiana."

"Georgie. No one calls me Georgiana."

"So that's where George comes from?"

I smiled. "I'm named after my grandfather, George Edward Rutherford, the Viscount of Northrup." His eyebrows shot up. "I know what you're thinking. Why would the granddaughter of a viscount possibly want to live on a ranch?"

When he laughed again, it surprised me. Twice he'd laughed, now. "Why would the granddaughter of a viscount pretend to be a boy?"

"How else would I get to Texas to find my brother? Do you honestly believe that I could have joined you had you known otherwise?" I shook my head. "You would have never allowed it."

"Wasn't my decision. Rooke woulda taken you anyway."

I scoffed. "Surely you know Rooke values your opinion, Geezer."

"Yeah, well, that boy . . . " He trailed off, staring at me.

I waited for him to finish, but he merely looked at me. It appeared he saw me for the first time then and had to figure his choice of next words. I could have assured him he could speak plainly, but I patiently waited.

"Rooke is smarter than any of us."

"I agree."

"He knew you weren't a boy."

Although Geezer didn't know the entire story of why Rooke knew I had been in disguise when arriving at Abilene, he didn't need to know it unless Rooke had told him.

"Looking back, do you think you'd have been able to tell if you really would have looked at me?" He squinted as though he tried now.

"These old eyes ain't what they used to be. So, no."

"That day I'd been sick?" He nodded. "I lost my baby. The one I'd found out I'd been carrying only a few days after we'd left Abilene." His eyes widened. "Please, don't feel bad. You wouldn't, couldn't, have known. I would have left when I figured out I was pregnant, but Rooke stopped me before I could leave."

"Is that . . . ?"

Suspicious that he'd start asking questions about my life, I quickly stopped him. "That part of my life is over and done. I'm here now, and I mean to stay. Thank you again for coming to talk to me today."

Geezer gave me a half smile, then a nod before turning to stroll away. After having an earnest conversation with him, I felt a weight lifted from me. I'd misjudged him, as he'd perhaps misjudged me.

Chapter Forty Nine

I stood in the kitchen, fixing myself supper, when I heard the familiar thunder of riders coming up the lane. I couldn't move fast enough to the front of the house and out the door to see Matthew, Wyatt, and Anthony ride up and stop in front of the barn. Bare feet slapping against the dirt lane, heedless to rocks and other dangers, I launched myself into Anthony as soon as he dismounted with Matthew's help. We'd have toppled over if Matthew hadn't caught us.

Once I got done hugging Anthony, I pulled away and noticed he didn't use a crutch but had a cane. He had a full pair of trousers on, without one pulled up and tied halfway up. I looked up at him in confusion.

He pulled up one leg of his trousers to show me a strange-looking piece of wood shaped similar to a leg stuck into his boot. It looked smooth, and although I could only see a portion of it, I figured someone had attached it to the stump of his leg somehow.

"It's called a prosthetic," Anthony explained. "Less than a couple hundred people have them. People have known about it for a while, but it is not widely used. They're working toward getting more amputees such as myself fitted for such things."

"Took him a while to figure out how to walk with it," Matthew said, grinning while he stepped around him and earned himself a glare. "Seems to get along fine with it now."

"Indeed, I am."

Since I'd arrived, I'd not seen such a glow in Anthony's eyes. We had a good start in mending not only our relationship but getting him better. With his haircut, and some new clothes that he must have purchased while in Austin, he'd looked like a new man. "Oh, Anthony, say we'll go to church services tomorrow." I said. "Please, say we will."

"I'm not sure that would be wise, Georgie."

"Please. I know Owen is after your land, and it would be a good idea to establish yourself in society again. Take a stand."

Anthony stood straighter. "Has Owen come here while I was away?"

"No, but that doesn't mean he won't. All the more reason for me to keep myself protected."

His eyes narrowed. "Rooke has been staying away from you?"

"Please do not start on that, Anthony. He's been teaching me how to shoot, and I'm actually quite good. Now, please say we'll go to church tomorrow."

"Rooke had to leave anyhow," Levi said, coming out of the barn to care for the horses.

With Cade gone, most of the care for the horses fell to him. Billy could help, but he had his hands full, taking care of the cattle that hadn't gone to the market on the drive. Now that Wyatt had returned, he'd resume helping Billy, and they'd need to divide the work between them.

"Where'd he go?" Anthony demanded.

"Cade and Rooke had to bring Nora to Austin," I responded tightly.

"Leanora? His wife?"

"The very one. She came to town, demanding money from him in exchange for a divorce."

Anthony stared at me in stunned silence. I couldn't be sure he believed me. When he looked at Levi for confirmation, Levi gave him a nod.

The scowl that crossed Wyatt's faced couldn't be missed. "I always knew that greedy bitch would come back for some reason."

I couldn't stop the smile, even if it was small. Wyatt made it impossible for me to dislike him.

"My brother is entirely too soft for a woman in need. He'll do anything to help a woman in need, even if it makes him poor in the process." He shook his head, then met my eyes. "Of course, he knows how vindictive she is. He won't take her back, Georgie."

Wyatt saying it gave me some reassurance, but hearing his description of Rooke doing anything to help a woman in need hit me deep. The truth to that was evident in the way he'd helped me.

"We'll go to church tomorrow," Anthony told me. "Is there supper?"

Although happy to hear we'd be attending services, I couldn't help but feel Anthony had abruptly changed the subject to get Wyatt to stop talking.

Levi, Matthew and Wyatt led the horses away while Anthony and I walked toward the house. I couldn't help but notice that Anthony didn't use the cane as much as I thought he would. Surprised he had gotten used to using his weight on the fake leg so quickly, I smiled at his bravery for trying something so new.

"When did Rooke leave?" Anthony asked, waving his arm at me to proceed before him up the steps.

"This morning. He won't be back for a while yet."

"She asked for money, you say?"

"Yes."

The house, sparkling clean from my efforts while he had been away, felt less empty now that Anthony had returned. While both Anthony and Rooke had been away, sleeping had been difficult. Even knowing there was a bunkhouse full of men a short distance away. With Anthony home at last, I'd be able to get a decent night's sleep.

"How much?"

I turned to look at him while we entered the kitchen. "Really, Anthony. Do you think Rooke would tell me such a thing? And why does it matter?"

"It matters to me," he grumbled, sitting down at the table and laying his cane on the ground. "Rooke helped me when I needed him the most, Georgie. I won't see him penniless because some hussy decided to shake him down for everything."

Warmth swelled in my heart. That Anthony would help Rooke settle the amount Nora demanded overwhelmed me with knowing deep down my brother cared what happened to Rooke, regardless of what they'd been through in the past.

I set a pan on the stove and heated some leftover stew I'd made. After picking vegetables from the garden and adding some herbs I'd been growing, it didn't taste too bad. I hoped he'd think so.

"Stella will be pleased to see us tomorrow."

"And?"

"You really are a dunce sometimes, Anthony. Stella doesn't come here just to see me." His pinched eyebrows said enough. "I think she likes you!"

"Why?"

I leaned against the counter, crossing my arms. "Oh, I don't know. Perhaps she thinks you are a pleasant man, pleasing to the eye and suitable in age. You know that she's been an immeasurable help to me here. I'm not sure I would have been able to do it on my own, not knowing the first thing about keeping a house."

That brought forth a chuckle from him, at least. "Our mother would look upon the both of us in horror."

"I have no doubt."

◆

Arm in arm, Anthony and I walked across the dusty road from the wagon to the church where townspeople gathered to attend services. We'd arrived early enough to catch Stella before going in, and the delight on her face had been well worth begging Anthony to get a move on at home.

"Georgie!" she said, hurrying toward us with Tanner in tow. "And Anthony, what a surprise to see you here as well. You look much better since I last saw you."

"Thank you." I elbowed him lightly in the ribs, a subtle reminder of his manners. "You look fine today, Miss Stella."

The blush that rose to her cheeks betrayed her feelings, at least to me. Anthony didn't know how to decipher such things, apparently.

"Anthony," Stella stepped closer to him. "Have you gotten yourself a new cane?"

Anthony lifted the shining black accessory, admiring the replacement of the crude crutch he'd been using these past several years. Triumph lit his brown eyes. "I've returned from seeing a doctor in Salado who fitted me with a fake leg called a prosthetic to move about better. The cane is to help until I grow more accustomed to walking."

Listening to him have a conversation instead of arguing lifted my spirits. While I didn't wish to continue to listen, the service would begin soon. I tilted my head.

"Tanner, would you escort me in?"

That should do it! I thought. Anthony will have no choice but to be a gentleman and lead Stella into the church, continuing their conversation while I keep Tanner occupied. Tanner inclined his head, offering me his elbow.

I linked my arm into his. "How is business?"

"Ah . . . business is always good on these dry days when people seek to slake their thirst out of the heat of the sun." He chuckled, his blonde head tipped back in good-natured humor. "Has my sister given you the help you've needed?"

"I hope it hasn't inconvenienced you, taking her away as I have."

Together, we stepped up and into the shade of the church. Townsfolk had already started sitting in the pews, women fanning themselves to ward off the heat. The interior of the church, painted white like the outside, had dark wood benches lined up in front of the podium. The preacher standing front and center, smiled at me in greeting while we approached. I'd not yet met him, but from what Delilah had told me, the preacher hailed from Alabama after the war and intended on staying here.

"Nonsense. I will gladly lend my sister to you any time." He released me, giving me a slight bow while I sidled into the row behind Delilah and Thaddeus.

She turned and greeted me while Stella and Anthony sat down beside Tanner. Gracious. The heat sweltered within the building, though each of the four windows on the sides of the church were open. My fan hardly did anything to keep the heat at bay.

The service began with a prayer and soon we were singing joyfully to the praises of the lord. Although the town hadn't grown large in residents in the years since its founding, it took a considerable amount of time to shuffle everyone out the doors into the fresh air.

Delilah cut a path through the crowd directly for us, regardless of who I might be engaged with. Thaddeus trailed helplessly behind her, a tiresome look in his eyes yet a smile beneath his whiskers.

"My, oh my, but you look like a vision, Georgie!" she gushed, reached for my hands while she approached. "Now, let me see you in this dress."

Warm hands closed around mine, bringing me out of my circle and stretching my arms wide to make a show of the fine yellow dress I wore that morning. The light color I'd thought would be pleasant with the absence of clouds that morning, accenting the darkness of my fast-growing hair that already reached my shoulder blades. I'd done the best I could that morning by pinning it up.

"Thank you. Though, it is only because of your talents that I look this way. I can only be grateful for your fast work in getting me these dresses in time, which allows me to attend church services."

She looked over at Anthony, talking with Tanner and Thaddeus nearby. "And I see you've brought your dear brother out of his shell."

"I am trying, but lately he's expressed a desire to be helped."

At that moment, Anthony looked over at us and I smiled quickly. His brows furrowed, knowing I'd been up to something. Anthony knew me well enough to know that. Sure enough, he cut his topic short and started over, his cane only tapping once every so often along the way.

"Dearest sister, might you tell me what you are up to?"

"Up to? Why, Anthony, I'm not up to anything."

He folded his arms. "Doubtful." He looked at Delilah. "You were talking about me?"

"Only how fit you look. It is truly wonderful to see you, Anthony."

Anthony merely smiled and when he did, my heart lifted. I wasn't the only one who wanted to see Anthony out of his house more. The people of the town liked him, that much had been clear.

"As much as this has been an adventure, it has been taxing and I fear I must be returning home. Georgie?" He bowed to Delilah, then Stella.

"Stella, you'll come to supper tonight, won't you?" I asked quickly, not willing to let the opportunity to get away from me.

Tanner had all but told me he could get by without her. It was all I needed to get Stella out to the ranch and in front of Anthony. It may take time, but someone to occupy his time other than me might help.

Her eyes fluttered. "I'd be delighted."

Anthony smiled, albeit crookedly. "Agreed. Stella, I believe Georgie has attempted to bake a pie with apples she picked from the grove of trees in the back."

I grinned. "I did. And I used the recipe Stella gave me, so she must come to supper and try it."

She nodded, a twinkle in her eye. "I shall be around this evening. Shall I bring anything with me?"

"Only yourself."

The urge to clap my hands in excitement swept through me, but I merely smiled and offered Anthony my arm to take while Stella went with Tanner. He had the good sense to stay silent until we were well away from the crowd before he chastised me for my mischief.

"I see what you are trying to do," he said, handing me up into the wagon.

Sitting down, I smoothed out my skirt while he pulled himself in and took up the reins. "I can't see what you might mean. I only asked Stella to join us for supper since she's been so kind to give me recipes and tips. If not for her, we'd be eating bland vegetables and drinking tea."

At his scoff, I shot him a glare. The wagon lurched into motion.

"I don't know the first thing about cooking, and you know it."

"Yes, yes. I know how you were raised. There is no need to

remind me of it. I understand fully the need for female companionship, but need I remind you that you had a city full of them you've left behind? You needlessly drag me into this when I've done nothing to encourage it."

Infuriating man, I grumbled. "You know full well why I left. I'll not rehash it with you. Do you like Stella?" He glanced at me, eyes flashing annoyance, before looking away again. "It might do you good for you to have female companionship, you know. She is not the same as Helene."

His jaw clenched. "I know that."

"Then why not give her a chance?"

"Because she may not want to be with only part of a man," he snapped.

The reason did not surprise me as much as the fact that he believed Stella would see him differently for such a thing. She was not the type of woman to judge him for it. If anything, she'd admire him more because of it. Anthony and his hard head only needed to see it.

"I can assure you, Stella does not think of you as part of a man. No one does. Only you think that way."

"The last I looked, you aren't broken."

There had been so much happening, so much to deal with. I'd kept it buried deep since, and although the hurt had faded some, I still thought about having my own child. Fate had taken away the one thing I had wanted most since I'd been married. I tried not to think about Rooke, the thought of having his child sending a wave of warmth through me.

"I can assure you, Stella does not think of you as part of a man. No one does. Only you think that way."

"The last I looked, you aren't broken."

There had been so much happening, so much to deal with. I'd kept it buried deep since, and although the hurt had faded some, I still thought about having my own child. Fate had taken away the one thing I had wanted most since I'd been married. I tried not to think about Rooke, the thought of having his child sending a wave of warmth through me.

Chapter Fifty

Tears sprang to my eyes when Anthony released the reins with one hand and covered my hands. When he squeezed, they flowed more freely, like a hot rain against my cheeks. This was the brother I knew.

"Georgie, I did not know."

Irritably, I swiped away the wetness on my cheeks. "You couldn't have. Only Rooke and Matthew know."

"How . . . how did Rooke help you?"

I told him of that night I'd woken in such horrible pain and what Rooke had done for me. If he hadn't already known of my womanhood, he would have known it then. Matthew accepted it graciously. It might have been my emotions, but Anthony's feelings toward Rooke may have changed after that.

Anthony's genuine concern gave me hope for the future. I'd not given much thought about how we would live together when I found him, only that I'd been intent on seeking his aid. We may have turned the corner where he had changed his mind about sending me back.

Would I continue to stay in the house with him? Cook supper, clean the house, tend the garden and chickens? What would happen if Anthony took a liking to Stella and something further happened? I'd not given any thought to what might happen if Anthony were to remarry.

Thoughts continued to plague me long after we'd arrived home. I had only a few moments to make myself presentable before I heard the clop of a horse up the lane and Stella knocked on the door a few moments later. The deep blue dress she wore, the delicate lace scoop neckline daringly low and quite becoming. I ushered her in and brought her into the parlor, where Anthony stood at the fireplace with a cup of tea.

"Could I get you a cup of tea or cider?" I asked. "Supper will be ready shortly, if you'd like to sit and visit with Anthony."

"I'll take a cup of tea, if you don't mind."

Leaving them alone together, I hurried out of the parlor and into the kitchen. Once in the kitchen, I took my time boiling more water and seeping the tea in a cup. It would give them ample time to start a pleasant conversation before I interrupted again. I wished there was somewhere else I needed to be that evening so they could be alone.

Bringing Stella's cup of tea, I warmed at the thought of Rooke. Anthony had allowed me to go to Rooke's house to check on things, so long as I didn't linger overly long. But while there, I couldn't help but to stretch out on his bed, breathing in his scent. I missed him terribly, couldn't stop thinking about him and wondering what he might be doing. Was he thinking of me? I sobered immediately, apologizing when I handed Stella the cup.

"Anthony was telling me of some cattle arriving in a few days." Stella took a tentative sip.

I nodded. "A ranch in the south needed a home for the cattle when the owner died with no children to take over, having lost his sons in the war. We'll need to separate them from the rest of the herd until we know they carry no diseases. Another cattle drive will need to be planned for spring, a bigger one this time."

Anthony raised his eyebrows. "You've been learning."

Beaming, I sat in the chair next to Stella. "I told you I wanted to learn about ranching. It's been more than learning how to cook and clean."

He jabbed the end of his cane into the floor. "Seems you've been talking to Rooke. There aren't too many others who know where the cattle are coming from and why."

I inwardly groaned, looking down at the fading rug in front of the fireplace.

"What Rooke did for you on the trail . . ." My head snapped up. "I may forgive him for . . . certain transgressions."

Stella looked confused. "Should I leave you two for a moment? This seems to be something I shouldn't be privy to."

"No, no." I waved my hand. "Anthony, we can discuss this another time."

To my surprise, Anthony smiled. "Georgie, I've given it some thought. I would like you to stay."

I wanted to dance around, twirl about the room in joy. Stella merely raised her eyebrows at me, not having known my leaving had been a possibility.

I rose. "Supper should be about ready, if you follow me to the dining room."

I'd set the dining room elegantly and poured cider, lighting the tapers to give some ambience to the room. Anthony took his place at the head of the table while Stella sat to his right. It would have been perfect to have Mack here attending supper, since he cooked much better than I, but I was eager to try out my pie.

"Tanner never found a wife, did he?" Anthony asked, buttering his biscuit.

He used his flatware with impeccable manners, unlike those I'd traveled with on the trail pushing around their beans with their fingers. He used his knife instead of his fingers. At least he'd not misplaced those along with his moods.

"Tanner's wife is his saloon." She laughed. "Unless he finds a woman who will work at the saloon as hard as he does, there won't be a woman worthy enough to turn his head. But my brother is as stubborn as an old goat. "

My lips pursed, giving Anthony a side look. "Mine as well. It must be a male quality."

He scowled. "Not all men are looking to fill such a role just for the sake of doing so. Helene was . . . " When he looked up at Stella, a lump formed in my throat. "She and I both changed. Suppose fate had a hand in it, but what's done can't be undone, and she's gone now."

Stella blushed. "I hope you don't think that I am trying to trick you."

"No." He reached over and touched her hand. My eyes widened. "I think nothing of the sort. Not of you."

I felt as though I'd been intruding on a private interlude, even after Anthony withdrew his hand. When I planned to get them to spend more time together, I never imagined it would progress so quickly. It didn't occur to me how lonely Anthony had been since Helene left. His bottle had been his companion.

The conversation turned to a livelier topic of the weather and the end of summer town celebration, in which Stella was part of the planning committee. When I brought out the pie and cut into it, I was delighted when it didn't crumble. I watched Anthony bite first, and when I didn't see a sour face, I turned to Stella. She smiled.

"This is wonderful, Georgie. I think you've mastered the art of baking apple pies."

I clapped my hands. "That makes me so happy. I may struggle with meat, but at least I know I can make a decent pie."

Anthony's slice disappeared within moments, his fork clattering to his plate. He wiped his mouth with his napkin and leaned back in his chair.

"You've outdone yourself, sister. I must say, you make a fine homemaker."

"Don't get used to it." I stood up, gathering up the dishes.

"Let me help you with these."

I shot her a look. "You're a guest and not here to be put to work. You do that enough when you come to visit."

We laughed, and she stayed put, pulling Anthony into talking about horses. I puttered around the kitchen, cleaning the dishes and wiping down counters until Anthony appeared in the doorway.

"I'll need to see Stella back since it's growing dark. Will you be good here alone?"

I swatted at his arm playfully. "I'll be fine. You go on ahead and bring her home, Anthony."

Stella appeared beside him. "Thank you for supper, and the pie, Georgie. I do hope you'll invite me back again."

When I turned and leaned against the counter, I took in the view of them together. Amazed at the vision they made together. "You're welcome anytime you want, Stella. If my brother had any good sense, he'll invite you next time." I winked.

By the time I finished cleaning, darkness had fallen. I missed Rooke, wondering when he'd return from Austin and hoping it would be soon. The night air hadn't cooled at all but still a good evening to sit on the porch.

Crickets chirped when I stepped out, leaning over the porch railing and watching the twinkling of the stars coming out.

Laughter drifted out from the bunkhouse, giving me a pang of jealousy of the companionship within. I now knew most of the men on the ranch, knew they'd not hurt me and of those I didn't know as well as the others, I had those who would protect me. But I'd made Anthony promises I'd intended to keep. As much as it hurt me, I would stay away in my solitude.

The lights of the barn shined in welcome, but I couldn't go there either. Cade had his quarters in the barn where the rest of them had quarters in the bunkhouse. Being in charge of the horses, he needed to be closer to them.

The crunch of footsteps on the dirt alerted me, my hand immediately going to my pistol. Carefully, I unsnapped the holster but kept the gun inside. Odd that I hadn't heard a horse approach. Only footsteps, as though someone meant to sneak up on me.

I straightened, stepping into the shadows as Owen came into view. My heart thundered. I should have known he'd try to sneak around. Did he not have better things to do than wait around for Anthony or Rooke to leave? With the men occupied in the bunkhouse, he likely thought he'd have a chance to what? Carry me off?

"Hello, pretty lady."

His words slurred, a sign he'd been drinking. After having spent such a good night with Anthony and Stella, this man would not dampen my mood.

"Go home, Owen. You're drunk."

He hurried up the steps toward me, nearly stumbling. I withdrew the pistol. I didn't point it at him, but I kept it firmly in my grip. Not sure I could put it to a person, but I had my hand on it.

"I mean to court you, Georgiana Rutherford." He came closer.

"You will not do such a thing without my say so, and I will never allow it."

He tossed his head back with a laugh. "You will. And if I say you'll be my wife, you will."

Of all the high-handed things to say! "That will never happen."

He moved toward me. This time, I leveled the pistol at him. "You will step back away from me before I put a hole through you." He held up his hands but grinned, like he doubted my ability to shoot him. "I won't think twice about it."

"You won't kill me."

Quickly, I pointed the pistol into the dark sky and pulled the trigger until it blasted a shot into the night. He jumped, but he still grinned. Even when I aimed it back at him as quickly as I'd shot. Inside, I shook violently.

"I'll do it, and I won't even feel bad about it."

I cocked the hammer back again, daring him to take another step toward me. The bullet would go directly between his eyes if he dared to move again. The sheriff would likely come and take me. Committed to an institution be damned. If I killed him, they'd hang me.

Running footsteps across the dirt reached my pounding ears, the men from the bunkhouse coming to a skidding halt in front of the porch to see me with my pistol aimed. But my eyes were only on Owen, narrowed and daring.

"Georgie." Geezer's voice drifted toward me. "Don't do it, darlin'."

"But he thinks he can force me into becoming his wife," I said, eyes unwavering.

"Shooting him won't solve the problem. The law don't take kindly to murder 'round here."

I stepped toward Owen, continuing to move forward until I saw his eyes widen. The barrel of the pistol stopped only an inch from his trembling chin. This is what I needed. I needed him to know the seriousness behind my words. If he tried this again, I would kill him. I pushed it until the cold steel of the barrel nearly touched his chin.

"If you dare to come on this land again, I will kill you on sight," I said between clenched teeth. "You, Owen Appleton. Trespassing is still against the law, and I've every right to defend this land. Do you understand?"

He didn't move.

"Do you understand me?"

With more vehemence behind my words, he nodded vigorously. Slowly, I stepped away from him. I kept the gun on him even when he lowered his hands. Watching him slump, I uncocked the gun and holstered it. Geezer and Billy came up to grab him off the porch, dragging him away.

Wyatt stood below, watching me. The rest of the men, laughing, walked back to the bunkhouse. With a snap, I secured the pistol for Wyatt's benefit. I couldn't be sure how afraid of me the rest of them would be, as much as I'd scared myself.

"You good?" he asked, stepping over until he could rest his booted foot on the first step.

I stepped down to him, sitting on the top step and resting my arms on my knees. Only after I released a shaky breath did I realize my entire body shook. Quickly, he shifted until he sat beside me, throwing his arm around me and pulling me close. Tears didn't come. I needed someone to hold me while I shook out the adrenaline.

"Damn, woman," he said, his voice smooth. "I ain't never seen a fire like that before. Not in a gal."

I smiled. "A man won't control me. Not anymore."

"Not even the boss?"

"Not even my brother. If you hadn't noticed, he's changed since I've been here. And he's going to keep changing as long as I can help it."

He nodded. "I've seen it. We've all seen it. Hell, he's got his leg back."

"And he's not drinking."

Giving me one last squeeze, he released me and leaned back with his elbows resting on the porch. "Takes a lot of courage to do what you do. You've a lot to be proud of."

Courage, I mused. I'd been taught not to need that. A woman could rely on her husband for that, not herself. But now that I thought about it, I'd had it all along. I had it when I'd agreed to join Rooke on a journey south. When vigilantes ran us down, I had it.

"Thank you, Wyatt."

"For what?"

"Coming for me. Showing me I've got courage."

A deep chuckle rumbled from him. "Pretty sure Owen woulda left here in a box if we hadn't . . . " He frowned. "You *didn't* shoot him, did you? We heard a shot. That's what got us out of the bunkhouse."

"I shot into the sky. A warning shot. I'd do it before I let him put a finger on me."

"Well then. I stand by my statement. He'd have left here in a box if we hadn't come out when we did."

"He would have. Thought he'd force me to become his wife." I sighed, my trembling ceasing and my bravery returning. "I have six bullets that say otherwise."

Wyatt pushed to his feet, laughing hysterically while he walked away. I sat on the porch step for a while longer before I felt safe enough to go into the house. As much as I could use a slug of whiskey, I couldn't be happier that I couldn't find any in the house. Instead, I sat in the kitchen and had another cup of tea with the pistol on the table in front of me until I heard the familiar sound of a horse returning. When the front door of the house opened, I knew it had to be Anthony. When he turned the corner to find me in the kitchen, his eyes widened at the pistol on the table and demanded to know what happened.

And once I told him what had happened, Anthony admitted that when Rooke had taught me how to shoot, the pistol might have saved me.

Chapter Fifty One

Days later, Rooke still hadn't returned. I knew it didn't take this long to get to Austin and back, and concern settled in. Did Nora purposely delay them? And why hadn't Cade returned?

Anthony had been spending more time in town. Stella swore he hadn't been drinking anything other than cider. It made me tremendously happy for both of them to be getting along so fine.

When I heard approaching horses one night when Anthony had spent supper in town with Stella, I knew it could only be Rooke and Cade. I dropped my needlepoint and hurried from the parlor so quickly, I might have lost the needle on the floor.

Heedless to my bare feet and lack of petticoats, I ran across the lane and nearly tripped when I watched Rooke and Cade riding up. My heart plummeted to my toes when I stopped, breathless from running. Rooke dismounted first, grinning at me.

He took two large strides toward me, pulling me into his arms. I hadn't taken the time to see who else had come out to see the arrival, but I knew Cade still stood there.

"I'm a free man."

Immediately, I stopped struggling against him. Did I hear him right? Hanging limp in his arms, I met his hazel-blue eyes. He'd been serious. "You are?"

"I am, darlin'."

"What now, Rooke?"

Fingers entwined with mine, the warmth of his skin against mine sending tingles along my spine. "Darlin', I'd take you to my bed and never let you leave if it were up to me."

My lips curled into a grin, my hand sliding up his neck and pulling his mouth down to mine. A sigh escaped, only to be swallowed by his mouth, tongue sweeping against mine in a kiss that sent heat flaring into every crevice of my body.

The galloping of an approaching horse had us apart in seconds.

"I can't leave for one minute without you getting into trouble!"

Rooke and I turned to see Anthony dismounting, still struggling with his new limb. He set his good leg on the ground first, straightening, before turning to glare daggers at Rooke.

"It is not what it looks like, Anthony," I said, moving toward him. "Rooke and Cade just arrived home."

Anthony stepped back, but he folded his arms in front of his chest. "You expect me to believe that when your face can't be any more red?" He turned his glare to Rooke.

I watched them equally, unsure if this would cause a fight as heated as they were both becoming. Having seen enough fights lately, I didn't want to cause this one. A crowd gathered, having heard the shouting of the two men. Cade stood back, wary of the two men.

"You can never marry her."

Rooke bowed his head, defeated. No one knew I'd been married before except Anthony and Rooke. We could go away and tell people we'd been married, and they'd believe it. I knew it would be far-fetched, but it could be possible. There had to be a way for us to be together without ruining either of our good names.

"There must be a way," I said. "Perhaps we can petition Charles for a divorce."

Anthony looked at me. "You don't think the minute he knows where you are, he won't come to retrieve you?"

"Why would he?"

Anthony stepped over to me, handing me a sealed envelope. My brows drew together when I took it from him, but when I flipped it over and recognized the seal, I stumbled back. Rooke's arm caught me, making sure I didn't topple over.

"Charles?" His voice had taken on an unhealthy tone.

Slowly, I shook my head. When he came around in front of me, I raised my eyes to him. I looked first at him, then Anthony. "It's from Benjamin."

Part of me wanted to burn the letter rather than read what he could want to say to me now, two months after I'd left. I split the seal, opening the letter and quickly scanning his neat penmanship. I gasped, his words sinking in.

"Well?" Anthony asked. "What does he say?"

I raised my eyes, meeting his troubled gaze. "Charles knows where I am. He's coming for me."

Everyone started talking at once. I shook my head. Too many voices coming at me in different directions. Knowing Charles was coming for me only heightened my anxiety.

Rooke reached out, not touching me. "There's something you aren't telling us."

"When he . . . the reason he did what he did was to get me away from Charles. Yes, he would have taken me as his mistress, but more than that, he wanted me away from Charles any way that he could. He told me that, but I really only believed that he wanted me to become his mistress. Why else would he have said such things?" I looked at Anthony. "He tells me that his sister's death may have been by her own hand, but . . ."

Anthony moved toward me swiftly.

"I know it's true. I overheard James and Charles when they were talking about Violet and how Charles said she'd gone crazy. James didn't believe it, though. He may not have killed her, but he was responsible for her death. She didn't want to be committed, so she took her own life. I refused to speak with him, and he didn't intend for Charles to go after me." The paper fell from my fingers, floating down until it landed in the dirt at Anthony's feet. "When Sybil was fired, she went to Benjamin and told him where I'd gone in complete secrecy. Benjamin found her a position elsewhere."

My hand came to my throat, fingers trembling. If he convinced his sister to take her own life, why had he taken my gun?

"We need to get you out of here," Anthony said.

"No! I'm not running from him. I will face him, if I must. But I will not run again. I'd just as soon end this once and for all."

"And if he refuses to divorce you?" Rooke took a step closer to me.

My eyes scanned the crowd we'd gathered, wondering why they all seemed so interested in this. "I'll be fine. He has much more to lose than I." Rooke arched an eyebrow. "Trust me. He does."

Chapter Fifty Two

The cattle arrived the next day and, along with the herd, a mad amount of activity. Abandoning my housework, I donned a pair of trousers and a white shirt rolled up to my elbows against the heat. Tying my bandana around my neck and slapping on my cowboy hat, I went out to help.

Every available man on the ranch, aside from Anthony and Mack, had launched into action to take over the herd from the drive team. I joined them to drive the herd out into the pastures to graze well away from the herd already on the ranch. Levi, who supervised the herds, would instruct when the herd was allowed into the pasture for branding and health checks.

According to the men who had driven the herd up from San Antonio, they only lost five along the way. Typically, herds were driven north during springtime for fertile grass to graze, and before the spring floods. Summer was hot and dry. Yet, five losses was not a bad number, Levi said.

I kept my bandana around my mouth from the clouds of dust that surrounded us, trying to keep the cattle in a group. If I thought the smell of cattle strong when I first arrived, it had grown much worse with the new additions. The bandana served to keep out the smell just as much as the dust. Fascinated, I watched Billy and Wyatt run down and rope a cow trying to escape. Since I hadn't been able to join them on their journey north, I was amazed by how much the men had to work as a team to prevent the cows from straying from the herd.

Dark clouds were gathering in the west, flashes of lightning followed by faint booms of thunder promising a storm. I would welcome a break from the dust, but not yet. Following the group, even though I only watched from the sidelines, is what I'd been ordered to do. Even after fat raindrops fell, I wanted to continue, but Rooke motioned for Wyatt to take me back.

Stubbornly, I declined.

Rooke wheeled his horse around, stopping next to me so I could face him. He reached over and pulled my bandana down, heedless of the increasing rain falling. "Darlin', don't argue with me about this."

When he looked at me like that, my knees weakened, and I couldn't argue with him. Not submissive, but agreeable. He leaned over, pulled my mouth to his in a searing kiss.

"Go."

Pulling the reins to the right, I rounded my horse in a circle and kicked him lightly in the flanks until we were galloping across the fields. Wyatt caught up with me, but I shouted at him. I knew the way back. They needed him more than I did. After a few seconds of contemplating it, he listened to me and turned back around.

By the time I reached the ranch, the skies had an ominous look with a mixture of dark and light gray clouds, some with a greenish tint. This would be one hell of a storm, I thought. With Cade still busy with the herd, I would need to tend to the horse myself and bring him right into the barn out of the rain. I took my time unsaddling him, then brushing out his coat before leading him into his stall.

I finished up as I heard a rider approaching and assumed they were returning. When I hurried outside, I could not have been more surprised, watching Charles dismounting from a horse instead. That he'd decided to set out and retrieve me in the middle of an incoming storm only made me wary of his intentions. I circled wide, hoping to be closer to the house rather than the barn in case I needed to run. My gun belt hung around my waist, but the last thing I wanted to do was use it.

"Georgiana, my sweet," he said, removing his riding gloves and shoving them in his pocket while he stepped around the horse toward me. "I've been looking for you. You left so abruptly."

I froze, halfway between the barn and the house. The rain soaked us both, but it didn't stop him. "Why?"

He laughed, the laugh that caused chills. Dark, mocking. His hair, trimmed perfectly and absent of a top hat like he always liked to wear, seemed a little gray at the temple.

"You're my wife. Why wouldn't I look for you?"

"I left you, Charles. You would have been rid of me otherwise."

Stepping toward me, the smile stayed on his face, but he laughed no more. "I could have gotten rid of you, yes. But you're my wife. Benjamin may have tried to steal what's mine, but I am the one who gets to say what happens. Not you. Not Benjamin."

I blanched. He still sought to control me.

His eyes traveled from my scuffed boots up to my cowboy hat and back down. The derision in his eyes was clear, disdain for this way of life or the way I'd dressed, I couldn't be sure.

"And I find you dressed like this." He waved his hand.

"This is my life. I live here."

"You don't belong here. You belong in New York by my side. Your Mother agrees."

I couldn't be surprised that he'd written to my mother to find my whereabouts. That was why it had taken him so long to come.

His jaw flexed, eyes sharp. "You leave when I allow you to leave. And as for your gun, the one you sought to hide away from me? Women shouldn't be allowed to handle such power."

His eyes traveled to my gun belt. If ever there had been a time

I'd been prouder to wear trousers with a gun belt slung around my waist, complete with the Colt tucked within, it would have been now. My chin tilted up. "Is that what you told your sister?"

The fury that came over his face made me take a step back. "That bitch deserved whatever hell she ended up in. She got pregnant. And when I told her to go away, to keep it a secret until we could find a good home for the child, she refused."

"Wasn't that for your father to help her with? If she was not married, he should have been the one to help her. Why would you . . " My mouth fell open, and for a moment I thought I might be sick. He couldn't be alluding to what I thought he was. Why he had been so controlling with his sister, even though I hadn't known her. "You were the one who got her pregnant."

Rain pounded down in earnest, the thunder and lightning increasing. I knew we shouldn't be standing out in this weather, yet I couldn't move.

The look on his face could only be of pride. "Yes, the child was mine."

I grimaced. "How could you? Your own sister?"

He laughed again. "She wasn't my sister. My parents adopted her. But the child was mine. Still, it would have been frowned upon since she'd been adopted as my sister. I told her to go away and take care of it, but she refused. My father gave the baby to a family who could care for it. But she went crazy, threatening to tell everyone of our secret unless I got the baby back." Pure evil glazed his eyes. "I did what I had to do to shut her mouth. And I'll shut yours, as well."

"Georgie?"

Anthony stepped onto the porch, a shotgun cradled in his arms. I'd never seen my brother with a firearm, even though I'd seen the serious side of him. He knew I'd been in distress before he stepped outside. As soon as he stepped out, the rain soaked him through.

"Go back into the house, Anthony. I'm fine here."

I sidled closer to Anthony, only to have Charles reach out and grab my arm painfully. Anthony brought the shotgun up, leveling it at Charles.

"Unhand my sister."

"Your *sister* is my wife. She and I still have a few things to discuss, such as why she left when I did not give her permission to do so. She *knows* she needs permission to leave." I pulled against his hold, only hurting myself. My free hand nearly reached for my pistol, when his other hand came up to my other arm, immobilizing me.

Dear God, I thought. Don't let Anthony shoot and kill him. Let him take me. I will get away again. I swear I will. Charles shook me, and my teeth nearly clattered together from the force.

"Why would you want a wife who cannot bear you children, Charles?" I cried. "I thought I would do you a favor by leaving so you could set aside our marriage and marry another. Another could give you an heir."

Charles pulled me closer, his hand coming up to cup my face as though tenderly caressing me. I winced at his touch, his anger returning. "You do not get to make those decisions for me. I decide when, and where, you go. Should I decide that you are not in your right of frame of mind and need to be put in an institute, I will do so. Until then, you do as I say."

"What do you intend to do now?" I whispered.

"While my mother could not make the journey, my father awaits in this dump of a town. We'll be leaving for New York immediately. I don't expect any further trouble for you, or I will bind and drug you for the duration." He leaned toward me. "Trust me."

"I'll never trust you. You told me my parents had died!" I renewed my efforts to escape his iron grasp, without success. "Instead, my grandfather did, and you kept all of this from me! Why?"

"You were better off without your family."

I managed to pull away from him enough, his hand still banded painfully around my one arm. No matter how much I tugged, he would not release me. I stood straight, facing him and hoping to have enough courage to see this finished.

"Bastard. Perhaps I should have become Benjamin's mistress."

The back of his hand connected with my face so quickly, it stunned me and I stumbled against him. The action only allowed him to tighten his hold on me. Hanging limply within his grasp, the burning of my face where he'd struck me only gave me little hope I'd get away from him.

"I'll put a bullet in you if you don't let her go," Anthony growled, stepping down from the porch carefully without removing the gun from aim.

"Anthony, let him take me," I begged. "Please."

"He doesn't deserve someone like you."

Charles laughed. "I'm all she deserves."

Renewing my efforts, I pushed against him, but it only made him squeeze my arms harder. Gritting my teeth, I lifted my leg to kick at him and dislodged him enough to release one arm. It granted me enough space to withdraw my gun, except he had me pulled back an instant later. I unclasped the holster and no more. I could see Anthony getting closer to us. I knew he did not want to pull that trigger. I prayed he wouldn't pull it. Let me deal with this, I silently begged.

I twisted again, but Charles would not relent. Instead, he dragged me toward the horse like he would throw me up and ride off with me. That wouldn't happen. I had the pistol handle gripped in my hand but with my hand pressed between us, I had no leeway to draw it. If I could threaten him like I did to Owen, he would perhaps leave.

His hand found the back of my head, pressing his mouth against mine in one of his brutal kisses. "You'll pay for this," he growled. "I swear I will never let you out of your room again."

My heart thundered beneath my shirt, the handle of the pistol slipping in my hand. The rain had slicked everything. Anthony shouted at me to move, and I knew he would pull that trigger. I couldn't move. Charles had me clutched to him, much stronger than I. It didn't matter that I struggled, less hindered in trousers than a dress. He still overpowered me.

Then I heard another shout, trying to turn my head and seeing the ranch hands returning, Rooke at the front and riding hellbent to get to me. Charles must have seen he had little time. He gave me another pull, enough to put distance between us. He pulled the gun from my hands, my eyes widening when it went off.

Chapter Fifty Three

The power of the shot made me fall away from Charles, landing painfully on my backside in the wet dirt. My hat fell off, landing behind me and slinging my hair against my face with a wet smack.

My ears rang, the pistol being so close to me instead of having held it away. All the times I'd shot it before, it had never been this deafening. With wide eyes, I looked at Charles. He lay on the ground, staring up at the sky. I scrambled to my knees and crawled to him. Red quickly appeared on his gray shirt, washing away from the force of the rain. His horse had spooked at the shot and taken off at a mad gallop down the lane toward the road.

I looked down at him, kneeling at his side. His eyes met mine. "I loved you, Georgiana."

I narrowed my eyes. "Benjamin wanted me to become his mistress to get me away from you." His eyes widened again. "That is what Maddie overheard and spread the rumor of deceit. He never touched me."

He coughed, blood speckling his lips. I saw his arm struggle to rise, attempting to wipe it away but not having enough strength to. Having mercy, I withdrew his pocket handkerchief and wiped the blood away though it would do no good. He would die.

Charles could say nothing else, the blood filling his lungs, stealing his breath and eventually his life until he lay unmoving on the ground. I stood up, looked down at him one last time, and walked over to Anthony, who still held the shotgun aimed at him. He dropped it, throwing his arm around me.

"Dear God, Georgie."

"His father is going to be furious," I said, starting to shake violently. "I'll tell him what happened."

"No," Anthony said. "We'll take the body and bury it. His horse has already run off. When Cash comes asking, we'll say we never saw him."

Rain pelted my face when I looked at him. "He'll never believe it."

Running footsteps approached us, and powerful arms locked around me, wrenching me away from Anthony. Rooke's hands swept over me as though he were looking for injury. His hands cupped my face, studying the blood at the corner of my mouth where it had already begun to swell.

"Bastard," he said beneath his breath.

That close of range, his blood splattered the front of my shirt. He lifted my shirt away on each side to reveal angry welts where Charles had grabbed me. He looked at the lifeless body near the barn.

"I will confess," I said.

"No," Anthony and Rooke said at the same time.

"They'll hang you for this," Anthony said. "I won't let that happen."

"Nor will I," Rooke added.

"We all saw it." Wyatt stepped out from behind Rooke. "You tell us what to say and we'll say it."

"Get the body out of here and bury it somewhere. If we get caught, you say I did it," Anthony said, his eyes sweeping from man to the next with a seriousness I hadn't seen for weeks. "All of you."

"No!" I cried out, the weight of the world spinning out of

control and taking my vision with it. "I won't lose you again, Anthony! I did this and I will face what I did."

"You don't have a choice. They'll string you up without a second thought, woman or not. No one can save you, then."

A wave of queasiness swept through me, causing me to sway on my feet until Rooke's arms swept under me and lifted me up. "Anthony and I will handle this. You'll rest, darlin'."

"Don't you dare put me to bed," I snapped. My eyes searched his while he carried me toward the house. "You can't let him do this, Rooke! Promise me you will not let him do this! I can't lose him again. I can't!"

"You need to calm down." He brought me up to the house, setting me down on the porch chair. He was smart enough to stand in front of me, knowing I would move the minute I had a chance.

Rooke turned, whistling at Wyatt, who came running. "Is there something I can help with?"

"Go make Georgie some tea."

Wyatt scrunched up his face. "I don't know how to make no damn tea."

"Heat water, put the tea in it and bring it out here," Rooke said with a growl.

When Wyatt didn't move fast enough, Rooke grabbed the front of his shirt and gave him a shove toward the door. Better than a boot to the britches, I thought as Rooke shouted at him to bring a blanket with him.

Rooke squatted in front of me, still ensuring I wouldn't move soon. Tenderly, he smoothed the hair caught near my mouth back, his fingers lingering. My hand came up, fingers threading through his while my eyes burned into his. What had I done? Although now free of the bonds of marriage, it had come at a terrible cost. I wanted to scream in frustration at my stupidity, shake Charles awake and tell him to get the hell out of here. But he'd been responsible for a young, innocent woman's death. A woman his parents had adopted. I clamped my eyes shut, trying to block out the unsavory things I'd learned, what damage had been done, and the repercussions coming.

Wyatt's boots clomping down the hallway roused me from my thoughts. A moment later, a cup of tea pressed into my hands and a blanket tucked around my shoulders. Rooke and Wyatt stepped away from me for a moment to speak in hushed tones, and I could see Anthony speaking with others near the paddocks. The rain had lightened; the storm having passed. I couldn't see the body now, but I could hear the fast approach of horses.

When Rooke returned to me, he took up his position at my feet again. "I should take you up to bed." I raised my eyebrows. "You know damn well that isn't what I mean."

"Pity," I whispered. "But I must decline."

"Georgie." His low growl made my heart flutter. Something it had no business doing considering what I'd done. "I'm not sure how in the hell Cash is here, and Robert Appleton right behind him, but we're about to find out. I don't think our plan worked."

I sighed in reluctance. "Will you allow me to stay here if I promise to stay quiet?"

Although he didn't immediately say no, his eyes did. I couldn't blame him. Still disinclined to allow anyone to take the blame for my foolishness, especially Anthony, I didn't know if I could keep that promise and sit idly by. I hoped Cash would listen to reason and believe it had been an accident. My hand had been on the gun with the purpose of getting away from him. I hadn't planned on shooting him. Just threatening him to leave.

When trembling overtook me, Rooke squatted down in front of me again and rubbed my legs to calm me but to no avail. Through the shrubbery, I could see Anthony speaking with Cash and using his hands animatedly. Every so often, I would see Cash pinch the bridge of his nose. Anthony disappeared with Cash following behind him through the barn for a while, returning several moments later in another heated discussion.

Cash looked toward me. I sat up straighter when he strolled my way. Every muscle in Rooke's body tensed. My hand found his, squeezing. His other hand slid along my jaw, cradling my face.

"Don't do it, darlin'."

My heart felt like it was splitting into two. A choice. Between staying here with Rooke and feigning innocence while Anthony took the blame for what he hadn't done, or speaking the truth for Anthony to be free and facing my own possible death.

Cash propped his boot up on the step. "Afternoon, Miss Georgie. Had some excitement here today, did ya? Want to tell me about what might have happened to your husband?"

"Didn't Anthony already tell you?" Rooke snapped.

The side of Cash's mouth twitched, annoyed with the interference. "I'd like to hear Georgie's accounting of what might have happened. Owen Appleton said he saw Charles coming here, as he was on the road. Anthony has already shown me the body they were going to try to cover up. Were you here, Rooke? Did you see what happened to Mr. St. John?"

Rooke's jaw flexed. "I was too far away, but from what I could see Anthony had his shotgun out and aimed, and Mr. St. John looked to be dragging Geor... *Miss* Rutherford away."

"Is that so?" Cash murmured, but his eyes were on me. "Was your husband hurting you, Miss Georgie?"

"You can see by her face that he struck her."

Cash glanced at Rooke, his eyes narrowed at the second interruption. "One more word from you, Rooke, and you'll need to step away." He looked back at me and I numbly nodded. "What happened then?"

"It... all happened so fast. I can't... I remember only that I fell from Charles, and he lay on the ground staring up at me. If Anthony did it, I'm positive he didn't mean to."

"He put bruises on her, too, Cash."

Rooke carefully pulled down the blanket to reveal the angry marks on my arms. Cash blew out a heavy sigh but leaned closer, then rocked back to where he'd been. He shook his head, pinching the bridge of his nose. Blood covered the entire front of my shirt. Charles's blood.

I held my breath to see if Cash would send Rooke away as he'd threatened to do. I had a feeling Rooke would not stop interrupting this conversation. But I needed him by my side.

"It's not a crime for a man to bruise his wife, Rooke."

I couldn't be certain, but I swore I heard another low growl come from Rooke. "I don't give a goddamn what any law says. She isn't a belonging."

Cash cocked his head to the side. "You sure you didn't pull that trigger, Rooke? You seem mighty angry at the man for how he treated his wife. Angry enough to murder him?"

I sat up straighter, but Rooke put his hand out as though to stop me from doing anything rash. He waited until my back pressed into the chair.

"I didn't kill him, Cash. Would I have, had I been closer?" He shrugged. "All I'm saying is that the man was hurting her, and law or not, he had no right to."

"That man's father won't rest until someone pays for what happened here today, I can assure you." Cash stepped down from the porch, hooking his thumbs into the ridge of his gun belt. "If Anthony says he's the one who did it, I'll need to take his word for it."

"Even if it was an accident?" I asked.

"For his sake, I hope it was, but from where I'm standing, it doesn't look good. I'll do whatever I can to make sure he's treated fairly."

With that, Cash turned and strode away while Rooke and I watched helplessly. Once he reached Anthony, I nearly lost my composure. Anthony mounted a horse on his own, and once Cash straddled his own horse, they started their journey to town. I knew my brother wouldn't give Cash any trouble. But my heart tore right down the center, knowing he went only to protect me. Coming here, I'd turned his life upside down and now he'd pay the ultimate price for it.

By the time they'd disappeared from view, sobs broke loose and Rooke drew his arms around me, pulling me into the strength of his embrace like he'd done countless times before.

Chapter Fifty Four

I assumed I'd wake to an empty house, but to my surprise, I wasn't alone in my bed. Rooke's arm curled beneath me, cradling my body against him while his long legs hooked between mine beneath the blankets. The even rise and fall of his chest, warm against my hand, comforted me. He'd been nothing short of gentlemanly the night before.

I had struggled to fall asleep, but with Rooke there, I finally did. But it had been fitful with horrible dreams, and each time I woke in terror, Rooke had been there to soothe my fears.

Sensing me awake, Rooke tightened his arm and brought me closer. His lips found my temple, breathing in deeply. I sighed, slipping my hand along his ribs until a groan rumbled through his chest.

"I want to go to town," I whispered. "Since James is here, I'll need to speak with him. See if I can persuade him to drop any charges."

Rooke had gone to town last night to speak with Cash, to see if he could get any information about what might happen with Anthony. Wyatt had been left to watch me. His return hadn't carried good news. James wanted Anthony to hang for what he'd done, and he'd promised not to rest until justice had been served.

"Can I convince you not to?"

His hand drifted over my ribs, thumb brushing the underside of my breast until I gasped. With heightened awareness, heat rose to my flesh when his leg moved. It so happened when he moved his leg, it moved mine. Wider.

"This isn't something we should do while my brother rots in jail," I murmured, all thoughts drifting away when his mouth caught mine.

"I don't think he's rotting, Georgie. In fact, he's rather enjoying himself with Cash's company." He nipped my lips, hastening to my ear while swiftly pulling me beneath him at the same time. "When I got there last night, they were playing cards."

I released a long, drawn-out sigh, pulling his mouth down to mine. "I need to go to town, Rooke. You may accompany me if you insist, but it might not look good if you do. I need to go alone."

When his eyes searched mine, I knew he understood. Just as I knew, he'd relent and allow me to do this. There wouldn't be any taking back what had happened, but he knew I'd do whatever I could do to convince James, or Cash, not to do anything rash. Charles had hurt me. In many more ways than one. He didn't deserve death, but it had happened and I couldn't take it back.

After another quick kiss, Rooke allowed me to slip out of bed and ready myself for a day of serious battle. I selected my dress carefully while Rooke went down to the kitchen to fix me something to eat along with tea before I left. The ivory dress, although well-worn, complimented my complexion and dark hair the best.

The look in Rooke's eyes gave me all the approval I needed when I went to eat a biscuit topped with fruit and honey and have some tea. He stayed with me while Levi saddled a horse.

A short time later, I found James in the saloon with a cup of coffee at the table nearest to the window. The saloon had only a few people in the morning. Tanner gave me a sad nod. I darted a glance at Stella, who sniffled but couldn't meet my gaze. Her eyes betrayed her sorrow, clearly red and puffy from crying. I wanted to ask her if she had been to the jail to speak with Anthony, but it would need to wait.

When I headed toward him, James lifted his head. The severity of his eyes and mouth matched the situation at hand. He didn't provide a greeting to me until I stopped near his table.

"This wouldn't have happened had you not run away," he said, bitterness thick in his voice.

I sank down into the chair beside him. I'd always thought James had a soft spot for me, but perhaps I'd been mistaken. Everyone had thought me guilty of falling prey to Benjamin's charms. There had been doubt James had believed it. Until now.

"You're wrong. This wouldn't have happened if he hadn't threatened to throw me into a hospital for the insane, which I am not."

Sorrow replaced the severity in his eyes, deeply embedded. If I would get through to him, I would need to dig further in.

"He wouldn't have done such a thing, Georgiana. I would not have let him."

"I heard him. That night. When Benjamin interrupted our family dinner. He said you'd already dealt with Violet not so many years ago."

"You must not have heard me tell him that I forbid it."

My heart sank. Would I have stayed if I'd known that James wouldn't have allowed it? Our marriage seemed irreparable. Benjamin wouldn't have denied the lies spreading of our affair. Benjamin wanted me to get away.

"I felt I had no other choice but to leave." Maybe not the entire truth, but James didn't need to know that. "He should have set the marriage aside and let me go if he truly thought I'd been unfaithful."

"Your brother had no right to murder him in cold blood."

I bristled. "It was an accident, James. Charles was hurting me, and..." I took a deep breath. "I did it. Not Anthony."

James laughed darkly. "You would say anything to save your brother. I will not allow you to pay for someone else's crime. No. He will pay for this. Not you."

"I swear!" I cried. "Please do not do this. He's been through so much. I cannot lose him, too! You will take everything from me!"

Burying my face in my hands, I wept. Losing Anthony a second time would devastate me. I didn't know how I would get past this.

Only when I felt a hand on my shoulder did I lift my tear-stained face to James, his eyes filled with pity. Pity I didn't think he had in him. I'd not known my father-in-law for long, but I knew him to be a serious man. He didn't take being cheated kindly. And someone had cheated him of his son. His only son. "I cannot take this lightly." His voice, though strong, came out hoarse. "I'm sorry."

Straightening, I swiped my hands across my cheeks to rid myself of the weak tears. They would do no good. When I stood, I smoothed out my dress and looked down at James.

"My brother would not murder anyone in cold blood. Not now. Not after the war."

With as much dignity as I could muster, I swept out of the saloon without looking back. My back ached with how rigid I'd held it while walking across the street to the jail, and I'd hoped his eyes followed me the entire tragic way. He would take away the one person who deserved to live the most.

Cash and Anthony weren't playing cards like Rooke said they had been last evening. Instead, Anthony lounged against the wall on his cot, his good leg pulled up and dangling his arm over it, while his wooden leg was propped up on a chair next to the cot. Cash sat with his booted feet on his desk, whistling and whittling a piece of wood. He stopped abruptly when I swept in.

"Miss Georgie," he drawled. "Didn't figure we'd see you here today."

"Go home," came the surly voice from inside the cell.

I shot a glare at Anthony. I'd get to him in a minute. Instead, I closed the door firmly behind me and stepped over to Cash. He dropped his legs, set down his piece of wood, and gave me a quirky smile.

"I've come from speaking with Mr. St. John. He's not inclined to listen to reason."

"Didn't think he would."

"You cannot blame me for trying," I snapped. "I've come to speak with Anthony. I'd like to do so alone, unless you think I'll try to break him free?"

Cash rose to his imposing height, at least a full head taller than me. If he thought to intimidate me, it wouldn't work. He had to know how alike Anthony and I were. He set his hat on his head and sidled from the building, closing the door with a light bang.

"I told you to go home," Anthony repeated. "There is nothing you can do here."

I sighed, wandering over to the thick bars and wrapping my fingers around them before leaning my forehead against the cold steel. "Why are you doing this?" I whispered. "You know you don't deserve this."

His head snapped up. "We know you didn't deserve what that bastard did to you. Had I known that, I would have never argued with you all those times to send you back."

When he pushed to his feet and walked toward me without the aid of his cane, I smiled proudly. He'd come so far. Too far to end up like this. I lifted my head as his hands came over mine.

"I swore after the war that I'd never take another life so long as I lived," he said. "But I'll be damned if I shouldn't have killed him myself so you didn't have to suffer like this, Georgiana Victoria. This is the least I can do for you. Now, Rooke has been given instructions—"

"No." I pulled my hands away. "I do not want to know what

you told Rooke to do when you are gone. I'll do everything to make sure they do not hang you. They can't. Even if I confess to having done it."

His jaw tensed. "That won't happen, Georgie. I've seen to that already."

"Wh . . . what do you mean?"

"I signed a confession." I gasped. "Cash already has what happened yesterday documented, and I will not retract it."

I stumbled back until my back hit the wall, covering my mouth. How could he have done such a thing? We might have found a way out of this had he not written an entire confession. We could have argued that it had been an accident, as I had told James.

"How could you?"

"I did what I had to do to protect you. And Rooke would have done the same thing. Any man on that ranch would have done the same thing to protect you. Don't you see? The only man that wouldn't protect you is the man you are now free of."

◆

On my way back to the ranch a short time later, his words still followed me. When I returned, my formidable mood kept everyone away from me. Ranch hands followed me with their eyes, saying nothing when I dismounted and handed the reins to Levi without a word. Taking my bottle of whiskey, courtesy of Delilah, I went straight for the house where I intended to stay.

I didn't want to talk to anyone. I didn't want to see anyone. I wanted only to succumb to my own dark pit of despair, wallowing in my own self-pity.

I looked down at it, understanding what Anthony had gone through when he'd returned broken. He had nothing to turn to except the taste of the bitterness in the burn. And that had been my intention, not even waiting to get to the ranch before taking a pull from the bottle.

The entire ride back, I thought about James. There had been no doubt in my mind that James would see that Anthony hanged for this. He would not leave town until he saw it himself. Justice would be served. I had no way of knowing how long it would be. So until then, I'd stay in my own hell. Away from anyone who could witness it.

"Georgie?"

I stopped, my head whipping over to see Matthew sliding over toward me from the paddock. He looked about as unsure at approaching me as anyone else that watched from afar. It didn't occur to me to look around for Rooke. I didn't care.

The narrowing of my eyes had Matthew holding up his hands and backing away from me. "You will leave me alone," I said, an edge to my voice I'd never heard myself. I said, louder for everyone to hear me: "You will all leave me alone until I say otherwise."

I continued walking, not looking back. Anyone who dared stop me again would regret it. That, I'd make sure of. I marched into the house and settled into Anthony's chair in the parlor.

Late afternoon arrived, along with voices becoming increasingly louder outside my door. I looked at the bottle in my hand, not drinking nearly as much as I thought I would. After the first time I'd vomited outside the barn, I never could stomach the stuff. But I'd had enough to have a slight buzzing in my head, a numbness in my body that gave me a reprieve from everything in the world going wrong.

The slam of the front door followed by bold footsteps in the hallway gave me a good enough reason to take another pull from the bottle. Rooke stepped around in front of me, folding his arms in front of his chest while he looked at me with disapproval. I looked down at myself, my leg hooked over the arm of the chair and my body twisted sideways across it. Slung, I thought sleepily. I'm slung in the chair.

He leaned toward me. "Should you be drinkin' that if there's a chance you're carrying my child?"

My eyes snapped to him.

"Go away, Rooke."

"No." He snatched the bottle out of my hand.

I straightened, my boots thumping to the floor. He didn't move an inch when I pulled myself up to him, my nose inches from his. "I want to be left alone. Now, leave."

"You think because you killed a man you're calling the shots now?"

My palm caught him flat across the face while my eyes blazed. My heart pounded in my chest for having hit him. I couldn't believe he'd said such a thing to me. "Get out of my house."

"You want to sit alone, pitying yourself instead of trying to fight? You go on ahead. But I'll tell you something. I've buried more men in my life than you've ever known. Innocent men. And I'm telling you that sitting here drinking is not the answer." He shoved the bottle back into my hands. "Fight back, darlin'."

"I'm tired of fighting, Rooke."

"The woman I fell in love with would be fighting back with everything she's got. I want you to think long and hard about what you'll do next because sitting here guzzling whiskey isn't the answer. Didn't you just save your brother from it?" I didn't look at him when he moved toward the door, whispering: "Fight back, Georgiana Victoria Rutherford."

I fell back into the chair while Rooke slammed out of the house, leaving me in silence again. All but the heavy thundering of my heart. His words haunted me. Was my courage misplaced because I'd killed someone? Because I murdered my husband? I threw the bottle into the fireplace, glass and amber liquid spraying like an explosion within the unlit chamber.

Slumping in the chair, I leaned my head back. I'd pushed away the one person in this world I needed the most. And he'd been right. I needed to fight back. But right now, I didn't know if I could. I needed to sober up to fight back, and by God, I would.

Chapter Fifty Five

The following day, I heard raised voices again and prepared myself to do battle with whoever had invaded my sanctuary. No one would find me drunk, although I likely looked it having not bathed nor changed out of my dress. I'd destroyed the only bottle of whiskey to be found. When I'd looked in the mirror, there were dark circles beneath my eyes and my hair was a mess. I hadn't slept much, lying awake in fear that if I fell asleep when I'd wake, it would be the day Anthony was taken from me.

I'd sat in Anthony's chair to come up with a plan to fight back, as Rooke had suggested. Sitting here, drinking and feeling sorry for myself, wouldn't do any good. And he was right. If I wanted to lose another child, sitting there drinking probably hadn't been a good idea. I'd suspected recently that I was pregnant with Rooke's child, but didn't know what to do about it. And I certainly didn't want to tell anyone.

"Miss Georgie don't want to be disturbed." I heard Matthew's voice outside. "I can't be responsible for what she'll do if you go in there. She's upset, and . . . "

"I'll handle whatever Georgiana does. You leave her to me."

My ears perked up. Why had James St. John come here? When I stayed in the chair in the parlor, hearing the front door open and close, I thought he'd been rather presumptuous to allow himself into my brother's house.

"Georgiana?"

I stood, slowly facing him. Surprisingly, he looked about as awful as I did. Rumpled suit, unkempt hair, and dark circles beneath his eyes. "I see you've let yourself in."

He inclined his head. "You would have allowed me in? After I threatened to see your brother hanged?"

"Unless you're here to tell me you've changed your mind, see yourself out."

The corner of his mouth lifted. "May I sit?"

I crossed my arms. "Give me a reason to allow it."

"That is what I'd like to discuss with you. Please."

I'd never heard him use that word before. Not to anyone. After considering for a full minute, I waved him over to the other chair. Hoping he would not stay longer than necessary, I did not want to offer him refreshments but, being a wonderful hostess, I knew I should.

"I don't have coffee, but I have tea. Would you like a cup?"

He shook his head. "I don't intend to stay long." He moved around me, easing himself into the chair near the front windows.

I glanced out to see if anyone lingered outside. Sure enough, Matthew and Wyatt stood outside. Guarding. Too fidgety to sit, I had a hard time forcing myself to. But in the end, I did. I had to fold my hands together to sit still.

"You've changed," he said. I raised a brow. "I have always had a fondness for you, Georgiana. My son was . . . harsh with you. Controlling and cruel." He jerked his chin. "I assume he did that to your lovely face?"

Gulping, I nodded.

"Yesterday, you mentioned Violet."

"Your adopted daughter."

Surprise lit his eyes. He didn't think I'd known. "How did you know about her? Did Charles tell you about her?"

I contemplated whether to tell him what Charles had divulged to me. I didn't want to cause him more pain. He had done nothing to deserve it. But Charles had fathered a child, a blood relation to them. Did James know?

"Do you know who fathered the child she bore?"

A look of perplexity passed over his facial features, first in his eyes then in the set of his chin. "I see Charles did not leave much out when he told you. Violet would not divulge the father of the child to us, but I'd never seen Charles angrier during that time. I believe after the baby was born and given to a good family to raise, it changed him. And when she died, the anger seemed to have lessened a bit."

I inhaled a deep, shaky breath. They deserved to know, even if it cast Charles in the worst possible light. "James, Charles told me that the child was his."

He gasped.

"He said he tried to get her to go away, but she refused. They could never publicly come forward because she was your adopted daughter. Shame would have been brought to the family."

I watched him cover his face. "She took her own life." He held my gaze, and I saw how deep the sadness within him was. "Charles had many faults. I believe he may have spoken to her before she died. He said she went crazy. That's why she did it, isn't it?"

It broke my heart to have to tell him what Charles never had. "I don't know why she did it. If her child was taken from her, then she was accused of being crazy, I might have done the same. Who knows what she might have been thinking." I slid to my knees in front of him, covering his hands with my own. His head bowed, but he made no sound. "I am so sorry, James. To Mary as well. But I thought you should know that Charles does have a child out there somewhere."

His shoulders shook, but as quickly as I'd noticed, he straightened and looked at me. "We have always been such a proud family. I should have told Charles to let you go. This would not have happened."

"James," I whispered. "You cannot think that we meant for this to happen. I told you . . . "

"I know what you've told me, Georgiana. Charles was hurting you. As much as I want justice for Charles, I truly believe you are telling me the truth, and it happened by accident."

My heart lifted. James stood, pulling me up with him.

"I'll not take another life in place of my son's. And that, I intend to rectify."

"I'm not sure I understand."

James kissed my knuckles on each hand. "I will not press charges for an accident." My knees nearly buckled beneath me from relief. "You have been the most gracious person I've known. Everyone loved you. Even Benjamin, who loves no one except himself. But I look upon you now, and I see a courage that I never saw before. I see a woman who deserves happiness."

He released my hands, moving swiftly toward the hallway. I followed behind him, afraid to say anything that might cause him to change his mind. That he told me he wouldn't charge Anthony only made me more cautious. He wasn't out of jail yet.

"I intend to find my grandchild. My heir." He put his fingers beneath my chin, lifting my face up. "Take what life has given you here and have the courage to live it to the fullest."

With that, he turned and left. I stared after him, unsure of what to think. I wanted to run after him, ask to make sure I'd heard him right. Would Anthony be able to come home? Instead of asking, afraid he'd change his mind, I waited until I heard his horse galloping away before I dared show my face outside.

A crowd had gathered outside the house, eager for news about what Anthony's fate might be. The man who held it in his hands had come and gone. Surely I would know. I eyed them all cautiously, seeing nearly everyone, including Geezer, but not Rooke. My heart twisted. I'd hurt him.

Matthew and Wyatt wasted no time in stepping up onto the

porch to make certain I hadn't been harmed.

"Georgie, are you good?" Wyatt asked.

I nodded, numb with relief sweeping through me. Anthony would not die. My knees nearly knocked together, they were shaking so badly. But I walked toward the edge of the porch. Wyatt and Matthew moved closer to me, hovering.

"What'd he say?" Billy called out.

I stepped off the porch, aware that I looked terrible. Rumpled and unkept, having barely slept and eaten. Though it hardly helped, I smoothed down the front of my dress.

"Anthony will not hang," I shouted. "I cannot guarantee he'll come home from jail. I know he won't hang for this. We'll need to wait and see what Cash will do."

"What're you going to do?" Matthew asked.

I hadn't given it much thought. "I'm going to take a bath."

No one moved. No one said anything or asked me anything else. They stared at me while I looked at them, one by one. After a few more minutes, they started back to what they had been doing. And I went about what I'd said I would do.

I heated several pails of water and filled the tub with as much water as I could. The water stayed hot in the lined tub, so by the time I stripped off my dress and undergarments, the heat of the water against my skin felt wonderful.

I sank in, letting the heat coax me into a state of relaxation. After several minutes of lying motionless to ease my tired body, I picked up the bar of soap and lathered the sponge with it.

A shadow fell over me as I lifted my leg out to run the soapy sponge along my skin. Rooke pulled up a stool and settled himself beside me. Our eyes met, holding as I sucked in a breath.

I had so many things I wanted to say to him, but the way he looked at me stole every thought from my mind. Desire as hot as the water reflected in his eyes, breaking away from mine to sweep the length of my body and back.

Reaching out, I watched his fingers trail up my wet leg, from my ankle to above my knee, his dark tan contrasting against my pale skin. A sigh slipped from deep in my throat, watching his fingertips retain soap from my leg and linger there by my knee.

"Anthony made me promise to take over the ranch should anything happen to him," he murmured. I tensed, but didn't move my leg. "Made me sign the deed."

"When did he do this?"

"After he came back from seeing the doc in Salado."

When he looked back into my eyes, my gaze searched his. He'd known that Anthony had planned to give him everything in case something happened to him, and he'd said nothing to me. Anthony had signed the ranch over to someone else, someone he'd been angry at for trifling with his sister, and no one had seen fit to tell me. I bit back my rising anger.

"He made me promise to take care of you."

"Did he know Charles would come for me?"

Rooke shrugged, curling his fingers around the inside of my leg. "Anthony is a smart man, darlin'. What man in his right mind would let a woman like you get away?"

Before I could argue, he leaned over and captured my mouth with his. His other hand slid around my neck, holding my lips captive against his while he kissed me senseless.

"I love you, Georgiana Victoria Rutherford. It tears me up to see you hurting like this. But you are a strong woman. Stronger than you think you are. In fact, I'm not sure I've met a woman who's been through what you have. Had the guts to leave an abusive marriage before it ended her life. There ain't a woman more suited for me in this world than you."

I would have apologized to him for my behavior, for slapping him, but he released me abruptly and left before I could utter a word. Stunned, I slowly continued my bath while I mulled over what he'd said. I thought about what he'd said for a long time before getting out of the long-since cooled water.

Chapter Fifty Six

"Levi," I called out, walking across to the barn with purpose. "Saddle a horse for me. Now."

Levi scrambled to get a horse from a stall and saddle for me without question. Wyatt, coming out from the paddock, raised a brow. I'd finished my bath, dressed hastily and gone out to find Rooke nowhere in sight. Everything I'd wanted to say to him came back in full force. Such a force that the raw energy consumed me, threatening to explode until I did something.

"Mighty demanding, aren't you?"

"Yes."

He chuckled. "Does Rooke know about it?"

"About what?"

"About you being so demanding?"

I sighed and hung my head. "Wyatt, I don't know who I am anymore."

He stopped in front of me. "I think you do. You just need to find her again."

I stared at him while Levi came out of the barn, leading a beautiful stallion. He handed me the reins. "Careful, Georgie. I know you've been feeling out of sorts. Please, be careful."

I nodded, turning to Wyatt. "I won't be gone long."

When I mounted, I looked down at them and didn't miss the exchanged looks between them. I knew they silently asked each other if Rooke knew where I might be heading. No, I wanted to say. No one knew. I didn't know. All I knew was I needed to ride. I couldn't clear my head staying around here. I needed to feel the wind in my hair and the air in my lungs.

With the urge of my heels, me and the stallion galloped forth toward the west. I knew enough to not push him too fast too soon, so we galloped for a few minutes before I urged him faster and faster, pulling off my hat until I felt my hair whipping around my face. I could feel the power of the horse beneath me as we burst forth together, flying across the landscape until I could feel the freedom at my fingertips.

Anthony would stay alive. And I no longer had the constraints of marriage stopping me from anything. All my life I'd been told what to do. No more. I would not live like that again. Never again. If Rooke would have me, he wouldn't make me live that way.

Feeling the stallion shuddering beneath me, I slowed down and eventually stopped to let him rest. A small creek nearby allowed him to slake his thirst while I sat beneath a shady tree. I knew what I needed to do. When Rooke had told me to fight back, he'd been telling me to fight back in more than one way. I needed to fight for him, as much as I'd needed to fight for Anthony.

I'd traveled hundreds of miles, done countless things that all my life I'd been told ladies couldn't do. Smiling, I stood up and shouted to the wind. It felt good to shout. I had the freedom to do whatever I could, grown into a woman who knew what she wanted in life, and by God, I would take it.

"Let's go back, boy. We know what we've got to do. I'll fight for it if I need to."

The ride back proved to be as exhilarating as the ride out. Although we hadn't gone far enough to be lost on the rangeland, it had been enough to get the pent up energy out of me. All thoughts of doubt were gone. The words James gave to me when he'd left came back to me. Have the courage. By God, I had it.

I slowed down as we neared the paddocks, spotting Rooke standing near Levi and Wyatt with his hands on his hips. He didn't look the least bit happy. As I neared, I swung out of the saddle and handed the reins to Levi. He gladly accepted them and beat a fast retreat out of the way while Rooke turned toward me.

"Are you out of your damn mind? You can't take a horse and ride out into land you aren't familiar with."

I strode over to him, took off my hat and threw it before I put my hands on his face, bringing his mouth down to mine. I couldn't be sure if he stopped talking because I'd stunned him or if he enjoyed my mouth on his. After a moment, I felt his arm slide possessively around my waist and his lips take control of mine. Strong, insistent and if I had my way, mine.

Whoops of joy in the background curved my lips into a smile, even when he growled at the intrusion. I threaded my fingers into the hair at his nape, nipping at his lips.

When he pulled away, he opened his mouth to say something, but I put my fingers against his lips. "You can lecture me later. I'm sorry for hitting you. No matter what you said to me, it didn't give me any right."

He growled again, despite my fingers remaining against his lips.

"Shush. Rooke, you were right when you said I might carry your child. I am pregnant with your child." His lips curled into a grin so wide it seemed the first time I'd seen him smile so big. I dropped my fingers away. "And what you said yesterday about loving me, I lo-"

He pulled me against him, his mouth covering mine and sucking the words right out until it left me breathless. And only then did he continue. "I've never loved anyone in my life as much as I love you, darlin'. From the moment that Indian was spying on you bathing, I knew. I knew it then as much as I know it now."

I buried my head against his chest. "Thank you for telling me to fight back. If you didn't know already, I'm fighting back. Fighting for you. For us."

He chuckled. "Fight all you want, but you can bet your sweet backside, you won't be riding so carelessly with you carrying my child."

My eyes widened. "I won't fight you on that, but I can't guarantee I won't fight you on other things. I've spent too much of my life complacent. I won't be anymore."

"Holy hell, but I won't expect you to be, darlin'. Fight back all you want, but you have to know that you'll be marrying me."

"I won't fight you on that, either."

He grinned. "Now. About you riding hellbent out of here. . ."

Chapter Fifty Seven

Three months later . . .

I looked out toward the west. Land as far as my eyes could see. Land that would eventually be my land, land that already technically belonged to me. Me and my darlin' wife, who consented to marry me in a small ceremony two months ago.

I hadn't been lying to Georgie when I'd told her Anthony had signed the deed over to me. He always saw her for who she was instead of others seeing her for who she could be. Georgie was much more of a woman than I thought I'd ever meet. For now, Anthony and I would run the ranch together. But he knew in his heart he'd be moving on eventually. Perhaps north to start a ranch in untamed land again.

Bracing my arms against the railing of the porch, I watched Anthony where he stood talking with Levi. He had proposed to Stella, and although this house wasn't meant to accommodate four grown people, immediate plans to build a second house closer to the main road had begun. Anthony claimed to have grown tired of climbing the stairs to seek his bed, but I knew it was to give Georgie and me the bigger house. Truth be told, this house wouldn't be big enough for as many kids as I intended to have with her. We'd be building an addition before long.

Anthony had been sleeping in my old house since we'd been married, stubbornly he'd refused to move until after marriage vows had been spoken. I knew Stella sometimes kept him company, although Georgie and I only laughed and whispered behind our hands. If he noticed, he never said.

I felt Georgie's arms slide around my waist and a second later, ducked under my arm and pressed her head against my chest. I kept my arms around her, admiring the slight swell of her belly. As much as she fought me, I made certain she rested and had no chance of losing this baby. So far, it proved to be working. I rested my chin lightly on top of her head, looking down at Anthony as he looked over at us. He paused in whatever he'd been saying to Levi and smiled up at us with a wink. After his release from jail, he'd arrived home a new man with a new outlook on life.

When she turned up at me, winding her arm around my neck and tilting her head up to look at me with that sparkle in her eyes, I felt like a young boy again. Her lips curved into a gentle smile. "You know me better than I know myself sometimes."

"I'm an excellent judge of character, darlin'."

"I got you, didn't I?" she teased

I grinned, lowering my mouth to hers, pausing to say: "And I will never let you get away.

Author's Note

Writing about this time period has been an exciting experience. If you couldn't tell by the length of this novel, there was a lot going on during that time period. Too much to put into words, however hard I tried.

You might notice that I don't outright confirm whether Rooke, Anthony, and the rest of the men fight for the north or the south during the American Civil War. I did that on purpose. Yes, they lived in Texas, a Confederate state, when the war started in 1861, but that didn't mean that all of those who lived in the southern states supported the south. That being said, those that lived in the south that were 'Union sympathizers' would be hunted down and shot. For that reason, many still fought alongside friends, family and neighbors no matter what they believed. It's a controversy I didn't want to get into, so I'll leave it to your imagination what you want to believe.

As for the Civil War battles I mention, which are only a couple of many, Antietam was the single, bloodiest battle of the war, resulting in the heaviest losses of both sides.

The Union destroyed much of the train tracks in the south, an effort to halt or slow supplies from getting to Confederate troops hoping to weaken them.

I also mention a couple of historical figures. Jesse Chisholm, famous for his cattle trail from the San Antonio area to Abilene, Kansas, where cattle prices were much higher. Men from Texas drove thousands of heads of cattle up the trail during the late 1800s. The Reno Gang, led by brothers Frank, John, Sim [Simeon], and Bill [William], started robbing trains in 1866 until they were all eventually caught and hanged in 1868. They did famously rob a train in May 1868, getting away with $96,000 without hurting anyone.

At the beginning of Chapter Eight, while Georgie is eating breakfast, she is reading from an actual article from that day in 1868 that I found a copy of online.

This is one of my favorite time periods in history, and I hope I did it justice for you!

Acknowledgements

It would be virtually impossible to thank everyone personally for their support and dedication to what I do. I continue to do daily what you allow me to do, and that is write. To me, it's like breathing.

As usual, I would be remiss if I did not thank those who have supported me. Family, friends, neighbors, acquaintances, friends of friends, followers on social media and other channels, friends that come to see me at shows, community . . . so many have been there. There are not enough words to express my gratitude to those who have helped me along.

Emily, Tonya and Jessica, my rockstar beta readers, thank you for being patient while I pumped this one out. I'm impressed with how fast all of you read it and provided me with insight.

And to my editor, Becky Wallace. Without you, I wouldn't be able to hone my books into the shining stars they are. Thank you for the dedication you put into my work.

Find more books by

Jodie Leigh Murray

by scanning the QR code below

Books are also available through:

Amazon

barnesandnoble.com

Bookshop.org

Tertulia

Select Bookshops